Praise for Alena Graedon's

The Word Exchange

"Combines the jaunty energy of youngish adult fiction with the spine-tingling chill of the science fiction conspiracy genre. . . . [Graedon achieves] the singular feat of turning the alphabet into a cliffhanger."
—*The New York Times Book Review*

"Dazzling. . . . A snappy, noir-inflected vision of a future New York. . . . Sparklingly inventive."   —*Slate*

"A sobering look at how dependent we are on technology and how susceptible we are to the distortions of language."
—*The Washington Post*

"Alena Graedon makes what sounds like a preposterous premise believable in this clever first novel, a mystery set in a dystopian near future."   —*Chicago Tribune*

"Imaginative, layered, and highly original."
—Karen Thompson Walker, bestselling author of *The Age of Miracles*

"[Graedon] knows how to ratchet up mystery. In [her] dystopian future, face-to-face interfacing is finished and even email is a fading memory."   —*Esquire* (UK edition)

ALENA GRAEDON

The Word Exchange

Alena Graedon was born in Durham, North Carolina, and is a graduate of Brown University and Columbia University's MFA program. She has worked at Knopf and PEN and taught at Columbia. *The Word Exchange*, her debut novel, was completed with the help of fellowships at several artist colonies. It has been translated into eight languages. She lives in Brooklyn, New York.

ALENA GRAEDON

The Word Exchange

Alena Graedon was born in Durham, North Carolina, and is a graduate of Brown University and Columbia University's MFA program. She has worked at Knopf and PEN and taught at Columbia. The Word Exchange, her debut novel, was completed with the help of fellowships at several artist colonies; it has been translated into eight languages. She lives in Brooklyn, New York.

THE WORD EXCHANGE

A NOVEL

Alena Graedon

Anchor Books
A Division of Random House LLC
New York

FIRST ANCHOR BOOKS EDITION, FEBRUARY 2015

The Library of Congress has cataloged the Doubleday edition as follows:
Graedon, Alena.
The word exchange : a novel / Alena Graedon. — First edition.
pages cm
1. Young women—Fiction.   2. Missing persons—Fiction.
3. Technology—Fiction.
4. Transmission of texts—Fiction.   I. Title.
PS3607.R3286W67 2014
813'.6—dc23   2013033165

Anchor Books Trade Paperback ISBN: 978-0-345-80603-1
eBook ISBN: 978-0-385-53766-7

www.anchorbooks.com

Printed in the United States of America
10 9 8   7   6   5

For my parents, who have never disappeared

I am not yet so lost in lexicography as to forget that words are the daughters of the earth, and that things are the sons of heaven.

—Samuel Johnson,
preface to *A Dictionary of the English Language*

"When *I* use a word," Humpty Dumpty said in a rather scornful tone, "it means just what I choose it to mean— neither more nor less."

"The question is," said Alice, "whether you *can* make words mean so many different things."

"The question is," said Humpty Dumpty, "which is to be master—that's all."

—Lewis Carroll,
Through the Looking-Glass

As a boy, I used to marvel that the letters in a closed book did not get scrambled and lost overnight.

—Jorge Luis Borges,
"The Aleph"

CONTENTS

PART I: THESIS

PART II: ANTITHESIS

I
THESIS
NOVEMBER

A

Al•ice \'a-ləs\ *n* : a girl transformed by reflection

On a very cold and lonely Friday last November, my father disappeared from the Dictionary. And not only from the big glass building on Broadway where its offices were housed. On that night my father, Douglas Samuel Johnson, Chief Editor of the *North American Dictionary of the English Language,* slipped from the actual artifact he'd helped compose.

That was before the Dictionary died, letters expiring on the page. Before the virus. Before our language dissolved like so much melting snow. It was before I nearly lost everything I love.

Words, I've come to learn, are pulleys through time. Portals into other minds. Without words, what remains? Indecipherable customs. Strange rites. Blighted hearts. Without words, we're history's orphans. Our lives and thoughts erased.

Before my father vanished, before the first signs of S0111 arrived, I'd reflected very little on our way of life. The changing world I'd come of age in—slowly bereft of books and love letters, photographs and maps, takeout menus, timetables, liner notes, and diaries—was a world I'd come to accept. If I was missing out on things, they were things I didn't think to miss. How could we miss words? We were drowning in a sea of text. A new one arrived, chiming, every minute.

All my life my father mourned the death of thank-you notes and penmanship. The newspaper. Libraries. Archives. Stamps. He even came to miss the mobile phones he'd been so slow to accept. And of course

he also grieved the loss of dictionaries as they went out of print. I could
understand his nostalgia for these things. The aesthetics of an old
Olivetti. A letter opener. A quill pen. But I'd dismissed him when he'd
spoken darkly of vague "consequences" and the dangers of the Meme.
When he'd lectured on "accelerated obsolescence" and "ouroboros"
and foretold the end of civilization. For years, as he predicted so much
of what eventually came to happen—the attenuation of memory; the
ascendance of the Word Exchange; later, the language virus—no one
listened. Not the government, or the media, or the publishing industry.
Not my mother, who grew very tired of these plaints. Not me, even after
I went to work for him when I was twenty-three. No one worried about
the bends we might get from progress; we just let ourselves fly higher up.

  Well—not quite no one. I later learned that my father had conspira-
tors. Those who shared his rare beliefs. But I didn't find them until after
the night he departed. Or, in fact, they sort of found me.

My father and I were supposed to meet for dinner at the Fancy Diner on
Fifty-second Street, a childhood ritual revived only a month before—
the night my boyfriend, Max, had moved out. Our four years together,
turned to dust. Maybe the breakup shouldn't have come as a shock; we'd
both tried ending things in the past. But I'd thought we'd finally bound
ourselves to something solid and strong, and then—Max was gone.

  When I'd stumbled into my father's office, reeling with the news, he'd
proposed that we knock off early. I was my dad's assistant—what he
called his "amanuensis"—a job I'd thought would be temporary when
I'd taken it more than four years earlier, soon after college: just until I
could finish my painting portfolio and apply to grad school, I'd assumed.
But I'd come to really like my life. I'd relaxed into it, like a bath. I liked
having time to watch movies: long, plotless, and Italian; short, violent,
and French; action ones, especially with steely heroines; and my favorite,
thanks to Dad, anything starring sweet Buster Keaton. I liked stalking
the Thirty-ninth Street flea market for vintage jumpers, leather bombers,
shirts for Max. Liked inviting friends and family over for lasagnas and
soufflés. I liked walking the High Line and the Battery Wetlands with
my mom and volunteering with her sometimes in the parks.

  And the truth was, I also really liked the job. It wasn't that hard, maybe,
but it was fun: combing through contributors' notes and importing edits

to the corpus; filing quotation paragraphs; drafting memos. Even taking editorial meeting minutes wasn't so bad. On days when I felt a little torpid or bored, I still liked the routine, having somewhere to be, with combed hair, not spattered in paint or clay (or uncertainty). I liked my colleagues, some of them as strange as me. And maybe most of all, I liked the time with my dad—whom I got in the habit of calling Doug along with the rest of the staff—even when he made me crazy, which was often. He'd spent a lot of time at work when I was growing up, and I'd sometimes felt as if he were off on an extended trip even when he was sleeping each night at home. I'd missed him, without always realizing it. Getting to spend so much time with him as an adult—coming to know him in all his generous, larking, exacting glory—felt very lucky.

I still spent most weekends in the studio, painting, sculpting, making what Max called my "installations": tiny dioramas, clothes of Kevlar or tinfoil or leaves, animated glyphs of Max and me doing odd routines. "Living in the now," in Max's words. My portfolio never felt quite done, which Doug often gently chided me for. "Are you sure you're not just being hard on yourself? You're capable of far more than you seem to think you are," was a recurring refrain. But it always seemed that I had a little more to do and that finishing could wait.

Max's plans—the MBA, the internships, Hermes Corp.—seemed more pressing, especially to him. "Once I start raking it in," Max would say, "you can be whatever you want." He'd say it to get at me. All my life I'd vexedly accepted other people's money. My grandparents', mostly. (They had a lot, and I had none, and I'm their only grandchild; I still tried to find polite ways to turn it down most of the time.) But there was more truth in what Max said than I'd liked to admit. And I did take it for granted, that we'd get married and start having kids. That was among the things I had to face when he left: myself.

But on the afternoon it happened—*My stuff will b out 2nite,* the text read—I wasn't quite ready for that yet, which Doug sensed. (The tears rilling down my face as I braced against his desk may have been a hint.) That's when he suggested the Fancy. "Let's just see if I'm available," he joked, browsing through his blank calendar. Doug was also single. He was almost always available.

In the month since then—as the Fancy's specials cycled from pot roast to meatloaf to filet of sole to turkey, in anticipation of Thanksgiving— Doug and I had spent every Friday night in the diner's front-corner booth. We liked it there because it still had a waitress, Marla. She was orange-haired and surly. Brought our food as if she were doing a favor. But even she was mostly for show; we'd order with my Meme, like anywhere. Still, it felt comforting. Mild abuse while we chewed.

We'd meet at seven-thirty, me coming from home, Doug straight from the Dictionary. He'd never been even a few minutes late. He'd usually be the one waiting. Hunched over a sheaf of pages, oblivious to the stares of small children unused to seeing such sustained, public use of pens and paper, he'd edit until I swept in, breathless from cold and the sad, lingering agitation of missing Max. "Give me a full report," Doug would say as I slid in beside him on the tacky vinyl.

But on the night in question, I arrived to find our booth empty.

At first I was unfazed. Vaguely remembered Doug saying he had a late meeting. I tried to order tea, but my Meme changed the order to a hot toddy. When Marla sloshed the foggy glass down in front of me, I relaxed and sipped it gratefully. After twenty minutes, though, my pulse started racing. I thought I'd mixed up the dates—that this was the night of Doug's big party and I should be home getting changed. My father had recently overseen a twenty-six-year revision of the Dictionary—by far the largest project of his career—and the forty-volume third edition was scheduled for release in just over a week.[1] But before my fear of being late could fully bloom in my brain, my Meme trilled with a reminder that the party was the next Friday. Relieved, I turned back to the toddy as the words faded from the screen.

In the end I stayed half an hour, mobbed by sadness, Marla's artless curiosity—"He ain't coming?" were, I think, her exact words; words that inexplicably cut me to the quick—and a growing sense of irrita-

---

1. The second edition, published in the early nineties, had been Doug's first coup: twenty volumes, and weighing in at 748 pounds. The *New York Times* had raved: "A scholastic Delphi; the *new* Dr. Johnson proves he's not just standing on the shoulders of giants." But the third edition had received unprecedented interest, probably because it was initially being published only in print, not as a limn. The launch, which would be held at the last remaining branch of the New York Public Library, had become a major social event of the season, surprising me, Doug, my mother, and pretty much everyone. Except, allegedly, Chandra in marketing.

(I feel compelled to disclose that these footnotes are part of my linguistic rehabilitation. I'm told that if I annotate this document, I can cut back on my hours in conversation lab—footnotes are kind of like a conversation with yourself. They can also help improve memory.)

tion. I placed half a dozen calls to Doug's office. Then, feeling slightly tipsy, I beamed Marla the check. I thought of heading home, but instead I trudged the few blocks east and north toward the Dictionary, buffeted by gritty winds.

As I turned the corner onto Broadway, hair lashing my face, I could swear I saw Max retreating off the avenue in a black cloud of suits. My heart beat faster. I thought of hiding, or turning back, but he was going the other direction and didn't seem to notice me.

I'd seen a lot of Max lately. Ordering coffee. Waiting for the train. Resting his arm on someone stunning. Only it was never him. Just a phantom, made from the smoke of old memories. Real Max had moved to Red Hook, deep in the leafy reaches of Brooklyn, to that stretch known as the Technocracy Sector. When I saw that night's version of him in profile, I decided I was wrong. Then I hurried on to the Dictionary.

The glass door to the lobby pushed back bodily when I lurched to open it, and let in one low, ghostly scream of wind as I made my way to security. Rodney was alone behind the desk. "Evening, Miss J," he said. Dipped his grizzled head politely.

"Is he still up there?" I asked, dabbing my nose with my mitten.

"Haven't seen him come down," said Rodney. Looked at me quizzically.

The twentieth floor was dark and desolate. It was after eight p.m. on a Friday and everyone, even the lowliest, loneliest etymology assistant, had left hours earlier. Everyone, it seemed, but Doug. I shuffled down the dim corridor toward his office. Past my cubicle. Past the conference room, which was a disaster. Chairs everywhere. Table littered with cold coffees.

Light spilled from under Doug's door, and I opened it without knocking. Started to ask, "Where were you?" as I stepped in. But then I stopped talking. Because he wasn't there.

I can't say what atavistic anxiety shivered through me, but I suddenly didn't want to leave the bright oasis of my father's office. I also didn't want to stay. But mostly I didn't want to go. I locked the door and dialed the lobby.

"Hmm," said Rodney. "You want someone to come get you? I can't leave the desk, but I could call Darryl down from twenty-two."

I almost agreed, but I felt crazy. And Rodney sounded strange—angry, maybe. Then I spied a familiar item on Doug's armchair: his brown leather satchel. "Forget it," I told Rodney. Wherever Doug had disap-

peared to, I thought, mollified, he'd be back soon. And in the meantime
I had a rare opportunity.

To be in Doug's office without Doug was extremely unusual. And
unlike his apartment, which was still unnervingly spare more than a
year after his separation from my mother, this room was filled with my
favorite father detritus. The jackalope hunting license that Aunt Jean
had sent from their hometown—and my father's namesake—of Douglas, Wyoming. The glass canister by the phone stocked with both sweet
and salted licorice. And next to the desk lamp, the small, stoppered bottle of well-aged sherry vinegar that Doug said was for salad but from
which I'd many times seen him take a straight swig.

Near the door were his pneumatic tubes, which emptied into a bin
marked "In." This label always struck me as gratuitous. But the same
could maybe be said of the whole system. One of the first things Doug
had done when he'd started at the Dictionary in 1974, at just twenty-
seven (my age), was campaign to have pneumatic tubes installed, for
fast, secure transport of "sensitive data" (e.g., neologisms, disputed
antedatings, particularly thorny etymologies, etc.). Also the occasional
fortune-cookie fortune. Comic book. Chocolate egg. The Dictionary
had occupied two floors then, and Doug had argued that the tubes
would increase efficiency. He decried the idea that they might be anach-
ronistic, costly, and inconvenient. Dismissed the "rumor" that computers would soon allow the electronic shuffling of information. And
against all odds, both his board and the building executives had okayed
it. Doug could be extraordinarily persuasive. (Though my mother might
disagree.)

It hadn't been easy; the Dictionary shared the building with different entities—in those days, mostly publishers. As a nonprofit run on
government and other grants, the *NADEL* was fairly separate. (It also
got a bit of a break on rent; executives liked having its prestigious name
on the directory.) But after the tubes' success at the Dictionary, they
were soon put in throughout the building. And initially nearly everyone
used them; stations on each floor, as well as a few offices, like Doug's,
were set up for direct delivery. An operator in the subbasement routing
terminal directed documents back and forth, and it was a boon to get
contracts, memos, notes moved so quickly and easily. Later, when computers had indeed become prevalent; the Dictionary "streamlined" to
one floor; and the operator started splitting his day between the terminal

and the (also obsolescing) mailroom; tube use, already dwindling by then, stopped almost completely.

All of this was familiar to me. What I didn't yet know that night in my father's office was that ours wasn't the only building in the city with tubes; at least a couple of other places had them as well—and had installed them far more recently.

Wending past Doug's in-tray, I surveyed his books, too. He was one of few people I knew who still read that way, from a book, instead of streaming limns from a Meme or some other smart screen. Even Dictionary staffers didn't do much analog reading. Except Bart, I should say. Bart was my father's protégé. (I'd always envied that slightly.) He was head of Etymologies—what Doug called the Department of Dead Letters—and the Dictionary's Deputy Editor. Bart also had lots of books. He and Doug weren't alone, completely. There were other holdouts. And collectors, of course, who hoarded all kinds of antiquarian *objets*.

On one of Doug's shelves, in front of a Samuel Johnson biography,[2] was a half-empty bottle of Bay Rum aftershave, Doug's preference for which, he claimed, required a visit every few years to Dominica, the West Indian island where it's made. Seeing it that night, I felt a deep pang. It reminded me of a trip Max and I had taken there once, right after we'd fallen in love. That bottle, in fact, was probably an artifact: we'd shipped Doug back a case. "An offering for my future father-in-law," Max had said then.

While we were there, we'd also stocked Doug up on pineapples. He had a special affection for them. There were a few pineapple etchings in his office—I could see two from where I stood—and a big bronze pineapple bookend. He also had a small stash of pineapple-print ties, some pineapple-patterned shirts and socks. A small bowl of stale oblong chocolates done up in yellow and green foils. He kept eight potted pineapple crowns under special lamps. That night they were a little dry. I'd tell Doug, I thought. If he ever showed.

I was getting antsy. I checked my Meme. Sneaked a licorice pip from

2. This other Dr. Johnson had authored the first comprehensive English dictionary in the eighteenth century. He and Doug shared lots of affinities: curiosity, doubt, physical rotundity, heartbreak, and a genius for lexicography. Doug often said the name had been his destiny. And he'd come by it honestly: Gram and PopPop Johnson had learned of Doug's eponymous literary ancestor only when he'd begun his undergraduate honors thesis.

Doug's jar. Followed it with a pineapple-wrapped chocolate and squirreled a few in my coat pocket for later, along with a pen of Doug's I'd been coveting. And I tried, for about two minutes, to read a book, until my mind collapsed in boredom.

I also started to feel a tiny twinge of unease, like an invisible hair tickling my cheek. To brush away the feeling, I fetched water for my father's pet bromeliads and soothed myself with the rich, nutty scent of damp earth. Then I felt the delicious frisson of transgression creep over me.

For as long as I could remember, I'd been curious about what Doug kept in his desk. Siphoning off some of my attention to listen for the sound of his tread, I sat and tried all the drawers. Most were filled with work chaff: loose papers, crumpled notes, broken pencil leads. But then I tried the top drawer on the left. Tugged it. And tugged. Shimmied, a little crazily. Finally it came loose with a crack—a pen wedged at the back, I soon learned, had snapped in half—and the drawer released with a rattle.

To say I was surprised by what Doug had hidden there wouldn't be quite true. But it did disappoint me. It was a cluttered (and newly ink-smattered) cache—probably the largest private collection in the world—of photographs[3] of Vera Doran. My mother. Douglas Johnson's soon-to-be ex-wife. And I felt very bad for splashing them with ink. But I also felt a tiny, unfair burst of reprisal. As Max would have said, there are no accidents. She was my mother, and I loved her, but sometimes I wished Doug didn't anymore. Watching him suffer had been agony.

Looking back on our whole family life through a new dark lens also hadn't been easy for me. Had my mother really been so unhappy? It hadn't seemed that way. My parents had never been one of those gloomy couples like some of my friends'. They'd hugged and touched and said "I love you," to each other and to me, and it had seemed so obviously true that the words were almost a superfluity. Doug would belt *Don Giovanni* to Vera in the kitchen as she laughingly roasted a chicken, trying not to spill her wine. He'd write love notes and scrawl funny drawings on grocery lists and receipts. Vera would mambo through the living room for Doug and me, or pretend the hallway was a catwalk. It's true that when they'd fought, it had been fulminous—things sometimes went flying—but I'd always taken that as a good sign. And maybe it

3. Doug hadn't made the switch to digital in this realm either. When I was a kid, ca. 2002, we used to make prints together in one of the city's last darkrooms, down in Chelsea.

was, in a way. Over the past few years those fights had slowly come to an end.

Regardless, there was no denying that Doug's photos of Vera were gorgeous. There was Vera Doran as Blanche DuBois in her high school's all-girl production of *A Streetcar Named Desire*. Vera wearing beautiful bell-bottom flares, hair to there, and in huge orange platform sandals, relaxing near a stage (at Woodstock), joking with some shaggy-haired men (Creedence Clearwater Revival) who were about to perform. Vera in nothing but painted-on jeans bordered by the blocky phrase THE JORDACHE LOOK, in an outtake of an ad, ca. 1978, when she and my father had been married just a few years and she was still modeling to augment their income. Vera on her sixth birthday, a formal princess fantasia at the Dorans' on East Sixty-eighth Street, comporting herself in a tiara encrusted with real diamonds. And my favorite—now tragically dappled with thick black splots—their wedding photo: Vera at twenty-one, a recent Bryn Mawr grad, bedecked in a curtain of blowsy dark-brown hair and a silver lamé minidress. (On seeing it, Mrs. Doran told the bride that it was lucky there was something silver at the ceremony, as she wouldn't be inheriting any.) In it, Vera's being fed a glistening bite of pineapple upside-down cake by her groom, a ruddy, pleased-looking man who was nearly twice her size, hairy,[4] smiling, in enormous thick-lensed glasses, and sporting a wide pineapple-print tie.

I held that picture for a long time, trying to dab it clean. In it, Vera is arch and easy, laughing out loud as Doug forks cake into her perfectly plump-lipped, large, smiling mouth. She's lolling sideways, considering something invisible to me. He, in contrast, is watching her with adoring absorption, oblivious to all other witnesses at the scene of the crime— a 1975 backyard wedding at the Doran estate in East Hampton.

I was seized then by what my father would call "an attack of sadness." The photos made me queasy. They seemed like more proof that devotion fades. That everyone you love will someday, in some way, disappear.

There were a few other pictures, these of Doug—all of which would be confiscated later by police. There was one of him as a teenager,

4. His nickname at Oxford, where he'd gone for a master's, had been Ursie, for his resemblance to a bear. Curly reddish blond hair grew on nearly every inch of him, from finger and toe knuckles to chest, back, and ears. The abundance of it had sometimes spooked me on childhood trips to the beach.

with Aunt Jean, each posing with a fat brown trout on the North Platte River. Another of Doug delivering the Graduate English Oration when he received his Ph.D. from Harvard, having also delivered the Undergraduate English Oration, "Johnson & Johnson: A Love Affair with *A Dictionary of the English Language*." Doug punting on the River Isis in Oxford. And one of him and a twelve-year-old me posed with the Alice in Wonderland sculpture in Central Park. I'd starred in the school play, and he'd made me wear my costume.

There was also something else in the drawer, buried beneath our family history: Doug's Aleph. I miswrote if I've implied that Doug didn't have a Meme. He didn't *use* a Meme. (He hated that I had one, but that battle had long been fought. He *had* gotten me to forgo the optional microchip; it made me a little nervous, too. But I was intrigued to see what the new Meme would do—it was supposed to be coming out soon—and I'd contemplated getting one when I upgraded.) Doug did have an Aleph, though, which I'd forgotten about. It was the first model of the Meme that Synchronic, Inc. ever manufactured. It wasn't widely distributed, but a few had been given to key publishing people when it came out.

From what I understand, Synchronic chose the name Aleph because it represents the number one and the first letter of the Hebrew alphabet. But the name tested poorly—no one could pronounce it—and the device was full of bugs. It had a very early version of Sixth Sense software, and its Crown, called a Diadem at the time, had almost no sensors; it could only roughly gauge basic mood states. Even after training it for weeks to recognize preferences, the smart technology could guess what you wanted less than 10 percent of the time. "It's not actually very smart," Doug had said, "but it does have a good personality."

It didn't, though: lots of users complained that a Chinese weather page loaded during games of Ping, or that they were redirected to Russian gambling sites while trying to watch live poker. When the software and hardware had been fixed about a year and a half later, the device was aggressively rebranded as the Meme, and Synchronic offered a steep discount to anyone willing to trade it in. As a result, very few Alephs remained in circulation. Doug's was one of them. But the significance of finding it was initially lost on me.

It was massive, nearly the size of a book, with clumsy raised buttons and keys. I flicked it on, guessed the password on the third try—one of Doug's many pet names for my mother—and while I waited for it to load, I crossed back over toward Doug's window. Wondered where he could be.

The sounds of streets that blinked red and white below were blocked out completely by the nineteen floors beneath me. Sometimes high winds could send our building creaking, as if on high seas. I looked into the window glass, my reflection rising from the surface like an emerging silver gelatin print. The pane became a parallax. For whoever might look in, it made a still. For me, looking out, it was a mirror, my face floating over all the dim shapes outside. And maybe it was my distance from the ground. The sense, from that height, that human life was illusory. But I felt for a moment as if I were falling a long, long way down. As if the girl reflected on the inside of the glass were merging with the one being watched.

The sensation faded but left a residue of sweat. I stepped back from the window with a shiver. Blood rushed through my ears in a kind of nautical orchestra, and I thought I heard a door slam shut somewhere. My heart surged. I grew still, listening for sounds in the hall, and felt the powerful urge to run. But I stayed where I was. Looked again at Doug's satchel. Reassured myself that he'd *be right back*.

Then four things happened more or less at once.

First I heard a familiar sound: the soft *shrr-tunk* of a metal delivery cylinder whirring through Doug's pneumatic tube and the melodic metal ting it made as it struck another one already in the bin. Out of habit, I collected both cylinders and slid open the lids. The messages looked normal. But then I read what they said. The first had been typed on a typewriter.[5] It was a definition. I still remember exactly how it read: "di•a•chron•ic \ˌdī-ə-ˈkrä-nik\ *adj* : a method of looking at language that's becoming extinct." That made no sense to me. It didn't even seem correct grammatically. Was the method fading or the language? It also wasn't clear who'd sent it; there were no initials. Strangest of all, it was smudged with a fingerling smear of dirt.

Hoping to get a clue from the other note, I unrolled it, too. It said, "Received your SOS. Standing by." It was handwritten and blind-

5. I'd only learned to recognize the brisk, erratic letters recently; a few weeks before his disappearance, Doug had dusted off an ancient Olivetti. I later tried it, to see if its typeface matched this enigmatic note's. It didn't.

stamped *Phineas Thwaite, Ph.D.* I knew the name; he was an outside contributor to the Dictionary. Nonplussed, I prepared to leave both missives on Doug's desk, and I lifted the Aleph to make room. That's when I noticed it had finally loaded. And it was open, curiously, to a page of the Dictionary. It was open, in fact, to a specific page: the one in the *J*'s on which Doug's entry appeared.[6] Self-involved as he could sometimes be, that surprised me: that he'd leave the limn open there.

Although it surprised me more that he'd used the Aleph at all— I thought it had been years. He'd told me that after his last assistant, Sam, had optimistically programmed it for him, he'd tried it for just a few months before abandoning it. But it occurred to me that it wouldn't even have turned on if it hadn't been at least a little charged. I wondered why Doug had bothered—and of course why he'd been looking at his own entry. Thinking I'd rib him for it when he turned up, I scanned the screen, planning to quote from it. But it wasn't there.

I clicked forward and back through the pages. Scanned again. The entries skipped from Andrew Johnson to Earvin (Magic) Johnson. No Douglas Johnson. No toothy thumbnail photo of my father. No pithy biographical facts. He had vanished.

Feeling the uncomfortable prickling of a premonition, I opened his satchel—and except for one natty brown shirt, it was empty. No pens or papers. No books. No wallet. The thought I had, unbidden, was that the bag was a decoy. He wasn't coming back for it.

The room began to shrink, and the red lights of tiny cars on the ground below seemed to rise up to blink in tandem with the red light on Doug's desk phone.

Which began, at roughly that moment, to ring.

Panicked, but thinking that it must be Doug calling with an explanation, I leaned in to look at the ID screen. There was no photo, but the caller's name appeared: Phineas Thwaite. Before I could decide whether

---

6. Not all dictionaries published biographical entries—they were absent, e.g., from the *OED*—and Doug would have preferred to omit them from the *NADEL*, too. But bowing to certain trends in the North American lexicographic community, as well as pressure from our board, Doug had allowed entries on some notable people into the second edition. He'd never approved inclusion of his own entry, however—he was nowhere near notable enough to warrant it, he said—and considered making a correction when he saw the "error" in the final printing. "We define words," he'd written in an angry memo to the staff. "We should leave the defining of people to them." But he'd ended on a softer note: "I enjoy laboring in obscurity (with all of you)."

to answer, the phone stopped ringing. The screen quickly blinked fifteen, the number of missed calls. It also said something else. Something that helped me decide—if an impulse can be called a decision—to flee.

All office phones were set up with speed dials between bosses and assistants. That night the display on my dad's phone looked strange to me. When I peered at it more closely, I saw it had changed. It said, "Hotline to Alice." And I knew something was wrong. Because my name isn't Alice. Alice is a fiction. One I never thought I'd hear or see again.

Not long before Doug disappeared, he began behaving in a way some might say was strange. But my antennae, tuned to my own sorrows, hadn't picked up the signals. In retrospect I could see that he seemed more secretive than usual, edgier, and withdrawn. On a few days, for instance, he'd wanted to talk only on the train. That presented logistical problems.

One night the week before, as we were waiting for the downtown 1, he began explaining in a whisper that he'd recently received a spate of odd emails. They had different senders and subjects, but all were composed of incomprehensible strings of words.

"Oh, Doug," I said. "You're not supposed to open those. Did they include ads for things?"

"Things?" he whispered, looking guilty.

"You know, for . . . enhancement? Or, like, pain pills?"

"No," he said, discomfited. "Nothing like that. But I wonder why no one told me. I had to stop using my computer. It started going berserk."

"Dad, yeah," I said. "You can't open those. They're not real."

"So you've gotten them, too?" he said. He seemed concerned.

"Of course. Those scams have been around for years. They're as old as me, I think."

"Oh," he continued, shaking his head. "No. Not that."

"No?" I said, unconvinced.

"No," he said. Then, changing the subject, he added, "But that's not the only thing that worries me." That was when the train had pulled into the station. As we boarded, he lowered his voice even more. I could barely hear him when he said, "I looked up our advance sales earlier, and they're hard to believe. At one point before noon we were up to number 213 on Synchronic's sales list. The second edition, too—up to 448."

"Dad!" I said, clapping his shoulder. "That's incredible! Congratulations!"

"No—but it isn't!" he hissed, glancing at our fellow passengers. They mostly seemed indifferent. "It's actually very suspicious," he said more gently.

"*Doug,*" I said, struggling not to sound annoyed. "Can't you just be happy? This is *good* news. We should be celebrating."

He glanced cagily again around the train car. "If only that were true," he said.

I was expecting him to add more, but just then we'd arrived at Fiftieth Street—my regular stop, where I would have gotten off if I'd been headed home and not to an event with my father—and he nodded emphatically at the platform. I looked up. But all I saw was a motley stream of people on their evening commute. He strained his neck toward the graffiti-scratched window and whispered, *"Tiles."*

"Dad, what are you talking about?" I said in a normal voice. Vera and I had long since learned that the best method for managing Doug's eccentricities was benign neglect.

The train started gliding from the station, and he murmured, "The mosaic—look!" I peered out at the pattern, which I'd seen so many times I couldn't see it anymore.[7] In blue, black, red, and white lacquer chips, the Queen of Hearts accuses the White Rabbit, whose top hat hovers in alarm.

"Okay," I said, twiddling my jacket zipper. "And?"

Doug waited until we'd rumbled back into the tunnel. "Did you notice?" he whispered.

"Notice?" I said. "No—what?"

He sloped in close to me, and I could smell the apothecary scent of licorice on his breath. *"Alice,"* he said. "In Wonderland?"

"Doug," I said, "could you please just spell it out?"

"Alice," he insisted. "If anything should happen to me—which it won't—but if it does, I want us to use the name Alice. To communicate."

"Uh," I said.

"Got it?"

"Roger."

"This is serious," Doug said, sounding impatient.

---

7. The image had transformed, for me, into a harbinger of home: the two short blocks from the subway to our apartment and, as I walked in the door, Max calling out a pet name that I'll omit.

"Okay. And what do I call you?" I teased, feeling a tick of disquiet. I wondered if I should worry—if Doug had slid into a manic state while I'd been cocooned in heartbreak. When under stress, he was sometimes prone to swerves in mood. Frenzied activity. Paranoia.

He looked a little startled, as if he hadn't gotten that far. "I don't know," he said. "Just indulge me, please."

I nodded absently, trying not to betray my vague trepidation. And then something else happened. Something that laid the track for a certain fate. Though at the time my meter reading of our exchange hardly registered any spike in strangeness.

Doug, likely sensing my concern, changed the subject, tossing off some light remark about the talk we were on our way to attend. I don't remember what he said. I wish I did. But the way it faded so quickly from my mind, like a text wisping from a screen, is in fact one of the primary reasons I'm recording this history.

Whatever comment he made, buried inside it was a word I couldn't quite place—a little reservoir of meaning I'd once known that had at some point cracked and drained. And in my brief moment of confusion, I made a stupid, careless mistake: I slid my Meme from my coat pocket and quickly peeked at the screen. (I knew that the Meme, having sensed my small mnemonic lapse, would have logged me into the Word Exchange to retrieve the forgotten term, displaying it in a brief, discreet definition that would quickly melt away.)

I'm sure I thought I was being surreptitious; I knew that if Doug saw what I was doing, he'd give a dire jeremiad. But I'd become so habituated to this routine—one whose frequency had gradually increased without my noticing—that in fact I probably barely bothered to hide it.

When I looked up again, Doug was grimacing. "Not you, too," he said quietly, face blazoned with dark alarm. "The Word Exchange?"

I felt my face spackle with heat, ashamed he'd finally learned my "secret." "Dad, yeah," I said brusquely, looking away. "So? Like most mortals—not you, I realize—I forget the meanings of obscure words sometimes, and I look them up—"

"*Obscure?*" he repeated, nearly bristling. I could tell he was gearing up to elaborate—I was bracing for it—but then he didn't. We'd roused the interest of a few fellow passengers (Doug's wary glances alerted me), and as we slid into our station, he stopped talking.

But I didn't find his silence very comforting; a mild reprimand would have unsettled me less. It meant he was truly worried, which worried me. Did he really believe I was forgetting things—losing my mental acuity? It wasn't a good thought. And it spurred me to remember the way I'd once made fun of friends who were dependent on the Exchange.[8] I half hoped Doug's lecture would come later that night, or at work the next week. But we were madly preparing for launch, and it didn't. Then it never did.

That wasn't entirely the end of our conversation, however. "Just one last thing," he said, frowning. "You're not going to like this." Quickly, furtively, he took two small bottles of what I soon realized were pills from his satchel. They were mottled with characters I couldn't read, and he pressed them on me in such a way that I all but had to take them.

"You'll never need these," he said. "But they're good to have. A few years expired, but it shouldn't matter."

"What will I not need them *for*?" I asked, disturbed. "Do they make me bigger or smaller?"

"Neither, I hope," Doug said wearily. "But knowing you have them will make *me* feel better. And in the *extremely* unlikely event that you start to feel sick, and like something's just very . . . wrong—you're tired or confused, you have muscle aches or fever, even mild hallucinations, and especially if you're having trouble speaking clearly, or if you have a very, very bad headache—just start taking these within forty-eight hours—the sooner, the better—and you should be fine. I'm giving you two courses just in case."

"In case of *what*?" I asked, getting very worried. Doug's behavior was officially off the charts. (Although in my defense, not entirely without precedent: every few years he'd press boxes of old flu medicine on me. So even this, hard as it is for me now to believe, didn't raise the red flag as high as it should have.)

But now I'm digressing. What I meant to say was this: we (he) had

---

8. "Can you pass the, um . . . the, um . . . the—" Ramona would say, gesticulating. "I think the word you want is 'fork'?" I'd tease, handing one to her. Flustered, she'd sigh and say, "Just—my Meme." But at some point it had started happening to me. I began relying on my Meme to anticipate when I'd need it to beam me a word or meaning I'd forgotten "temporarily"—while reading, writing, listening, speaking—often barely registering that it had logged me on to the Word Exchange.

settled on Alice,[9] and I'd stored this conversation on the shelf in my brain where I keep certain stories about Doug.[10] Then I sort of forgot it—until the following Friday, when I found myself alone in his office, staring frantically at his phone.

Barely thinking, I scrolled through Doug's missed calls. Wrote Phineas Thwaite's number on the back of his blind-stamped note. Then, abandoning Doug's satchel, trying to make as little sound as possible, I unlocked the door and peered out into the dark hall. It took all my will not to make a break for it: run flat out. I forced myself to tread quietly, cursing the husky rustling of my coat. I could barely breathe.

As I neared the elevator I passed Bart's office, and decided, almost as an afterthought, to leave a note. His door was open, and I didn't bother with the light. I meant to hurry in and hurry out. Get to the elevator and pump the button. Descend to Rodney in the lobby. Visit Doug's apartment and, if he wasn't there, call the cops. But something stopped me in the doorway.

Sticking out from beneath Bart's desk was a skinny pair of legs.

9. Nicknames, I should note, were one of Doug's things. Growing up, I'd been Apple and Aps, Pin, Needle, and Nins. Vera was Veils, Vittles, Nibbles, and a million other things. Bart's real name wasn't even Bartleby, which was a Melville reference. But Doug had given me the name Alice with none of his usual ebullience.

10. Normally this one would have been cross-referenced under the subcategories "subway," "Alice," and "crazy."

Bar•tle•by \\'bär-təl-bē\ *n* **1 :** a scrivener **2 a :** a man with many friends and casual acquaintances **:** BART **b** *slang* **:** life of the party <here comes ~, the life of the party>; a person who is never lonely, especially not on Friday night

Friday, November 16

Has this happened to you? You're taking a nap. Maybe you're having a dream about someone you know, and maybe you don't feel like revealing all the particulars right now, but let's just say it's a nice one, very vivid, that you'd like to go on dreaming for a while. You don't get that chance, though, because just when you reach the nicest part (praying later you weren't making any incriminating sounds), you're wakened by what turns out to be a woman's screaming. And what happens next, or roughly at the same time, is that you sort of forget where you were napping, which was underneath your desk, and when you try to rise up quickly, you clock yourself so hard in your (admittedly large) forehead that while you're still half asleep, you nearly concuss, and the screaming seems still to be going on and on, like a siren song, until it reaches an apotheosis, and it isn't until you've managed in a bruised approximation of panic to crawl out from below your desk (maybe with the vestige of an erection) that you realize the person standing there in the dark is the star of your once pleasant, now departed dream.

"What the fuck, Bart?" she says when she sees you, which seems a little unfair, considering.

You can't help but notice what she's wearing, because you always can't help but notice. Tonight her sartorial choices are regrettably voluminous: baggy red pants—pajama bottoms?—and an olive-green coat quilted in figure-swallowing chevrons. Her hair looks unwashed, though you can't really call the kettle black on that one, and she seems to have on two different shoes. This change in mien is pretty recent; in fact, you think you can date it to the day Max moved out of their Lilliputian apartment in Hell's Kitchen. (A lamentably apt neighborhood for Max, less so for this variegated seraph.)

Not that your heart doesn't still do an ovation each time she walks by your open office door. And in fact, on those rare occasions when you might shut said door to concentrate, just the buttery clop of her clogs on the carpet outside is enough to carbonate your blood. Her congenital restlessness, thank God, tempts her from her desk a couple times an hour—to check on Doug (and, on the way back, chat with someone, usually Svetlana or Frank), to visit the kitchen for endless cups of tea (and subsequently the ladies'), and, more often than really seems possible, to take covert trips to the cafeteria for candy.

In the month since Max left, though, her restlessness has changed. These days you sometimes see her slowly come to a bewildered halt halfway down the hall. She'll shake her head as if lost, then turn around and go back—sometimes only to stumble by again a few moments later, muttering something unkind to herself, face beset with disappointment.

And what a face. A face that (if it weren't so chauvinistic to think it) you might find yourself believing should be exempt from mortal disappointments. The kind of face that one could easily make the mistake of describing, e.g., as a "radiant, pre-Raphaelite cynosure" (as you may have done on one of this journal's earlier pages). It does conform to a paint-by-numbers kind of cardinal "beauty." You could imagine it atomized by the teen blogs you're sometimes forced to consult for neologisms, with its [sic] "perfect heart shape," "rich, golden complexion," and high "crabapple cheeks," its huge "sea-green" eyes, straight, slender nose, and pointy chin, lips so ridiculously full they could be in an ad for tire gauges, and the long, blondish hair that "halos" the whole thing, nearly condemning it to simple, plasticine convention. But it's saved, naturally, by its defects. I.e., her slightly crooked front teeth; her unusually dark brows, which help perpetuate confusion about her hair's natural color (you've seen it in shades of brown, black, platinum, red, and, once, blue); her oddly cramped smile, the tightness of which is somehow accentuated by a peculiarly pleatlike and asymmetrical dimple; and especially the small, brownish pink, strawberry-shaped mark on her left cheek. It's always the scuffs in the marble that make its inner light seem to glow more brightly.

(Twice you've heard her described as "plain": once by Ana herself, which was a little grating, but once also by Svetlana, which you found far more mystifying.)

So, no. It's not the neat collection of ideal features that makes your guts do a little leap. It's the way her upper lip tends to dew with sweat, especially when she's nervous, e.g., during a book launch, or when she has to give a Dictionary tour to someone kind of famous. It's how Doug's Dougish little jokes and pranks can get her to bray with bona fide mirth, and the ambrosial if tuneless songs you sometimes catch her humming in the hall. In other words, it's the way your insides feel when she sees you and smiles.

(Okay, enough. I'm now officially embarrassed by much of the above, but especially of writing in the second person. Somehow it seemed so much more evocative and—ugh—literary a few months ago, when I finally succumbed to Doug's aggressive encouragements and started keeping this journal. But let's face it, I'm no Camus or Faulkner or Calvino. And anyway, my use of "you" derived not from an interesting effort to "subvert narrative expectations"—i.e., call attention to the consentient artifice implied by the act of reading—but probably just from a misguided attempt to short-circuit my own neurotic self-censoring tendencies by sort of pretending I'm someone else. But now I'm stopping, officially.)

Hence: "Ana," I say, rubbing the lump rising on my forehead.

"What were you doing?" she asks, in what I can only describe as a suspicious tone. I notice she's holding something crumpled in her purple mitten.

"Well . . ." I begin. But it's at about this point that I realize how not only small and unwashed but how truly *harrowed* Ana is looking, and it doesn't seem worth explaining about the train up to Washington Heights taking 30 minutes, times two to come back, and having at least another few hours of work for tomorrow, rendering the cost-benefit analysis of napping in the relative comfort of my sagging, squeaky full mattress at home versus (as I generally do) on the floor beneath my desk to lead me most often on weekends to the latter course. (I occasionally sleep in the guest bed of Dr. D's apartment, in Ana's old room, but I'm not sure she knows.)

It goes without saying, of course, that Ana isn't merely pretty. Both in the sense that she supersedes mere prettiness (see above) and in that she's not *merely* pretty. It wouldn't be an overstatement to call her, as Dr. D once did, "a boldly sapient creature of divine enchantment." Form, I think, is dialectically related to content. And in fact it's perhaps her not-mere-prettiness, her intellect and sense of style and kindness and competency and good joke timing and infectious joy for life, etc., that have, to my mind (and, believe me, many others'), elevated her from the more crowded and clamorous ranks of the pretty to the rarified stratum of the beautiful. Something about her suggests the endless unfolding of possibilities. Ana qua Ana is, basically, flawlessness qua flawlessness, sui generis.

Maybe, before launching into an accounting of tonight's events, I should start by explaining how my acquaintanceship with Ana began. Maybe. But as Hegel teaches us, beginnings are necessarily problematic. (As are endings.)

How can I describe my first encounter with Ana fairly, when my understanding of her essence has passed through infinite iterations over the past four and a half years? My early impressions, if I could even accurately access them, would come across now as vulgar. Not in the sense of lewdness, of course, but I'm ashamed to admit that some of her subtler and more refined charms—maybe, e.g., her brains—were a little lost on me when Dr. D introduced us in the hall outside his office, Ana wearing just a yellow slip of sundress.

Unfortunately, in one of the more disappointing turns of my early adulthood, Ana met Max soon after. (His appearance, like Ana's, tends not to elicit a neutral response. He has sort of woundedly Rimbaudian eyes, oddly paired with a warm, impish, slightly gap-toothed smile. That, and he's tall and blond. Honestly, he and Ana don't look altogether unrelated. A fact I'll diplomatically refrain from remarking on further.)

He turned up at the Dictionary unannounced—to visit me, funnily enough. I think it would be fair to say that Max was also less attuned at the time to the sapient-creature side of Ana's nature. Unlike me, though, he didn't really outgrow his first impressions. In part because he didn't have to: within a week, as he'd crassly wagered several friends, he and

Ana were "together." Also, though, Max is incapable of anything more probing than first impressions. He claims his powers of perspicacity are such that he "gets" everything—women, philosophical precepts, etc.— from the most superficial of initial perceptions. Any deliberations one might undertake beyond the seminal "gut reaction" should be dismissed, he says, as perseveration.

(On the afternoon Max and Ana met, when it was already clear where things were headed, Max cornered me outside the office men's room. "Going in for a grunter?" he said, very loudly, which made me blush. The men's room is near Neologisms, and several women work in Neologisms. I don't like calling attention to these visits, especially given how often they occur. Once he'd embarrassed me, Max gripped my shoulder in a way I found menacing, and oddly intimate. "Don't tell her about me," he said quietly. "I don't want to fuck this one up. So don't *you* fuck it up for me." I promised him, of course, that I wouldn't say anything, which I wouldn't have anyway, because of the sheer unpleasantry of divulging an unattractive truth to an attractive person.)

Let me begin instead, then—yes, appreciating the irony—with Hegel. First, it bears acknowledging that G. W. F. H., born in Stuttgart at the end of August 1770, has enjoyed only fleeting upticks in popularity. Depending on whom you ask, his work is part of the canon or it isn't. He's been hijacked by the left or the right. Some claim he's an apologist for the abuse of state power, even totalitarianism. At the moment of his death, he's supposed to have said, "And he didn't understand me."

GWF is often remembered only for the reductive thesis-antithesis-synthesis triad, when that phraseology wasn't even his but Kant's. Carl Jung (of all people) called him crazy. And more philistines than one could count have accused his writing of being inelegant or difficult— or incomprehensible. As every serious scholar knows, to read Hegel in anything other than the original German is an amateurish offense. There really is just no appropriate translation for *Begriff, Urteil,* or even *Geist,* let alone *Aufhebung.*

According to my reading of Hegel, language is our servant, submissive to the master of reason. Max, among others, likes to remind me that this judgment is considered conservative; it apparently fails to account for historical context. And I guess it *could* seem contradictory to argue that Hegel is only Hegelian in the gusty vigor of his native German. It might be more rational to make a concession here to at least the weak version of the Sapir-Whorf hypothesis. (I feel a certain kinship with this version, frankly, if weakness is its defining feature. The day Max bench-pressed me was a humbling day indeed.)

So, okay: I give in. Language can *influence* the content of communication. But really I was defending Hegel against charges of inelegance, not difficulty. What's *Aufhebung* in English? Only "to raise up." In German it connotes (i) raising higher, literally and figuratively; (ii) taking away, i.e., canceling or annulling; and (iii) (thanks to Hegel) sublation. Viz., this one small, soothing word and its multifarious meanings are in some ways the kernel from which Hegel's whole philosophical enterprise springs. Its aleph, if you will. *Aufhebung.* Aleph. They even sound like simulacra. (I don't mean, of course, the electronic device. Although I'm sure that's why the word is on my mind—from the strange conversation Ana and I had a couple hours ago.)

I guess all I'm trying to say is that language may be large, unwieldy, and in a perpetual state of transformation—in other words, language is like love—but, unlike Dr. D, I don't think it's greater than we are. I think it's our duty, in fact, to corral it into coherence; to suppress its more unruly tendencies; to verify its meaning and, more importantly, its efficacy; to test its subjectivity-bridging potential. (Again, we should treat it very much like love.)

And on this point maybe Max and I aren't so far apart. We both think love (and language) are interesting but taffylike diversions: soft, simple, perhaps a little salty. If either one takes over your life, you're an ass.

I met Hermes Maximilian King and Hegel at roughly the same time, in Professor Lockhart's terms four and five seminar on the mythologization of the philosopher, in which Lockhart argued that Hegel was one of the most important—and misread—thinkers of the past 200 years. (Max remained skeptical. His attachment was to Sartre. Who, by the way, was also influenced by Hegel.)

You might think the thin coincidence of two people sharing a syllabus wouldn't automatically occasion some kind of lasting friendship. But to understand my relationship with Max, it's important to know that, apart from us and David Lockhart, there were only two other people in that class. And 24 other students on campus—total. No girls at the time. No distractions. No chances for escape, or much escapism. An actual *policy* promoting isolation. Such was the nature of our college, way over yonder in that lonesome California valley.

I didn't really know how lucky we were to be at Deep Springs. Even then, a decade ago, professors at other schools were slowly being replaced by computers and machines. Now, with the Meme, kids just download everything. For us there were nights we stayed up until four in the morning reading. And you could *feel* the work we did: an afternoon of hefting alfalfa bales will leave you sorer than a beating. That's why it's hard for me to understand Max's plans to take over the world. (Kidding. Kind of.) But I guess it fits on the logical continuum. Let's just say he can claim an inimitable and, to many, intoxicating admixture of volubility, rigor, pathological charisma, and dismissiveness. He was—is—worshipped. Then, by Professor Lockhart, by probably 22 of the 26 pupils at our school, by *all* their moms and sisters and girlfriends, and yes, debasing as it is to admit, by me, even if my hero worship was shot through with a note of very serious doubt. The first thing Max ever said to me? "You look like my great-uncle Gustav, man. I think he has those same suspenders."

The truth (and I find this maddening) is he just has that thing. I can't explain it; I just know what it is. I've studied it. But it's proven hard to replicate. It partly has to do with eye contact, and the ease and frequency with which he touches people. Partly with how he smiles when he says names. And partly it's a scintillating skill he's perfected: of first showering you with, and then withholding, affection. But there are other variables, too, beyond human ken.

Over the course of that semester, it was functionally impossible not to get to know Max well. Far more intimately, I thought at the time, than anyone else ever had—including the (impressive number of) women with whom he's been involved. (As it turns out, Max has an almost alchemical ability to morph nearly every relationship into one the other party feels is the closest they've had.) Because fate dictated that we serve together on the Curriculum Committee (Max was, of course, Cur-Com chair) while we also both had Boarding House duty (somehow I always did most of the dishes), we spent more time together in those two months than I've spent with almost anyone. And I'll say it: I was honored to be his friend.

For all his faults (and faults happen to be a specialty of mine), Max is something of a marvel. That observation clearly isn't very new. But while others might try to explicate Max by listing what I see as carefully cultivated traits (e.g., that blend of magnetism and energy that together convey "authenticity"; his fearlessness; his weird, somewhat contingent brand of integrity; or even his blazing and unconventional intelligence, which probably constitutes real genius), I consider all that secondary—just part of the mythology. When I met Max, what impressed me most was something far more essential and surprising: I imagined I recognized a true generosity of spirit.

In retrospect, I realize he kind of reminded me of Florian Reiter, my closest friend from Carbondale Community High. Florian spent just junior year in Illinois; he was on exchange from Salzburg, and I wasn't sure at first that befriending him was the best idea. My stock was pretty low already; I was afraid if I joined forces with a brash, fashion-challenged foreign kid, we'd plummet through the earth together.

But Florian had an outsider's willful blindness to social boundaries, and he had confidence. As it turned out, he could get along with everyone—and he chose to get along with me. (When I understood that later, it was humbling.) Also, he was hard to avoid; he was in most of my honors and AP classes, in Science Club and on Math Team, and soon he started coming to the couple of college courses I audited at SIU. Later I helped line him up with some waitering shifts at the Lodge. (They loved him there. I think the accent helped.) He even joined Debate, which was maybe the one thing he didn't really excel at, but which he did with the same ribald enthusiasm with which he did everything.

Because he was stuck with the god-fearing Knupps, he was never free on Sundays. (He was also forced to wear sweaters, courtesy of Mrs. Knupp, featuring reindeer and snowflake fantasias, which quickly keened his American slang, esp. inc. the phrase "your mother.") When he could get away, he was the only person able to convince me to go camping in Trail of Tears State Forest or fishing and hunting at Horseshoe Lake with my dad and Tobias. He called everything a "woodlands adventure," even visits to the shooting range.

Florian was also the only other person my age I'd met who could operate a record player, and the things he listened to blew me away: the Goldberg Variations, Shostakovich, *Mozart*. But Slick Rick, too, and the Notorious B.I.G., Fela Kuti, Joy Division, Siouxsie and the Banshees. He'd engage in endless rounds of Which Is Better with me: Johnny Cash or Dolly Parton, Pantera or Slayer, *Vertigo* or *Rear Window, Best of*

Youth or *The Wire, Settlers of Catan* or *Advanced D&D,* deep-fried pick-
les or deep-fried bacon, Hemingway or Fitzgerald, etc., ad infinitum.
After a while, sort of reluctantly, I gave him things I was writing, and
he'd tell me what he thought. (Sometimes crushingly, sometimes not.)

But I was most impressed by the casual way he dispensed wisdom.
Here, e.g., is some Florian mint: "If your brain is smart but your body is
stupid, you will be a very sad man." "The most important thing in life
is to be decisive; what you decide matters not as much." "Interesting
women get more attracted by humor, dark humor, and—how do you
say?—*geschicklichkeit,* plus true capacity for intimacy, than some big
red trucks and hulk muscles." And: "Meat: this is the best gift God gave
to us. Maybe after sex." One he lived by (and that I did not at the time):
"You must be willing to take a punch." Admittedly, these aphorisms
might sound a little unnuanced to an adult ear. But at 16, just sitting
with him in my living room felt like prospecting for gold.

And I guess the point is this: until I met Max, I'd never met anyone
who seemed as real, as fully himself, as Florian did. But more than that,
he was a really good person. The day he left, I drove him to the airport,
and I teared up a little on the way home.

A friendship like that was what I thought I'd signed on for with Max.

After our term together in the Boarding House, Max went on to be a
Feedman, Butcher, and finally Cowboy. I followed a different trajectory:
as Dairy Boy; then assigned endless alfalfa duty; until finally answering my prescribed calling, as Librarian. Because I have a slight self-
loathing streak, I ran against him for student body president. Max won
(if I remember correctly, it was 21 votes to 5) and served popularly and
well—until he was suspended, disciplined, and stripped of the position.
(Some of our classmates were actually crying as they cast their ballots
to unseat him.)

Basically, it came down to embezzling fairly insignificant sums of
grocery money for drugs. Our college has only two self-enforced rules,
established with the school's founding a century ago. One: you can't
leave campus during term except on official school business or matters
of religion or illness. The other? Drugs and alcohol are strictly forbidden. When Max was ousted, I asked him why he did cocaine (and, it was
rumored, crack). Most of the other stuff I could fathom—the drinking
and pot, bribing the visiting writer to drive him to the town of Bishop
for trysts, even the prank with the pinball machine and Samantha, one of

our pigs. Some of it I'd known about before it was exposed. But maybe because I'm from a part of the country where there are more meth labs than drive-throughs, anything harder than cough syrup always makes me nervous.

(When several of your cousins, and even an uncle, have been arrested for possession, and when, in the middle of the night before debate finals, you've accidentally stumbled on your mom quietly weeping in the kitchen over an empty carton of Neapolitan ice cream, wondering where she and the family went wrong and how she'll come up with Uncle Jack's bail—should she see about being a greeter at the mall? [my mom is a retired history teacher and part-time librarian, and while she absolutely loves people and has an impressive threshold for boredom, I think a greeter job might crush her soul]—and you offer her your small nest egg earned from grueling hours of waiting tables and tutoring, and she tearfully accepts it, which both of you regret, and when her tear-striped face is the first thing you picture whenever someone mentions drugs, this anxiety doesn't seem so wildly misplaced.)

But all Max said, smiling, was, "It's fun." We were in the Boarding House; I remember he was chugging milk, which irritated me for some reason. Like everyone (and maybe more than everyone), I felt betrayed, but also slightly complicit. As if the fun part had been fooling us.

And it made me mad. Madder, in fact, than I could ever remember letting myself get (including the time Tobias accidentally crashed my car even after I said he couldn't borrow it). The feeling was strangely fortifying, like a vitamin. Compounded with a noxious mix of righteousness, disenchantment, worry, and curiosity. (I'd never really done more than drink—beer, parental spirits, the occasional wine cooler. The couple times I'd smoked pot, it had rendered me jangly rather than high.)

My forearms were tingling. I felt light, and larger than myself. I felt, in other words, like I could take a punch. Or throw one. But I also felt just the tiniest flicker of doubt. Despite the overwhelming evidence against him—much of which I'd seen—I was in an interregnum of belief. Maybe Max had done some of the alleged things. But for him to *steal* from us? I just couldn't accept it yet. I mean, Max *loaned* money all the time. It didn't make sense. And questioning that aspect of the charges against him made me question everything.

So on that afternoon in the BH, I wanted him to explain himself. Or at least pretend to try. But he just squinted into the distance. "Man," he said, laughing, "you think too much." He had a milk mustache, and his laugh was loaded with heat-seeking derision.

"Yeah," I said (and I still regret this). "Well, that's kind of the point."

Max just shook his head, said, "Jesus, Horse—keep it *light*," and walked away, taking his milk glass with him. Through the window I watched him toss it in a hedge.

And that was it. All his "complications"—the paradoxes that had once made him seem so exceptional—fell away. It was the end of any real friendship that existed between us. After that it was mostly soap and shadows, as Ana might say.

That was nine years ago. Not much has changed. Like everyone who imagines he's a hero, Max has a fatal flaw: he likes to tempt fate. If not lashed tightly to the mast, he'll always cast himself overboard. He's convinced he can swim, but he nearly drowns every time. After a while, though, he'll surface again and walk from the water unharmed. It's the rest of us trying to figure out what just happened.

To illustrate, let me offer a more recent example, from about four months back. It was late on a Friday night, around ten, and I'd fallen asleep again on a scrap pile of neologisms. The desk started gently rumbling (maybe a 2 on the Richter of insect earthquakes), and through cracked lids I could see my cell phone bluely shimmying toward the edge of the desk. I picked it up, thinking, *If it's Ana, I'll die*. It was Ana. But of course (as if on purpose?) I missed the call.

I sat starkly upright in my swivel chair, gulped a few times, smiled, felt sick, promised God I'd say 10 Ave Marias if Ana left a message— this all took about 14 seconds—then decided I'd call her back regardless. As I flipped open my phone, though, it started vibrating again; the screen said it was Max, and should I Answer or Ignore?

Against my better judgment, I answered. I almost always answer, which Max knows.

"If Ana calls, don't answer," Max yelled into the pink domicile of my ear. The juggernaut tones of a party or bar thundered from behind his yelling to crush several dozen cells of my auricular hair.

"What?" I said, hoping to play dumb. It never worked. Max was inured.

"Or actually, dude, come meet us," Max shouted. "This party's pretty talented" (one of Max's many euphemisms for noting a given venue's density of attractive women). "We're at SoPo." Then he hung up. And since Max was fond of "losing" his Meme ("Can't have the old lady always calling," he'd enjoyed saying in front of Ana), my tenuous connection to him (and thus possible escape from a lie/Friday night ad nauseam) was gone with a beep. I headed to SoPo to meet him, annoyed before I'd even buttoned my coat.

The walk from the Dictionary was short and gloomy, scattered with chicken bones and profane requests for cash. When I arrived at SoPo, the first thing I discovered was Max, ringed by several more and less beautiful women, doing lines in the bathroom.

Max and his partners were celebrating: that afternoon, after weeks of secret negotiations, they'd sold their start-up, Hermes, to Synchronic, Inc.—for more than $100 million, I think. (Actually, I'm trying very hard *not* to think about it.)

Maybe it sounds uncouth that Max named a company after himself. But really it's apt: Hermes was the god of words, commerce, and thieves. And Hermes Corp. is in the business of selling language. (Like me and Dr. D, I guess. But a little more profitably.) At least their new parent company, Synchronic, certainly is.

I don't actually quite get why Synchronic was so interested in Hermes. Although I also don't know that much about what Hermes *does*, per se; its nebulous mission statement—"Redefining communication for a changing future"—isn't exactly a decoder ring. They initially did some stuff with voice commands or something, working on better ways for Memes and people to "talk." And I know they've had a few big successes with online games, too, which they did seemingly on the side: Word Warcraft™, Wordloxx™, Whorld™. But that doesn't really explain it. I think they're maybe designing an interface between Synchronic's Meme and its Word Exchange? (To be fair, this has been explained to me several times.)

In the bar, the Hermes boys were in full swing: Floyd, calling "Strippers for everyone!," was getting lap-danced by a bleached, sinewy, possibly Belarusian teen; Johnny Lee was drunkenly slumped over the *Time Crisis* console, his girlfriend watching graciously nearby; and Vernon, garishly waving his cane, was chatting up some girls who claimed they really liked to read. (One waggled her Meme at me flirtatiously, and when I said, "How do I know you don't just use it to watch movies?" she said, "Same thing.")

Apparently no one had thought to inform Ana of the night's festivities. When she called me again later, I was pretty much swaying on off-brand lager and a few/four bourbons bought for me by Max. (Max was in one of his generous/jacked-up moods, and I was in one of my—extremely rare—drunken moods. I'd even spent a couple hours speaking to a skinny but otherwise comely Meme developer with very pink lipstick. I was feeling like a wine-knight. I was having a good time.)

"Heeeeellllloooooo, Ana," I answered. Max, who was sitting beside me at the bar, his hand inside the shirt of some squash-blossom blonde, turned around to flash a warning glance. I winked back conspiratorially (which, I confess, made me sick).

"Do you know where he is?" said Ana. "Did something happen?"

From the twangy tension in her voice, I guessed she'd been crying. The sick feeling redoubled, punched up by a feeling of panic. For some reason I don't really understand—had he come up earlier?—I thought she was talking about Doug. It took me, evidently, too long to reply, because she whispered, "Oh, God," and then she did start to cry, and I knew those were Max tears, always kept on reserve, and I wanted to die.

"No, no," I said, waving agitatedly. My skinny companion raised a skinny eyebrow and took a long, challenging sip of her sloe gin fizz. Scissoring off my stool, its duct tape sticking to my slacks, I exited the bar almost at a run, then breached the pocket of smokers loitering near the door to reach a quietish bubble down the block.

"Sorry about that," I said, sounding, I thought, cartoonishly sober. "I was just passing a very loud bar. I was at the office late"—I looked at my watch and discovered with an ulcery pain that it was three—"and, you know, the trains at this hour." Then I thought, morosely, about the trains at that hour. It would be four-thirty at least before I got home.

"So you haven't heard from him, I guess." Her voice then was so Ana, so quavering, conjured her so perfectly, that I imagined it as an audible strand of her DNA. If I could only capture it somehow as it passed through the tiny holes of my phone and make it manifest, I could re-create her whole there on the sidewalk, probably wearing a leather vest or a silk kimono or a pair of vintage orange velvet hot pants (not that I've been keeping track), something else impractically fashionable for the July night, and I would kiss her.

Instead I said, "He's here. We were working on something—I've been helping him with a project—and he just decided to stay."

"Can I talk to him? For a second?" The relief in her voice made my elbow weak. I didn't want to go back in that bar, guide the phone into the hand of Max's not cupping some other girl's breast. Watch while he lied to her. Like *I* was lying to her. My dulcarnon status became painfully acute. "Oh." I coughed. "You know Max."

After a pause, during which I pondered what this meant (and worried that she might, too), she said, "Comatose? Snoring?" She tried to sound cheerfully rather than neurotically proprietary. It was hard to tell whether she was pretending for my sake or hers.

"Like a rhinoceros," I said, not sure if rhinos even make noise, just thinking of sleep apnea and rhinoplasty and working up a sweat, a little resentful of Ana for reminding me of my place in the moral universe. "I'm sure he'll call first thing. And I'm pretty tired myself."

"Of course," she said, sounding a bit peeved. "I'm so sorry. I was worried. Couldn't sleep. He's been, you know, disappearing a lot lately. I just wanted to make sure he's still alive."

I found it odd, bordering on disturbing, that she didn't know Max was out celebrating Hermes's sale. Was it remotely conceivable that she hadn't yet heard the news? But what I said was, "You worry too much," trying to imagine for a moment it was true, that her worry was unfounded. (If she were in love with me, it would be.) "Goodnight, Girl Friday," I (apparently) added. "I never even knew what you were wearing."

And as she asked, "Bart, are you drunk?" I closed the phone, delicately and of course sadly, waiting on the pitching curb for the world to stop slow-dancing with me.

But that's not really where I want to end. If we're talking about love, it seems only right to return now to the very strange story Ana told me earlier tonight after waking me from my Ana-soaked reverie. Ana, who seems so very alone these days, and who, until this evening, has resisted my solicitous (though perhaps silent) offers of aid: an ear, a shoulder, etc.

We sat thigh-to-thigh in my dark office, the door locked, her whispering. In other words, I was finding it somewhat difficult to concentrate on the actual sounds she was forming rather than on the warm, breathy sensation of them exiting her mouth and entering, so sweetly, my very vivified ear. And I admit that I didn't really start to listen until she said, "Bart, are you listening?"

"No," I said, prudently.

For a moment she looked like she might cry, which was a very terrible thing, but then she touched my knee, which was a wonderful thing, and said, "That's why I like you, Bart. Honesty is a virtue."

This declaration made me think back to, e.g., the Night of Slow-Dancing on the Curb, and I temporarily felt very terrible again, but she resumed talking shortly after that, and we got to do the whole thing over from the top, so I had to quickly swap my terrible feelings for something like focus. When she showed me the *J* page in Dr. D's Aleph, I assured her that there must be some simple explanation.

"Like what?" Ana asked in a tone of hopeful skepticism.

"Remember, there's a reason Synchronic recalled these things," I ad-libbed. That seemed to have a slightly ameliorating effect. "Or maybe he finally made that 'correction,' like he always threatened."

"Maybe," she conceded. (I was a little curious about that myself.)

The pneumatic messages were similarly easy to dismiss. Dr. Thwaite, I told her, was almost certainly crazy, but also harmless. And the fake definition was probably a prank.

"A prank?" she said. "But it's not funny."

"Define 'funny,'" I said. She didn't laugh. "Get it? Define?"

"I get it," she said.

The Alice thing was harder to refute. I proposed we go together to look at Doug's phone, but she refused. Even when I offered (bravely, I thought) to go alone, she said no, which I found kind of flattering. When she said, "Bart, let's get out of here," I was feeling so emboldened that I offered to escort her to Dr. D's apartment. And she agreed.

In the lobby Rodney unwittingly undid a lot of my good work when he said, "Y'all find him, then?" Ana, looking panicked, turned to me, and I invented a story (which I happen to believe) about how Doug must have slipped out while Rodney was on break. "Haven't taken a break since five," said Rodney, looking at me oddly. (Maybe he was offended? Thought I meant he'd been shirking? Or maybe he just wondered how I'd gotten Ana alone on a Friday night.) But somehow, through a combination of chuckling, making expressive gestures with my arms, and wishing Rodney a good night, I managed to keep Ana calm and (crucially) get her out the door. (And I have to admit, I liked taking charge.)

When we got to Doug's and didn't find him in, I barely remember what I said to hold back the storm. I think I may have promised to call the police if he didn't turn up by morning. (That could be awkward. Especially when D confronts me about letting things get out of hand. But tonight is tonight. The morning's not until the morning.)

When Ana and I stepped back outside, I had no time even to hope: a cab passed; she hailed it with her Meme and said, "Come with me?" I was so overwhelmed that I got in first, before it even finished braking. Then she also clambered aboard, almost into my lap, and suddenly there we were—here we are—a few short blocks later, at her apartment, alone together. ("Alone together" is a phrase I once had no appreciation for.)

Before tonight I'd never been inside. This only really struck me as strange during my ascent of the fourth and final flight, at which point my heart (maybe just taxed from the climb, or maybe in thrall to the bewildering thought that I was about to enter Ana's apartment) began to beat violently. After we summited the stairs, I had to grip the wall for a second.

Until fairly recently I wouldn't have found the ongoing noninvitation to what was formerly Max and Ana's place in any way surprising. But as Ana finally led me, somewhat apologetically, inside (to insinuate that I'm judging *at all* would essentially be a crime, but the myriad mounds of clothes and other breakup detritus piled pretty much everywhere actually made it hard just to open the door wide), I realized, with a mild sense of astonishment, that Max has already had me over to his new house twice. Once in the summer, right after he bought it (I'm not sure Ana knows he's had it so long; I certainly don't intend to apprise her), and then again a few weeks ago, for a putative "housewarming" (an event so ennui-inspiring that I'd barely unzipped my coat before deciding to leave).

Tonight, standing in the middle of Ana's living room–cum–dining room–cum–study, I couldn't have been more shocked by the contrast between their living quarters if I'd licked an electric socket.

Max's place isn't without charm. I mean, it's a 19th-century carriage house in Red Hook's beating heart, mere blocks from the water. (And hence, alas, that monstrous new Koons sculpture, theoretically meant to keep the water back.) From Max's roof deck there's a view of the bay and that great, insensate goddess whose green-patinaed majesty has heartened New World comelings for ages. He also has: two working fireplaces, a small home sauna, a manicured backyard, a regulation-sized billiards table, etc. The master bath boasts a large mural on a crumbly chunk of wall, allegedly painted by Banksy back before we knew who that was. Beneath one set of stairs is an enchanting, antediluvian film-screening nook. (Of course in his office Max also has a CubeYMax 3D printer, a glyph projector, a simulator, and an eerie, "immersive" gaming booth that hooks up to the Meme.) In other words, Max resides in an advertisement from some heirloom men's magazine.

But the apartment he shared with Ana for more than three years? The place she still calls home? Stepping across the threshold left me more or less dumb. For one thing, it's *very* small. (Conceivably smaller than my apartment.) There's the room you step into, referred to above; the tiny kitchen, off to the left; and past that, a bathroom. Then, to the right, and not even shielded by a door, is the bedroom. (A room it gives me jitters just to think about.) But that's it. Le tout. You can see almost the whole thing from the welcome mat.

Also, though, and maybe even more amazing, it's kind of full of crap. I mean *not* crap—so much of it is irresistibly *great*—but *stuff:* light fixtures with weird, wattled textures whose referents on the flora-fauna spectrum are fairly ambiguous; mismatched dishes (many on display in the sink); lovely little glasses ringed in old, worn-off gold; plants in varying stages of vitality; a dusty vacuum bent with scoliosis; a small ceramic rhino head mounted to one wall; ancient musical instruments (dinged French horn, dulcimer [?] lute [??]). In a corner, a scary scissor mobile hangs, sword-of-Damocles-like, over an "easy" chair. (Ha.)

All the chairs—and the number beggars plausibility (seven, maybe?)—are mounded with throws and faded tapestries and pretty flattened pillows dense with flowers and ladies and fleurs-de-lis. There are hooks dripping with scarves—plaid, tasseled, silk—alongside coats and towels. Shelves crammed with sweaters, sheets, tennis rackets. A messy shrine to boots and shoes. A veritable explosion of hats spilling off a rack on the back of the door (pillbox, cowboy, bike helmet, fedora). Dresses from every decade loll on a clothing rack with wheels. (The shivery fabrics feel almost animate, as if they could slither from their hangers.) In the kitchen, skull-shaped salt and pepper shakers grimace beside a fat ceramic man with the word "COOKIE" on his stomach. (If one squints, he bears a slight resemblance to Doug.) Even the windowsill has tenants: a wind-up robot, a plastic archer, a tin ziggurat, a rabbit eating a carrot, an empty flower vase, a bourbon bottle (also empty).

On one of the overflowing shelves I was astonished to see some old

CDs, and even more dumbfounded by which ones: mixed in with a few I assumed to be Max's were many I knew were not: Joan Jett, The Avengers (!), Kim Gordon, Bikini Kill, and a bunch of jaw-droppingly great old country and blues vocalists, too—Wanda Jackson, Loretta Lynn, Rose Maddox, Lefty Frizzell, Nina Simone, Robert Johnson, Sister Rosetta Tharpe. I was agog. (Ana saw me looking at the music and laughed a little self-consciously. "I know—who still has CDs?" she said, misinterpreting my scrutiny. "Getting rid of stuff is sort of hard for me. I bought all those in high school.")

But I was even more amazed by the art—*her* art—which is everywhere, and nearly all on paper. I always thought Ana worked mostly with glyphs—I could swear that's what she told me once—and there is, in fact, a big glyph projector in the bedroom, beneath the sim's massive screen. But there are also scrupulous, photo-realistic drawings in black and white: of thunderheads curdled over spent, empty fields; of the burned-out chassis of old cars; of giant, silent glaciers, calving ice; of thin women in slips, ecstatically dancing, the whites of their eyes almost seeming to shine. Excruciating drawings. Stunning. Almost paralytic. (I actually wobbled on the edge of a worry that I might lacrimate.)

And the paintings were just as fucking good. Richly saturated hues, stylized and bare. Strange angles that implied occlusion. A fixation with words in bygone form: newspaper headlines, shredded phonebook pages, haunting half-bare billboards. When I made some observation about linguistic affinity and heredity and Freud—so obvious, I worried that I sounded like a philistine—Ana gave a startled, gargled laugh. Her already enormous eyes grew even wider. And I was immediately engulfed in a warm, prickly compunction.

It was the photos from her past, though, that totally clobbered me. Some were actual snapshots, patchworking the walls. (Those were old, of course, mainly family tableaux; there's no such thing as candid photos anymore.) One—of Vera, Doug, and a young Ana chasing each other with pies, Ana with a whipped-cream beard and Vera wiping laughtears from her eyes—caused my hand to rise unbidden to my chest. And not only because they all looked so *happy* then, but because I found myself searching the frame for other kids, and I realized with a cold, jagged jolt that Ana's childhood must have been extremely lonely. I literally can't imagine growing up—turning into a person—without little Emma bumping constantly along behind me, like a blond tetherball, trailing her tattered blue blankie and calling "Hossy! Wait for me!" Or, for that matter, without Tobias's ongoing barrage of minor physical assaults, which kept me adorned with purple hearts. (And which my gentle parents rendered still more painful, and confusing, by penalizing with a tepid, paradoxical form of corporal punishment on us both.)

I also saw lots more "snapshots" via Ana's profile on Life. (N.B.: I didn't open it; she'd left it up on the sim.) While Ana was making us some ziti, I wandered into the bedroom and scrolled through some of them. Most were of A with her friends—whose names, embarrassingly, I seem somehow to have gleaned. I.e., Ana's Saint Ann's friend, Ramona, a balletically thin, milk-skinned brunette who's maybe a little plain but who comes across as very striking. (After several of her visits to A at the Dictionary, I've decided it's [i] her glaring, strobelike sense of humor, which is borderline frightening, and [ii] her incredible eyes, which burn with a vivid, sort of satyresque fire.)

Her closest friend seems to be Coco. (My sense is that A often stayed at her place when things with Max hit a patch of black ice.) Coco's more classically beautiful than Ramona—I'm pretty sure she's half French, half Ethiopian—and like Ana, she's a visual artist. She appears to be doing quite well for herself. (Apparently she works mostly with lard.) I think it was Ana, in fact, who introduced her to her gallerist and helped her secure an artist visa.

Then there's Audrey, 2L at NYU. I don't know much about her, but I do know she has an evocative tattoo: a large prawn, discreetly curled on her tiny upper arm and captioned "Imperial Shrimp." (Ironic commentary, so Ana has said, on being second-generation Shanghainese, and, more apropos, on the inverse relationship between her physical size and the size of her trust fund.)

I've never met the fifth woman in their group. Jesmyn, I think. From the photos, I can see only that she's tall and pale and sort of gawky, with a prominent jaw and a weird, serrated fringe of reddish black hair. Kind of punk rock. (My type, in other words. Except that Ana is the only type on earth.)

Images of Max are noticeably scarce, which I can't say breaks my heart. But there are still a few pictures of them together (the ones she hasn't been able to part with, I guess): side by side on bicycles, going in for a shaky kiss; laughingly flattening each other on an ugly brown couch; waving from an old, mustard-yellow convertible, top down, in some little New England town. A black-and-white one of them glamorously dressed for a friend's wedding, looking like the stars of a Godard film.

And the point is this: wandering awestruck through Ana's apartment, I felt a surprising, enlivening *ease*. Its cramped and cluttered and sane domesticity, its humble, humid *plainness*—its allusive symmetry, i.e., with where I live—had the palpable, heart-palpitating effect of causing my love for her actually to grow (if that's possible) like a Mylar balloon. And it gave me a grudging new respect for Max, too.

Anyway, I'm getting sidetracked. Because for me, even given everything, the night's most exciting discovery came in the form of a bulging, broken box. Needless to say, it didn't look like much. Dusty. Crammed with old trophies and books. (Ana trucked it from under the kitchen table to make a bed for me on the floor.) Naturally I assumed that the things inside belonged to Max and had been scuttled aside for easy dispatch. This inference seemed fair enough; one trophy displayed two figures fighting (or, as I later learned, practicing judo; in the moment, I failed to note their tiny ponytails). It wasn't until I'd doubled over, bemused, to excise an old *Black Hole* (#2, "Racing Towards Something," November 1995, Chris's POV) that my sense of the box and its contents began to change.

I whistled, and delicately balanced the book on my palm. "I can't believe Max *has* this," I said, laughing, in what may have sounded like a derisive tone.

Ana instantly appeared at my elbow. Firmly—very firmly—she took the book back.

I felt chastened, afraid she thought I was making fun of Max. (Also a little aggrieved, or disappointed, that she was still so protective of him.) I started to say, "Oh, no, I didn't mean—I just meant he always gave me so much shit—"

"It's not Max's," she said tersely, her pretty cheeks pinkening.

But still it took me another long moment of staring dumbly at the battered box, which I only then saw was filled with dog-eared collections of amazing early-20th-century comics—*Krazy Kat, Max and Moritz, Little Nemo in Slumberland*—before I got what she meant.

"He gave me shit for it, too," she said. Then quickly backpedaled: "Well, not really." Her face had taken an even lovelier shade, approaching scarlet. "He said he thought it was cute. Every time he'd see them on the shelf, he'd joke about it with me, or any guests who might be over. It was always the first thing he pointed out. The trophies, too. He loved trying to startle me into a judo throw." She gripped my sleeve and did a sort of dancey hop toward me. My heart fired like a cannon. But then she let go and with a sheepish shrug added, "I almost hurt him really badly that way once, actually." I shivered.

"Anyway," she went on, "after a while I just got a little tired of it. I knew it wasn't malicious—just Max being Max. And I thought if I put everything in here"—she gently kicked the box—"he'd get bored and shut up. And he did, eventually. But I guess I sort of forgot about it all, too. I haven't looked at this stuff in years." She shook her head, smiling, and covered half her face with one hand. But nestled in with the extant embarrassment was a note of wistfulness, maybe a little defiance. And I felt a tiny, irrational bubble of hope. Which was further buoyed when, after making this confession, she peeked between her fingers at me and held my eyes for a gratuitous beat.

But now it's quite late, and Ana has kindly offered to put me up, as I said, and even clothe me in some of Max's old things. And that's the sort of offer I'm far too wise, and too weak, to refuse. She's softly snoring so close to where I'm sitting writing this, at the kitchen table, and I'm really very tired. I'm afraid the lamp might wake her, and that she'll find me writing, which would discomfit us both. (She might ask certain questions—who am I writing this journal "for," e.g.—that I'd rather not answer, since I don't really know.) I'm afraid, too, that this will all end. I'd like, for one moment, to feel the feeling I'm having.

So—adieu.

C

com•mu•ni•ca•tion \kə-ˌmyü-nə-ˈkā-shən\ *n* **1 :** the successful bridging of subjectivities **2 :** the act of spreading disease **3 :** something foolhardy, to be avoided

"Alice," rasped Dr. Thwaite. "Is that you?"

I was thrown into a tense, cottony confusion. I'd called him not from my Meme but from the pay phone down the block.[1] My name and photo shouldn't have come up. Not to mention which name he'd used. It didn't occur to me that he'd been waiting for my call. When I heard him wield the alias before I'd even said a word, I imagined I was being watched. I scanned the corner of Forty-ninth and Ninth, glancing nervously from the bodega to the lightbulb store, the glass fronts of both shops sparkling in the hard late-morning light. But all I saw was a man in a black overcoat crouched on a curb, clutching a paper bag.

"No?" I said, after a pretty robust pause.

"No?" asked Dr. Thwaite. "Are you sure?"

"Yes?" I said. But without much heart.

My name, though, as I've already noted, isn't Alice. My name, in high Doug style, is extremely obscure. When I'd been in this world for less than a day, he began calling me Anana. I've never met another one. And though I've come over time to accept it, to think of it as a totem of me, for years I heard a bumpy nasal mountain range where my father saw balance and beauty. Anana: a palindrome—a reflection—a synthesis of

---

1. It was one of few left in New York. In Hell's Kitchen, still home to a few XXX peepshows and lots of corporate law firms, the demand for anonymity remained high.

paradoxical extremes. *Masculin féminin*. In Africa it's used for girls; in India it can be a boy's name. In Swahili it means "soft," "gentle," "mild." In Sanskrit, the prosaic "face." Doug claimed it means "lovely" in Inuit, and in Gweno "harmonize." It also rhymes, with "banana." Add an *s* to make it many of me and it's another fruit. My father's favorite. Ananas, which means "pineapple."

So what did it mean that Dr. Thwaite had called me Alice? That he'd guessed who was on the phone? Was he a friend of my father's? Or somehow implicated in what I'd come to think of as Doug's abduction? Did he know anything about my father's whereabouts?

"Who are you?" I asked, deferentially clearing my throat.

There was a crinkled silence. Then, as I'd somehow known he would, Dr. Thwaite asked, "Who are you?" And for a moment I was eddied in a cold swirl of déjà vu: twelve years old, posed on a scuffed black stage in stiff blue dress and ruffled pinafore, Doug's flashbulb firing white lightning from the dark front row of Saint Ann's theater, Tobey Ringwald plucking the brass pipe of a true hookah from his pudgy, spit-glossed lips. "*Who* are *you*?" he asked, nearly shouting the last word. *I hardly know, sir,* Alice tells the Caterpillar.

I wasn't sure how to respond.

A bitter gust stirred the man slumped on the nearby curb, and I was grateful for the windbreaker of the booth. "Dr. Thwaite—"

"Please," he said. "Don't call me that."

I waited for him to say something else. Explain. Supply another name. When he didn't, I was struck by an absurd thought: that I was talking to an unknown man who also imagined I was someone I'm not. I searched my purse for my Meme, to scan the number I'd dialed and confirm the man's identity. But I realized with an unpleasant jolt that I'd left the Meme in my apartment. That wasn't like me.

Meanwhile the pause dragged on. And something else strange happened: a woman in red glasses with a steely silver bob trolled past and glared at me in a way that felt very direct. Startled, I shifted my gaze to the man propped on the curb, who'd started drinking from his bag. With a strange squiggle in my gut, I squinted, to make sure it wasn't Max. But the man was smaller. Skin tinctured gray. When another squall flapped his black hood back, I saw a small skullcap of dark hair. All of which I remembered in a flash when I saw him on the block again later.

"Alice," Dr. Thwaite said at last. "If that's who you in fact *are*. I think you should come here. We need to talk about your father." That made me shiver. I'd spent the time since I'd discovered my father's absence trying to take Bart's advice and not worry. Cajoling myself that I'd been infected with Doug's paranoia. That everything was fine.

But in fact I'd slept terribly. I kept replaying the conversation I'd had with Doug the previous week in the train, about the strange emails he claimed to have gotten; the surge in Dictionary sales; that name, Alice, which had later turned up on his phone's display; the bottles of pills he'd given me. My head had started to ache. The blankets felt too hot; just the sheets too cold. I'd wanted to get up. *Do* something. But I'd already tried calling Doug dozens of times. There'd been nothing *to* do in the middle of the night. And I hadn't wanted to wake Bart, asleep on my floor.

Eventually, around three, I'd put on my Crown, snugly tucking in the Ear Beads, and programmed my Meme to release SomnEase®—strictly verboten by Doug. But I'd streamed the smallest possible dose and slept only five or six hours before getting up again.

And when I woke, there was still no sign of my father. Well before I went out to call Dr. Thwaite, I'd rung Doug's office and apartment. Talked to both overnight doormen. A few of his friends. Even considered trying my mother.

I hadn't spoken to Vera in weeks—since before Max had moved out. For most of that time she'd been abroad—in India, China, southern Europe, and South Korea, visiting parks and gardens and doing some shopping for her no-longer-new East Side apartment—and I hadn't wanted to savage her travels with my broken heart.

Or so I'd told myself. In truth, it was also by design: as much as I loved my mother, she wasn't often the person I sought for comfort in hard times. She disapproved tacitly of crying. Preferred "helpful advice." But her advice wasn't always that helpful for me. I don't do yoga; don't have her green thumb; don't really like window-shopping—especially not in stores where I can't afford even the candles they burn to make you calm enough to take your wallet out—and am unmotivated, in times of sorrow, to host dinners or attend social events. I *had* been drinking more than usual, sometimes alone, sometimes with Audrey and Ramona, who tried to cheer me up with stories of all the egregious parties I kept not going to with them.

I'd also been trying to force myself to meet Coco on weekends in Greenpoint; her studio was next to mine, and she could almost always make me feel better, whether I wanted to or not. She sang Bob Dylan and Sylvie Vartan songs across our shared wall and recited e. e. cummings poetry. Sometimes a scrap of paper weighted with an old coin would come sailing over with a note, e.g., "Do you still love me? Check the box: □ Yes □ No." When it got late, she'd wander in with ramen and beer.

I hated distracting her—she had two shows coming up—but I'd been having trouble making work, which she knew. She often found me curled on my studio couch, streaming B movies through my Ear Beads, and she'd make me scoot over and rest my head in her lap. Then she'd stream the same thing on her own Meme even though she hated aliens and monsters. She also often gently suggested that I call my mom. "I'm just jealous, Nans. You can see her any time you want." Coco's own mother lived in Paris.

And there *were* lots of things I really loved to do with Vera. My favorite ways to spend winter weekends were with her. Going down to one of the city's last movie theaters on Houston to watch all the brassy fall blockbusters that we both so enjoyed. Prowling the Union Square Greenmarket for anything that wasn't a root vegetable. Taking greedy gulps of air as we wandered through the redolent rows of listing Christmas trees. (Vera didn't believe in chopping them down to appreciate for just a few weeks, so we'd never had one when I was growing up. But we did both adore the smell.) Discussing my most recent projects or a biography Vera was reading during our volunteer shifts in the park. Taking the Q train all the way to Avenue J for wedges of the greatest pizza on earth, a sojourn we made just once a year. And—maybe the very best—we spent hours together baking: scores of shortbread wheels and linzer hearts, *sablés,* truffles, meringue. Ostensibly they were for friends and family, and we did ship lots of wax-paper-lined tins. But our muse had always been Doug, who was an enormously appreciative audience. ("And growing more enormous daily," he'd say, slapping his gut.) The thought of melting butter and dusting things with sugar without his constant interruptive "help" seemed inordinately sad. And honestly, I was having a hard time just feeding myself then; after Max left I lost my appetite, which I'd previously disbelieved could happen.

There was another, more salient reason I hadn't been in touch with my mom: she'd never much liked Max. ("It's not that I don't like him," she'd say, unconvincingly. "I just worry that he doesn't really make you happy.") I hadn't told her yet that he'd moved out—I wasn't quite ready for her commentary—and the thought of keeping up a front seemed very tough.

But maybe even more than that, I also didn't much like the man she'd been seeing, Laird Sharpe. Before he'd shacked up with Vera, Laird had long been one of Doug's best friends. They'd been freshman roommates: Hollis Hall, Harvard class of '72. They'd formed a trio with a man named Fergus Hedstrom, who was soon to resurface in all our lives. (I'd never met Ferg; he didn't spend much time in New York. But all through my girlhood I'd heard filigreed stories of adventures he and Doug had taken—and occasionally still took—in places as far-flung as Norse Lake, Ontario; Barra de Navidad, Jalisco; and Angkor Wat: catching walleye, surfing, visiting shrines, drinking insalubrious amounts. For whatever reason, Laird never went along.)

I was confounded by Laird and Doug's ongoing friendship. And I likewise didn't get why Laird was beloved by the audiences of PI News, the station he anchored. Before he'd found his calling, reporting small and large tragedies to the public, he'd done a stint for several years as an investment banker; he still often covered financial stories. And watching him, I always felt like he was still selling something (beyond what was required). I didn't really enjoy the thought of him and Vera on their jaunt overseas, pitying my fate in some Beijing teahouse or Jaipur gem boutique.

On the morning after Doug went missing, though, it wasn't so much my pride that kept me from calling my mom; a slightly battered ego seemed like a fair trade for her advice. What welled up instead, swallowing everything—rationality, a desire for comfort, consideration of Vera's feelings—was a powerful wave of protectiveness. I didn't want Laird to have the satisfaction of knowing that Doug was gone, or wondering if it had anything to do with him and my mom.

And to be candid, strung out as I felt from sleeplessness and worry—even before I talked to Dr. Thwaite—the person whose voice I wanted to hear most that morning was Max's, despite everything. Despite a month of embarrassed crying in the stairwell when attacks of sadness would hit on my breathless ascent, picturing the poor neighbors rolling their eyes as they lifted pasta lids, wiped kids' noses, turned up the volume on things. A month of rashly commanding my Meme to erase his number and most of his photos, texts, beams, only to bitterly regret it later and try to get them back—an operation the Meme claimed was "not actionable." A month of inane incantations—"I can't believe this is happening," "I don't understand"—to each of my (also progressively less understanding) friends.

Despite everything, and of course knowing better, I still wanted to feel Max's massive arms around me. His pointy chin jutting into my head. "Such a cute, cute nutjob," I could almost hear him say. "I'll bring you lots of nice chocolates at Bellevue." Right away I reprimanded myself; even in my fantasies Max was an ass.

Doug, the teasing king, had always disapproved of Max's brand of it. When I pointed out that I teased Max, too, and noted Doug's own affinities, Doug would shake his shaggy head, face drooping in sad folds, and say, quietly emphatic, "It's not the same, Nins. His isn't generous. He tries to discredit you." I usually thought that Doug was missing the point, or that I'd misrepresented things. I tried to explain that the difference between my own blithe imitations of Max's lumbering, athletic stride, the halting way he often talked, and his relentless befriendment of nearly everyone we met (bartenders, dry cleaners, lots of girls on the street) was a difference only in method from the way Max teased me. But Doug didn't miss many points. And I'd been revisiting this theory.

In recent evidence to the contrary, for instance: after Max was done breaking up with me, he tried to shake my hand, as if we were business associates. That had upset me (obviously). In part because I blamed his work for our estrangement. And there was no denying that things got worse after Hermes was sold in July. He'd had a lot more nights out and coming home trashed, or not at all. He started traveling all the time—Shanghai, Rio, L.A.—and spending money like he'd won a game show. He could waste $16K on dinner, including guests he'd just met. Soon he had a motorcycle and a car. He bought himself one of John Lennon's guitars, a fur coat, a *gold-plated toilet*. (That was a joke, allegedly.)

He naturally began to resent "my" tiny apartment and started looking at listings. "You wouldn't get it," he snapped when I asked, bewildered, what was happening. "You've *always* had money." (Which wasn't totally fair—I remembered lots of successive nights of beans and rice as a child when my parents hadn't felt like going begging to my grandparents. But the underlying point was sound.) Max bought things for me, too, of course. Perfume. Spiky jewelry. Electronics. I gave most of them back. Faster than I knew what was happening, he'd turned into a person I didn't know, or like. Our life became a never-ending fight. But it was because of Hermes's sale, I told myself. I just had to wait. For how long, I wasn't sure—he didn't like to talk about work.

In truth, we'd had only two really good years. But the first had been transcendent. We'd been together barely two weeks when Max asked, over glasses of rum, if I'd ever been to Barbados; he had to go for business, he claimed, and the thought of a beautiful, secluded beach without me was "just too sad." Flattered and flustered and caught off-guard, I opined in a bad British accent that my favorite former island colony was Dominica. (I'd been exactly once.) It was a stupid quip, and kind of mean. (I'd assumed at first, like nearly everyone Max met, that he came from money; I thought I was calling him out.) But I wasn't self-conscious; with Max, I felt completely at ease. "Okay," he said, laughing. "We'll go there instead." But when he sent me a hotel reservation later that night, I was shocked. Thrilled and nervous and a little offended. But mostly gripped by a fit of excitement so intense I almost thought I was coming down with something. When I next saw Max, I could tell he felt the same way: his eyes were ragged with agitation and amazement and disbelief. (I didn't know that his anxiety was at least as much about money: he was broke.)

From then on we couldn't stand to be apart. We moved in together after just three months. "You need to get a life," I'd say, laughing as I tried to tear myself from our bed to visit the studio, or have dinner with Coco, or ferry Ramona through her latest crisis. "You *are* my life," he'd say. And even though I knew it was mostly a joke, it worried me. It didn't seem smart, letting him give me so much of his time. But I couldn't help it; it was the happiest I'd ever been.

Ineluctably, though, things began disintegrating. He did start to feel trapped, did often resent me, sometimes for good reason, and there were times I resented him. We'd both done stupid things. Yet despite the many reckless ways we'd alienated and betrayed each other, I still loved him. And none of our previous attempts to break up had stuck. I'd known right away, though, that this one would. But I'd always believed, even to the end, that he loved me, too. I nearly convinced myself that the final split itself had been a gift: his callousness crafted so I could stop loving him. It just didn't work.

But on the morning after I discovered my father missing, I managed not to call Max, thanks largely to Bart.

It was just after nine a.m., and I hadn't yet gone to the pay phone to try calling Dr. Thwaite. I was balanced on one leg in the bedroom, frowning at my Meme, wondering how to override its "not actionable" setting, when a groggy voice floated up from the floor in the other room. "Very graceful," it croaked, startling me so badly I lost my balance and nearly dropped the Meme.

"Sorry," Bart mumbled, sounding still snared in the nets of sleep. "I wasn't watching. Just opened my eyes. And there you were."

The back of my neck petaled with heat. I wasn't quite sure why. I wasn't attracted to Bart; he wasn't my type. ("Bastards?" Audrey would say. Which wasn't totally inaccurate, unfortunately. Historically I'd fallen for men with a little more . . . audacity.) I also knew Bart wasn't interested. Shortly after I met Max, Doug dropped hints about how Bart made the better catch, and I wondered, with the placid detachment of someone newly in love, if Doug had been told (or imagined) that Bart had a crush on me. But then I heard Bart was in love with our colleague Svetlana, and that made more sense. She's more beautiful than I am, and far smarter. And if there's one thing that ever made me insecure around kind, funny, slightly odd Bart, it was my intellect. Several Dictionary staffers could read at least three languages; Bart could read eight; Svetlana: five. I struggled to read Spanish even with the Word Exchange. Bart also read lots of philosophy, which he discussed with Svetlana. Next to them I felt like what I was: a genius's relatively average daughter, hired out of family loyalty.

Speaking of filial ties, part of the reason I was so aware of Bart was because of his friendship with my dad. They ate lunch together most days—at the Fancy, or the weird sandwich place down the block—talking constantly about work. Doug solicited Bart's opinions on nearly everything. I knew because Doug often cited Bart's stellar insights. They also occasionally played squash on weekends when Doug's regular partner couldn't get away. I think they even went fishing once, upstate.

There was one thing, though, that had kind of come between Bart and me: I'd gotten the sense he didn't think so highly of Max. Max respected him and thought they were friends, and Bart was otherwise so nonjudgmental that it seemed a little unfair. So out of my own sense of loyalty, I'd always felt a small degree of distance from him.

But that was before Max and I broke up. Before Doug started acting so strange—and then vanished. And seeing Bart that first morning, steeped in sleepiness on my hardwood floor, I suddenly felt shy; I couldn't quite believe I'd asked him to come home with me the night before. And I didn't want him to hear me beg my Meme to call Max. *You're better than that,* I told myself. I'd had a shortage of those kinds of thoughts since being dumped, and it gave me a grateful little rush of fortitude.

Instead of calling my mom or Max, I was on the verge of calling the cops. I wasn't quite sure what I'd say; I was already afraid, though, that they'd be involved eventually. But Bart blearily convinced me that they wouldn't take us seriously until we waited at least twenty-four hours. Repeated what he'd said the previous night when we hadn't found Doug home, about him maybe having plans he'd forgotten to mention. (Doug did have a few friends, like Ferg, who sometimes spirited him away.) Or maybe, Bart suggested, something had come up with the launch, and Doug had "gone into one of his tunnels" and hadn't thought to be in touch. "I bet he'll call in a few hours," Bart said with a yawn. Then he rolled over and went back to his dreams.

I'd tried to distract myself for another couple hours—streaming some of the music Bart had pointed out the night before, doing a quick sketch of him asleep on the floor, willing Doug to call—but the thought of waiting, pacing, trying not to panic, was making me feel unwelcome to myself. And that's why, after running out of other ideas, I'd carefully crept outside to call Dr. Thwaite and found myself, coldly huddled in an old phone booth, agreeing to go to his apartment.

I wrote the directions on my skin. That felt strange. I couldn't remember the last time I'd used my hand for transcription.[2] I examined Doug's pen, which I'd been surprised to find still in my coat pocket. It was branded with some kind of seal, an open book ringed by crowns. But soon I turned my attention back to writing; the directions turned out

---

2. Dr. Thwaite scolded me for this later, when I took off my mittens. But I couldn't tell if he was angry because pens "release toxins into the bloodstream" or because I'd published the location of his apartment on my body.

to be very involved: when I got to Dr. Thwaite's building on Beekman Place, I should see Clive, the doorman, who'd send me right up. But if Clive wasn't in for some peculiar reason, I should turn around and walk back toward the door, where I'd see a painting of a wintry scene. I should lift it to reveal a panel of buzzers and press Dr. Thwaite's, gently but firmly. He'd be waiting on the sixth floor, a point he underscored. Then he hung up without saying goodbye.

I hurried back home to collect Bart, but Bart wasn't collectible: he was gone. In his place I found the faint, ferrety smell of boy. On the floor, a messy nest of blankets. Several poorly washed dishes in the rack. A dusting of coffee grounds on the counter. A bouquet of purple deli roses and a note on a scrap of paper bag. "A— Thank you," it began in his slanty left-handed script. "I'm sorry the flowers are sort of forlorn. It was the best they had at that place on eighth. Hope you like purple. Hope you find Doug today. Talk soon? —B"

Worried as I was about Doug, I smiled. Its taciturnity—so un-Bart-like—made me wonder if it said more than it said.[3] When I'd seen him curled on the floor that morning, sleeping in all his rumpled clothes, I'd felt a warm, pleasant shock. He was the first person to stay the night since Max had moved out, and the nearby beating of another heart did something to sort of reset mine.

As I'd started to sketch his face, I noticed for the first time that he looked a little like Buster Keaton. He had the same long, almost Gallic nose and small, bow-shaped mouth. Same dark, lightly waved hair gently receding from his forehead. His large, wide-set eyes bulged slightly under the lids, as if that were the price of closely observing things. I was so glad he'd stayed. Glad, too, that the night before, when he'd discovered my Box of Shame—relics of the nerdier person I'd once been—he hadn't mocked me, had in fact seemed interested. As I'd carefully stepped over his legs and seen his soft pink heels exposed by holes in his dark socks, I'd felt a web of tenderness spring from me to engulf his whole tall, lean frame.

Anyway, I was sad he'd left. And without him, I was also less sure about the trip to Dr. Thwaite's. But the flowers, still hemmed in plastic, gave me a little boost of strength. I put them in a vase. When a bud fell

---

3. Max used to buy me roses, too. But he always got red ones, never purple. And purple is my favorite color.

off, I tucked it in my pocket. Kicked the gamey blankets beneath the table. Poured myself a black coffee—Bart had finished the soy milk—and made my way east.

Clive, of course, was not in the lobby. But when I turned around to face the entrance, I discovered two paintings of wintry scenes; specific as Dr. Thwaite's directions had been, I thought they might have included this detail. So my mind began to spin a little, especially when Clive didn't turn up after several more minutes and people passing through the lobby started to look at me with twin glimmers of interest and distrust. I almost wondered if Dr. Thwaite was laying some kind of trap. Colluding with kidnappers, even. Maybe I was next.

For a few moments I very seriously considered leaving. But to do what? Before I called the police, I thought I should at least speak to him, find out if he knew anything. I also thought my worry was irrational. It had been clear from his voice that he was an older man—a lexicographer; I was a former judo champion (a decade ago, it was true). Bart's word for him, "harmless," echoed in my head, which had started hurting again.

The first painting opened after I fumbled a bit with its clasp, and buzzer 6B read P. THWAITE. Yet when I arrived on the sixth floor, no one was waiting, which again tested my resolve. I wandered the hall twice, then stalked outside B like a rookie thief. I'd forgotten to bring Dr. Thwaite's phone number, and my Meme couldn't seem to find it.[4] I almost knocked—but, remembering his firm admonition to *wait outside,* I refrained. Finally, frustrated and confused, I turned back to the elevator. As if on cue, the door flew open.

"I kept waiting for the bell," said the man standing there. That could have been annoying, but his tone was so ingenuous and flustered and kind that I just mumbled, "Sorry."

He was older than I'd imagined, though not so much older than Doug—maybe mid-seventies. Daffy white hair. Petite as a jockey. The stooped posture of a person who reads. I liked him instantly. He offered me a Coke before I'd even crossed the threshold, then another when he took my coat a minute later. I declined both, my affection for him growing.

---

4. *"Cannot confirm existence,"* the pop-up informed me.

For himself Dr. Thwaite poured a tall glass of water. Decanted some into a silver bowl on the floor. "Canon," he called, and a shaggy calico dog with one brown eye, one ice blue, shambled in from around the corner. I reached out a hand, but Canon barely raised his head. "I'm surprised he's not hounding you for treats," Dr. Thwaite said, apologetic. "Your father spoils him rotten."

He led me to the living room, Canon clacking quietly behind us, and I could see that the apartment was palatial. Not quite as big as my Doran grandparents' up on East Sixty-eighth, but much less cumbered with gilt and brocade things and so more spacious. (I think this had to do with the vintage of his family's money: the older the gold, the less shiny it tends to be.)

To the right of the foyer was a large, scarred, rustic table. It flanked the kitchen, which was paused on the early sixties: baby blue and cream, outfitted with a Formica island, knotty pine cabinets, stippled linoleum. Outside the kitchen, parquet floors unfurled in a glossy, endless chessboard: starting at the door, veering right, and disappearing down a dark hall, partly obscured in the living room by big red kilim rugs.

Dr. Thwaite installed me on an L-shaped leather sofa. It faced a fireplace burning with a modest blaze. The wood gave off an earthy, turbid smoke. Music was playing—Brahms, or maybe Debussy. I'd heard it in the kitchen, too, but in the living room it was louder. (I'd expected a view of the East River and the mop-bucket gray sky, but all the drapes, heavy red velvet, were drawn, which I found a little odd.) The coffee table was cluttered with crumbling newspaper clippings and defunct magazines. Bookshelves lined every free wall, volumes with gold-stamped bindings beside fuzzy paperbacks. But while the room was large, its shape seemed off. The layout lopsided. Almost claustrophobic. At the time I couldn't put my finger on why. Assumed it was a trick of my sleep-starved and anxious mind.

Dr. Thwaite stoked the fire with an iron poker that looked too heavy for him. I watched his thin back heave. He said something I couldn't quite make out over the music. Then, after a moment of silence—maybe waiting for me to speak—he turned and slowly lowered himself onto an ottoman. "I presume you haven't heard anything," he said.

I hesitated. For a moment I wondered again if there was any chance he'd had a hand in Doug's departure. I studied him. Rumpled shirt. Worn velveteen slippers. Canon lobed at his feet. He reached down absently to scratch the dog's ruff, his eyes clouded with what looked to me like real worry. I decided I should try to trust him.

"I haven't talked to him," I said, shaking my head. It was throbbing a bit worse by then. "Not since yesterday, when I left work. We had dinner plans, but he never showed." I felt a little loop of sadness, and something like regret. As if I could turn back time, wait longer at the diner, and make Doug appear. "You probably know this about my father," I went on, "but that's—that doesn't happen. He's very punctual." Dr. Thwaite nodded. "After that, I went to look for him in his office . . ." But then I trailed off, not sure how to describe the sequence of events, if there was anything I should leave out. I wanted to ask him about the message he'd sent. I started to say, "Dr. Thwaite—"

"Please," he interrupted. "Call me Phineas. Phin, if you prefer. That's what your father calls me. Also Thin, Phinny, Thimbleman . . . You get the idea." He laughed.

And that tiny revelation crumpled my heart. It was pure Doug. And it meant that my father had another life. Friends I didn't know about. That I'd been neglecting him, or he'd been keeping me out. I felt selfish and jealous and guilty at once. And also relieved, and grateful to this odd, small man. Thankful that for the past year, since my mother had broken Doug's heart—so much worse than Max had broken mine, I realized, as if I'd been moaning to a war veteran about a sprain—he'd had people in his life besides me.

I'd done my best to support Doug. It had been hard to know how, and so sad. My mother still loved him, she said; she "just couldn't do it anymore." I'd be lying if I claimed I hadn't taken sides. Vera started dating Laird so soon after she moved out.

But my father, it's only fair to note, wasn't all panicles and dappled light. He could be very difficult. Overbearing and precise. Prone to fervors but also dark spirals. Both quiet and loud. And for a long time he'd all but vanished from their life. My mom got, she claimed, "the worst leftovers" of Doug. In happier times she'd complained about the hours he and I spent together at the Dictionary. "*You* try being his assistant," I'd joked. She'd laughed, waving a wallet fat with dry-cleaning tags. "Oh, I have," she'd said, a drop of acid in her voice. But how could I pretend I didn't understand her side? Max and Doug were very different, of course. But the echoes were loud. I knew pretty well what her loneliness was like.

Seated across from Dr. Thwaite, the leather of his couch squeaking under me, I swallowed hard. Doug had been "missing" for less than seventeen hours then, and while it was extremely unlike him to vanish so abruptly, he was capable of being both thoughtful and oblivious; he might call home every quarter hour if he was running late for dinner, but he'd forgotten his wedding anniversary at least once. With the impending launch he'd been under a huge amount of pressure, and I was still trying to hope his disappearance could be plausibly explained. But then I thought of Dr. Thwaite's note to Doug's office the night before, and those nerve-frying letters *SOS*.

"This might sound crazy," I said, my voice quivering slightly. "But I'm—I'm really worried about my dad." I probably said it hoping that Phineas would reassure me. One of my methods for warding off destiny is to voice my fears.

But instead he'd sighed. Kneaded the ottoman. "My dear," he said softly, "so am I."

And a tiny white star of panic shot behind my right eye. "When was the last time you spoke to him?" I asked.

"Your father and I had a different . . . method of communicating."

"Do you mean email?" I asked, worry stirring my sarcasm.[5]

"No."

"Text?"

"Almost never."

"What, then?" I asked. But it was disingenuous. Of course I knew what he meant. I'd seen his blind-stamped note come through Doug's pneumatic tube myself. I probably had it in my purse. I just had a hard time believing they pinged paper missives back and forth. It's true I had only a hazy sense of how the tubes worked. But wasn't Dr. Thwaite's building a co-op? It seemed unlikely that the board would have approved the infrastructure. And what about the City of New York? Nearly a dozen blocks separated Dr. Thwaite's apartment from the Dictionary. I'd always assumed tube operations were confined to our building on Broadway, not to long underground expanses that tangoed with trains and rats and pipes.

---

5. Doug remained committed to email—claimed it was the last, best bastion of "civil discourse." He'd always threatened to revert to letter writing—until mail delivery was cut to twice a week.

What I didn't know then—what it would take me weeks to learn—was that in fact there once *were* miles of tubes beneath the streets, used by the postal system. In the early twentieth century, more than twenty-seven miles of them had connected New York's general P.O. to stations stretching from Harlem to Battery Park and on to Brooklyn. Operators known as rocketeers sent twenty pounds through the tubes each minute, sixteen hours a day, from five a.m. to nine p.m. They conveyed telegrams and letters. Light packages. Supposedly once even a cat, who survived.

The tubes had been considered a wonder technology. Acres of lines ran under Europe and in four major U.S. cities outside NYC—Boston, Chicago, Philadelphia, and St. Louis—with initial plans to install them in at least eleven more, including Denver, New Orleans, and D.C. In Manhattan there were hubs at Madison Square, Penn Station, Grand Central, Wall Street. Station H was at Lexington and Forty-fourth, Station P in the Produce Building. There were Stations S, W—up to Y. For a time, in other words, the system enjoyed great popularity, and its developers had big dreams: to shuttle packages from department stores to housewives in the suburbs; to deliver hot meals, and "fresh flowers to one's sweetheart"; to link every home in the country. They hoped one day to transport heavy freight, and eventually people.

But in just a few decades the infinitely looping tubes found their end. Cars and trucks superseded them. The system faded nearly as quickly as it had come. (Ouroboros, Doug would call it: the serpent of progress eating its own tail, as it always does.) When the next decades rolled in, just a few vestiges remained—in hospitals, e.g., and banks. Some even lingered into the twenty-first century, like dinosaurs outliving their time. Komodo dragons coexisting with swimming pools. The tubes were all but forgotten, at least by most of us. What I didn't know then was that some infrastructure was still extant, parts of it old, parts less so. And while I thought I was savvy about what New York money could buy—helicopters, things from the Ming Dynasty, a new nose or kidney—I still had a lot to learn.

But on that day in Dr. Thwaite's apartment, I had no hint of this. "I don't like email," was all he said. Then he eased gingerly off the ottoman, stood, and walked away. I was baffled. Half afraid I'd offended him, half convinced he'd just gone off to do something else. I waited on the couch, but minutes passed. I began to wonder if I should let myself out. It wasn't until he finally reappeared and said, "Are you coming or not?" that I realized he'd expected me to follow. I understood then why I liked Dr. Thwaite: he showed signs of wear, like me. He was a little careless, like me. And like me, he didn't put much stock in language. He knew words were fairly futile things. Best used sparingly.

In the hall he started, in his cryptic way, to tell me something. It was hard to hear—the music, I discovered, was pervasive, invisibly floating through the whole apartment. What I thought he said was, "He was most afraid of a pandemic." But it couldn't have been.

"Pandemic?" I said. "You mean—of a disease?" As I said it, I thought of the bottles of medicine Doug had made me take, and I shivered reflexively. But then another, terrible thought occurred to me. I'd heard no warnings about a disease—no news bulletins, no public health announcements. And suddenly I was scared. Was it possible, I remember wondering, that my father had become sick—mentally? That his paranoia had morphed from a quirk to a pathology? Maybe something latent had surfaced, catalyzed by months of sad anxiety and stress. Was there a chance, even very small, that he might have hurt himself? Or someone else? That he was hiding out? How exactly did he know Dr. Thwaite? I shivered again, acutely aware that I was in a stranger's home. Walking down a dark hall to a back room.

Dr. Thwaite stopped and turned to study me. Frowning, he said, "You're serious?"

I nodded numbly, chastened into silence by his grim, dismissive poise.

"I wonder," he muttered to himself. "Why wouldn't he . . . ?" His eyes wobbled over my face. "The flu?" he tried. "Word flu? You're sure he never mentioned it?"

I nodded again, submerged in a molasses of nameless dread. My head started to pulse harder with brilliant, light-edged flowers of pain. And then something unlucky happened: my Meme rang. It hadn't sounded in so long I'd forgotten it was on. Canon, who'd been standing silently behind us, began to growl.

The little dram of color in Dr. Thwaite's pale face leaked out. "Is that . . . ?" He raised his brows. "You brought a Meme into my house?" he asked in a flat, distant voice that made my stomach drop. I didn't know why.

"Sorry," I said. "I thought I'd turned it off. I'll do that now."

He shook his head. "I should have explained. You'll have to leave it out in the hall." He sounded calm, but his eyes were on fire. Rattled, I nodded, and he escorted me to the door. Once outside, I considered bolting. But I'd left my coat in his apartment. And I still wanted to know what he knew.

Because he was watching, I powered down my Meme without looking closely at the screen. But I did see I had six missed calls—four from the same 800 number, all unknown. Of course I thought—hoped—they were from Doug. But Doug always left long, rambling messages, and this caller hadn't recorded a single one. It wasn't until later, seized with horror, that I realized my voicemail was still full of old messages from Max that I hadn't yet been able to let go. Too late, I erased each one.

There were also two texts. One from Bart, which said, "Any news?" The other, like the calls, anonymous and indecipherable. "PT will have more. Don't use this": that was it. It was the second message, tagged *urgent,* that had made the Meme ring; sensing that Dr. Thwaite was hostile to its presence, it had turned itself silent until then. I considered asking Dr. Thwaite if he knew what the text meant. But I thought better of it. Or maybe worse, as it turned out.

"You really shouldn't use that thing," Dr. Thwaite warned from the door. It was a familiar refrain; in my mind's ear, I could almost hear Doug launch into Lecture #449: "No reliable, double-blind, placebo-controlled trials have tested the long-term consequences of Crown use or Sixth Sense technology. We do know users become not just psychologically attached but physiologically dependent on Memes in a very short time . . . We *don't* know if the device poses other risks . . . Norwegian scientists have just discovered [blah blah blah] . . . Consequences for memory and language . . ." And on.

"Where should I leave it?" I said softly, glancing around. He pointed at the welcome mat. I thought he was joking. He was not. Awkwardly hunched, head pounding as I bent down, I tucked my Crown and pretty silver Meme beneath the scratchy tan sisal on the floor. Then, not sure it was the smartest course, I followed Dr. Thwaite back inside.

In many ways his office seemed derivative of Doug's: the clutter, the calendar still turned to September, the magnifying-glass collection, the wooden head with its leggy pairs of bifocals. Floor-to-ceiling dictionaries and other books, including the *North American Dictionary,* one of its volumes open on a lectern. He also had antique machines: typewriters, giant cameras, a record player, and what I thought was a tape deck—things I couldn't identify. Slanting stacks of spiral pads and *International Journal of Lexicography* back issues. Old scraps of quotation paragraphs and neologisms. Relics of the way dictionary-making once was for everyone.[6]

But there was a way in which Dr. Thwaite's office differed from my father's: it was filled with framed photos of naked women. Or of one woman, actually, shot many times. And in fact I was afraid at first it was my mother. She had the same swirling dark hair as the young Vera Doran. Same creamy skin, high breasts, violin-thin waist. I've been ambushed by her likeness all my life. I have her memorized. But the woman wasn't Vera. I was relieved but still uneasy. For Dr. Thwaite, though, she was wrapped in the modest mists of iteration. He seemed blind to her nakedness, the coyness in her shining eyes. Blind, at least, until he noticed me staring. Then, with a hint of diffidence, he said, "You'd be surprised how long it can haunt you." The pictures did look old—forty years or more. "I was sorry," he continued, "to hear of your own recent heartbreak. Certainly it's for the best. But it must be very hard."

"Wait," I mumbled, stunned. "What?" I felt a cold tremor of shame and indignation. I was shocked that Doug would breach my trust. Confide in this strange stranger. Our father-daughter privilege apparently worthless.

Dr. Thwaite's brows went up, pleating his forehead. "Oh," he said. "No?" His voice was strained. "I thought I'd heard you were alone now, too."

"No," I said, trying to sound fine. "I'm not alone." I don't know why I lied. Maybe it was lingering embarrassment, or wishful thinking. Maybe reflex—protecting my privacy behind a seemingly small untruth. I'm not sure, because it just came out, unpremeditated, and then I felt committed. I wish I hadn't said it. The consequences were surprisingly

---

6. Dr. Thwaite, a relic himself, was probably retired, or at best freelance. The *NADEL* was the last of its kind. All other U.S. dictionaries had of course been folded into Synchronic, Inc.'s Word Exchange by then—all language reference "tools" consolidated in one digital "marketplace." And even Doug acknowledged that the third edition, about to be published, would be the final one. He'd reached the end of the end of a cycle of grants. From then on it would exist only online, in constant flux. "Edition" would lose its meaning.

serious. But at the time it didn't occur to me that Dr. Thwaite might have mentioned my breakup on purpose. "I'm not at all alone," I repeated, evading his eyes.

"I see." When I looked back at his face, it had clouded inscrutably. "Well, my apologies. I must have misheard."

"Yes," I said stiffly. "Well, that's all right."

We lapsed into a scratchy silence. I felt my face grow hot, and I reached down to stroke the dog. But that wasn't enough to break the static. And Dr. Thwaite wasn't helping out. I glanced again around his windowless study. That's when I saw his pneumatic tubes. The familiar brass matrix tucked in a crowded corner, which emptied into a large, shellacked bin marked "In." In my father's handwriting.

Suddenly I was exhausted. My brain smogged with anxiety and concern. The pain in my head was getting worse—I was afraid it was a migraine—and my Meme, with its new Pax® prescription, was in the hall. I was tired of being in Dr. Thwaite's apartment, and I felt in my pockets for the folded scraps of paper that had come through Doug's tubes the night before. "What can you tell me about these?" I asked, handing them over.

He hefted a magnifier that gave him the eye of a giant. Read in silence. Then, gravely, lowered the glass. Slid out a drawer in his desk. Removed a folded slip of paper and pressed it into my palm. It read: "diachronic: a method of looking at language that's becoming extinct." This, Dr. Thwaite claimed, was Doug's SOS. The phrase they'd all agreed on.

"All who? Agreed to what?" I asked. I felt ill. The white light behind my eye flashed brightly. It wasn't impossible, I realized, feeling a little faint, that Dr. Thwaite had typed both notes himself—that I was in the company of someone crazy, and not harmless at all. How else to explain the circumlocutions, bizarre references, vacillating mood? And yet. He struck me as sane. But he didn't reply. He studied me for a long time, eyes tightening. It occurred to me that he was covering for Doug, or someone. And I was flunking his character assessment.

"Dr. Thwaite," I said. I was fed up, afraid. "Is my father in trouble?" It made me breathless to get out the words.

After a moment he said, "I don't know." I thought that would be it. But then his eyes softened. "He might be," he said gently, turning up a corner of his mouth. "I think so."

My heart started to pound, the hammer of my headache striking with it. "And this little slip of paper—it's supposed to be proof?" I volleyed back, fear sharpening my tone.

Again Dr. Thwaite's eyes narrowed. "I sense you think I'm engaged in hyperbole," he countered. "Is that right?"

"I'm sorry," I said. "I'm just very scared, and I don't understand what's going on. I don't know what the police are going to be able to do with these . . . SOS's. And I'm really worried about my dad." I tried not to, but I choked up a little.

Dr. Thwaite seemed to tense. He passed me a hankie, looking away. "It's all right," he fretted, sort of raking my back with his hand. Added, "No need to involve the police just yet." And the strangeness of this statement coupled with the strangeness of his touch worked to sober me up. He asked me to tell him again exactly what had happened the night before, and I did. Only this time I mentioned the Aleph. And when I described how Doug's entry had vanished from the Dictionary, Dr. Thwaite became completely still. The words "My God" flew from his bloodless lips.

He wouldn't tell me why he was so upset. But he didn't have to. Because as I watched him, the nameless dread I'd been feeling coalesced. The Aleph, of course, had been custom-programmed for Doug, to map the fluctions of his brain: preferences and decisions, spending habits, reading history, walking routes, contacts' names. I'd heard rumors that people's Memes sometimes froze at the moment they died. Or deleted their profiles on Life. Purged files. And that's when I knew that Doug's disappearance from the Aleph's Dictionary had a meaning in the real world. All of a sudden I was sure I'd never see my father alive again.

Our devastation seemed to knit us in a fragile, cobweb trust. After we'd calmed down enough to talk, Dr. Thwaite asked if he could see the Aleph for himself. I wanted to see it again, too. But I'd left it at home.

When I said I had to go, he nodded kindly. Put a hand on my arm. "Alice," he said. In his craggy voice, the name felt right. "Would you like a Coke for the road?"

I said I would. Kept the cold can pressed to my aching head most of the bus ride back instead of downloading Pax® from my Meme, getting gently jostled among a noisy passel of kids dressed as Pilgrims. I hurried the last few blocks by foot. Ran, panting, up the four flights to my door. Went straight for the Aleph, plugged in beside the toaster.

When I flicked it on, though, I noticed something wrong right away. It was still open to the same place in the *J*'s. Same curled, feral letters crouched on the glowing page. But this time Doug was *there*, neatly tucked between the seventeenth president of the United States and a former point guard for the L.A. Lakers. There was Doug's pale, short-sleeved button-down with a welter of hair spilling from the neck. And there was the tiny dot on his pocket that I knew was a pineapple lapel pin. There were the massive glasses, a ghostly prick of glare glinting whitely in each lens. And the signature smile of a man overflowing with exuberance. And there, most reassuringly, was the lemma: "Johnson, Douglas (1950–)," with no death date.

I felt a swell of gratitude. I was filled with the uncanny certainty that Doug was alive. But I didn't know how to contextualize my discovery. At first I assumed I'd just overlooked his entry the night before, unsettled as I'd been. Then I remembered that Bart had seen—or not seen—it, too. His theory that Alephs are defective seemed most plausible. But that left me wondering again if Doug was all right. And where he was.

I wanted to ask Bart what he thought. I turned on my Meme, hoping there'd be a message from Doug. There wasn't—just a beam from my friend Ramona of a RoBoLoVe song, tagged with the poetic caption "Ware r u slut?" I told my Meme to phone Bart. But even before it dialed the final number, I was struck by another thought—bitten, even, as if by a pinched nerve.

Doug was *back inside the Dictionary.* Last night he'd left our Broadway office for some reason. But now he was back. Not missing at all.

The idea was so risible I blushed. Even without witnesses to the workings of my mind, alone in my tiny kitchen. But as I dialed Doug's extension, I held my breath. It rang three times. Four. I kept waiting for his rich bass voice to come on. Give a shaggy-dog account of where he'd been. Suggest Fancy lentil soup with rye. But then the ringing stopped. And a pocky, awkward recording of my own voice told me Doug was unavailable. I tried the office lobby, but no one picked up.

I *knew*, though, that Doug was in the Dictionary. The feeling was palpable, like warm wax. I was so sure that I rehearsed my rebuke. Planned to propose he start seeing a shrink. Indulged in imagined apologies to

Bart and Dr. Thwaite. Sighing, I zippered back into my coat. Braced for the eight cold blocks up to the office.

But as I neared the Dictionary, I became less convinced. Slowed. Caught a glimpse of myself in the building's black glass. I looked frail and frightened. I wasn't used to seeing myself that way. But just as hearing an unexpected tremor in one's own voice can turn, unbidden, to stage fright, that nervous, shadowy likeness undermined my assurance. The lobby looked darker and bleaker than it had ever seemed. I wished Doug had answered. Or that I'd asked Bart to come with me. I lingered on the sidewalk. But it was freezing out, and gusting. I told myself that what I felt was just the sticky remnants of last night's nervousness. So I took a deep breath and held my Meme to the door's ID reader.

Inside, I thought I smelled the tiniest note of smoke; I assumed I was imagining it. The security guard on duty was a woman. I'd never seen her before. I said, "Where's Rodney?" with a mouth that didn't feel like my mouth, and she said, "He ain't here."

I went up to twenty. Circled the whole dark floor. Called, "Hello? Anybody here?" But there was only silence. I was shaking by the time I reached Doug's door. I tried the knob. It wouldn't turn. And I realized, heart surging, that someone else must have been there. Maybe still was. I balked, and nearly ran for the exit. But then I remembered that I'd been the one to lock up the night before. I raised a hand to my pounding chest and exhaled. Fumbled in my purse for the keys, fingers trembling so badly I dropped them on the floor. They struck the carpet with a muffled bang that burst my heart all over again. The blackness swarmed. My vision pinholed in. I heard the sandpaper sound of my own breathing, and when I finally got the door open, I was alone: Doug wasn't there. No one was.

But everything else also seemed unchanged. The phone blinked red in accusation. The desk drawers were shut. Doug's satchel was limply slumped on his armchair. As I scanned the room, my eyes rested on his pneumatic tubes, the in-bin a perfect double of its East Side twin at Dr. Thwaite's. I thought of sending a progress report, if I could. But then another thought popped up, like a cork: I should visit the routing terminal in the subbasement.

I don't know why a chill went through me, like a too-cold sip of water, or what I hoped I'd find. At the very least, I thought I might learn if Doug's distress signal had been sent from within the building or outside.

It's probably no surprise, given the strange wind that had blown through my weekend, that I did find something down there. Much more than I'd intended.

I'd been to the subbasement before, but I couldn't recall ever visiting the terminal, where the few pneumatic messages that still got sent went first, to be hand-sorted. It was also used for storage of what was called "dead matter"—old passes of print manuscripts—and occasional shipments of books. The idea that I should go down there, alone, conjured a heady mix of courage and fatalism, and at an even stronger titration than at Dr. Thwaite's. Like the hot, robotic bravery that would overtake me before judo tournaments or stepping onstage for school plays.

Which is how, after riding the elevator back down to the lobby, then walking the two flights belowground to the subbasement and tracking the tubes past the server room, Repro, and Security, I found, at the end of a long hall, on the second-to-last door on the left, the Creatorium.

D dic•tio•nar•y \\'dik-shə-ˌner-ē\ *n* **1 :** one of several commodities aggregated on a privately held exchange **2** *obscure* **:** a reference book used for decoding arbitrary linguistic signs; a culturally significant artifact

As I descended the stairs, I once again thought I smelled something burning, which was odd—I knew the furnace must be off; it was Saturday night. There might be no one in the whole building but the woman up at lobby security and me. And it was cold in the stairwell; my breath ghosted out in front of me. My teeth clattered like cabinet china.

When I opened the subbasement door, though, the air felt a bit warmer, and the burning scent intensified. Confused and a little alarmed, I stepped into the hall. My footsteps rang loudly on the concrete. I craned my neck up to the exposed ceiling, eyes shrinking from the white honeycomb of light. The brass pneumatic tubes hung down like fat, dusty snakes. They lazed the length of the hall, then curved abruptly left, out of sight. I followed beneath them, my head trained slightly up, ears tuned to my resounding progress. Splashing once or twice into the shallow puddles, ubiquitous in the subbasement, that I'd heard were the result of groundwater seepage after renovations, requiring everything down there to be stored on pallets or shelves.

But that night I barely noticed the water. As I turned the curve, the sound of my steps was soon swallowed by another noise: an indistinct thudder. It got louder as I neared the spot where the metal snakes stopped, heads plunged hungrily in plaster. It had also gotten smokier and hotter, my breath evanescing as I walked.

I found myself outside a blank door. That surprised me. I'd expected arrows, cues, signs in blue, as at ID, REPRO, and SECURITY. But the whole scuffed hall seemed unmarked. Signs may have existed once—there were a few small holes drilled in walls, squares where paint seemed slightly brighter—but someone had removed them. Then I noticed a drooping piece of paper tacked up. When I flattened it out, I saw a single word scrawled in red: CREATORIUM. And beneath it the door was hot. The roar and hum I'd heard from down the hall was clearly coming from inside.

I was scared, but I was still being carried by the sinuous energy I'd once depended on to compete and throw opponents bigger than me. A feeling that had largely lain dormant in my adult life, partly because when it did appear—as in especially fierce fights with Max—it had earned enmity, not match points. But it was a feeling I'd missed, and I held it, exhaled, and knocked on the door. There was no answer. After a moment I knocked harder. But still nothing happened, so I tried the knob. And to my surprise, it turned.

Almost instantly I wished it hadn't. Because the door swung in, shifting a towel lining its bottom edge, and what I saw on the other side was very strange and unsettling. Twenty or more workers, all in identical dark blue jumpsuits, were locked in a fast, agile dance. Several sets of eyes darted toward mine, then quickly glanced off, the people they belonged to hurriedly turning back to their tasks.

I didn't know, of course, that the man who'd been stationed outside— the one they must have expected to see when the door opened, and to whom they might have reacted differently—had gone out for a few hours. Compared to him, I doubt I seemed very frightening. And yet even though I was careful to move with purpose as I stepped inside, I was surprised that no one spoke to me, or tried to keep me back, or even stopped what they were doing. Someone hurried past me to shut the door—that was all.

Even now, more than two months later, I find it hard to believe I wasn't turned away immediately. I can only speculate that the workers didn't know the guard had left his post. They must have assumed he'd let me in. And maybe my feigned authority also worked; they were willing to believe I might belong. But I think there's another, more relevant reason: that whatever threat hovered over not finishing their night's work was far more menacing than me. (A person running from a pack of wild dogs might not worry if a bird suddenly appeared and started circling.)

There's also a final possibility, the one I find most troubling: that many of the workers were already too sick or stunned to notice me.

Once I was inside the room, I was mesmerized. It was very large—four or five times the size of my art studio—but it felt cramped and chaotic. Thick concrete support pillars made the space feel crowded, smaller; the pneumatic tubes and exposed pipes brought the high ceiling down, and I felt again like Alice, suddenly taller—and as if I'd stepped into a dark, elaborate dream, one littered with large orange trash barrels and white-tiled walls streaked with dirt, the reverberant clang of pipes and pounding feet. And one in which the light, which jangled down from bare bulbs high on the walls, was filtered through a gray spume of smoke. Because the most vivid sign that something was very wrong, that made me wonder if anyone upstairs knew what was happening in that room, was that it was sweltering, the air thick and acrid.

I unzipped my coat and coughed into the liner, and right away I was jostled by a man hefting boxes from a massive, messy cairn of them stacked on pallets near the door I'd just walked through, and piled high above my head, almost up to the tubes. With a low grunt, the man heaved a box and carefully swung it to the worker next to him. A line of men in dark blue suits undulated along the left wall as they passed boxes hand to hand. I couldn't see where the row of them ended; it vanished into a cove around the corner.

The man at the head of the line nodded that I should move—I nodded curtly back—and as I stepped away from him, I tugged the neck of my shirt over my nose. It was hard to breathe through the smoke and heat, almost hard to see. My eyes burned, and I blinked back tears as I tried to interpret the shadowy movements around me.

I could make things out well enough to tell that in contrast to the thronging motion along the wall nearest me, just one man was standing on the room's opposite side, next to what must have been the message-routing station: the pneumatic tubes curving along the ceiling came together in a confluence of dull brass gills resembling a large church organ. Each tube had a small placard that I couldn't read from where I stood—their origins and destinations, I guessed—and they all emptied into a long sorting trough. A few empty metal stools were dispersed along its length, but the lone man stationed beside it stood. He had his back to me and seemed absorbed in his Meme, which glowed with a rabid, colored pulse. From my position, half hidden behind one of the support pillars, I watched him intently for several long moments, but I saw him glance over his shoulder just once, at a long table in the center of the room that separated him from the men moving boxes, who were nearer to me.

Of all the room's activity, it was the unfathomable work taking place at that cluttered table that most confounded me. About a dozen laborers sat staggered around it. I couldn't see them all—where I stood, pillars blocked some from view—but each seemed bent at the same crimped angle, tipped into the indigo glow of monitor screens, heads floating like tired ghosts over awkwardly perched bodies. Several had white masks over their noses and mouths, which made their faces hard to read. But I thought I saw something disquieting: the dead-eyed expressions of people dulled by mindless computation, or hallucinating. Or maybe that's what I see only now, with the eyes of memory. But then I was distracted by an even more distinctive trait they all shared: affixed to each of their foreheads was what looked like a coin, a little larger and thicker than a silver dollar. (Or so I'm told—I've never seen one of those.) When I got closer, I saw it was emblazoned with a coil intermittently glowing different colors: red, white, blue, gold, green. I was transfixed.

Cautiously, first studying the man watching his Meme near the tubes' terminus—from his solitude and idleness, I deduced authority—I walked over to the table. The girl sitting closest to me was tiny and silent and must have been ferociously focused; she didn't seem to notice me standing just a few feet away. Two enormous open books were balanced on her delicate knees, one nested inside the other. She looked down at each of them in turn and at another volume open on the table. Then she peered up at her monitor.[1] The screen was filled with populated fields laid over dishwater gray. And it looked a lot, actually, like the corpus of our Dictionary.

While I watched over her shoulder, a field on her screen turned a pale, pretty green. Then a word—I think it was "paradox," but I couldn't quite see—disappeared. And in its place strange characters emerged: б-а-у-д-о-к-с. Then the blocks of text below—its senses and textual examples—also vanished. Replaced by the single phrase "that which is true."

---

1. I didn't think to wonder then why they were bothering to use monitors; it occurred to me only later that the screens must have been for actual monitoring—so their foreman could watch their progress.

I learned only later what I'd seen: the manufacture of a term that would be used to increase traffic on the Word Exchange. For some users of the Meme—those whose devices had been infected with a new virus that had recently started circulating—terms like this one would replace "obscure" words—"cynical," "morbid," "integrity"—that those of us who'd grown dependent on our Memes no longer fully trusted to our memories. But I knew nothing then about these neologisms, or the virus, or why this "word" had just been fabricated.

The new, alien string of letters had no illustration. No etymology. No pronunciation guide, even. It was just a hard-hearted, ungenerous little word whose whole use was in its uselessness, cut off from human thought and history. A sad, sterile birth, prefigured by the death of paradox. It was ouroboros made manifest. The snake eating its tail. Facta non verba. My father's worst fears come to life, in other words. But at the time I just watched, silently entranced, as the next field on the girl's screen flooded green.

I looked at her again. Saw the silver coil on her forehead morph from blue to purple back to blue as she stooped to peer at the thick book resting more on her left knee, glance up at the screen, look at the one on her right knee, peer up again. Then she bent to mark a check with a pen next to one of the columns of text in the book open on the table, which had been annotated heavily in what I thought might be Chinese.

I leaned in to get a better look, and the girl, finally seeing me, gave a start.

I tugged my shirt from my face. "What are you doing?" I asked quietly, trying to sound curious instead of accusatory, not sure, but not unsure, that she'd understand me.

She was silent, replying only by blinking her eyes. Her coil began to glow red.

Without asking, I picked up the defaced book and flopped it closed. Hauled it over to inspect the gold letters on its spine and saw what I'd already suspected: it was volume P of the third edition of the *North American Dictionary of the English Language*. I more closely examined the girl's screen. It *was* our corpus. "Paradox" was gone. I felt dizzy.

"Wh-what's going on here?" I asked, shaking the heavy volume, then gesturing at her screen. My voice had gotten louder and harder than I'd meant it to, but my pulse was surging, my face getting hot. And when she tensed but still didn't speak, just kept blinking under the ember glow of her device, I nearly yelled, "Do you understand?"

But it was clear she didn't. Terrified, she flinched, and one of the books fell from her lap. It hit the floor with a loud report, and we both recoiled, me partly out of guilt and shame for the way I was treating her. I was also still vibrating with confused agitation, but that was no excuse.

Shaking, I bent to recover the volume. Before I could, though, the woman next to her dove for it, and as she leaned forward, the coil on her own forehead came off, maybe loosened by sweat—my face was dripping—fell to the floor, and rolled a few inches toward me before spinning to a stop.

I reached to pick it up. And on impulse I turned my back to the women and took a few steps away. I rubbed the device on my jeans, swiped my arm across my forehead, and pressed the disk to my skin. The side not raised into a coil seemed almost adhesive, like an electrode sticker— or more like the feet of a fly, I thought later; there wasn't any tape or glue. That's how I came to test the latest model of the Meme, the Nautilus. Not yet released.

I don't know what I expected. If I thought I'd experience anything— in the tiny shell of an instant I may have considered it—perhaps I half imagined I'd see a replica in miniature of what had appeared on the girl's monitor. But I think I assumed I'd feel nothing. What I did feel, though, right away, was a tingling, almost needlelike stinging on my forehead and an incredible warmth that quickly spread through my head and face.

But that wasn't the most remarkable effect. As I watched, it seemed that several glowing, golden columns of calligraphic characters faded from before my eyes like lovely, dispersing sun phantoms. It was as if I'd seen them projected on some sort of screen, the impression so strong that I patted my face to feel for something—lenses. But of course there was nothing there. And stranger still, as the characters faded, I felt a residue of indignation and fear, as if induced by whatever had been written there.

It's possible, of course, that this memory is false; I now know the Nautilus has an extraordinary power to distort—to flatten and rewrite experience and thought. And although the older woman quickly snatched the device back, scratching my face a little as she did, I later spent several hours lost in the fog of a different Nautilus, which also might have augmented my impressions of that night.

Before she removed it, I do remember being suffused with calm. An elating, almost paralytic sense of destiny and becoming—absurd (and dangerous) as that now sounds. Then I saw the angry face of the woman whose Nautilus I'd taken right in front of mine, and in an instant I felt a painful ripping and perceived noise and blinking light. She gripped the device in one hand, and in the other, a silver case, which she quickly opened. It seemed to be full of liquid. Carefully she placed the device inside, closed the lid, and violently shook it from side to side.

She was speaking loudly and quickly in Chinese. Everyone had stopped to stare at us.

"Listen," I said, shivering, still a little anesthetized. "You can't do this." I stepped back over to the girl, and I pointed at her monitor, shaking my head. Continuing to speak English to them seemed not only useless but antagonistic—patronizing. But I couldn't seem to stop myself. "I don't know how you got the passwords," I babbled on. "And I'm sure this is all saved somewhere"—I had the unsettling feeling that I was reassuring myself—"but this is bad. Very bad. You have to stop." Again I pointed at the screen and shook my head, embarrassed by my condescension. But also upset, and overwhelmed.

What was happening? These weren't building employees, that much seemed clear. So how did they get in? How long had they been there? Hours? Days? And what were they doing? On whose orders? Even if their intention wasn't to destroy the *NADEL*—and how could it be? It was an insane thought—accidental deletions would also be devastating. Each term represented untold hours of painstaking labor. Nearly three decades of Doug's work. And Bart's and mine. And dozens of others'.

And insane or not, nothing about what was happening looked accidental.

If many words were tampered with or erased—my mind went blank. The scale of the damage could be tremendous. Especially, I thought, my stomach getting tight, if the backups had also been harmed. The server room was down the hall. The Dictionary offices, with all the files of our digital archive, were just upstairs. The third edition was supposed to launch in less than a week. The first copies had been printed. But after that? How would we restore the missing terms? Every scenario I imagined, even the best ones, would require months or more of monumental effort to replace what had been lost. Time we didn't have—our funding was already almost gone. I wasn't sure any of us besides Doug would even know where to start.

As I thought of Doug, I felt my breath evaporate. I coughed again, violently, eyes watering. A sob lurking near the surface. "Dad, where *are* you?" I whispered to myself, wiping my eyes. Looking down the table at the line of laborers who'd gone back to inking up volumes, I finally let myself believe the worst. I found myself gripping the table edge, not sure I could stand. Staring into the frightened face of the girl I'd interrogated, who was still blinking. Now blinking back tears.

But it was at about this time that the man who'd been standing near the pneumatic tubes hurried over, shouting at the workers as he approached the table. I couldn't make out most of what he said—he was speaking something incomprehensible to me—but I thought I heard the English words "How? Who let her?" as he jabbed his hand through the air at me, a few white dots of spit jumping from his lips as he looked toward the door a little frantically. Then, with a final flurry, he motioned with both hands that they should get back to work. And he stalked toward me, anxiously glancing once more at the door.

I steeled myself. *Wood and glue,* I thought. It's what Doug would have said to me.[2] *You don't know anything,* I reminded myself. *Never let uncertainty get to you.* I swallowed hard and stared at the man's eyes. Unlike most of the other workers, he looked Slavic, with a strong nose and cleft chin. And he was short—about my height—but very solidly built. "Everything is all right," he said gruffly. "Naypek problems here. Yes?"

I still had a hand on the edge of the table, and he put his next to mine, setting something down: a silver case like the one in which the older woman had just forcefully cleaned her device. In the other hand he was holding his Meme, with whatever he'd been watching on mute, but when he noticed that I'd noticed it, he put it in his pocket.

"Look," I said, trying to sound reasonable. I found myself peering at

2. When I was eight, he made me a dazzling blue and silver sword encrusted with sequins (which soon fell off). Amazed, I asked how he'd made it. "Wood and glue," he said, shrugging. It had become one of our tropes, with different meanings—it could be used to signify something either magical or very prosaic. But mostly we said it when we meant "toughen up": that we can fashion our strength from whatever we want.

the silver case. Wondering for a moment why he wasn't using the coil inside it. "I work here, upstairs. My father is Douglas Johnson, Chief Editor of the *North American Dictionary*." As I said it, my voice crumbled a little, like a dune, a warm sluice of pride spreading through my chest. (*Wood and glue,* I repeated to myself.) "Can you tell me—what is all this?" I stared at him. "It looks like they're in our corpus. And as I'm sure you know—"

"Nothing," he said, cleanly scything my line of inquiry. "Myno is happening." The specter of a smile played on his lips. He looked again at the door, and the smile slipped away.

Exasperated, I shook my head. "I don't mean to contradict you—" I started to reply. But he placed a hand firmly on my shoulder. A shiver flickered down my spine.

"Everything is okay," he said, a bit more brusquely. "You don't see what you think you see. Time tyaz for you to leave." But then he grimaced strangely; letting go of me for a moment, he gripped his head in both hands. Very quickly, though, before I could process what was happening, the odd fit subsided. He reached across my body and roughly turned me toward the door.

And that unexpected shove ruptured some psychic membrane that had been convincing me I was safe; it made me freshly aware of where I was: two floors underground on a Saturday night. No one in the outside world knew I was there.

But I didn't move any closer to the door. I held my ground, tensing slightly but nodding. Looking over my shoulder at the foreman, I said, "I'm sorry," relieved to hear that I sounded calm. "I just need to know what's going on."

He studied me, eyes sparkling. He'd stopped pressing my back. But his hand lingered there lightly, as if on a horse's flank. The heat in the room was amazing. I felt shaky. Turning again to face the door, I tugged the neck of my shirt back over my nose for a few breaths. Sweat tickled my temples and the back of my neck, and I watched the men toss boxes in an inky curve through the shifting scrim of smoke. Stuck here and there to the concrete floor were boot-smudged pieces of paper. Pages from books. I watched the weak light dance in a few shallow puddles, and I tried to will the man's hand off me. I found myself wondering if I could use a judo throw to take him over my shoulder if it came to that.

I'd thrown men larger than me, but not in a very long time. And if I did, what then?

I didn't have to, though. Finally he lifted his hand. "I think it's better we don't call Dmitri. You agree?" I twisted again to face him. "He's coming back yankor. He doesn't like when we call." Then he lightly patted the baggy pocket that held his Meme—or something else. And that implied threat, together with the mention of another man, finally, fully pierced my armor. Maybe he was bluffing, maybe not. But he seemed very agitated, and insistent that I should leave—worried, I imagined, that he'd have to account for me to the other man: Dmitri. And frightened people can do very frightening things.

"All right," I agreed, groping in my pocket for my own Meme. Mentally filing details I could tell police. "I'm going."

"Yes. Good. You need help?" he asked.

I shook my head and smiled. He smiled back. Our smiles said vastly different things.

What he didn't know was that mine was also a feint. He'd left his silver case exposed on the table, and while we spoke, I very slowly edged my hand closer to it. As I demurely agreed to leave, lowering my eyes, I slid my palm over it. In one quick twist, as he glanced again at the door, I slipped it into my pocket with my Meme.

On my way to the exit, stepping over puddles and sheets of sullied paper, weaving quickly through the dirty concrete pillars, I looked back. He was still standing at the head of the table, watching me, one hand pressed to his head. Any moment he'd notice what I'd stolen. My pulse was thrumming so fast it made me sick. The floor seemed far away and pitched. Each screen I could see glowed with a smearing nimbus, and the smoke seemed to grow hotter and thicker. The room's loud thunder softened, as if it were coming through cotton. Time dilated.

But he wasn't following me. I turned back to face the door; it seemed to have crept farther away. Stumbling, I hurried past the last pillar, the ziggurat of boxes, the men shifting them, who were watching me. When I finally reached the exit, I forced myself to look over my shoulder one last time. The foreman made a shooing motion, and prickles of relief stung my face. I nodded. He turned back toward the tubes, reaching into his pocket to retrieve his Meme. And I stepped out into the bright, cool hall.

But I didn't shut the door all the way. And I didn't leave. I waited a few minutes, doing my best to get calm. I tore my coat and sweater off, fanned the hem of my shirt. Coughed. Leaned shakily against the wall. Closed my eyes against the painful light and pressed hard on my eyelids until I saw a luminous snow that lingered a moment after I opened them. I counted to twenty twenty times. Took a few ragged breaths. Glanced up and down the hall. All I saw were dingy white walls, blaring fluorescent bulbs, exposed ceilings busy with dusty tubes and pipes, gray concrete floor.

For a moment I thought I heard an impossible noise, like running water. But it was hard to hear over the pounding drone of the Creatorium. I peered farther down the hall—not in the direction I'd come but the other way—and the floor did look wet; I saw a glittering reflection of the overheads. But I was more concerned that no one was coming and quickly turned back.

I flapped my shirt a last time and tugged my dark sweater back on, leaving my green coat husked at my feet. Pulled the sweater's hood up over my hair. And slipped quietly inside the Creatorium again. There was something else I needed to see before I'd let myself leave.

The workers passing boxes in a line along the wall weren't wearing lighted coils, but a few had safety glasses on, and most wore cotton masks to filter out the smoke. I watched a man slide a box from the towering mound near the door. Sine it in a flowing motion to the next man down, who tossed it gracefully to the man nearest him, and so on.

As I hurried along the line, looking over my shoulder every few seconds at the foreman—he was back on the room's other side, again turned toward the tubes, watching his Meme, but at any time he could look my way—I felt the temperature rise and the air grow even harder to breathe. By the time I reached the apse where a hunched worker was slicing boxes open, I was coughing without stopping. Sweat slid off my nose.

Gazing through wavy lines of heat, eyes stinging, I made another awful discovery. As I watched in horror, barely swallowing a shout, books were wrested from boxes and tossed into the raging orange mouth of an old and badly ventilated coal furnace. I squinted at one of the boxes arcing by, and my heart ballooned. A white sticker affixed to the side read: N. AM. DICTIONARY OF THE ENGLISH LANGUAGE: 3RD—R. The worker who'd just caught the box looked up at me, eyes widening over his white mask. Before he had time to miss a beat, I placed a finger to my mouth.

Shook my head. Scurried back toward the door. Cast a last glance, before hurrying out, at the mountain of boxes. Each with a white sticker.

Back in the hall, I pressed a hand to my chest. Wiped wet ash from my eyes. Leaned into the wall, coughed, and struggled to breathe. Putting on my coat, I tried to understand what I'd seen. I felt as if I'd just stepped out of a limn on twentieth-century book burnings: gaunt, vampiric Goebbels screaming beside a seditious inferno; Stalin; Mao and his Red Guards; Iranian forces in the Republic of Mahabad burning anything in Kurdish; midcentury New York school kids incinerating comics in Binghamton; Ray Bradbury's firemen; apartheid-era librarians; Pinochet; Pol Pot; Serbian nationalists setting fire to the National and University Library.

But this was no ordinary book-burning. Our digital corpus was also being dismantled, by pale, nimble hands. Who, I wondered, would want to destroy the Dictionary? Did Doug know? Was that why he'd vanished?

I wanted to get out of there. Call the cops to report Doug gone. Describe what I'd just seen. But I was addled and not thinking clearly, and I started walking the wrong way—not toward the stairs but in the other direction, which I only really noticed when I heard splashing and looked down at my feet. And as I snapped back to consciousness, I saw that the large puddle I'd noticed a while earlier wasn't a puddle; it was a very small stream. And it was being fed by a few black hoses peeking through holes drilled in the walls. But it also seemed to be coming straight up through the floor. A little channel had even been dug into the concrete to let it flow down the hall, where it veered left into an open door.[3]

Cautiously I peeked inside. It was just a dark, dank storage closet, cool as a cave and plangent with rushing water. I hesitated for only a moment, to search for the light switch; I wanted to see where the water went. But before I could find it, I heard a man's hard Russian voice call from down the hall, "You want to know what we hide there? Keep snooping and you'll find out."

And that was it; I knew I'd been caught by the Slavic foreman. I felt

3. Like most New Yorkers, I'd heard the rumors about underground rivers and streams; the subbasement puddles were the only proof I'd seen. When I was a Columbia undergrad, I'd heard kids claim that water was running under Prentis Hall. But a far more famous subterranean brook had been discovered beneath the New York Athletic Club more than 120 years earlier—just a few blocks from the Dictionary.

oddly calm—the resolved, green tranquillity of waiting for a hurricane. Slowly I backed out of the closet, trying to invent some kind of story. But as soon as I turned around, I saw what my ears had already sensed but not yet quite transmitted to me: it wasn't the same man. And when he saw me, he seemed surprised. But not as surprised as I was when he said, "Ms. Johnson."

I'd never seen him before. He wore the uniform of one of our guards. Introduced himself, in an accent thick as cream, as Dmitri Sokolov— the man, I deduced, whom the foreman didn't like to disturb. He was massive: a dense three hundred pounds, six six or six five. The same physique and sad, soulful eyes of my favorite painting professor from college. I put him in his mid-forties, hair less pepper, more salt, but with eyebrows so dark they looked drawn in with charcoal. Clear blue eyes. Chin glinting with a scurf of day-old beard. His nose looked like it might have been broken once or twice. But he had a puckish, lopsided smile. And he teased, "I wasn't expecting the pleasure of seeing you tonight. What are you doing here?"

No story had materialized. "I got a little turned around," I said. My mouth felt unreliable and dry, as if I'd been eating salt. But I was still keeping a diamond focus.

"Yes," he said. Winked. "And where did you think you were going?"

Trying to think quickly, I blurted the wrong thing. "I was looking for Security," I said. Or meant to say.

He studied me with cold confusion. A dimple appeared in his forehead. And after a viscous pause, he said, "I do not know what this means, 'obaysin.'"

I had no idea what he was talking about. "Security?" I repeated, my voice crumbling out from under me.

He frowned. Scratched his chin. The rasp of nails on stubble set me on edge. Staring down at me, he slowly cracked the knuckles of both hands. Then, enunciating, he said, "Closed."

My stomach shrank as if it had been trussed with string. All I wanted was to leave. Get to the street. Call the police. Find my father, alive.

"Look, I really should be going," I said, reaching into my pocket. Surprised for half a moment by the presence of the coil case, and hoping it didn't show in my face, I gently removed my Meme. But there was no signal; strangely, it was asleep.

He glanced down at my screen, and I could tell he saw what I saw: the half glow. No connection. "Really?" he said. He seemed amused. "You should be going?"

"Yeah," I said, trying to bridle my voice. "My boyfriend's waiting." I shook my Meme.

"Boyfriend?" he mocked, eyebrows rising. "So you are meeting your boyfriend now?" He nodded lightly, the corners of his mouth dipping down. With a sickening tremor, I realized he didn't believe me. As if he knew no one was waiting.

Furtively I glanced up at the ceiling, and I realized, chest tightening, that there were no cameras in that hall. If Dmitri decided to take me back to the Creatorium, no one would know. It would be days before anyone even noticed I was gone. I could see the headline: "Father and Daughter Both Assumed Dead."

Dmitri said nothing for a long time. I tried to read his face, but it was illegible. Like a letter in a dream. I braced myself, every particle trembling with potential energy. I might not be able to fight him, but I wondered if I should try to run. If I made a mistake, I knew I'd be in much more trouble. I was in the rubber-band lag of a decision, imagining pushing past him and pounding down the hall. About to do it.

But then the long, murky silence passed. He gently clapped his big hands, gave a sly half smile that brightened his blue eyes, and said, "All right, Ms. Johnson. Go see your boyfriend. Give my best wishes to him."

We hovered there another few seconds, him blocking the hall. Then he took one small half-step to the side, not enough for me to get by without our bodies touching. He smelled of cigarettes and fried onion, a trace of cinnamon. I shouldered past with tensile force and made myself walk with steady, resounding power. I felt his eyes on my back, almost felt him smiling. But I didn't turn around.

And I didn't start running until I reached the stairs—then sprinted all the way up, heart feeling like a thing struggling to be born, holding my Meme like a torch. When I reached the lobby, I ran so fast across the marble floor I nearly fell. I realized only later that the woman who'd been at the front desk before wasn't there anymore. No one was.

Out on the street, I coughed and coughed on the wind, eyes tearing. Lungs sloughing off the inhaled atoms of my father's life's work. Signal restored, my Meme buzzed with two texts from old cell phones. One, sent by Bart, felt like a tiny life raft: "Any word? Hope you're okay." But the other was from Dr. Thwaite. "Alice," it said, "do not use your Meme. And stay away from the Dictionary." I tried calling, but he didn't answer.

My Meme hailed a cab, and once I was inside, it locked the door. It was a car with a live driver, and I saw him study me in the rearview mirror. We had trouble communicating; I had to give him my address three times before he finally nodded, unsmiling. I didn't know what was wrong with me, but I didn't feel well; I was sweaty, lightheaded. My Meme rolled the back window down. But I still got a little sick on the floor, and when I arrived outside my building, the Meme beamed my driver a 40 percent tip.

I thought I was just depleted. After I made it up to my apartment, I was so exhausted that I climbed into bed in all my clothes.

But tired as I was, I couldn't sleep. My mind kept taking me on punitive loops around a gruesome track: terrible things that could have happened to Doug, that might have happened to me if the night had gone differently. I begged my brain to stop, told it I needed rest so that I could get myself together enough to call the cops and keep looking for Doug. I even tried conjuring good memories, which sometimes helped me drift off. But most were quickly hijacked by anxiety, and after a while I reached into my coat for my Meme.

That's when my fingers brushed the coil's case again. And I wondered if *it* could stream something to take away my consciousness. Dr. Thwaite's warning, to avoid Memes, floated up in my mind. With a small stab of bad faith, I told myself that he hadn't said anything about this device. I doubted he'd approve of it either. But my stomach dipped as I thought of the heady serenity I'd experienced in the Creatorium when I'd taken the older woman's coil. I felt an almost compulsive need to use the foreman's.

It didn't seem to have an on switch; I just opened the case, removed it from its strange, clear solution, and placed it on my forehead. Once again I felt pinching, buzzing warmth. And I soon had a flurry of impressions that weren't quite mine, far more distinct than before. A thin, topless woman rippling in one corner of my vision called up a twitch of lust and mild languor. It almost seemed I could smell her perfume—juniper and fruit. On a different visual plane, two boxers bludgeoning each other stirred me much more: I felt a strong pull of excited rage; optimism, as if I were about to win something; a vague throbbing in my jaw.

In another corner I saw a pair of small children paw each other, vying to tell me a story in squeaky singsong, in a language I somehow nearly understood—maybe about a horse that had stepped on someone's foot. (I sensed that I preferred the girl to the boy.)

All of these memories—my memories, "our" memories—fluttered away very fast, like ash. But one thing vanished before I was ready: eerily lovely music so familiar I could almost name it—not quite. I wanted it back.

And the strange thing was, after waiting what felt like only moments—it must have been far longer; maybe as much as half an hour, I was later told—there it was again. A flashing caption said it was *Spiegel im Spiegel,* a piece for piano and violin by the Estonian composer Arvo Pärt. Vera had fallen in love with it for a while when I was a child and played it over and over for months.

That music unlocked the gate to a menagerie of sensations and memories, some that I'd been trying to summon to lull myself asleep, others that I'd forgotten, or that were half invented by the machine. But all incredibly rich in vivid, sweetly melancholic detail. Afterward I could recall only a few of them.

In one Vera hummed along to *Spiegel im Spiegel* as she baked lemon bars;[4] nearby I lay stretched on my stomach on a sun-warmed patch of floor, drawing a many-eyed dragon-wolf and occasionally glancing up at thrashing green trees outside the window, utterly absorbed, content, and sure of my place in the calm, perfect world.

In another, even earlier one, from what must have been my fourth or fifth birthday, she and Doug took me on the train from the Upper West Side to the East Village for my first real art supplies. As they swung me between them on the sidewalk, Vera joked, "I think they sell colored pencils in our neighborhood," and I felt a little guilty and happy and giddy with excitement.

While this memory played, other images arrived on different planes: a subway map from that year, side by side with the most recent one, glowing with the changes (the Second Avenue line, the M, the extended G, the T and U). The weather report for that afternoon appeared (partly

---

4. The smell appeared: melting butter, lemon zest. But so did a recipe, along with a link to a "shopping cart" already filled with all the ingredients. I had to think *Not interested* for it to go away.

cloudy and 62°), morphing into current conditions (windy, 38°). I saw saturated color swatches alongside ads for glyph projectors that could re-create them faithfully. And some works I loved floated past—by Gerhard Richter, Vija Celmins, Ed Ruscha, Kiki Smith, Louise Bourgeois, Francis Bacon, Isamu Noguchi, Picasso, Caravaggio, Rubens—with the names and locations of their museums and collectors. There were even other memories, playing on smaller "screens" simultaneously: my first excruciating college crit, the tannic wine served at my thesis exhibition, tossing rolls of grasshopper cookies to Coco over our studio wall one night when we were both camped out before a group show. (I heard a muffled "Ouch," and winced; then, a moment later, "Thank you, amour," mumbled through a full mouth.)

There was a freezing one, of Vera, Doug, and me flapping on the powdery ground of Riverside Park, making what Doug called "snow hippies," not angels, because he claimed they always looked like they had bellbottoms on. (For the same reason I called them snow moms, after jeans Vera had once modeled.) In another few, Doug drew elaborate maps to the Natural History Museum and the Seventy-ninth Street boat basin—three and seven blocks away, respectively—rubber-banded them to my wrist, and made me recite the routes back aloud. In yet another, my favorite, Vera had the flu and Doug and I tried to make her chicken soup. We took her a bowl in bed, and she tasted it bravely, but when Doug said, "It's terrible?" she nodded, laughing, tears running down her cheeks, soup spilling on the sheets, and she set down the bowl and opened her arms and we both crawled into bed with her.

There were lots of others, including many of Max and me. Our first kiss, beside a busy Hell's Kitchen handball court to a noisy soundtrack of hooting kids. Max insisting that we find a place to go fishing the first time he went to my grandparents' house in East Hampton and then making everyone, even my grandmother, eat our meager catch. Riding our bikes over the Brooklyn Bridge at night, handlebars jumping in my hands, and nearly being crushed by a car on the Brooklyn side, heart surging with the twin intoxicants of survival and love. Max singing Donny Hathaway's "A Song for You" in the shower of our Dominica hotel room one morning when he thought I was still on the beach.

All these memories—most of which skewed toward sentimentality— were elaborately layered, sprouting "added content" and ads. And the experience was strange in other ways. At one point, when Ramona appeared in a sequence from a middle-school field trip to the Bronx Zoo, I thought I even started to place a call to her—I heard a series of beeps followed by ringing—but the device said it was 2:37 a.m., and I made sure to "hang up," which I did just by willing it (feeling very relieved that it hadn't dialed Max).

At the same time I was also aware, if less distinctly, of my body in my bed, the coil stuck like a third eye in the center of my forehead. I could feel its pulsation on my skin, like a constant, low-grade jellyfish sting. Although in fact it didn't feel like only surface prickling; it felt somehow *deeper* than that. Which I later learned it was, in a sense.

One thing I did feel was that my head hurt. Tremendously. More and more, until I couldn't ignore it. And not a normal headache, like the kind I'd had at Dr. Thwaite's. It was as if my brain had been plunged in ice. My forehead, though, was warm. Very warm, and getting warmer. Finally a moment came when not just my head but my whole body was burning, and I discovered I'd been sweating—for some time, it seemed: I was bathed in it.

And then suddenly I swerved toward feeling very cold. My teeth started to rattle, hard. Head bursting with white shocks of pain at each clatter. And a message that I sensed I'd been evading suddenly got larger and started throbbing red. It said my temperature was 101. (The diagnosis, though, came back *"unknown."*) With barely any warning, I felt violently ill; I hardly made it to the bathroom before beginning to retch.

I don't know how long I stayed curled on the cold tile; it felt like I was sick for hours, intermittently flushing the toilet, rinsing my mouth with water from the tap. It wasn't until I finally sort of came to, splashing water on my face and toweling dry, that I made what was at the time a very upsetting discovery: I felt nothing on my forehead anymore.

Helplessly I searched the sink and floor. Then all over the apartment. Until, panicking, I rushed back to the bathroom and stared, defeated, into the empty toilet. Slumped to the floor. And thank God I'd flushed it, half delirious, by mistake. If I hadn't, I might have gotten much sicker—it could even have killed me. But at the time all I felt was annihilating regret.

I crawled on all fours back to bed and slept straight through to the next afternoon. But I woke up still unwell: fevered, joints aching, my head staved by pain. I'd slept on my arms; it felt like I'd held hands with an electric man. Needles and pins.

With my Meme I made a round of calls from bed. There was still no sign of Doug at his building or in the office or with friends. Aunt Jean hadn't heard from him, and I couldn't reach my mom.

All these calls were strange. I kept being asked to repeat things. The last person I dialed was Bart, who answered instantly, before the phone even rang. He offered to call the cops, and I agreed, tearing up a little from gratitude and worry. "There's something else you should tell them," I said, and began to describe the Creatorium. But from the silence on the other end, I could sense that Bart didn't understand what I was saying. Self-conscious, I tried to yoke myself to telling. But the story kept slipping its reins and running away from me.

"I think you should get some rest," Bart suggested gently. "Stay home tomorrow."

After I hung up, the pain in my head became so intense that I did start to cry. I wondered if I could die from it—if something had burst. I thought of calling Bart back, or dialing an ambulance. But in a tiny, crumpled pocket of my brain I remembered Doug's obscure warnings about a sickness—a very bad headache, I thought I remembered him saying—and the vials of pills he'd had me take.

With my last remaining strength, I dragged myself back to the bathroom and swallowed a blue pill with a cold handful of tap water. Then, my legs collapsing out from under me twice, I struggled again to bed, a slightly bitter, metallic taste in my mouth.

That's the last thing I remember before I fell back to sleep.

OP-ED CONTRIBUTORS

How the Meme Is Replacing the I

By The International Diachronic Society
Published: November 20

For many of us, it's hard to remember a time when print books were in wide circulation. So hard, in fact, that the word "book" sounds antiquated and quaint when applied to a bound rather than "beamable" document. (Most people, of course, now use the word "limn" even for print volumes. But we authors hope you'll forgive our small anachronism.) Yet as difficult as it is to recall, it wasn't actually so very long ago that books, magazines, and even news appeared primarily on paper. Certainly, when considered against the vast, varied curtain of human civilization, it's been barely any time at all.

It was nearly six hundred years ago that German inventor Johannes Gutenberg created the printing press, thus enabling the mass reproduction of inexpensive, uniform texts. A library, no longer the sole province of clergy and kings, was something common men could aspire to amass. Within decades books became ubiquitous, reading a veritable phenomenon. Gutenberg's innovation led directly to the Renaissance, the Protestant Reformation, and the scientific revolution. And the bound codex proved surprisingly enduring as a technology: books persisted more or less in their original form until the beginning of this century.

Even today a few books and periodicals are published on paper. But they're certainly the exception. And media executives who make this choice often do so to evoke nostalgia or spark publicity, as when this newspaper's editors celebrated its sixty thousandth "printing" a few years ago by putting out a supplement only in ink. Another example would be Marcus Hapgood's recent national bestseller, *Book: How Bound Volumes Unbind Minds,* which sold nearly half a million copies in print—although, notably, it was made available in only print form for the first six months after publication.

In contrast, readers—what we once called "e-readers"—have been commonplace for little more than a decade. And as unbelievable as it may now seem, Synchronic, Inc.'s popular Meme™ was introduced only four years ago. While safety concerns over the patented Crown™, Ear Bead™, and Sixth Sense™ technology have restricted sales in some parts of the world—i.e., Canada, the United Kingdom, and most former EU countries—Memes are nonetheless hugely popular worldwide. More than 100 million units have been sold globally to date.

Even the controversial microchip, introduced last year, has been a surprising—some might say alarming—success. Exact implantation figures aren't available; technically, of course, microchips are intended only for people with specific physical or neurological limitations, and Synchronic has been reluctant to release data on off-label use. But we all know that the chip's reputation for enhanced "neuronal efficiency" has resulted in much more pervasive adaptation—by at least 12 to 15 million people, some experts claim. (Memes utilizing microchips are reportedly far better at exploiting the devices' EEG technology to decipher and transmit electrical signals between the device and its user's brain.) It's rumored that the next generation of the Meme, slated for public release very shortly, is even more "efficient." Allegedly in development for years, it's supposed to function in a wholly new way.

The apparatus, it seems, has lived up to its name. (The word "meme," coined by British scientist Richard Dawkins in 1976, means an idea, pattern of behavior, practice, or style that spreads quickly from person to person within a given cultural context. It's derived from the Greek μίμημα, "that which is imitated.")

In just a few short years the Meme has completely transformed the technological landscape, influencing everything from how we interact to how we're entertained, how we shop and pay for things to how we receive certain medical treatments, how we're educated to how we express ourselves creatively. Even how we eat and sleep. Some might say that machines and users have become so intimately entangled that to presume any boundary would be fallacious.

In many ways these remarkable changes have been a boon. The switch from print to digital media has of course saved tens of millions of trees. (Even though discarded devices are damaging the environment in other ways, this step toward protecting forests seems worth underscoring.) And the Meme's advances in medicine, child and elder care, education, transportation, security, even prison reform have been much and duly lauded.

Memes have done everything from reducing traffic deaths, with Chauffeur™, to revolutionizing security, thanks to Safe™. This year Artiste™ was largely credited when the Artes Mundi went to a twelve-year-old girl. The controversial Ware™ helps monitor the movements of small children and the elderly, not to mention parolees. Some claim that Substitute™ is responsible for increasing student test scores in underfunded schools. Memes' contributions to the field of medicine are perhaps best documented: MD™ has unburdened doctors by facilitating many diagnoses. And Memes have obviated the need for some pharmaceuticals by offering a wide variety of treatments for everything from anxiety to pain, high blood pressure, ADD, and even addictions. The therapies are especially effective, ostensibly, in microchipped users. One small clinical study published in August (*J Affect Disord*) suggests that they might decrease the risk of suicide in certain populations by nearly 60 percent: interceding when they sense negative thinking and calling family and friends, or, in extreme cases, suicide hotlines and 911. They can even deliver mild electroconvulsive therapy. For many, Memes are life-saving.

But naturally, as with any new technology, they also have their detractions. For example, several highly publicized lawsuits have been settled in cases of Meme "misfires," as they've come to be known. Instances when Memes have commandeered user data not simply to predict but to *guide* behavior: gestures as innocent—and difficult to prove—as generating vindictive beams and tempting one to send them, ordering more drinks when you should go home, or purveying a wink to a lovely young woman—who isn't your wife. But Memes have also been known to precipitate disastrous outcomes: destroyed credit, bankruptcy, eviction. Or worse.

Rather than catalog a long litany of the Meme's dangers, however, we'll focus on the sphere of our greatest concern: communication. How we write and read. How we listen and speak, including to ourselves. In other words, how we think. It's comforting to believe that consigning small decisions to a device frees up our brains for more important things. But that begs the question, which things have been deemed more important? And what does our purportedly decluttered mind now allow us to do? Express ourselves? Concentrate? Think? Or have we simply carved out more time for entertainment? Anxiety? Dread?

We fear that Memes may have a paradoxical effect—that indeed, contrary to Synchronic's claims, they tend to narrow rather than expand consciousness, to the point where our most basic sense of self—our interior I—has started to be eclipsed. Our facility for reflection has dimmed, taking with it our skill for deep and unfettered thinking. And another change is taking place: our capacity for communication is fading.

In the most extreme cases, Meme users have been losing language. Not esoteric bits of linguistic debris but everyday words: ambivalence, paradox, naive. The more they forget, the more dependent on the device they become, a frightening cycle that only amplifies and that has grown to engulf another of Synchronic's innovations, the Word Exchange.

As most of you will know, the Exchange is a proprietary online marketplace that consists of hundreds of thousands of terms, downloadable as definitions, translations, synonyms, and antonyms, at 2 cents per word (as of this morning's publication). It seems to have been modeled on early digital music stores and Synchronic's own wildly successful Internet bazaar for limns, encompassing both a web presence and attendant device applications.

Once—and not so long ago—the Exchange was considered fairly useless and fringe. It certainly wasn't aimed at logophiles, or those of us who study words for a living. The quality was poor, for one; when Synchronic began to gather content, making mass word acquisitions, it watered most of them down and jettisoned "redundancies." Moreover, legitimate resources are still extant (as of today): specifically, the *North American Dictionary of the English Language* (*NADEL*) and the *Oxford English Dictionary* (*OED*). Professionals (the few of us that remain) tend to prefer these.

But the Exchange also didn't seem to be a site most civilians would have much cause to use, particularly since free online dictionaries and other reference tools existed until very recently. (We confess that when these sometimes less than rigorous resources started disappearing over the past year or two, we didn't necessarily mourn their loss as we ought have, and we may not have given enough thought to the cause: whether their developers simply lost interest in keeping them up or in fact they were being systematically dismantled.) Of course, some people encountering unknown words may also occasionally have looked them up in old print dictionaries. But it seems far safer to assume that more often they skipped over them—back when they could. When it was still possible for them to make themselves understood and comprehend the words around them without the Exchange or Memes.

A few years ago, if we'd been asked to name the Exchange's target demographic, we would have been hard pressed. We might have guessed college freshmen, analysts "punching up" time-crunched reports, perhaps those in need of a quick translation—of a warning label, say. What we absolutely failed to anticipate was that a day could come when average intelligent adults would be forced to consult the Exchange simply to get through the day's e-mail, parent-teacher conferences, the news. (Perhaps some of you are deploying it right now, to read this.) Suffice it to say that as our idiom shrinks, the Word Exchange has become far more lucrative.

We hope you'll forgive us a brief history of the Exchange; we gather that for those outside the very small (and shrinking) precinct of the publishing industry, it remains fairly opaque. Seven years ago, when Synchronic was still a relatively modest start-up, its chief executive, Steve Brock, approached the CEOs of several major publishing conglomerates and offered them a deal: a significant one-time payment for the digital copyright to all dictionary, thesaurus, and other word-reference tools; an annual remittance every year thereafter (not to exceed 25 percent of the initial payment nor fall below 12.5 percent) for access to and ownership of any new terms; and point-of-purchase royalties (not to exceed 10 percent nor fall below 4 percent) for each downloaded term. Many of them refused outright at first. But most eventually capitulated as the one-time remuneration settlement was adjusted upward and as they watched their competitors relent.

The fact is that the publishing industry was then in dire straits. While it hadn't yet collapsed, it was on the brink. And though most publishers were loath to sell even the digital copyright to their content, their parent companies' executives exerted pressure on them. In the end most publishers agreed primarily because they didn't think there would ever be a real market for downloadable definitions. In a sense, Synchronic's money seemed free. And the promise of royalties, should things work out otherwise, helped make the deal seem more appealing.

But most of us know money is never free. One publisher after another shuttered dictionaries in an effort to cut costs and keep other enterprises going. Later, as more and more houses filed for bankruptcy, more and more words passed into the sole domain of the Exchange. Eventually publishers lost their definitions by default. (The only holdout in the United States was the *NADEL*, protected from shareholder pressure by its status as a nonprofit.)

Before the end of dictionaries, it seemed to all of us that publishers were right: users would never pay to download meanings from the Exchange. All that changed, however, with the advent of the Meme. Suddenly users could get definitions right on their machines: tap a term and a pop-up appeared, the word charged straight to their Synchronic accounts.

At first people tended to use this service sparingly, such as for science and medical vocabulary. But more quickly than we could have imagined—as Meme users' own language began to corrode, we only later speculated—they embraced the new interface, weaving it seamlessly into their experience of language. (Some might even argue that as the devices became ever faster and "smarter," seeming almost to foresee wants and needs, users' consciousness over the decision to download words depleted.) And the price of words is so cheap—fifty for a dollar—that it must have seemed worth looking up any term that was even slightly unfamiliar (the number of which, as already noted, has increased exponentially).

And indeed, the words *are* cheap. But ironically, "adding value" to words has only *decreased* their worth. By putting a price (a very low price) on language, Synchronic has depreciated it immeasurably. Over time, attitudes toward words have changed. Now, rather than commit them to memory, many simply use "memory," relegating that chore to their Memes.

This is how we've arrived at our current crisis: our capacity for language—and perhaps, then, thought—becoming so seriously compromised that even scanning headlines, telling bedtime stories, greeting family this week for Thanksgiving, have become tasks requiring help from a device.

This is probably as opportune a time as any to parse the meaning of the word "synchronic." According to the *NADEL,* the term was developed by Swiss linguist Ferdinand de Saussure in 1913; applied to the study of language, it means that which is descriptive of a particular fixed moment in time, generally the present, rather than considered in light of historical precedent. It's a remarkably apt name for a corporation that, wittingly or not, promotes an ethos of accelerated obsolescence, shortsightedness, and privileging of the present over future or past, promoting the potential erasure not just of individual reminiscences but of our collective human memory. "Diachronic" means essentially the opposite. Perhaps it's not surprising, then, that when it came time several years ago for the authors of this editorial to adopt a name, we chose the Diachronic Society. The analogy is inexact—in linguistics, these terms are value-neutral—but we nonetheless thought the appellation fitting. When it comes to lexicography, as with most things, we prefer a long view. Words are alluvial, like rock formations. Phonemes are arbitrary. Meanings aren't: they accrue from shared experience.

These two seemingly disparate trends—the increasing predominance of the Meme and the growing popularity of the Word Exchange—have converged to create a new concern with the impending publication of the *NADEL*'s third edition, slated to hit stores next week. At present the *NADEL* and the *OED* in the U.K. are the last trusted English dictionaries not yet under Synchronic's jurisdiction. Allegedly, deals have very recently been proffered that would finally bring both institutions' terms onto the Exchange.

The consequences of these deals would be swift, irreversible, and cataclysmic. With a corner on sales, nothing would prevent Synchronic from adjusting the price of words up. And the company might well be able to influence the market in such a way that terms would be available only through Memes—no other device, no print reference books—further changing the calculus of supply and demand.

But far more worrisome: as language slides from people's

minds and begins to be stored more and more in just one place, the Exchange, accessible with just one machine, the Meme, it might conceivably become possible for people so motivated to begin manipulating our words in certain subtle ways that many people might not notice very quickly. Perhaps that sounds fantastical; not long ago, we thought pervasive Exchange use did, too. Many things that once seemed like fiction have come true. There are experts who also fear other hazards, even sickness. (We're prevented from sharing more details about potential public health risks by a voluntary agreement between this paper's editors and the U.S. government.)

As more and more of our interactions are mediated by machines—as all consciousness and communication are streamed through Crowns, Ear Beads, screens, and whatever Synchronic has planned next, for its newest Meme—there's no telling what will happen, not only to language but in some sense to civilization. The end of words would mean the end of memory and thought. In other words, our past and future.

It may seem to some readers that the dystopian future we're imagining is exaggerated or, at the very least, a long way off. We can only hope, for all our sakes, that they're right. Because if not, then these and all words may very soon lose their meanings. And then we'll all be lost.

E

em•pa•na•da \ˌem-pə-ˈnä-də\ *n* : a source of considerable digestive discomfort

Wednesday, November 21

It's been a weird and trying few days. But despite being single (pretty chronically), I've learned to make good on my promises. E.g., I still think Doug is fine. I grew up in a part of the country where men vanish sometimes—like my own father and Tobias, who occasionally drive my mother crazy by forgetting to mention that they're going camping or hunting—and I know it's not so different where Dr. D grew up.

But I agreed on Sunday, per Friday night's Devil's bargain (glimpsing Ana in her pj's ipso facto denotes that he was involved), to call the cops and report Doug as a missing person. (I think Ana may have a fever, or a mild case of shock. We had an exceedingly odd conversation Sunday— she was totally incoherent, mumbling something about creation or a basement or . . . ? I'm more worried about her than D right now, frankly. Though she does seem *maybe* a little better, at least linguistically.)

The bizarre thing is, it's been three days since I made the report, and Doug still seems to be gone. Granted, the cops didn't really opt in until yesterday. I'm sure he'll turn up. Honestly, I wouldn't be that surprised if he were just lying low somewhere, waiting out Friday's party for the third-edition launch. (I would: 600 people! I'm starting to panic that if he doesn't show, *I* might have to make some remarks. God, I hope he turns up soon.)

Yesterday they interviewed Ana, Rodney, and me at the station. (Rodney was acting pretty strange—he tried to pull me aside to tell me something about the office surveillance system that I didn't really understand.) Today police are investigating the office and I'm working from home. Well, sort of working. Trying to. But I'm having trouble focusing, which isn't a problem that often afflicts me, so I'm not sure what's going on. Maybe I really am worried about Dr. D. Or maybe it's that Mom just left another message with the unsubtle observation that I won't be home tomorrow for Thanksgiving. (It was lengthy: a cheerful, furtive guilt trip of the kind, slung with the ammo of banalities, that's indiscernible to a lay ear. The same kind she deploys nearly every year, even though I'm following her advice by saving what little I can, which means staying here.)

Honestly, it *is* hard not being in Illinois. Not attempting to split logs in the yard with Dad while we exchange almost no words. Not being force-fed warm ham biscuits by Mom while she tries to ask about my "love life." Not getting punched in the chest by Tobias and handed a wad of chaw that I'll deposit later, unchewed, in the hedge. Or playing Scrabble with Emma, who's home on break from ISU. Being apart from them this time of year always does something a little twisty to my heart.

But maybe my aberrant lethargy has a different antecedent. Maybe (okay, this is why) ever since I stayed the night at A's place, I've been thinking about her a lot. Which has naturally prompted an inner inquisition into what she saw in Max.

Not, I'm sure, his taste, which almost couldn't be worse. He likes the hazy, sunstroked sixties oeuvre—Bob Marley, the Beatles, Jerry Garcia (he prefers songs exceeding 25 minutes), etc. Clearly very different from A's musical proclivities. And, needless to say, mine. My favorite records from high school/the reason I survived southern Illinois are by Wire, the Jam, Television, Gang of Four, the Only Ones, et al.; Neil Young, Gram Parsons, the Stooges, Amon Düül II (whose 1969 record, *Phallus Dei*, kicked off the Krautrock movement); strange, sylvan Bulgarians singing the liturgy, etc.

Max, like most people, also no longer really reads. When I had to dump a box of favorite volumes last year after a basement flood, and (trying to keep calm) recounted the terrible, tragic loss to the Hermes crew—a natty copy of *Lolita* I'd read at least three times; *The Brothers K* and *The Thin Man* and *The Man Without Qualities*; *The Society of the Spectacle,* Hegel's *Elements of the Philosophy of Right* (or, as Max would argue, of *the* right); *Black Hole;* and, e.g., (fittingly) Bernhard's *The Loser*—Max's bemused response was, "Tell me again why you don't have a Meme?" (He espouses—and truly practices—a disavowal of attachment to "things," including, for instance, people.)

I didn't even mention the saddest loss of all: the bloated, boggy death of Samuel Johnson's *A Dictionary of the English Language.* I attempted, fruitlessly, to dry it on the roof, and succeeded only in crackling the pages. It wasn't a first edition, of course. Just some abridged 20th-century selection. Vera spent practically a home down payment on the 1755 edition as her wedding gift to Doug. My lowly imitation was the poor, toothless cousin to the two volumes Dr. D keeps under lock and key at home. But my mother had given it to me, in a rare bout of Midwest-transcending perspicacity, and I'd loved it for that reason.

There's more to life than music or books, though, I'm told. And I guess in some ways I'd like to be a little more like Max. There've been times, i.e., when I've wanted to tell Ana why I've devoted myself to this big, puddinglike language of ours, explain the reasons I chose to enlist at a dictionary instead of, say, start a start-up. But I think she'd be pretty unreceptive. And I'd like to save her, at the very least, from boredom.

If I *were,* however, to enumerate a few of my motives, I might give her something like the list below. Although I'd never give her *this* list, specifically. For obvious reasons, I have no plans to share this journal with her.

But speaking of this journal: first, a short apostrophe. During the most recent of what are fairly frequent exchanges between Dr. D and me, this one a month ago—or no, it must have been earlier, because we were celebrating having finally gotten everything off to the printer, drinking whiskeys at that Irish pub way over on Tenth—D was once again waxing overgenerous about some ancient *Yale Lit Mag* short story of mine, which I'd made the mistake of letting him read five years ago when he saw it on my résumé.

I'll gloss most of it—he made several embarrassing, overblown literary comparisons, per his wont, and while of course it's nice to hear, he's not exactly a paragon of subdued, unbiased judgment. (God knows I love the man, but he's pretty easy to dismiss with stuff like this.) And yet over the course of his apology re: why I should "collate my pensées," he said something that managed to sneak past my expertly laid defenses and actually *get* to me.

Well, *first*, actually, he made his standard case: that the reasons no one reads these days are (i) so much "media" is now generated by algorithms and machines and can't induce true "stirring in the soul" (I happen to agree), and (ii) because of the Meme, people are losing not just interest but the *ability* to engage. Then he went on to limn some pretty batty conspiracy theories—that Someone or Something is trying to commandeer language, take it over, "infect" it, erase it from the face of the earth, and that keeping a journal might both insulate me in some obscure way, and, potentially, serve as an important (ha) record if in fact that comes to pass. (These rants have grown worryingly recurrent; I'm hoping they'll stop when he can get a little postpub rest.) For some reason he took that moment to invite me again—even though he knows it's really not my thing—to join him at those Samuel Johnson meetings he attends. (Although I've just remembered that he also asked me not to write about *any* of this if he managed to convince me to start keeping a notebook . . .)

But anyway, then he pointed out that we'd just achieved a monumental feat, which had taken nearly his entire professional life, and that I'd had the good fortune to help facilitate before turning 30. And he said this: "If none of that convinces you, Bartleby, just look at me. I wanted to do it once, too. Be a writer. Now I'm near 70, and the only thing I have to show for it is dictionary entries. Don't get me wrong—I'm incredibly proud of it all. But let me say this, and I'll say it only once: don't fool yourself into thinking you're just on a detour as you sail home for Ithaca. A little pit stop, if you like, with the Lotus-Eaters or Calypso. There's no Athena interceding on your behalf. No guarantee you'll eventually arrive. If there's something you really want in life—especially if it's something that scares you, or you think you don't deserve—you have to go after it and do it now. Or in not very long you'll be right: you won't deserve it."

Histrionic as Doug can often be, I have to admit: it made an impression on me.

He then offered a remark about how his daughter would never fall for a man for whom lexicography was the sole obsession, claiming that (even if it wasn't obvious from her most recent choice of mate) she was helplessly smitten by creativity. That also caught my attention—and made me blush so much I had to go to the men's room.

So—here goes, I guess. Some of my collated pensées on language:

1. HISTORY

Language is the only tie that binds us to the otherwise vaporized ideas of the dead. It lets us hear the clanging air of history and slips the links of our own epoch onto that long concatenation.

Every word is itself a memento of the past. Take, for example, the word "lousy" (a favorite of D's). We're all familiar with its modern meaning—awful, contemptible, etc.—popularized, e.g., by Holden C. c. 1951. That sense actually dates to at least 1532 and Sir Thomas More's *Confutacyon of Tyndales answere*. Perhaps you won't be surprised by a few of its earlier, more corporeal connotations (dirty, filthy, soiled) if we shuttle back to 1377, year of its first recorded appearance. Back then it denoted lice-ridden, beloused. The same expanded use has cropped up in other languages as well: *lausig* in German, *pouilleux* in French, *piojoso* in Spanish, and so on.

How about the lithe little word "larva," from the Latin, which had nothing to do with insects until the 18th century? In an earlier life it meant ghost or spirit. "Nightmare," too, comes from the spectral realm. Derived from Old English *niht* (night) + *mare* (incubus), it applied to an evil, female-type phantom that settled (like Ana?) on sleeping innocents.

"Buxom" once meant meek, "crazy" a thing cracked to pieces. And while some terms have undergone a painful pejoration, others have been plucky enough to rise, revived, from degraded ranks. There are also words that have enjoyed particularization: a deer was once any four-legged animal, a girl any child, meat any hunk of food. To be naughty was once to be worth nothing, while to be nice, in Middle English, meant to be stupid.

Words are living legends, swollen with significance. We string them together to make stories, but they themselves *are* stories, encapsulating rich, runny histories.

2. LINGUISTIC EVOLUTION AND DIACHRONY

Language is incarnate. It's the way our bodies evolved—to stand upright, to walk—that enables us to speak at all. And it's our senses that give us reasons to talk. We want to verify with others what we seem to perceive. It's also our bodies that give our words urgency: the tiny ticking clocks in each of our cells.

Words, then, are born of worlds. But they also take us places we can't go: Constantinople and Mars, Valhalla, the Planet of the Apes. Language comes from what we've seen, touched, loved, lost. And it uses knowable things to give us glimpses of what's not. The Word, after all, is God. Some might say in fact that our ability to speak proves we're made in the divine image (*Bildung*), as we, among all creatures, are the only ones that really talk.

The way that came to pass is really pretty remarkable. Human babies, like other mute mammals, are *incapable* of speech; their airways are separate from their nutritive passages so they can pound gallons of milk. The upshot is a facility only to emit noise. For our vocal cords and diaphragms to develop, humans had to stand. Now every time a child learns to walk, the laryngeal tract shifts, the soft palate closes, and the miracle of evolution begins again.

3. EXACTITUDE AND EVOCATION

Language is infinite. It can be as creative, and as chillingly precise, as the human mind. *Bombenbrandschrumpfleichen,* e.g., a word coined per conditions distinct to the 20th century, means incendiary-bomb-shrunken bodies. Less distressing (in a sense) is *shitta* (Farsi): leftover dinner that's eaten for breakfast. Or the Indonesian *jayus,* to bungle a joke so badly that your interlocutor feels forced to laugh. In Japanese, *koi no yokan* means the ineluctable feeling you have, upon meeting someone for the first time, that eventually the two of you will fall in love.

Words compress impressions into facts cold as frozen quarters. One single word—like EMERGENCY, or love—can revise a whole night. A whole life.

4. POETICS

Just as language can be pliant enough to create a word for faces caramelized by firebombing, it's elusive enough to mask them in metaphor. It can make disparate things seem alike, marry unwed ideas, hide things lying in plain sight (for instance, people, nations, wars).

Definition, like poetry, is the project of revivifying the familiar. Making things we think we know seem newly strange. To estrange, according to Hegel, is requisite to practicing consciousness. He also thought recollection requires interiorization of language, and to describe the place from which recollections are drawn, he used metaphor: it's a "night-like pit in which a world of infinitely many images is kept."

And from our pits we draw: a world like a stage, the number seven, small hands like rain, time like money, lions that lie down with lambs, whoopee cushions, broken hearts.

5. LOVE

Language seems to be the only means for linking consciousnesses, the most effective way to stifle loneliness and pull us from our night-like pits. (Maybe not the *most* effective. Some might argue on behalf of physical contact. But words are more accessible. To me, at least.)

Language also acts like love in form. The sign, according to Hegel, is a union between the external word and its inlying meaning. But this idea can also be extrapolated. A few years ago I read a quite compelling philosophical theory claiming that one could read in Hegel an argument for a universal grammar. The same argument can be applied to love. Underlying every lexicon is a hopeful faith in the existence of order: i.e., that words will be arranged to make sense. The feeling of love, likewise, presupposes the existence of an object of love around which to organize. Similarly, the concept of a universal grammar presumes specific lexicons (e.g., German, Hebrew, Japanese), just as the universal feeling "love" presumes a contingent, particular love (e.g., Anana Johnson).

6. DIVERSION

Finally, language is a good distraction; it shields us from thinking of other things (like love).

Okay, writing is hard. And now I'm starving. Going to the pushcart for empanadas.

November 21 (much later)

Here's what ended up happening when I went out to get food.

It was unseasonably mild, and I elected to eat on my stoop. Hot coffee (from a bag, wino-like) and a pair of crispy chicken empanadas. (This might seem an unfortunate combo for a person with IBS. But owing to the inflammatory nature of both comestibles, I find it more efficient to aggregate them.)

While sipping my coffee, I thought about work, in a sense. I.e., my mind went to A. You can imagine, then, my discomfiture when Max appeared on the sidewalk. He was suckling a toothpick and watching me with a roguish grin that made me very tense. Why had he come all the way uptown to materialize, like a warlock, before me? How had he known I'd be home? It didn't bode well. But all I said, non-nonchalantly, was, "Hey."

"Come on," he drawled. "We're going to meet those guys for lunch."

I frowned, unwittingly. "But . . . my empanadas," I said, gesturing lamely at the tined half-moons of food balanced on my knees. I didn't know it yet, but the grease had worked its way through the now translucent paper and into quarter-sized spots on each trouser leg.

"Forget it, man. You hate empanadas," said Max. His declaration was made with such conviction that for a moment I was confused. When had I told him that? Empanadas are the linchpin of my diet, such as it is. I felt compelled to say (to myself), *No. You, sir, are mistaken.* But by then we were almost at the A train and Max had eaten the empanadas.

The casualness with which he'd said we'd be having lunch with "those guys" belied the fraught nature of their four-man fraternity vis-à-vis me. In theory, we're all friends; really, though, we're all friends with Max. Over the years he's collected us, like mutant moths: Johnny, at Harvard, after Deep Springs; Floyd, of London, where Max accrued a quick master's at LSE; and Vernon, at Columbia University, the site of Max's MBA. Before he'd even shaken the dean's hand for that last *Hedera helix* degree, he'd assembled his Hermes Corp. team. (Not to belabor the point, but I'm the odd one out: he never asked me.)

I've spent a lot of time with Those Guys. Mostly I don't mind. I'd enjoy it more if they'd excise Floyd. He's like a chalk outline of Max: flatter, more cartoon-esque, and he leaves behind a residue that's hard to brush off. He's a man of unexamined tastes who believes they're charming and unique. He likes: large-chested redheads (also any drunk woman), whiskeys over ice, and, after the latter, starting fights. He cultivates giant, frazzy muttonchops—"face pets"—that he goads girls to stroke. A person could be forgiven for failing to infer that he's also sort of a genius who's won awards for game-theory work.

Given the competition, Vernon's pretense is pretty easy to stomach. He's a standard-issue Comp Lit ABD: short fro, stylish peacoat, and an only slightly affected cane for his bum knee, the result of a Vespa wreck back in '03 (on which I will refrain from airing judgment). He doesn't get total immunity, but he's a decent guy. And fun fact about Vern: his thesis, like Dr. D's, was on Samuel Johnson.

There's also one diamond in the rough: the best, most inoffensive of the bunch is the calm and cynical Johnny Lee, aka Hong Kong Johnny, aka Long John Johnny, aka Jack the Jackknife (nicknames © Floyd Dobbs). Johnny was in fact born in Hong Kong, but he grew up in Bergen County. His preternatural knack for programming gained him Hermes entrée—that, and his equanimity: "eh" and "whatever" tend to dominate his vocabulary. He falls more in my camp—i.e., shy and rangy—which is why he sops up some of Floyd's surfeit persecution. In theory, he's as ambitious as the rest of them. But his main penchants seem to be blue Gatorade, weed, games in the *Time Crisis* franchise, and music by the rapper Lil' Big. He's had the same girlfriend, Lizzie, since he was 20.

Anyway, as I said, I see those guys plenty. But it's not like the five of us "lunch." The fact that Max made a special trip up to invite me was incongruous, to say the least, and the timing seemed noteworthy. The Dictionary launch is in just two days, and it's been getting tons of publicity. I thought Max might want me to ask him along: an epoch-making role reversal. The thought was sweet. It was also fleeting. Because I suddenly, lurchingly, worried that he'd somehow heard I spent Friday night at A's. Maybe the lunch was actually an invitation to a beheading. Or maybe, I thought hopefully, he just wanted a report on how she's been. Whatever his motivation, I was feeling more than a little anxious as we lumbered down the subway stairs. "So why are we going to lunch?" I asked, trying to sound laid-back.

Max tossed the crumpled wax-paper rosette from my bygone lunch into the trash. Then he held his Meme up to the turnstile scanner and cannily replied, "We're just having lunch, Horse. Try not to be such a pussy about it." "Pussy" is a term I loathe, and that also often spurs me to action. Two facts of which Max is apprised.

When I still tarried, he gave an impatient jerk of the head and uttered a salient pair of phrases. "Just come on," he said. "We're paying."

A little while later we emerged in that carefully shabbied playground, the Lower East Side. Our destination, Premium Meats, delivered mightily on its titular promise. (Sadly, we were seated near the ladies', so the meal was sullied by Floyd. His sparkling witticism—"I've got some premium meat right here"—got kind of flat after the fourth time. And later, when I offered to share my lunch with Johnny, who wasn't touching his, I made the terrible tactical error of noting that I'd ordered more than enough meat for two people. "Funny," Floyd rejoined. "That's the name of my penis." And there went my appetite.)

When we arrived, the other guys were already there, drinking and updating their Life statuses. Our booth was a vigorous red-vinyl affair, the mottled table shot through with faux gold veins. Lithographs of handsome cuts of meat lined the walls, and dusty light filtered from dangly bulbs, casting a romantic glow over the six square feet we'd snugly jackknifed into. (I was smooshed up against the paneled wall, Vernon and Johnny beside me.) They all beamed their orders in—Max, a sporadic vegetarian, ordered snails, rabbit kidneys, and fried pork belly; Floyd got an ox heart; Vernon went for smoked eel; Johnny opted for a steak and fries—and I asked Max to get me black coffee.

"Come on, man," said Floyd. "Live a little. At least get it with cream."

"I'm lactose-intolerant," I informed him, for maybe the fiftieth time.

"Of course you are," Floyd said, shaking his head and snickering, as always.

"Keep it light, you two," said Max. "And really, Horse, get what you want. On us. It's been a good year for Hermes."

He had me there. I shrugged and ordered a steak and sweetbreads.

Then Max removed his tattered toothpick, trailed by a strand of saliva silk. "Horse," he drawled, "we called you here today because we want you to join our team. Hermes really needs you. So we all hope you'll say yes."

I'd been waiting so long to hear those words you'd think they might've lost their glow. His request also wasn't executed particularly subtly or well. And in truth, I'm not very familiar with their oeuvre. (Before tonight I'd never tried any of their games. I don't even have a Life profile. And I obviously don't spend much time on the Exchange.) But more importantly, I *have* a job. That I *love*. I wouldn't trade it for pretty much anything. Despite all that, I said, "What would that entail, exactly?"

Max explained that their new contract with Synchronic let them hire a lexicographer, and he claimed I was his top choice. (I wondered how many others he knew. Besides Doug, of course, who, as Ana's dad, I assumed wasn't on his list.) He said the first job would be freelance, so I could get a sense of things. Basically, they'd pay me to attend a party and write "on-demand definitions" of words—what Floyd called "money words"—that guests made up on the spot. ("What party?" I asked. Max shrugged. "Just this gala thing.")

Vernon, gently rubbing his glasses on his black sweater, offered, "It's essentially Meaning Master performed live."

I nodded thoughtfully, as if I got the reference. A tried-and-true method of mine. And one Max sees through every time. "He doesn't know what that is. Do you, B?" he said. I did something kind of non-committally shruggy. Max took a swig of lager and said, "Didn't think so," sounding nonjudgmental. "Doesn't matter."

I've since looked it up. The lamentably named Meaning Master™ is a game—Hermes®—downloadable from the Exchange. (I didn't even know Synchronic *sold* games now. I guess that helps explain its interest in Hermes.) To the degree that I've discerned its machinations, it seems a player's main goal is to coin new words. Each round is two minutes long. For the first minute, as letters stream by on the screen, you link matching colors by typing them in or pinching them together. In the second minute, you mint as many fresh definitions as you can, or just opt for automatic "meaning assignment." (I have to admit, it's kind of fun. High production values.)

Apparently the most "inventive" neologisms are featured on the Word Exchange and made available for download—and one "Meaning Master" a week receives $1K and is featured on Synchronic's home page. I think they even get a little PI News feature. I read that the first winner, Haley Rutherford, a 16-year-old from Cleveland, created the appalling word "now•y \\na ů-ē\ *n* : when everything important is happening." I also found an astounding Hermes press release that claims the game produced a threefold increase in Exchange traffic in the first half of this month.

But at lunch Max didn't bother to explain; being Max, he just started his pitch. And to explicate this party trick—of making up words, like cake, more or less from scratch—he invoked GWF. "According to Bodammer," he began, "Hegel calls for the mind to 'kick name and meaning away from each other, *treten Name und Bedeutung ausein-ander*,' to create 'names as such'—senseless words—which are blank, and ready to receive pure thought."

Which means, I *think,* that he's using Hegel to justify creating fake words, claiming that they qualify as "names as such," one of Hegel's lesser-known concepts. And I don't know if that's what Max actually believes, if he's being intellectually lazy, if he feels compelled to jus-tify profiting from manipulating language, or if he really thinks he can fool me—that I won't know the difference. But of course that's *not* what Hegel meant by "names as such." He precisely *wasn't* talking about inventing nonsensical "words." He meant words we've mentally stripped of all meaning so we can consider words qua words, in formal relation, as a practice of consciousness. The mind acquires language because it anticipates sharing in communal expression. There'd be no point to learning private words only it can use.

But I decided not to go into all that. I hate getting in pissing matches with Max. I always get peed on. Besides, his soliloquy coincided with the arrival of our food. I did wonder, though, what had happened to his longstanding concern with "context": his belief that language suggests a wobbly ecology of meanings and that words can never be divested from the who, what, where, when, and why of their use. That *I'm* a right-wing crank for proposing that words are molds into which we can pour thoughts. After I'd scarfed a few fries, I said as much.

"Well, Bart," Max said, fixing me with his freakishly lambent eyes, "I'm glad you said that. Because context *is* important. Very important. It's a big part of our motivation, actually." Then he launched into a sort of confusing treatise on how Hermes's methods offer the historically marginalized and voiceless a "new opportunity to enter the sociocul-tural conversation." By co-opting words and "creating more useful ones," disenfranchised people could "reclaim a language that has for centuries conspired to keep them in their so-called place. Think of how powerful it would be if 'primitive' morphed into 'sovereign,' or 'empire' became 'salt'—or some word that hasn't even been invented yet."

Then he pulled out the big guns. "I don't think it's a coincidence," he continued with a one-sided smile, "that Samuel Johnson compared cataloging English to taming a savage land. Johnson said"—here he wiped the rabbit-kidney juice from his fingers and picked up his Meme to read—"'though I should not complete the conquest, I shall, at least, discover the coast, civilize part of the inhabitants, and make it easy for some other adventurer to proceed further, to reduce them wholly to subjection, and settle them under laws.'" Then he looked up and pierced me again with the hazel lasers of his eyes. "Imposing ourselves on other people—our language, style of governance, way of life—it just isn't right. Even when the ends seem worth it—spreading democracy, more open lines of communication. 'Liberty' and 'free expression.' How free are people, really, when you make them say what you want?"

I thought of pointing out some of the more gaping holes in this rhetorical set piece, and also of asking how exactly inventing fake words at a "gala thing" would help upend the hegemony. Some people, though, can justify anything, at least to themselves.

"I wish the answer was easy," he said. "But we can't fix things with just skillful elisions, or by learning Urdu or Kazakh or whatever. Might not be a bad start. But if we really want to try to understand each other, we have to communicate not just better but differently. Invent a completely new kind of exchange."

At that moment Floyd leered at a girl on her way back from the bathroom, and (surprise) she recoiled, knocking into Vernon's cane. It clattered to the ground, nearly taking out a sprightly busboy loaded down with heavy plates. Vernon (not Floyd) began profusely apologizing; the girl turned the color of rare steak, and Max leapt heroically into the fray, gripping the busboy's shoulder, righting the cane, and reassuring the girl that it had been Floyd's fault and everything was okay. Later she looped back by our table and, flushing crimson again, passed Max a napkin, on which—in a cute nostalgic gesture—she had scrawled her number and name. (Normally girls just look at him boldly and say, "Share contact"—often when he hasn't even asked—and their information apparently then leaps right into his Meme. In fact, I think it was the Hermes boys who devised this app.) When she was gone, Max scanned her into his Meme—which told him, among other things, that she was 22, originally from Phoenix, and trying to make it on Broadway—high-fived Floyd, and unceremoniously handed him the napkin.

The interruption disoriented me. (The girl was really very pretty.) Instead of offering my planned rebuttal, I just said, "It's a nice idea. But how's it supposed to work, exactly?"

"Sounds like someone feels a little threatened," sneered Floyd, drooling on a mouthful of ice from the bourbon he'd just drained. "An interactive dictionary might just put you out of a job, bro." He winked at Johnny.

"An 'interactive dictionary,' whatever that means, is a *terrible* idea," I said, making sure to keep talking over Floyd, who was saying, "Why? They did it with the encyclopedia." "I mean, it seems like you're not really suggesting a new, shared language but a unilateral one that's constantly changing. You're emphasizing the *destruction* part—tearing down the old temples or whatever. But what would you erect in their place?"

"We'd erect *this*," Floyd grinned, wanking into space. Max gently stilled his fist.

"Okay, Horse," said Max, shifting in his seat. "Habermas would say that Hegel sees language as a means of submitting to the state. Which of course Hegel would have approved of. Language, like labor, like domesticated 'love,' is a means of subordinating the individual to the larger civic sphere. And what we're advocating isn't necessarily insubordination but freedom from subordination. We can get words to mean whatever we want."

I had so many objections I didn't know where to start. And I didn't get why Max was being willfully obtuse. Maybe that's why, at about that point, I ran out of steam for the debate. Besides, let's be frank: I wasn't weighing the job on the basis of ideology. The fee Max had quoted me was *obscene*. I could buy my mom a car with it—and still have some left over. I shrugged and told them I'd sleep on it.

"Great," said Max. "I'll send you deets in the morning."

Then he rummaged under the table and produced a small black box glinting with the words MEME on one side and NAUTILUS on the other. But it was also printed with a picture, and it looked nothing like the Memes I'd seen. I thought a Meme was just a slim silver screen and a little pair of fern-furled Ear Beads attached to a misnomed Crown (aka headband), its one weird little silver arm that hooks forward to lightly kiss the center of the forehead always seeming as if it might fall off. But this was different. It didn't look like much, just a small silver circle imprinted with a spiral that glowed in the photo with a bluish light.

"Here," Max said, holding out the box.

"Thanks," I said, shaking my head. "But no thanks."

"Sorry, brother," Max said, smiling aggressively. "It's a condition of employment. You're impossible to reach. Time to join the 21st century."

But when I still didn't comply, Floyd reached over, slurring, "Shit, I'll take it. I've been wanting one of these. Heard it works way better with the chip."

"You can get your own," said Max, roughly swatting Floyd's hand.

"No I can't," Floyd said, shaking the hand Max had smacked. "You know we don't have any of the new ones yet." Max, ignoring him, passed the box to Vernon, miming that Vern should tuck it in my hoodie hood. "Sorry," Vernon murmured very quietly, just to me, so close I could smell the cigarette smoke clinging to his sweater. "You don't have to use it."

That was a little odd.

But I had a question for Floyd. "Did you say 'chip'? As in 'microchip'?" I was incredulous. "I thought only people with, like, spine injuries got those."

"Naw, dumbass," said Floyd. He sounded sullen and therefore more lucid, his cheeks flushed at the edges of his furry face pets. "We've all got them. Except Vern. Pussy."

Aghast, I stared at Floyd's big, fatuous head. Imagined a microchip implanted under his skull. *Electrodes* embedded in his *brain*. I couldn't tell—as was so often the case—whether he was telling the truth or fucking with me.

"But actually," Max interrupted, "like with other Memes, you don't need the chip."

"Can I ask," I said, gingerly removing the box from my hood, "what does it . . . do?"

"What—the Nautilus specifically?" Vernon said, forking dressing-glossed arugula leaves. "Or you mean a Meme?"

I shrugged evasively. (I'd seen them up close and even held them, but I'd never actually used a Meme.)

Floyd, eyes goggling, laughed. "Are you fucking serious?"

But before I could feel too sheepish, Max coolly responded, "Everything." And together they proceeded to rattle off a list that did in fact succeed in blowing my mind. The Meme did all the "obvious things," they explained: anticipating wants and needs. "It'll do your groceries," Vernon said through his napkin. "That's pretty convenient. Oh, but taxes is the best. There's a pop-up sometime in March asking if you want them filed, and you just hit 'yes.'" That's the moment my interest increased.

But it also transformed life in more extraordinary ways. Max claimed, for instance, that anyone could create a "masterpiece." As proof, he nudged the least obvious artist in our party. Floyd put on his Crown, concentrated for a minute, and beamed the results to Vern so I could see. Astonishingly, it was true: the image, of women bathing, was *breathtaking*. Sort of Baroque, with golden, Flemish light, the figures drenched in pathos and grace. "And it's dialectical," Max explained, "which is part of what makes it so moving, or whatever—it senses what you want to see and augments those aspects. There's no fixed image. And you can do it in any medium—music, film, glyphs."

If I was willing to get a microchip—a minor, outpatient procedure— my Meme could do even more for me. Make it easier to remember certain incidents in full, lustrous color, or forget things I'd rather not revisit (again and again). It could change my visual field so that walking or driving or riding in the train would feel like performing in a video game.

"What happens if you want the microchip out?" I asked, looking around at all of them. "Is that—that's a minor procedure, too?"

There was an edgy silence. Vernon shifted next to me.

"Yeah," Max acknowledged. "That's a little more complicated." But he quickly changed the subject, listing more Meme functions: it could yield access to whole fields of study—macroeconomics, 17th-century Italian poetry, mixology. "You don't necessarily 'learn' the stuff," Max explained. "But it doesn't matter—it's all right there for however long you need." It could suppress or increase appetite. Help you focus. Coach you to enhance some physical abilities.

Needless to say, my defenses started getting worn down almost painfully—and Max hadn't even started to describe the Nautilus.

When he did, his face was deadpan. But his voice was a little too muted; I knew it was big. "It's the first commercially available device that integrates electronics with cellular biology," he said.

Obviously I needed to have that explained—and I suddenly had the uncomfortable feeling that the machine then nestled in my lap cost more than my childhood home.

Unlike his own Meme, Max said, which utilized electroencephalography; an abundant array of chips, sensors, and transmitters—"Enough for a small island country"—and (he tapped his skull) a microchip; my new Nautilus Meme required far less "messy hardware," because it utilized the already existing infrastructure of the brain.

He invited me to think of the brain as having all the functions of a computer. It has computational power; it can filter, sort, and rank data and stimuli (determine what to pay attention to, what to ignore). It has the capacity to visualize and conjure auditory sensations through imagination and dreams. By building strong neuronal pathways, it can become very efficient at certain things. But like a computer, it can also form new networks. "Which is how it's able to work with the Nautilus," Max said mysteriously.

Synchronic had spent years perfecting a device that, instead of maintaining separate, parallel systems that have to interface constantly, could simply integrate them—literally. The cellular components in the Nautilus combined with sensory neurons. That's why it didn't need a screen or mouthpiece or mic, or "any of the cumbersome light-to-sensor-to-signal transitions." (I jotted down a few hasty notes on my grease-freckled napkin.)

And with its electronic and digital elements, the Nautilus created a gateway that would convey information directly from the Internet to the brain. It required a little neural "rewiring," Max said. But especially with extended use, it could create what he called a new "relay center," exploiting the brain's plasticity and "changing native topology" to engage directly with visual, auditory, and other sensory systems.

That was how, Max claimed, you could get a "text" without a screen to see it on: it would simply appear, like a mirage. Eventually, he went on, you'd no longer even need any vestigial cues, e.g., a ringing sound to alert you to a call. After months, or maybe only weeks, of use, you'd simply sense the call—and perhaps be able to respond without words.

At my request, the guys went into a lot more detail about the Nautilus. It was named for its spiral design, reminiscent of the eponymous mollusk, and like its namesake, it has to be stored in fluid. ("Comes with enough for the first six months," Max said, tipping his chin at me.) Parts of the device are electronic. But it needs to be kept in special solution when not attached to skin because it also contains biological tissue. "Sort of a logical extension of biological computing," Max offered casually.

Apparently the Nautilus has a semipermeable membrane; when you put it on, its needleless "bioject" technology creates the conditions for cell "infiltration." That, naturally, sounded pretty unwelcome to me, but Max claimed it was completely safe; just the device's cells integrating with the somas of the nearest sensory neurons to create new chimeric cells that can communicate with their cortical counterparts in the brain.

"Whatever that means," I said, glancing around the table, expecting nods of solidarity. But everyone was staring calmly at Max.

"What it means," Max elaborated, pausing to sip his rum and soda, "is that the Nautilus creates its own point of entry for letting digital information in. Namely, it allows data to flow through the device to the user's skin, and then it employs existing neuronal channels to send signals from the skin to the brain."

"Where exactly are you supposed to put it?" I asked warily.

"The directions will say to put it on your forehead," Max replied through a mouthful of pork. "That's partly a marketing thing, so other people can see you have one. It's probably also a little more effective there; the signals don't have to travel very far since the forehead's so close to the brain." That made me flinch a little, which I guess Max could see, because he chewed, swallowed, and continued smoothly, "But you should be able to put it anywhere, as long as it's in the same place each time."

Floyd leaned across the table toward me, his eyes betraying rare excitement, and interjected, "That's only possible because the Nautilus uses biological computing, like Max said. It stores data in DNA code, not zeros and ones—although it's obviously always translating back and forth between the two. But also, instead of electronic logic gates, it uses proteins. So there's this . . . seamless integration between the device"—he held up one hand—"and the neuronal network it joins." He raised his other hand and clamped them together. "In other words," he said, smiling slyly, "between the outside world and your mind."

"We've all tried them," Max reassured me.

"You too, Vern?" I asked. I thought I felt him tense a little on the bench beside me. But he just nodded mildly. "Indeed," he said, scratching his throat.

Max then explained, lowering his voice, that I could tell absolutely no one that he'd given me a Nautilus. "I will hunt you down," he joked. (I think.) They wouldn't go on sale for several more weeks. But he expected a shipment within days of a version that fixed a few "tiny, superficial glitches." When they got the new ones in, he promised to hold one for me.

I shook my head. "Not necessary," I said.

Max sort of squinted at me, one corner of his mouth ticking up—his codified expression of disappointment—and said, "You're not going to use it, are you?"

I shrugged. Sighing, Max said, "Yeah, I thought you might be that way. You should really try it. It's pretty cool. But—" He reached back under the table and brought out a second box, this one picturing a standard Meme. "Here, Horse," he said, tossing it at me.

And then something else happened. Floyd interrupted. "Hey, that reminds me. Anyone else see that report in the *Times* yesterday on Memes?"

"It was an opinion piece," Vern corrected, and Floyd flipped him off reflexively.

Vernon seemed unfazed. He very plainly *had* read the piece (I hadn't), and in fact he seemed to have come prepared to dissect it: he offered a close reading of everything from use of the term "book" ("manipulative, maudlin") to a critique of the former EU. Most of all, he seemed disturbed by the lack of a true byline. "It's the end of journalism" were, I think, his words, which struck me as a bit overwrought. Max seemed to agree with me; he smirked through Vernon's oration. Strangely, though, he chose not to riposte.

But that wasn't the oddest thing about the conversation, which soon got far stranger.

It was all sparked, per Vernon's byline comment, by an argument over the so-called Diachronic Society, which had apparently written the piece. The guys all seemed convinced, for some reason, that I'd know what this is. When I assured them that I don't—"I never know anything," I explained—Floyd said, "Dude, are you lying right now?" But prompted by Max, Floyd soon ceded that lying is one of several things that fall outside my skill set. That, though, is not what surprised me. Rather, N.B. the following exchange:

"What do you think, Johnny?" Vernon asked, pointing one of my fries at Johnny.

"Yeah, little guy," added Floyd. "Your threshold of creepy silence is impressive today even for you."

Johnny shrugged, looking, I thought, a touch disquieted. "Eh," he said. "Whatever."

"Seriously, John." Vernon laced his long, aristocratic fingers and craned his head to the left to give Johnny one of his special supra-glasses stares. "It's the first public critique of the Meme that links it explicitly to the Word Exchange. I'm curious to hear your opinion."

It might sound naive, but this was maybe the first time it really sank in that my compatriots in meat are into something truly big. That what they're doing with Synchronic is on the national stage. And I, too, was curious to hear Johnny's judgment, since I'm sure he's the only one who really understands the technical aspects. And Johnny looked queasy.

What he said was, "Honestly, dude, I feel a little exinbo."

We all stared at him. I don't know why, but the hair on my neck stood on end.

After a moment of silence, Floyd said, "Exinbo? What does that fucking mean?"

Johnny looked nonplussed. "Exinbo?" he said, turning a shade greener. "Huh?"

Vernon cleared his throat. "That's what you just said," he offered gently.

"I-I did?" stammered Johnny. "Really?" He gave a lopsided shrug, wincing. Pressed his temples for a second. "Don't know what that means." Then he tried to laugh, but it was a strange and stifled sound, like a person laughing in his sleep. "Hungover, I guess I meant. Feeling hungovo."

"Nothing to be ashamed of, little buddy," Floyd said, hoisting a refreshed glass. "Hair of the dog. Nature's medicine." Ad hoc shtick seemingly meant to un-unsettle things.

But the exchange had profoundly agitated me, in ways I can't quite explain. It made me hearken again to the weird, brief call I'd had with Ana Sunday, when her speech was overrun with lots of these odd slips. Frankly, though, everyone seemed shaken. I could see it in their boozy faces.

But Max prodded us on. "Who do you think wrote it?" he asked, staring at Vernon.

Before Vern could reply, though, Floyd said something that set off another strange cascade of chain reactions. "I don't know, man," he said, gurgling his bourbon. "What about your ex? Doesn't she hate you right now? Maybe she'd want to discredit us."

The corners of Max's mouth dipped down, and a crease furled between his brows. "No way," he said, shaking his shaggy blond head. But his eyes had dimmed. He turned them on me and started to speak, and his voice was edged with the sharp teeth of worry.

The question he asked, though, had nothing to do with Hermes. "Hey, Horse," he said, trying (I could tell) to sound relaxed. "Has she heard anything, by the way? Or have you? I know she loses her shit if anyone goes missing for, like, 20 minutes."

I was chilled to the kidneys. Like I'd put on a pair of jeans taken too soon from the drier. "Who said anything about someone going missing?" I asked Max.

"Oh . . ." he trailed off, his brow crease deepening. "I thought I heard . . . in the news. About her dad?" We were all watching him by then, even Floyd, and Max's frown flickered into a small, embarrassed smile. I felt, if possible, even more rattled than I had after Johnny's slip. What did it mean, I wondered, that Max knew Doug had disappeared? Who would have told him? Ana? That seemed extremely unlikely.

"In the news?" I said. "Really? I haven't seen anything." In fact I knew, based on my discussion yesterday with the detective in charge of Doug's case, that the story hadn't been made public.

Max ducked his head and, trying to suppress his nervous smile, babbled, "Yeah, I heard about it somewhere yesterday. Or the day before, maybe." I saw him look pointedly at Vernon, who again feigned indifference at the scrutiny. Though again I could swear I felt his shoulder tense. Then Max took a long pull of his drink, and when he set down his glass, I could see he'd recovered his equilibrium. In a tactically offensive move, he pinched my last, runty fry from its wide slick of grease, met my eyes, and added, "Let's face it, Horse. You're not exactly known for your deft grasp of current media developments."

And as if to prove Max's uncontestedly superior au-courant status, his Meme chose that moment to chime. He glanced at it, peered up at the rest of us, and said, "Hey, did you guys hear someone just tried to hack the Pentagon again?"

I decided to let the Doug thing slide. Max's favorite insult for me is "milquetoast." And I do hate needless discord. Honestly, I was pretty drunk by that point. With some magnanimous donnings of his Crown, Max had ordered us all several rounds. So I shrugged, faking good-natured defeat. Vernon, our resident diplomat, maneuvered a change of subject by reviving the question of the *Times* op-ed's authorship.

Unfortunately, Floyd jumped in. "Maybe Douglas Johnson wrote it," he mused, spinning a coaster. Then, impishly eyeballing me, he added, "Unless he's dead or something."

I knew it was meant as a provocation. Normally I wouldn't have taken the bait. But I'd had one nutty, autumnal Märzen too many to simulate the appropriate level of apathy. (Also I was probably sublimating.) "You know, you're a real asshole," I responded. "That's a seriously uncool thing to say." (Floyd seems to understand me better when I use his vernacular.) Riled, I disclosed, "The police and Anana and I are all looking for him. He might be in trouble. So please. For once, can you just . . ." But I let the sentence die, shaking my head. I was beginning to feel the familiar urge to take off.

"What about you, Max?" Vernon asked, draping his napkin over the remains of his plate and gently pushing it away.

"What about me?" Max asked, seeming distracted. I couldn't really tell, though: he'd plucked a pair of Aviators from his shirtfront and put them on.

"Who do you think wrote the piece?" Vernon persisted.

Max broke out a fresh toothpick. Jimmied meat from his teeth. "Doesn't matter what I think," he said. (Which was clearly not what he meant.)

"Do you have an opinion?" asked Vernon, who is fluent in Max. As are we all.

"You really want to know what I think?" Max said. All I could see was the bowed reflection of me, Vernon, and Johnny in his dark lenses. But it seemed like he was once again glaring at Vernon, jaw set in a hard line. I could tell Vernon felt it, too: he squirmed a little. Dipped his long fingers into the neck of his sweater and stretched it away from his throat.

It was Floyd who obliviously negotiated the moment when he said, "Yeah, dog, I do."

Max stabbed his spent toothpick into Johnny's nearly intact steak. "I think Horse wrote it. Didn't you?"

And for no reason at all, I broke out in a sweat. Then I spilled beer on myself and pretty much everyone else.

After that I went sheepishly back to the Heights. And let me say this: I didn't write that op-ed. I don't know why my gadfly fingers made it seem otherwise, but Max has adapted some of the erratic methods of a dictator, and it makes me nervous. His accusation was obviously insincere. I don't know what he meant by it, or who it was most supposed to disconcert. It could just have been payback for my catching him out about Doug. But there's clearly something going on between him and Vernon. Guess I'll have to ask Vern about that.

As for the op-ed, which I just read: I don't believe it at all. Synchronic making a bid to co-opt the *NADEL*? Impossible. I'd even hazard to say that it seems like a publicity stunt—that Chandra in marketing has gotten even cleverer than she's always been. Maybe that's where Doug is? This is part of a whole thing, to ratchet up suspense ahead of Friday's launch? I guess that's pretty implausible. Why wouldn't Doug just tell me? And, more relevantly, A? Unless she's lying to me, too. God, *please* let that not be the case. Please?

Okay, this'll be ves for tonight. But a few super weird things just happened.

So I'm trying the Meme. I was a little hesitant, табен reading that op-ed, but they do all use them, ez Vern, and after what they described, I was also tychen curious. I figured I'd just quickly check email from bed, and if I didn't like it, I'd take it right off again. And the Crown takes a little getting used to, даш it *is* pretty amazing. I especially liked how it started eezow Neil Young on the stereo before I quite knew that's what I wanted to fall asleep to.

But when I checked my email, some of them were really chig. A few seemed like spam, full of random unintelligible words. I only opened one of them because it seemed to come from Johnny. *Really* hoping that doesn't bite me in the ass. There was also one from Ana, inviting me to Thanksgiving tomorrow at her mom's. Is that even possible? Did I make it up? Guess I'll check again in the зowshong. But it was the last one—a mass message to the *NADEL* staff—that disturbed me most. It said the party scheduled for Friday at the New York Public Library—the third-edition launch party, for *this* Friday, two nights from zyve—is apparently "postponed until further notice," due to "Douglas Johnson's unexpected absence" and "other factors." Holy. Fucking. Shit.

F

fa•ther \'fä-<u>th</u>ər\ *n* : Something sought but not often found; in some contexts: G–d; in others: D–g

As I scurried up to the blue door of the Midtown North Precinct on Tuesday, the familiar curl of Bart—hunched under the flagpole, hood tugged up against the cold, a white puff of breath clouding his face like an omen—made my stomach swirl with shy gladness, even given everything. I was so relieved to see him after the past few terrible days—to have an ally who cared nearly as much as I did about finding my dad.

I was also a little embarrassed. The last time I'd seen Bart, Saturday morning, the morning after Doug went missing, my dirty hair had been thatched in knots; I'd hardly slept; I'd had on no bra. Since then the only time we'd spoken had been Sunday, when I'd been so sick I couldn't roll over in bed. I barely remembered the call, but standing beneath the briskly whipping stars and stripes, I could tell from the startled, sheepish look on Bart's face—a mirror of mine?—that whatever I'd said had been in some way untoward. At least the call had done the job. There we were at the station, about to be interviewed by the cops.

Bart gave me a little, melancholic smile, looking more than ever like Buster Keaton. "How are you feeling?" he asked, and I felt a warm wave of blood flood my cheeks, which confused me. Since when did Bart make me blush? I had a flashback to his look of pleased surprise as he'd rummaged through the box of detritus from my earlier life, and to him slumbering on my floor, the soft pink soles of his feet showing.

As if to save me the trouble of answering him—or maybe, I realized later, afraid that I wouldn't be able to—he didn't wait for me to respond. (This was, of course, the day before Bart himself started to be aphasic.) Nodding, he said, "Come on, let's get you out of the cold. Rodney's waiting in the lobby."

But when we went inside, we were told that Rodney's interview was already in progress. Bart and I took metal chairs near the door. I was still shaky: I'd been laid out for two days. Maybe sicker than I'd ever been. It was only that morning that I'd woken feeling a little more like myself. I'd managed to shower and eat some dry toast. I'd even made a trip to TriBeCa, to an old cell-phone store on Church. That's why I'd been late to meet Rodney and Bart.[1]

When I started to describe my sickness to Bart, he looked troubled; then he leapt up and vanished. At first I was a little hurt, afraid he was trying to get a safe distance away. But I also understood: he had a lot of health problems—allergies, maybe asthma; I didn't know what else— and whenever anyone in the office started sniffling, he always kept a wide berth. That day at the precinct, though, he soon returned, gripping a white paper cup dotted with flowers, jostling water on the floor. "Here," he said, his trembling hand dribbling a few dark blots on my coat. And off he went again, to find a paper towel.

Diffidently, between sips of water, I tried to ask him about our Sunday call—whether it had been what I'd said or the way I'd said it that had thrown him off. But before I even mentioned the Creatorium, I watched his thin face hollow in concern, and with rising alarm, I wondered if I was still having trouble making myself understood.

I didn't have a chance to ask, though: a scrawny officer escorted Rodney out to the lobby and called my name. I had just enough time to nod to Rodney—and watch him step toward Bart—before the cop whisked me away. As we squeaked down the hall, he introduced himself as Officer Maroney. He was about my age, with a shiny, slightly under-baked face, a heavy mustache, and dark brown hair dense as turf. He

---

1. I'd texted Dr. Thwaite: "Is this phone okay? Have you heard from my dad?" But he hadn't replied.

stood aside to let me pass first into a tidy office done up simply, with no plaques or degrees.

A handsome man lumbered out from behind a large metal desk, hand first.

"Detective Billings," he barked, squeezing my palm into submission before pulling out my seat. His blazer was decked out in brass buttons and a special badge, and he had on a black tie, knotted tightly at the neck. His bald head gleamed with a star of glare. He had some extra padding beneath his jacket. Not as much as Doug. But I tend to trust a man of appetite, and I put implicit faith in the detective.

The interview, though, was short and discomfiting. It started straightforwardly enough. Officer Maroney stood back near the door, and Detective Billings asked me to describe the night Doug went missing. But as I spoke, Billings kept hooking his hand behind his ear and asking me to repeat myself. A few times he glanced over my head at Maroney. And at one point he interrupted to ask if I felt all right. When I nodded, he motioned for me to go on; he was recording notes, so I seemed to be conveying something.

But I was scared. I'd been taking the pills Doug had given me, and I felt better. It seemed I was still sick, though—with what I didn't know. Something that had come on as I'd used that preternatural coil. (It seemed crazy to link the two; also crazy not to.) I remembered Dr. Thwaite mentioning a disease—a pandemic, he'd said. And I felt my chest and neck grow warm even before my exchange with Billings took a more unsettling turn.

It happened as I was trying to explain that Doug's late meeting on Friday hadn't been in his date book (like about half his meetings). "But I'm sure his visitors are on the security tapes," I said, or managed to express after a few attempts. "You must have discussed all that with Rodney."

Detective Billings hitched one corner of his mouth to the side. Then, again, he looked at Maroney. After a moment he raked his bottom lip with his teeth. "Tapes are blank," he said flatly.

"Blank?" I said, incredulous. "Did you talk to Rodney?" My pulse picked up.

"Did we . . . ? Ah, talk to Mr. Moore. We discussed it with him, yes," Billings said, voice dry as flint. "We're interviewing him further—that night's visitors' log is also empty."

"That's impossible," I blurted. I saw his jaw tighten almost imperceptibly. I could feel him studying me, and I wondered if he was conducting a test. Trying to get me to say something that might discredit Rodney. Or myself. If I hadn't already. With a mouth of rubber, I said lamely, "Rodney's the best there is." Explained—or tried to—that even to get to the Dictionary's elevators, all guests had to sign in. That surveillance was always on. I'd even seen some of the recordings myself, when an intern-turned-pickpocket had stolen my necklace one summer.

He didn't interrupt me this time, but I didn't know whether it was because I was making sense or he'd just decided not to. I tried to press the detective for details—did they have any leads on when or how the recordings might have been erased? Had Rodney been able to identify suspects?—but that was it: by then Billings's lips were sealed. He politely deflected all my attempted questions, gently yanking at his ear as if he'd just been swimming.

"*Rodney's* not under investigation, is he?" I finally couldn't help but ask. Detective Billings put his big hands on his desk. Knit his mammoth fingers together. Said, "At this point, we're not ruling anything out."

My stomach flipped. I wanted to ask if I was being scrutinized, too, but that seemed impolitic. So I asked instead what they'd thought of the Creatorium.

Again Billings squinted, one brow dipping down. Same errant corner of his mouth ticking up. "The what?" he asked.

"Creatorium. In the subbasement?" I tried. "At the Dictionary?"

Detective Billings shook his head.

I said it again, and when his expression remained blank, I started to wonder if the problem wasn't that he didn't understand me but that Bart hadn't mentioned the Creatorium when he'd first talked to the cops. If not, *why* not? Had he thought I made it up? That I was delirious, maybe. Or nuts—like Doug. Maybe the police just hadn't followed up on it. But it seemed most likely—and unnerving—that whatever I'd said to Bart on the phone, I hadn't managed to convey the Creatorium at all. That at that very moment, no one knew it was there. Or had ever known.

I shivered, scrunching my neck in an uncontrollable twitch. Then did my best to explain what I'd seen Saturday in the subbasement. Described the hall where I'd found the hot, crowded room. Sweatshop workers in blue. The Slavic foreman. Our electronic corpus, overwritten term by term. Hundreds of books burned. The hulking, knuckle-cracking figure of Dmitri Sokolov. As my account haltingly uncoiled, I don't know how it sounded to Detective Billings, but to me it sounded more and more crazy. If he doubted its veracity, his mistrust had gone subterranean. He listened game-faced, stopping me only to ask for clarification, expressions stowed like carry-ons.

I thought of him the next afternoon, Wednesday, when I went in to work for the first time that week, late, and got a call from one of his colleagues. Cops were searching the twentieth floor for clues about Doug, so a few of us Dictionary staffers had been allowed down on fourteen. I'd just started combing through hundreds of emails, hoping to see one from my dad or someone who might know where he was, when my new cell phone rang, startling me.[2]

"I was just down in the basement," the officer said gruffly, his voice harsh through the metal holes of the alien earpiece. "There's nothing there. What'd you say you saw?"

I held the phone away, frozen for a moment. As blood surged through my head, I heard a faint rumble, like distant thunder. Had I *made it up*? What would Billings think, I wondered—what doubts about me would surface, or be confirmed—when this officer reported back to him? Which he probably already had.

"I want to go with you," I heard myself say. I said it twice, just in case.

Hesitantly the officer agreed—he'd just gone down to the cafeteria for a coffee and asked me to meet him in the lobby in fifteen. When I shook his hand next to the security desk, I hoped he didn't make too much of my palm's clamminess.

We plodded down the dim, echoing stairs, then traipsed along the damp, bleak hall below the dust-furred pneumatic tubes, exactly tracking my Saturday route. And it was true: the Creatorium was gone. All of it. Disappeared. The only signs it had existed were a black patch of soot on the floor near the furnace and a faint smoky scent. Everything else had vanished. The paper sign outside the door. Boxes, table, chairs. Workers. Even the message-routing station was closed down; a note hung from one metal tube that said, "Temporarily Out of Service." A few glinting delivery cylinders littered the floor. Again I felt the specter of sickness. And that my mind was cracking apart. The officer just shrugged, unruffled, and sipped his coffee.

2. It rang four times before I realized it was mine.

And that was just the start. In the cafeteria line, surreptitiously buying a bag of candy for lunch, I overheard some etymologists discussing an anonymous editorial on Memes published the day before in the *Times*. As I started reading it in the elevator back up to fourteen, I could swear it was in Doug's voice. I'd heard so much of what it said before that *I* almost could have written it. That was sort of reassuring. I hoped it meant he was okay—that I'd have an explanation very soon for where he was and what was happening.

But my peace of mind didn't even make it all the way to my temporary desk. As I rounded reception, biting into a soft licorice nib, Chandra from marketing came flying past. She looked pale. Mascara smudged. When I asked what was wrong, she seemed to understand what I said. Her hands went to her throat, and she blurted, "It's canceled."

"What is?" I tried to ask, swallowing the sweet mash. My teeth probably black.

"The launch," she said, voice teetering. Fingers finding her temples.

Silent alarms started going off in my head. Chandra didn't upset easily; I was sure she'd heard something about my father that no one had told me yet. Trying to stay calm, speaking as clearly as I could, I asked what was going on. When she tipped her head in confusion, I asked again, apologizing if I didn't make sense—I'd been so sick and anxious since Doug had been gone. She nodded, frowning, and put a hand lightly on my arm. She started to say that she didn't know why the launch was being called off. But then, quietly, after a tiny drag of silence, she leaned in a little and added that it might have to do with "the deal."

"Deal?" I asked, perplexed. The op-ed was still open on my phone; I hadn't finished reading it.

For a moment Chandra's expression flickered, a wrinkle trembling her brow. But right away her face reglazed. She swiped away the mascara. Said she'd meant it was because of Doug's disappearance. Then, stilettos clacking, she vanished, too, calling over her shoulder that she had to catch a train. The email she sent later that night didn't clarify anything.

Back at my desk, already shaken, I finished reading the *Times* piece. That's how I learned about "the deal": that all our terms might be sold to the Exchange. I found it very hard to believe. And yet. A wavy picture appeared, of the Dictionary crumpling into cinder and ash downstairs. Of nonsensical strings of letters smothering our corpus. I knew in my heart that these things were related. But I didn't know how, or what it meant. Where Doug's disappearance might fit in; if he was in danger. Or—maybe almost as bad—somehow involved.

Rattled, I tried calling Bart—someone had told me he was working from home that day. But I couldn't get him: maddeningly, my signal kept dying.[3] I sent another text to Dr. Thwaite. Again there was no response. Frustrated and on edge, I switched from the phone back to my Meme. Not using it was more than a hassle—I felt paralyzed. It was part of me.[4]

And there were things I felt I needed the Meme for, things that nothing else could do. I.e., when I got home later that night, I used it and the Exchange to translate the strange, faded instructions on the pill bottles Doug had given me—in Chinese, traditional characters—and learned that the pills were antivirals, to be taken three times a day "for abatement of symptoms"—if not symptoms of what. I'd been guessing and taking them only morning and night.

While my Meme had been switched off, I'd received a slew of texts and beams. Several were from Coco. One wondered why I'd never turned up in the studio Sunday; she'd sent a few invitations to things; and her last one, which made my throat tighten a little, said, "Are you all right, *mignonne*? I'm very worried. I love you." The beam from Ramona, who was the only friend I'd managed to speak to since the week before, said, "U alive? What about yr dad?" There was also a text from the doctor, who said she had something free in two months. (I'd noticed that as

3. Cell service didn't always work so well these days, the guy in the TriBeCa store had warned me ruefully.

4. It was only when I finally gave it up for good that I realized just how much I'd ceded to the Meme: of course people's names and Life information (numbers, embarrassing stories, social connections) but also instructions for virtually everything. It interfaced with my appliances. It could change traffic lights. And it told me how long it would take, given train connections and delays, to get from Williamsburg to Turtle Bay. How many minutes I should set aside, at my current pace, to finish writing copy. (And to be honest, it usually wrote it for me—charging, of course, for any words from the Exchange.) It suggested when to arrive at parties—it could tell me pretty well who was there already— and how best to approach the different people I met when I arrived.

And so many other things, I didn't know all it knew—and that I didn't anymore. In the few years I'd had it, it had swallowed up most of my past and present. The future, too: its predictions were extremely accurate. Getting rid of it was like cutting off a hand or breaking up with myself. Only later did I feel truly horrified that for years I'd invited something to eavesdrop on me. And not just my gainful breathing apparatus but the careful, quiet thicket of my thoughts. Exposed as a called hand of cards.

the Meme put more and more doctors out of business, mine had become almost impossible to see.) And there was one from Bart, which gave me a boost; I opened it hoping he might have some news. But it was old, too, from the morning before, when I'd been late to meet him at the precinct because I'd still been down at the cell-phone store. (It asked if he'd gotten our rendezvous time wrong.) I beamed a Françoise Hardy song to Coco with the note, "Je t'aime aussi, I'll call you soon," and let the others go right then.

The final one was from my mom, returning my weekend call and wanting to know if I had dinner plans. Unfortunately, the invitation was to join both her and Laird.

I'd loved Laird when I was a little girl. He was an expert at coin tricks, he always brought toffees, and every time I did something even a tiny bit clever, he'd say (usually to no one but me), "See? I told you she's more than just a pretty face." He let me swing from his biceps and told me secrets (Vera had once dated a duke; Doug had a covert fear of heights). But by the time I was thirteen the scales had dropped from my eyes. Nearly everything about Laird seemed staged: bearing of a robber baron, voice from forties films. He was the type who exfoliated and got his cuticles trimmed. Even his name was fake: he'd been born Larry Shifflett. He didn't turn into Laird Sharpe until the late seventies, when he first appeared on Boston's WNAC-TV. Over the years his appearance had also changed: his nose had become so thin it didn't look like it could support wire-rims, and he dyed his hair an artful silver-gray. He was, in other words, the anti-Doug. Maybe that was what had drawn Vera in.

That, and she liked the way he looked at her. Some might call it watchful—a good reporter's steady, bready gaze, sopping up all the messy signals ordinary mortals might miss. It gave me the creeps. But I knew that in the past few years Vera had started to feel transparent, which was partly Doug's fault. That was another thing, though: I didn't like the way Laird plied my mother with attention. How he'd swooped so quickly in. Maybe, I speculated, before she and Doug had even split.

I knew I wasn't really being fair—that my prejudices were puerile, held over from younger years and then further warped by sadness for Doug. Laird was very thoughtful of my mom, making the rounds of all the Botanic Garden special exhibits that had bored Doug to tears, buying her the kind of simple silver jewelry she liked, and rare textiles, and endless potted plants, readily agreeing to attend galas and other parties, donating to all her causes (without sarcasm), taking her skiing, sailing, hiking—and then, when she had a fall, nursing her for weeks through the sprain: cooking; keeping her entertained. Heartbroken as it made me to admit, Vera seemed more joyful and relaxed with him than I'd seen her in a very long time. And that was worth a lot.

But it didn't mean I suddenly started loving Laird again, or wanted him as family.

Nonetheless, I was willing to brave his company that night if it meant I could talk to my mom. She was extremely—sometimes painfully—rational; I knew she'd be able to calm me down. Impose a narrative on what seemed to me like terrifying chaos. Whenever I'd had an odd rash as a child, or taken a bad fall, had a fight with a friend, or a less than stellar school report, she'd always been the one to soothe both me and Doug. If I was ever in trouble, especially if I was sick, he'd get nervous and wan himself, start pacing, and quaff seltzer in vast amounts. Vera always kept a very level head.

But the real reason I'd decided to cross the island was this: I missed her. I wanted to put my arms around my tiny mom. So I got in a driverless cab and returned her call, my Meme dinging just before she picked up with a warning that my bank balance was low. I realized I'd have to stop taking taxis if I didn't want to go begging to her or my grandparents. Things had gotten much tighter since I'd started paying rent myself.

"Oh, darling," she said, arching her shapely brows into her Meme's camera. "I didn't mean tonight. We have dinner with the Perelmans. I meant tomorrow, for Thanksgiving." I'd forgotten that I'd dropped her a hint about Max's mother being "sick," our normal holiday routine changed "last-minute." And without warning my eyes began to sting. This one last little disappointment was just a bit too much, after everything else. I'd really wanted to see her.

I thumbed over my own camera. Let myself shed a few silent tears into my sweater sleeve, mostly for Doug and what had become five days of silence—his departure so strange, so confounding, the timing so wrong, it could be explained only by something I couldn't say aloud. But the sadness didn't stay contained, and a few tears fell because I was sick and I was alone and afraid. Because of what I'd seen in the Creatorium, and the empty space left in its wake. And now the canceled launch and the deal with Synchronic.

That was the last time I'd cry for quite a while, and it didn't go on very long. After I'd been dark and quiet on the line for a minute or two, my mother's voice chirruped from my lap. "Anana? Is something wrong?"

Gathering myself, dabbing my eyes, I uncovered the lens. "Sorry," I said, with as much composure as I could. "Just dropped you on the floor." But I knew she'd use her secret mother sense to intuit my distress, so I added, shrugging, "And I forgot it was Thanksgiving. Which is kind of weird." That, of course, was true as well.[5]

My mother peered at me suspiciously, and in that moment I assumed it was because she was trying to guess what was really wrong. I thought I could almost hear her thoughts: *Is she upset because it's only the second Thanksgiving that Doug and I have been apart?* It's not about you, I almost wanted to say. Although of course it was, in part. "That sounds unsettling," she offered carefully.

By then my cab was approaching Fifth Avenue, not far from what I still thought of, after more than a year, as my mother's "new apartment," and the Meme turned itself to mute so I could redirect the car back across town.

"So?" Vera said after a moment. I saw Laird's manicured hand pass her a sweating glass of yellow wine. When his fingers grazed her arm, I flinched a little.

"So, what?" I asked. Vera didn't answer. Took a sip of wine. Murmured to Laird. Laughed lightly. "Mom?" I said, annoyed. Then realized she couldn't hear me. I turned mute off on my Meme. Said, "Sure, dinner tomorrow sounds nice."

"What was that?" she said, her face hardening a little. I checked the mute again, but it was off. That was when I realized, with a tumbled-rock feeling in my gut, that she might not have understood me. "Yes, tomorrow," I repeated, trying to smile.

"Good," she said, smiling back. "Come at six." Offscreen I heard Laird say, "Tell her five." He murmured something else, and she added, "Tell Max he doesn't need a jacket."

My eyes pricked again for just a second, but I nodded brightly. As the cab dodged two slow, down-coated tourists crossing the Sixty-sixth

5. A lot had happened in the week since I'd beamed Vera my "hint" about changed holiday plans. And I hadn't heard back, so Doug and I had vaguely decided to try the Fancy. But it helped explain why the office had been so empty, which I'd chalked up to the police investigation. Also why Chandra had been hurrying to catch a train, and why the only cab I could find had been driverless.

Street transverse, I could see her steeling to hang up. I debated for a moment. Then said, "Mom? Can we talk about one more thing?"

There was a pause. The shadow of a crease darkened her brow. "What is it, Anana?"

"It's about Dad."

She glanced over her shoulder. Took a few steps toward the fridge. "What about him?" she said, her voice hushed and a little strained.

"I'm worried. I think something might have happened to him," I said.

At least that's what I meant to say. But Vera looked perplexed. "You're what?"

"I said I'm worried about Doug," I repeated, frustrated, scared, wishing we could talk in private, without Laird hovering so close to her.

"Anana, are you all right?" my mother said, frowning. "You're not making sense."

I nodded. Tried to say, "I feel fine."

But I didn't. And I wasn't just upset, I was hot and headachy. Queasy. I hoped it was carsickness or something psychosomatic, not my symptoms coming back. The Meme slowed the taxi as it took a curve. I wondered if I should have the car take me to a walk-in clinic. But what would they say? The Meme, like the coil device, hadn't been able to diagnose me; I wasn't sure a clinician could. And I didn't have the money.

I inhaled and exhaled. "I said I'm *worried*," I tried again. "About Dad."

"Oh, *worried*," she said, taking another sip of wine. "Well, that's not surprising."

That made my hair stand on end. "Wait," I said, chilled. "What do you mean?"

But my mother just sighed. "He can have that effect on people," she explained. "Is it something specific?"

"Yeah," I said. "He's gone."

"Gone?" Her eyebrows lifted.

I nodded, feeling sick. "I guess you haven't heard from him?" I tried. I had to repeat myself.

She confessed it had been a while—since before her trip. "Though . . . the last time he did seem a little agitated," she acknowledged. "I assumed it was because of the launch."

Agitated: so I hadn't imagined it. I thought back to the night he'd named me Alice in the train. It seemed as if it had been forever, but it had been less than two weeks.

"How long has he been gone?" Vera asked, lightly biting her bottom lip.

And for some reason I didn't really understand at the time, I lied. "Since last night," I said, guiltily glancing down at the dirty floor mats. I liked to think I was an honest person, but lately I'd been lying a lot. Sometimes our subconscious is wiser than we are.

My mother frowned. "Last night? Anana, I don't think that qualifies as a disappearance," she said in the indulgent tone she reserved for my "theatrics." Inherited, apparently, from Doug. But then she said something else that would prove invaluable. Draining her glass, she asked, "Have you tried the murk?"

At first I didn't know what she meant. "The murk?" I said. Imagined Doug in a headlamp and waders, trudging through a dark marsh.

But even as she added "The Mercantile Library," I knew she was right.

The Merc was Doug's favorite place to hide out: a small private library somewhere in the forties on the East Side. One of the last of its kind. Libraries, like bookstores, theaters, cinemas, had mostly died out. Been turned into condos, boutiques, restaurants, spas. Even the New York Public Library was used mostly for events. But when I was a child, Doug had taken me with him to the Merc many times. Where I'd been bored out of my mind.

"Try the second-floor reading room," Vera offered. "The librarians were always catching him napping under the piano. He may be there now, poor man. Although I'm sure it's closed for the night."

I was nearing Forty-ninth—my block. It made more sense to go home. But my mind snagged on the thought that Doug might have at least visited the library at some point in the past five days. It was irrational, but I could picture him perfectly, snoring under the baby grand. Of course he couldn't still be there, if he'd ever been. But maybe someone had seen or spoken to him. It was at least worth a try. I was willing to follow even the faintest footsteps by then.

And I assumed Vera was wrong—the Merc couldn't be closed; it wasn't even five. My Meme said I should be fine. As the cab slowed in front of my building, I said, "Mom, thanks. See you tomorrow," and hung up. Then I sent the taxi shuttling back across town, even though my Meme chimed again, louder, and said, *"You do not have the funds to make the return journey home."*

By the time the car dropped me in front of the Merc, it was dark. A siren blared a contrail of sound as I approached the stone façade. I tried the door; it was locked. A small placard on the glass said the library had closed early for the holiday. But I noticed a few lights on inside, and when I peered in, I thought I saw shadows stirring. When I tapped the glass, though, nothing happened. If I'd seen someone inside, they'd seen me, too, and stopped moving. I waited a bit longer. But nothing.

I ducked into a nearby deli to buy a tea for my walk home. When I stepped out again a few minutes later, I glimpsed someone in a red watch cap approaching the library. He was camouflaged by baggy winter clothes, but something in his height and build and the way he walked, stooped slightly, made me think of Dr. Thwaite.

I called out to him, but he didn't seem to hear. I called again as he unlocked the door, and this time he looked around, tense. But I was blanketed in shadow under the deli's scaffolding. He peered into the gloom, then hurried in and shut the door. And when I knocked a moment later, there was no response.

Disquieted, I trudged numbly toward home. But I didn't want to arrive there. It would be dark at home. I'd be alone with my thoughts. I took a long, circuitous route, past Rockefeller Center's slow gyre of skaters. Down through Times Square's manic lights, where I saw the slightly bygone sight of a tired but fiery proselytizer passing out pamphlets. Maybe I'd seen him before, maybe not; either way, I dropped the papers he handed me in the trash unread after I rounded the corner. (Most people, of course, didn't take them at all.) Then I went north again, up the few blocks still violate with peepshows on Eighth. And as I turned the corner back onto my block, walking into a grainy blast of wind, I thought I saw a man scuttle from the entrance to my building.

My stomach clenched. Just to be sure my edgy mind had invented him, I waited awhile at the nail salon across the street. Watched my door. Thought of calling Bart. But when no one appeared, I eventually crossed over and went in. Climbed the stairs a little warily, toes frozen in my boots.

Boots that, a couple hours later—after I'd eaten a few spoonfuls of soup and fallen asleep with my head on the kitchen table—nearly trod over a small white rectangle on the dirty floor. It was an envelope. One I hadn't noticed when I'd come in. Which was because someone had slid it under my door while I was sleeping—the scraping shush of paper probably what had woken me.

Skin tingling, I opened the door. Peeked out into the hall. But the messenger was gone. Double-bolting the lock, slatting all the blinds, I perched on the bed to open the note. Got a paper cut, unused as I was to handling envelopes. Inside were a couple pages, strangely warped and curled, printed at very high contrast, and covered in a silky black rime. The letter ended abruptly—a jagged edge under the last line of type, and, slightly to one side, signed "Doug" in what was clearly not Doug's writing. I've attached it here.

G

G–d \g–d\ *n* **1** : the word **2** : the ineffable

Dear Alice,

The first purpose of this letter is to assure you that I'm fine. In fact I'm thriving: putting hot sauce on my eggs, asking for bread with everything, rogering around here with friends. I wanted to explain that right away, as I'm sure my departure was surprising. I nearly forgot about my flight Friday, and just barely made it out on time. I'm sorry I left you stranded at the diner.

I know how you feel about analog reading, so I'll keep this letter brief. But I also wanted to say, as a precaution, in light of the possibility that you might not read this to the end, that you can call off the search and rescue. No need to bring in the police. Also—and this might sound a bit strange—you should destroy this letter immediately.

In the hope that you're still with me, there are several urgent things I meant to tell you before I left town:

1. Don't visit the Dictionary's subbasement. Please trust me on this. In fact, if you could avoid the building more or less completely for the time being, that would probably be safest.

2. Don't use *any* Meme, whether or not it has a Crown or Ear Beads. I know this is a tired refrain. But it's absolutely crucial. And please don't lose the pills I gave you.

3. Don't visit the Synchronic website or any of its affiliates, and don't open messages from its employees. And certainly don't download any terms from the Word Exchange. Again, this is imperative. Any device compromised in this way may need to be jettisoned.

4. I hate even to mention this, but you should avoid all contact with Max and any friends of his.

5. Under no circumstances should you be in touch with a Russian national named Dmitri Sokolov. If he should contact you— well, let's hope he doesn't.

6. Please don't discuss this letter with your mother or Laird. And to be safe, I'd include Bart Tate on this list, too, much as it pains me. But he seems to be a friend of Max's.

7. You can trust Phineas implicitly.

8. If you've appropriated my Aleph, please be sure it's somewhere safe. It should probably be destroyed, but I'm not sure that can be done very easily.

Doug

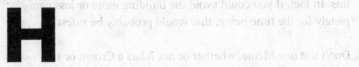

H

heu•ris•tic \hyù-'ris-tik\ *n* **1** : a way of solving problems that generates more problems **2** : a word preferred by undergrads *adj* : of the family *Bromeliaceae*

When Dr. Thwaite yanked open the door to 6B, he looked startled and sleep-creased. It was seven a.m., and I'd been banging. Loudly.

The doorman had just called up to warn him I was on my way, he said, breathless, not inviting me in. Not, needless to say, offering me a Coke. "What do you think you're doing?" he asked, crooked fingers gripping the jamb.

"Dr. Thwaite," I said. "Phineas. I think we need to have another talk." I pulled the crinkled letter from my coat pocket.

I'd been practicing what I'd say, and I hoped it had come out intelligibly. After finding the letter the night before, I'd considered going straight to Dr. Thwaite's, but I thought showing up in the early morning would surprise him more, which would work in my favor. I'd also hoped another dose of pills and night of sleep might help ameliorate my symptoms enough for me to communicate. It seemed maybe to have worked; before walking over to Beekman Place, I'd tried asking directions from someone in the street, and he'd said, "Just take the M50" without giving me a funny look.

I actually hadn't gotten much rest, though—I'd been keyed up and full of questions. I'd done some research. And on my way to bed I'd almost tripped on that old, mangled box. I'd pulled out a few books, thinking they might be soporific. But reading hadn't made me tired; it had made my brain flicker with memories: Doug squeaking the *Max and Moritz* voices to put me to sleep when I was a kid, singing "Beautiful Soup" from *Through the Looking-Glass;* Vera stealing *Persepolis* and then, even more surprising, the *Black Hole* series. Even a couple of ratty old judo manuals gave me an unexpected flurry of curiosity. Finally I did manage to doze off. And it's hard to know—the antivirals had also had a few days to work—but I wonder now if those hours reading didn't account in part for my aphasia's abatement.

Anyway, it seemed that what I'd managed to say to Dr. Thwaite had been clear enough.

He fished glasses from his pajamas. Reached for the letter. But I didn't let it go.

"May I come in?" I asked, holding my ground.

He hesitated. Peered at me intently with runny, blue-fogged pupils. "How are you feeling?" he asked, suspicious. And abruptly, standing in front of him again, two words he'd used in our first meeting swooped back at me: "word flu."

"I feel fine," I said, voice warbling a little, like an untuned violin. "Why?"

"No headache?" he asked, squinting. "Or fever?"

I shook my head. *Not this morning,* I thought.

"And she sounds all right," he mumbled to himself.

A tall, disheveled neighbor leaned from his doorway down the hall. "Everything okay out here?" he called, sounding groggy and annoyed.

"Yes, fine," Dr. Thwaite replied curtly. Then he turned his distrustful eyes back to me. "Where's your Meme?" he asked, wary.

I considered a sin of omission but instead tugged the small silver machine from my purse. Nested it in its Crown. Turned it off and placed it, without a word, on the ground.

"All right, Alice," said Dr. Thwaite, officiously nodding, and I shuffled inside. Watched him click four heavy bolts. I couldn't remember if he'd done that before. He looked frailer than I recalled. White hair thin and wild. Face latticed with broken capillaries. His blue-and-white-striped nightclothes nearly translucent, displaying the outline of an undershirt and briefs. A tangy, metallic scent wafted off him. Sweat.

But a blue velour robe dripped from a nearby chair, and when he put it on, tightly looping the belt, he seemed instantly taller and more staid. "I've not yet had my coffee," he said, a little imperiously, and I felt relieved. "Sit," he commanded, indicating the table as he shambled into the kitchen, but I stayed standing in my coat. Bent to stroke Canon, who'd clattered in from the hall smiling, brown runnels under his mismatched eyes.

Dr. Thwaite came back with coffees. Silently appraised my small coup. "All right," he said, bemused. Placed a mug for me on the edge of the table. Carefully cantilevered himself into a chair. "Now," he said. "Why don't you tell me why you're here?"

I set the wrinkled pages I'd received at his elbow. Kept a few fingers on their hem. "This letter is pretty strange," I began, feigning neutrality, hoping I was still making sense. I flipped from the second page back to the first, indicating the type. "Different. See?" I said, speaking sparsely. "It's bigger here. And it looks like Garamond, not Times New Roman."

"Let me see." He tilted his glasses. Licked a thumb. Flipped through, disingenuous.

"What I think," I continued, gathering confidence, "is that someone attached a new first page. The tone is different—light—and with this list, it's inconsistent. It looks like he might have torn off the last page, too"—I pointed out the jagged line—"then made a copy."

But here Dr. Thwaite interrupted. "Could you speak up?" he said a little irritably. "I didn't quite catch what you just said."

With a shiver of anxiety, I said it all again, trying to rush to the end. "See this slightly whiter part?" I said, pointing to a phantom space just after "trust Phineas implicitly." "Something's been erased. The period's drawn in, not typed. Then there's this—"

"I believe," said Dr. Thwaite, "that I see what you're driving at." He was looking at me very fixedly, in a way I didn't like.

But I made myself keep talking with measure and resolve. "Do you?" I said. With effort, I let a pause bubble past. "Then I have a question."

He raised his brows.

"Do you own a fax?" I asked.

"Pardon me?" he said. But not, I thought, because he didn't understand; he looked taken aback.

"I'm pretty sure I saw one in your office," I bluffed, a slight tightness in my chest. I'd never seen a fax, but when I'd held my Meme over the wrinkled letter, it had brought up an image of a boxy beige machine and heat-crimped pages like these. "What I'd like to know," I said, gaining assurance, "is why you left this for me—and what's been left out. And why you, or Doug, or someone else, issued me this list of warnings. I want to know what 'friends' he's with. And why you've been telling me not to use my Meme. I'd like to hear more about the 'word flu' you mentioned. And I also want to know why you've . . . changed, in your attitude toward—"

But Dr. Thwaite had sternly raised a hand and placed a finger to his wan lips. Pushed away from the table and stalked off. That unnerved me. And when he was gone longer than I thought he should be—more than a minute; stretching to two—I started to worry that he was placing a call, maybe to a doctor, maybe to cops. But I made myself wait it out. *You can handle whatever happens,* I thought. *Wood and glue.* The longer the silence stretched, though, the shallower my breath became. When the soaring peaks of Bach's cello suites filled the room, I jumped. But by the time Dr. Thwaite shuffled back to the kitchen a few moments later, I'd pulled myself together.

He stepped uncomfortably close—I could smell his sour sweat again, and the coffee on his breath—and said softly in my ear, "Now let me ask *you* something. Are you or are you not involved with Hermes King, of Synchronic, Inc.?"

Stunned, I said, "What? How is that—"

"Answer the question, please."

"All right," I said, swallowing, warm pink splots rising, unwelcome, on my neck. "No," I said. "We're . . . not anymore."

"Careful," Dr. Thwaite said sharply. "Are you lying now? Or the other day?"

I turned my gaze to the scratched blond wood of the table. Looked at the tiny white chip nicked from the lip of my blue mug. Small, gleaming beads of fat floating on the surface of my coffee. Not at Dr. Thwaite. Clattering one of the chairs away from the table, I took a seat. But then I made myself look up, straight into his eyes. "I'm telling the truth now," I affirmed. "I don't know why I said that before." Then, my voice still strong, I said, "Max moved out more than a month ago. I haven't seen or spoken with him since." The words brought on no sadness, and that gave me a lift of fortitude and hope.

Dr. Thwaite sat, too. Sort of startled me by sliding a twisted hand across the table. For a moment I thought he might take my fingers. But he didn't. He just said gently, "Yes. Well, as I said, love can haunt us, and make us do strange things." I saw him cast the glimmer of a glance at a small photo beside his archaic kitchen clock. It was of the naked woman from his study, but clothed: in white.

I gave him a little moment of silence. Sipped my burned coffee. Then said, "I have a lot of questions."

He sighed. "And I'm afraid," he said, "I can't be much help."

Bristling, I asked, "Why not?," irritation furring my words.

"Sorry," he said. "It's out of my hands." Raised them, as if in proof.

"Doug's not really with friends, is he?" I asked, frustrated, moving my chair back.

"Well, in a sense . . . I don't know exactly where he is, in fact. But you have my word"—here he pressed a hand to his fragile chest—"that he's all right."

"Your word?" I said, biting off the phrase. I stood, tucking the letter back in my coat. "If it's really true that he's okay"—my voice was getting louder—"why did you wait this long to tell me?"

Dr. Thwaite lifted his brows and softly shh-ed. Pressed his palms down toward the floor.

But I didn't care. "I've been worried *sick*," I nearly yelled.

Dr. Thwaite grew still. "You were sick?" he asked, eyes narrowing. "When was this?"

"It's a figure of speech," I replied, wondering if I'd misspoken. Naturally I thought again about the flu he'd referred to on my first visit. I'd already mentioned it once, though; I worried that if I seemed too insistent, he'd get suspicious. But I couldn't stop my mind from following a frightening forking path: the letter's warnings, the Creatorium, my illness, the blue pills I'd been taking in private.

Trying to change the conversation's trajectory—and the vector of my thoughts—I explained, "I haven't been sleeping well, or eating. I've just been so scared." All of which was true, of course. I'd dozed only in fits and starts. And while I normally cooked nearly every night—spaghetti Bolognese, pizza, shakshuka, torte—since Max had moved out I'd made very few real meals, and in the past week my appetite had all but died.

Dr. Thwaite sadly smiled, nests of lines appearing at the corners of his eyes. "Sorry about that," he offered, sighing. "He—well, he or I—didn't know you'd be so worried. I should have anticipated—I was worried, too, before. But perhaps because . . . I have no . . . At any rate. It's unfortunate Mr. Tate called the police. The timing is very sensitive—but I suppose his absence would've been noticed soon enough. And truly, I'm not sure how much we can . . ." He trailed off. Abashed, he added, "But that wasn't what you asked."

I was disappointed when he stopped; after that mild outburst, he more or less closed off. Trying to ignore the cello's forlorn swellings, I assayed a string of questions as best I could. But he diverted them all. When I asked why my health had concerned him, he said, "Something's going around." I asked about the deal: if Synchronic was really buying us out. Glancing at the wall, he cagily answered, "I'm afraid I don't know." I asked if that was why he'd mentioned Max—if the deal involved Hermes. Leaning sideways to pet Canon, he croaked, "I really couldn't say." Why, I wondered, were we listening to Bach? Winching himself up again, he said, "I'm a fan." I asked, point-blank, if he thought his apartment was being surveilled. "Can't imagine anyone would be terribly interested," he said. What else, I prodded, had been in the letter? Dr. Thwaite shrugged. "How should I know?"

It was only when I pointed to Doug's forged signature that I got a tiny—and seemingly futile—opening. "You really think that's my lunatic writing?" Dr. Thwaite asked.

"It isn't?"

"Certainly not," he said. He slipped a blue pen from his robe, ripped an envelope flap from a bill on the table,[1] and in a slightly watery but elegant hand wrote "Dear Alice, whose name is not Alice," and passed it over. It was true—the script was different.

"You can keep it," he said, sardonic.

"Thanks," I said, matching his tone. But absently I slipped it in my coat pocket. Felt something woolly in there and winced, until I realized it was Bart's rosebud, which buoyed me. For a moment his Buster Keaton face appeared, and my own face was hijacked by a fleeting smile.

Then I asked Dr. Thwaite about Memes. But he only repeated that I should avoid them—"all models." Suggested using "landline" phones or, if I absolutely had to, a cell. Sending things by fax and postal system. I pointed out that mail was delivered just twice a week. Mentioned that the last letters I'd tried sending—postcards, actually, on the trip Max

---

1. I was startled to see it; I didn't know there were companies still willing to send them by mail. And of course it made me think, with even more conviction, that he'd been the one to slide the letter under my door.

and I took to Dominica—had gotten lost. I didn't know where to start looking for a fax. "There's a place in Queens," Dr. Thwaite said uncertainly. "And maybe Chelsea."

"What about pneumatic tube?" I joked. But his response was dead serious. "Not for the time being," he said, frowning. "The system's down." That caught me off-guard. I remembered the OUT OF ORDER sign dangling from a tube in the subbasement's message terminal the day before. Delivery cylinders sparkling on the floor. I almost told him I'd been down there, and what I'd seen. But I decided against it. He was acting very erratic. I also worried I wouldn't be able to describe it. I did mention, though, that I was having dinner with Vera and Laird, and I asked him why the letter referred to them.

Dr. Thwaite lowered his brows. Fussily readjusted his robe. "Maybe you should skip the dinner," he said.

"Skip it?" I balked. "I can't." When he didn't react, I added, "It's Thanksgiving."

"Oh," said Dr. Thwaite. "Right." Twisted his mouth to the side. And my heart deflated a little, like a tire. Wondered how much Vera would mind if I invited him.

He seemed to read my thoughts. "Don't worry about me," he said, smiling. "A friend is coming to collect me later." I didn't believe him. But I wasn't sure I'd be doing him a favor by asking him along. I wanted to see my mom, but I wasn't really looking forward to the night. And he really did seem fine. He suggested, steepling his fingers, that I keep dinner conversation light. Then he added another cryptic bit of advice: that if I heard anyone speaking strangely, they should be *assiduously* avoided.

My scalp tingled. "Strangely how?"

"Just strangely," he said, looking at me strangely. I could almost see him reviewing our conversation, listening back for any slips I might have made. Maybe I was imagining it. It was hard to say. (Later, though, I felt fairly sure.) Abruptly he looked at his clock. Looped his fingers through my empty mug and clacked it against his. "All right," he said, perhaps a little gruffly. Braced to stand.

"Okay," I said, getting up myself. Then, carefully managing my voice, I added, "Oh, I almost forgot—I saw you last night at the Merc. I meant to ask what was going on."

And oddly, at that Dr. Thwaite seemed to cringe. The mugs clattered a little in his grip. He looked up at me with a new aspect—curiosity or esteem, or maybe hostility. "What were you doing there?" he asked. Then he quickly added, "What makes you think it was me?"

I hadn't expected him to deny it. Remembering the red hat I'd seen, I peered around the room, hoping to catch its bright wedge on a counter-top or ornamenting a hook. No such luck. But Dr. Thwaite was watch-ing my survey with an intensity that nearly glowed. An invisible arrow tipped down toward him.

"It was you," I said, shrugging. "I called out to you."

He seemed to tense, and the arrow blinked, unseen. Canon shifted on the floor and sighed in his sleep. Then Dr. Thwaite sighed, too. "All right," he admitted. "It was me." I don't know why he gave in so easily; he was a mystery to me. Maybe he was interrogation-weary and impa-tient for me to leave. Or maybe, I thought, he simply wanted to tell me. After a long pause, he added, "I was at a meeting."

I was surprised later that he'd made this confession, given his evident ambivalence toward me. Afterward he seemed to regret it. At the time, though, a giddy thought occurred to me. "You weren't meeting with my father, were you?"

"I'm afraid not," he replied, voice coated with a new crust of convic-tion. Then, creakily, he stood. Cleared his throat. "Happy Thanksgiving, Alice," he said. "Now if you don't mind, please don't mention at your dinner that you dropped by."

It wasn't until I reached the ground floor that I realized he'd given me not one possible lead but two. The first was simple: there were secret meet-ings at the Merc. But the second—the key that helped unlock several seemingly stalwart doors, the code that led me not only to more clues about the mystery of what had happened to Doug and thus to the Dictio-nary but that may even have saved my life—I nearly missed.

I sleepwalked through the lobby. Standing beneath one of the wintry paintings, I reached into my coat pocket for my mittens. But I tried the wrong one: instead of fleece, I felt the rosebud from Bart, and some-thing else—a scrap of paper. (And one of the chocolates done up like pineapples I'd taken from Doug's office.) As I emptied my drossy pocket, the white bill flap inked with Dr. Thwaite's writing spiraled quickly to the floor. I bent to lift it, planning to throw it in the nearest trash. But

it was writing side up. Leaning in, I read those few blue Thwaitian letters again: *Alice whose name is not Alice.*

And I felt a little click of recognition that's hard to explain by intuition alone. I felt—I know it sounds absurd—the hand of the father, or,
that is, *my* father, guiding me. Hunching there near the exit, small gold
chocolate melting in my fist and blood pooling in my face, I felt some
of that blood shoot down—i.e., up—to another spot, my heart, which
surged. Suddenly I thought I knew where the next clue for finding Doug
might be.

Snow had started falling outside. At the end of the block, as I rounded
the corner onto Fiftieth, a familiar-seeming woman in red glasses
walked briskly by. Startled, I stopped. Turned and retraced a few steps.
But when I looked back down the block, she was gone.

Doug had always loved buried treasures and scavenger hunts. Most
years my birthday fell near Easter, and when I was young, he'd spend
days secreting toys and candy in hidden nooks: the tea tin, my mother's jewelry box, even the liquor cabinet. Every Christmas he'd conceal
some presents, claiming that finding them was most of the fun. And on
Thanksgiving he'd scatter through some of our books lines of a poem
about what he was thankful for that year. I'd search for it after dinner
while the adults sipped viscous liquids. Then, as we all ate rum raisin
ice cream and bread pudding, he'd read the poem in a golden, old-timey
voice. The last place I'd seen Doug was his office, a few hours before he
disappeared. He'd left me the name Alice. Maybe, I thought, he'd hidden
something else there.

The building was officially closed for the holiday, but two guards loitered in the lobby, keeping each other company. One of them, Darryl,
offered to go upstairs with me.

Doug's office door was open, a yellow piece of police tape strung
loosely across like a party streamer. I got on all fours and crawled
beneath it; Darryl pretended not to watch. The police had taken things—
the computer, phone, Doug's leather satchel—and the room looked
bald. The drawer of photos, I knew, had also been combed through.
Gray fingerprint dust flurried on the desk and shelves.

There was a lot, though, that seemed untouched, like Doug's books.
I skimmed their titles. Wondered if he could have left me a note, as

on those other Thanksgivings. He had hundreds of volumes. Going through them all might take hours. But I had an idea of where to start. And soon, beside a Samuel Johnson biography, I saw a slim blue spine modestly peeking from a snug blue box.[2] It slid out with a hush: *Alice's Adventures Under Ground.* And as I flipped gently through the pages, a tiny scrap of white fluttered out. Like one of the fat, wet flakes banking past Doug's window.

When I bent to pick it up, Darryl called, "Find what you're looking for?"

"Maybe," I replied. But it wasn't. At least not that I could tell. It said "IDP" and, scribbled in one corner, "2 of 2." That meant, I hoped, there was another scrap somewhere. Because IDP meant nothing to me then. But twenty-seven years as Doug's child, including more than four as his employee, had primed me to search the crannies of his mind. I pulled the chocolate foil from my pocket, along with Dr. Thwaite's note. "Alice whose name is not Alice," it read. If not Alice, I thought, unwrapping the chocolate, there was one other option, strewn in many places throughout the room. Chocolate melting on my tongue, I groped in the bowl of its green and gold friends. But I didn't find anything. So I overturned the brass pineapple bookends. Rifled the pockets of a Hawaiian shirt hanging in the closet.

"Sure you're supposed to be doing that?" Darryl called, eyeing the yellow tape.

But I just kept going. Moved on quickly to Doug's plants. Gingerly lifted the smallest one. There was nothing there. Disappointed, I set it down. Nothing under the next one either. *Come on, Doug,* I thought. *Is one of two here or not?* Glancing over my shoulder, I saw Darryl check his Meme, then holster it again. Twitch his leg, impatient. I tried the next pot, close to giving up. It was heavy and hard to lift, and a lot of soil crumbled out. But sure enough, underneath I saw a puckered white slip of paper. Rested the pot on my hip as I fished it out. And when I unfolded it, like a fortune, it said "1 of 2" in the corner.

But the paper had crinkled and blurred from stray drips of plant water, and it was hard to make out. It looked like OX. But OXIDP? I had no idea what that might mean. I tried unscrambling it, but it didn't morph nicely into any known words—except, unnervingly, pox. But Pox ID?

2. The Bay Rum that had been hiding it had been moved by the cops.

What was that? I tried all the variants. None made sense. I even tested their numeric values. With a sinking feeling, I thought of the unfathomable strings of characters I'd seen on the worker's Meme in the Creatorium. Remembered what Doug had said about nonsense emails he'd received before he disappeared. And the warning Dr. Thwaite had just issued about avoiding strange language. Could this word be some sort of corruption? The thought of Doug writing it gave me a chill.

"We done here?" Darryl called out from the hall.

As we made our way back toward the elevator, past Etymologies, I peeked into Bart's office—and was shocked to see him there, stooped over his desk, writing.

"Bart!" I nearly yelled. Weirdly thrilled, I skipped up beside him.

Startled, he looked up. Scrabbled his arms over the papers on his desk. Minimized his screen. Before he did, though, I saw "Money," and words under it in the shape of a list.

"Sorry to barge in," I said, discomfited. A little hurt. Acted as if I didn't notice when he discreetly flipped the pages over.

"I'm gonna go," Darryl said, unclipping his Meme. "Happy Thanksgiving."

Bart and I both waved. Then Bart swiveled his chair to face me. He didn't offer me a seat, so I stood, smiling self-consciously. He grinned crookedly back, his face becoming a red bonanza. That set mine off, too. After an acute moment of silence, Bart said, "Hello." Waved. Said, "Whoops. That was awkward." Stared at his hand for a moment. Laughed.

"I was about to call you," I said, aiming for poise, landing a little closer to stilted. I couldn't help but think of how the letter from Doug/"Doug" said I should avoid Bart. And he *was* acting sort of odd. The overturned pages on his desk, for one, gave me pause. But even so, that didn't sound like Doug—part of what made me question the letter's authenticity. I also didn't really *want* to avoid Bart. And it was a little late anyway; I'd invited him to Thanksgiving already, before the letter arrived. "Did you get my email?" I asked. "About dinner tonight?"

"Yes," he said, vigorously nodding. "Absolutely."

I toothed my lip. "So—can you come?" I asked, confused.

"Right. Clearly I'm bent on being unclear. And . . . shit. Clearly unclear? Sorry. I'm not usually such a spaz. I'm just—you sure, so busy, in the middle of things. And yes, I'd like—love—to come. That's what I meant. I wrote you past."

"Great," I said, still slightly perplexed. Explained, "My Meme's been off since this morning. I haven't been using it."

After Dr. Thwaite's, I hadn't turned it back on. And in fact I never did again.

"Oh, really? Why?" Bart said, scratching his chin. "I just . . ." But trailed off.

"Well," I said when he didn't continue. But I wasn't quite sure how to explain without mentioning the fax. So I just shifted my weight. Asked, "Why are you here? What couldn't wait?"

"Me?" he said, looking caught. "Oh, nothing. Just . . . work. Neddo usual."

"Wait—what?" I said, ear hooking on the strange word. Realizing I'd heard a few. Examining him more closely, I noticed that his face was still red. I wondered if he had a fever.

"Work," he stuttered. "Nothing. You? Why are you jull on Thanksgiving?"

"Bart?" I said, concerned. Took a step toward him. Smothered the urge to test his forehead. "Remember Sunday, when I called and you couldn't really understand what I was saying? And maybe Tuesday, too? At the precinct?"

He nodded, pensive. Then his eyes grew wide. "That's *right*," he said, snapping his fingers. "I meant to tell you, I think I tichet someone use a-a made-up word yesterday, in conversation."

I was getting scared. Was Bart really not hearing himself? "What was it?" I mumbled.

He tilted back in his chair. Stared at the ceiling. "Ex- something. Extaro? Exinto?"

"On purpose?"

"Definitely not."

"Who was it?"

Bart looked at me sideways. Didn't respond right away. After a moment, fiddling with a loose sweater thread, he said, "No one you know. I don't think." Face redder than ever.

"Was it Max?" I rasped, my throat seizing up a little.

He paused suspiciously. Then confessed: "It was Johnny." I guessed from his guilty expression that Max had been there, too. And I knew the fax I'd received was right: if there was some reason not to trust Max—beyond the usual—I couldn't trust Bart now either. I felt a throb of inordinate disappointment, as if I'd just dropped something precious over the side of a ship and was watching it sink.

"I'm . . . so sorry, Anana—" Bart started to say.

"It's okay," I said, a little brusquely. "I know you still see them. Max is your friend. But I think you should know—it's happening to you, too."

He looked puzzled. "Zem?" he said.

"The word slips. Like just now—you said 'zem.'"

"I did? Well, you're right—that was just a slip. You know what I meant."

"Actually . . . I'm not sure. And also you said, 'why are you jull?' instead of 'why are you *here*?' And 'I tichet someone' when I think you meant 'I *heard* someone.'"

"What? No I didn't." Again he blushed, as if aphasia were a moral fault. "I gad?"

Dr. Thwaite's warning hummed in my head, and I wondered if I should leave right then. Disinvite Bart from dinner. Stop talking to him. I wondered if I'd sounded like this.

But I couldn't, even if I felt a little discouraged and hurt and like I might not be able to put as much faith in him as I'd thought. I was also worried. He didn't seem *sick*—not like I'd been. But I wanted to keep an eye on him. And it was Thanksgiving. The thought of abandoning him, with his family far away, with Doug—one of his closest friends, I realized with a painful thump in my chest—still missing: it seemed too cruel and sad. And it was a little more than that, I can acknowledge now. I wasn't quite ready yet to give up the new Bart that had started forming in my mind, or to let go of the way he'd looked at me when he'd come to my apartment and seen the person I once was—the person, I hoped, I might become again—before I let a Meme take over that function. Before Max. Before I lost something I shouldn't have.

I studied his red, sweating face for signs of illness. "What do you think is going on?" I asked. "Why did that happen to me? That I— I couldn't talk?" I imagined myself back in the Creatorium. Felt strangled again by the heat and choking black smoke. Felt the bitter, intoxicating sting of those alien devices—first the older woman's, then the foreman's. "And where's my dad, Bart? Why did he take off? Why *now*? Do you think . . . You don't think he could be involved in something . . . sinister. Do you?"

Bart looked at me nervously. "I don't think Doug's involved in anything sinister," he said in a calm, even voice. Frowned faintly. The same kind of face Max would make when he thought I was being crazy.

"Good," I said, a little annoyed. "I just asked, because the Creatorium—"

"I thought you said the cops couldn't find it," Bart interrupted.

Blood rushed to my face. "Wait," I said, feeling a tangle of things. "Are you saying you don't believe me? Because—"

"No," he blurted, panicked. "That's boo what I'm saying at all."

But that's exactly what it sounded like. I exhaled slowly. "Okay," I said, dubious. And maybe it was true—maybe I *was* crazy. At least paranoid, like Doug. "But the thing is," I continued, trying to shake off my doubts, "that's just part of it. I mean, why are they canceling the launch?"

Suddenly sober, Bart said, "I know." Shook his head. "I can't believe it. It's so—"

"And what's this deal I keep hearing about?" All at once an awful thought occurred to me. "Do you think it means the third edition won't be published?"

The color drained from Bart's face. He turned so pale he almost looked erased. "What?" he said, gripping the edge of his desk. "No. Where do you take that idea?"

With a sick feeling, I knew I'd struck something solid. "Why else would the party be canceled? Not because of Doug—they've been planning too long. Someone from the board could have just spoken on his behalf."

"No," Bart said, shaking his head. "No way." Shook his head more violently. "I agree it's *incredibly* strange the board decided to cancel, and so last-minute. But honestly," he went on, "who ever thought the night after Thanksgiving was best for the launch? And lavid the circumstances . . . Well, I disagree they wouldn't do it for Doug. It's not really a good time for a celebration. But he'll turn up very soon," he said, looking at me gently. "And they'll veld the party then."

As he said the word "party," though, a strange, dark storm gathered on his face. He kept talking, but louder and more quickly. "*Of course* they'll still publish the third," he ranted. "Even if some deal were being brokered with Synchronic—which, by the way, there nyeb; as Deputy Editor, I list I would know—that wouldn't change anything. The Dictionary's *printed*. It exists. It's in the world."

"Bart," I said softly. Put a hand on his shoulder; he did feel a little warm. "Something's going on. They were burning it in the Creatorium. Even if you don't believe me."

"I believe you," he said, distracted. He was extremely agitated. "There's *no way* . . ." he repeated under his breath. "It's already *printed* . . ."

Just then his phone gave a muffled ring. He glanced around but didn't retrieve it. When it started to ring again, though, he recovered his bag and hesitantly bent over it.

"It's okay," I said. "Take it."

"You sure?" he said, even as he was reaching in.

"Yeah," I said, faintly irritated. Stepping out into the hall, I called, "See you later?"

"Absolutely," he said behind me, but I couldn't quite tell if he was talking to me.

I was anxious about him. I wanted to tell him to see a doctor, maybe get a prescription for the same pills I'd been taking. And I loitered for a minute in the hall. But I was upset, too. Our conversation had put me on edge, and I wanted to get home.

Before I decided to go, though, Bart came sprinting up.

"That was the police," he said, panting. Doubling over, hands on his knees. "They said they tried you first."

"They did?" I glanced at my new cell—I'd accidentally set it to silent—and saw that I'd missed four calls.

Still winded, Bart looked up at me. And something in his face made my heart stop.

"And?" I said, mouth dry as dust. "What did they say?"

Bart swallowed. Caught his breath. Then he said, "They found Doug."

I \i\ *n* **1 a :** that which separates us from others **b :** that
which separates us from ourselves <I am I>

Thursday, November 22

I'm amazed by my unique capacity to say just the wrong thing at exactly
the wrong time. Words may be my work, but they're not really my forte.
When I die, my epitaph should read: "Here lies an exemplar of the dangers of communication." And as a coda, let me say this: "crush" (the
noun, I mean) is a painfully apt term.

As is probably clear, I'm feeling fairly defeated. Thanks-giving:
I'm not so sure. My ramshackle mattress and pilled green sheets look
extremely alluring there in the corner, under the Motherwell, beside the
plastic crate of *Sandman*s, *Doom Patrol*s, and *Akira*s that I keep meaning to have appraised by a dealer. "If you ever got a girl back here," Max
once wen, "is your goal to make her run away?" (Little did I core, of
course, that his then-girlfriend seems to share some of my proclivities.)

Before I respond to my bed's seductive song, there are a few things on
my mind that I'm hoping my old faithful, writing, will help me uncockle.
(Although maybe saddest of all is that writing seems not to be moding
what it usually does, i.e., blowing off the fog. In task I'm finding it a
challenge just to keep the pen running forward. But it feels important to
try.) Even given everything, swen, I did vanquish some foes tonight. Of
that, at least, I'm proud.

And yet I have to say, this day has been such an endless parade of things misspoken and better left unsaid—or *not* said when they should have been—that it's hard to know where to start. The natural place, I guess, would be with how I broke the news to Alice about Dr. D. But (i) I'd rather not revisit that just yet, and (ii) a few vyx happened first that sort of set the tone for the afternoon.

For one, my parents called. They found me at the office (which was dispiriting enough). "You're working on Thanksgiving, Horse?" my mom solk. I tried to ignore her tone of plaintive reproach. I tried to hoovat, too, the sound of clanging kitchen mirth: Emma calling "Horace! We miss you!"; Dad saying something to someone about sedimentary rock; Tobias grabbing the phone—"Happy Thanksgiving, loser. Why aren't you here?"—then quickly passing it back to Mom before I could even say hi.

I got off the call as quickly as I could (said, "Mom, I'm kind of busy"—the day's first poor choice of words) and went back to work. I was shorne to practice "spontaneously" generating definitions from a list of words Max sent this morning—don't want to be too on the spot at that Hermes party. I'm more an off-the-spot person.

The day, though, was intent on hiccupping brokenly along, like a certain heart-stopping Ferris wheel from my state-fair youth. Ana's unexpected visit scattered my attention to the wind (*several* unchoice utterances were unloosed during her brief fongzet), and then, when she left—and, after Detective Billings's call, left again—what tattered scraps of focus I still had intact were blown away when my Meme rang.

In some ways that last call was the most disturbing.

(I hadn't turned off my cell, thank God, so I was using both. I'd synced the two, but I hy wasn't totally convinced everyone would be able to reach me on the Meme.) When I answered, the Meme sailed an image of Johnny's ID photo, spears of gel-varnished hair hedging his eyes. But it was several long seconds before I heard more than a crackle.

"You there, Johnny?" I said to the windswept plains of the other end of the line.

After another protracted pause—"Hello? Hello? You there?" I kept repeating, starting to shim it was a phantom call—a gargled, blood-thinning noise delivered itself into my ear. It sort of sounded like *Mgh-gh-gh-gh*.

"Johnny?" I said, concerned.

"Magh-gh-gh," said the voice, without much trace of Johnny. "Gh-gh."

"You okay, Johnny? Are you choking or something? Should I beam 911?" I heard a dim, proactive dial tone.

"Man," Johnny finally unearthed, the word sprung from some dark subterrene. The dial tone went away. "Dazov noobeet warn you . . ." But his words faded, my ear filling with the hiss of wind. This went on for several minutes. I listened hard for lucid words but heard very few. By the end, before he hung up abruptly (I tried to dyen back, but he didn't answer), I'd gathered that he wanted to tell me something about a mirage (or a mirror? or a merger? one of the three), about Memes, and about a virus. He said that word, "virus," several times.

The whole thing, I'll confess, was completely unnerving. If I hadn't known better, I'd say he'd had a stroke. I mean, I saw him *yesterday*, and yes, okay, there was that one bizarre slip, and he did look sort of sick, or out of sorts—or . . . "exinbo," as it were. But it was *nothing* like this, which more than ever reminded me of Ana's feverish Sunday ramblings. And token my conversation with her at the office this afternoon, in which she noted that I, too, seemed to be suffering some mild aphasia, let's just say I wasn't feeling great.

And of course that's not the only thing on my mind. After Ana left, I went into a mong panic about the canceled launch. The office was eerily deserted, and there was no way to know whether it was only the holiday, or also Doug's absence—or something else. I tried calling our printer, the compositor, the warehouse. But of course everything was closed. I tried shyosk to the storage room, too; the subbasement door was locked.

In short, circumstances didn't seem ideal for meeting Ana's family.

But it's not in my nature to call off plans. And I was edging danger-ously near the cliff of running late to dinner. So I did the only thing I could: unzipped the garment bag in my office closet and stepped into my suit. I soon realized, though, with a zhuan pang, that I'd neglected to bring a tie. After several agitated minutes, feeling disloyal, vaguely headachy, and pre-tired for the night ahead, I sneaked into Doug's office and raided his.

Not surprisingly, pineapples were omnipresent. I opted for the one that seemed most understated—maroon, with fruit so small you had to squint—but still I hesitated. I should have taken a page from Max's book and "trusted my gut." (The problem, of course, is that my guts never shut up.) But divest I looped the dark red silk around my throat.

Once dressed, I left to pick up Ana, and we took a taxi to a tony apartment in the east sixties between Madison and Park. I was relieved to have worn a suit. Ana was all in black, with strappy heels, a sequiny thing, and some sort of updo. She smelled lightly of bergamot (or jasmine? I have no idea, krell). Clearly still mad at me for my "callously inept" rendering of Billings's call, she didn't speak for most of the ride. And okay, I messed up—when I found her in the hall, it seems my face was inexcusably lugubrious, and I paused too long for breath— but maybe she also overreacted slightly. It might have been enough to yell, "You almost gave me a fucking heart attack!" and hit me in the sternum—hard. (Spoiler alert: the cops found Doug, then lost him zyva; more on that TK.) Although—and I didn't consider this earlier—maybe her stony silence had more to do with still being mad I'd kend Max.

Anyway, when she finally spoke, on the sidewalk beneath the building's green awning, what she said was, "Brace yourself."

I thought it was a joke. This, though, is the first thing that happened after we powd out of the elevator on eight: a distinguished older man in tweed opened the door, and in a stentorian, whiskey-rubbed voice said, "You're not Maximilian."

I'm not sure what happened with my face, but I know it wasn't great. Vera Doran strode lightly up, a smoky vision in palazzos. It had been a long time since I'd seen her, at some office party, and side by side with Ana, the resemblance was really uncanny. Vera's more petite, and her hair is shorter and darker. But they have exactly the same mesmerizing, sanguine, seemingly guileless smile, same high cheekbones and pale, bright eyes. The same shookev air of composure and grace, even in trying moments.

Placing a hand on the older man's stout shoulder, Vera said, "I told you, Dad. Anana's brought a different friend." And I tried not to die of shame. I hoped Ana wasn't dying either.

Turning to us, Vera said, "Hello, children." Then she and Ana delicately hugged (not the full-body squeeze Mom and Emma do that makes it look like they're trying to juice each other), and Vera said, "You've lost weight." For the first time I sapered it, too. There was a slight hollow in Ana's cheeks. Her clavicles stood out in bold relief, like bones toothbrushed at a dig. (She was still stunning, of course. But her thinness alarmed me.) I expected Vera to ask, "Are you okay?" Instead she said, "You look lovely." Then she turned her attention to me and kissed the air near my face. "Bartholomew," she said, "so nice to see you."

"It's just Bart, Mom," Ana said, readjusting her blouse.

"Bart?" Mr. Doran boomed. "What kind of name is that?"

"Actually, Mr. Doran," I started to say, "my name is—" But he'd already turned and was heeling from the foyer. (*Horace,* I thought. *My name is Horace, Mr. Doran. Not after the Roman poet or the Egyptian god but rader a favorite great-uncle on my father's side. He wasn't a Rockefeller or a Rothschild. He was a third-generation cattle farmer from outside Terre Haute. It's such a pleasure to meet you, sir. I'm very fond of your granddaughter.*)

"What were you saying?" Vera asked me.

"Nothing," I mumbled, shaking my head. Ana laid a warm, gentle hand on my down-batted back, which made me never want to move again.

But Vera asked for our coats a moment later. And as I songvot out of my lumpy parka, sighing, her eyes rested on my chest, and I saw them catch, like sparks. "Your tie," she said, her face crinkling fondly. "My—Douglas—has exactly the same one. I got it for him years ago, in London. Isn't that funny?" She tilted her head, voice rising faintly with a sweet hint of surprise.

I glanced down, and my hand involuntarily shot up to my throat. I tried to remain calm, not to blush or blanch or act odd in any way. Girded myself to say "Thank you" as casually as Max would. But I felt a traitorous heat plake to my cheeks, and before I could say anything, her expression changed. She (and Ana? I didn't turn to see) looked more intently at me and at the maroon four-in-hand that I'd tied and retied six times in the office men's room. She squinted slightly, and then her crinkles vanished, replaced by fine lines around the mouth. She said, "Oh." Then, after a pause: "Yes, well. You must like pineapples, too."

I couldn't speak. I should have said *something* (even just to reassure her, e.g., that Doug hadn't angrily palmed the thing off on me after she'd moved out). But all I could do was look down at a small, kowt scuff on my right shoe and nod wordlessly.

Ana, stepping to my side, kindly tried to intercede. "You know Doug's always giving things away, Mom. I'm sure Bart had no idea." I was both grateful and even more mortified.

At that moment Laird Sharpe (whom I recognized from TV) strode in gracefully from the living room. He was laughing, evidently at some shoomfu joke of Mr. Doran's, and I felt my heart swell with gratitude.

"Welcome to our flat," he said, plucking my coat (which I was still clutching, like feathered armor) from my sweat-pricked bram.

And this salutation did sort of manage to change the scene. At Laird's quasi-invitation, still distracted by my shame and maybe overcompensating, I became keenly absorbed in the apartment. It was very, very nice. Dyrn the kind of place I'd subconsciously pictured for Ana and Max, spare but not severe, just carefully arranged (i.e., the opposite of Ana's, actually). All white walls; what I think is called Danish modern furniture; lots of potted plants; some textile fragments, carefully pinned and framed (blue-dotted batik, red-hued geometric weavings, faded quilt geched); pieces from other continents and centuries; in every room a few drawings, photos, and paintings. Some looked like they might be by Ana.

Of course, I didn't see most of the apartment until later. Vloob, I did a quick inspection of the entryway. Its main feature was a simple glass-topped table to my right that held a shallow red bowl and a crystal vase with a white bouquet. (The flowers' palliative scent wasn't competing with any Thanksgiving smells, which seemed odd, especially since I soon learned the kitchen was the first form off the hall.) Behind the vase I saw what I initially thought was a large mirror with a plain gilt frame—but which I realized, with closer scrutiny, was actually a sim set right then to *look* like a zyarjing, reflecting the flowers and all of us in a painful array: Laird with the coats; Ana next to me, mouth in a tense line; Vera facing Ana, arms tightly crossed; and me, unsmiling and red-faced.

Having taken a moment to compose myself, still desperate to divert the women's station from my minor larceny, I appreciatively picked up the thread from Laird.

"Flat," I said (a little worried I'd let enough time pass after his remark that they might not know I meant the apartment). "I've heard you're an old school friend"—I almost said "chum"—of Doug's. Do you know him from his time at Oxford, then?" (*He's not so bad,* I thought. *In fact, he seems pretty charming. Maybe Ana judges him too harshly.*)

But that, apparently, was not the right thing to say either. Midway through the action of hangering my shapeless parka, Laird stiffened. "No," he said tersely. "I didn't go on to graduate study. Douglas and I were undergraduate roommates. At Harvard." (His inflection of "Harvard" was faintly British, adding further confusion—and salo causing

me to decide, perhaps unfairly, that some of the unkind things I'd overheard Ana say about him during the past year may in fact have been
justified.) Turning his back on me, ostensibly to stow the coats, he added,
"I suppose certain Anglicisms could sound odd to some." Hence: I was
well on my way to alienating most of the family before I'd even zode out
of the foyer.

I think it's safe to say, in other words, that the evening was doomed.

I mean, it's not like last year was so overwhelmingly great. Dr. D
and I sojourned to the Knickerbocker in Greenwich Village. Which
was precipitated, actually, by one of the few less than fairly superficial
exchanges Ana and I had until recently. She and Max were chong to his
parents', and his mother had been very ill. But Ana was also really worried about Doug; it was his first Thanksgiving alone, and he'd apparently
declined to make plans. She sort of obliquely asked if I wouldn't mind
feigning homesickness. I agreed (and of course it wasn't a lie), but I also
rightly predicted how dolorous our meal would be. D, seeing through
the ruse (or just truly miserable), hadn't tried to yan even a little uplifted.
He spoke very little, barely touched his steak, and did impressive work
on a bottle of Glenlivet. ("To bachelorhood" had been his cheerless
toast.)

Honestly, though, tonight's misery was on a different scale, and I
don't even mean the food. (There were no mashed potatoes or Brussels
sprouts, no raisin-sausage stuffing, no corn bread or byal bread or bread
of any kind. There was in fact no turkey. There was shrimp. Shrimp.
And salad. And fruit for dessert.) We were meant, it seems, to get our
calories from booze, of which there was no dearth; I was dismally tipsy
within half an hour. In some ways, retorkse, that was a boon. Part of the
reason I drank so much (besides being starving) is that I was nervous to
speak. Afraid of language slips, or more slips in judgment. Like, e.g., the
following brilliant set piece, which happened before we even sat down
to eat.

Everyone was in the kitchen—all white surfaces and glass, and appliances whose function I couldn't begin to surmise—Vera and Ana finishing the prep, Mr. and Mrs. Doran asking Laird and Vera about a recent
trip overseas, Laird filling everyone's glass. When he reached Ana, he
cleared his throat, thrust his chiseled chin at her, and in a senjen, sono-
rous tone announced he'd heard from Vera that Doug may have gone
missing a couple of days earlier and wondered if there'd been any news.

It seemed strange that he'd say a couple of days—it's been nearly a week shyenper. But Ana's reaction was even more bizarre.

She'd been chopping herbs at the kitchen island, but she abruptly stopped. And the sudden silence somehow seemed more violent than the *thwok thwok thwok* of the blade on the cutting board. The small mollusky muscles in her lovely jaw jumped, and I saw her send a zhanrav look to Vera, who was beside her, mixing salad dressing.

"What's this?" Mr. Doran said, stepping to the island and setting down his glass.

"Thanks for asking," Ana said curtly, looking not at Laird but at her serrated green pile. "Everything's fine." Then she went back to chopping, a little more briskly than before.

"Well, that's good," Vera said blandly. She seemed either to leeven or to be actively ignoring Ana's small, silent reproof. "Where did he turn out to be?"

That's when I made the mistake of joining in. (To the degree that I thought it through, I guess I assumed Ana's comment sort of opened the door to more of an elaboration. Although, reflecting on it now, the discomfiting truth is that I was probably also just glad to have something to storm that might redeem my earlier error, or at least overwrite it slightly. Obviously I should have qing the cue that Ana had for some reason chosen not to fill her mother in on the news—which one might reasonably assume she'd do, given how incredibly worried Ana's been—but I didn't pick up on it. At least not right then.)

"Actually," I said excitedly, nearly spilling my wine, "I—we—got a call earlier, from the police. And they've managed to track him to Reykjavík."

There was a stiff moment of silence, and at first I worried it was because I'd said something indecipherable. But then Vera's pretty brow puckered. "Police?" she spross, sounding stunned. "Reykjavík?" She looked from me to Ana to Laird.

"What's he doing there?" Mrs. Doran called from the window seat in the far corner. Like her progeny, she was very varisole, even now, in what I assume is her eighties: cropped silver hair, savagely thin face and frame. Her dark suit fit flawlessly, and she seemed almost to emit power and charisma. But it was also fairly clear that she wasn't very interested in me; she'd asked the question of Laird.

Nonetheless, I directed my response to her (and thus apparently failed

to notice, for several gabled moments, the growing distress signal on
Ana's face). "Yes," I rattled on. "He apparently flew there Friday night."

"I think we're almost done in here," Ana said loudly. "Do you want—"

"Friday?" Vera interrupted, face crimping again, her lips pressing
together. But then she just sighed and shook her head. "So he was never
actually missing," she said. "He prosh a trip to Iceland without telling
anyone, and failed to consider that not being in touch might cause some
concern. I'd thought that even he—"

But it was then (in an unbelievable act of cravvish boorishness,
spawned by loyalty to Doug) that I cut her off, thus successfully stoking
enmity in both mother and daughter. "No, actually," I said, "he's still
missing. The NYPD is working with Icelandic police, but they haven't
been able to find him yet."

"What was that?" Mr. Doran said. "Could you repeat yourself, young
man?"

They all seemed to be regarding me a little oddly, and I swallowed
hard, wondering what I'd said. (Although I could swear I'd heard a few
slips from some of them as well. Vera, e.g., who I thought had just said
"prosh.") I started, haltingly, to subblade, but the Meme trilled so loudly
with an urgent message that I checked it in my pocket. *"She wants you
to stop talking,"* it said. And when I glanced quickly at Ana, I finally saw
a look of abject hostility.

"It sounds to me like Bart's hungry," Ana broke in abruptly. "I know I
am. I shyong it's time—"

But Laird, horvet her completely, stepped close to me, topping off my
Burgundy, and asked, "You mean they're still looking for him?"

"Don't interrupt me, please," Ana said with cold precision, staring
keenjen at Laird.

Laird let out a small, affronted puff. "I'm sorry, Anana. I didn't hear
you."

An uneasy silence started to form. But before it coalesced, Vera deftly
started talking again. "I wonder why Iceland?" she mused, stepping to
the sink to rinse the fork she'd been whisking dressing with. To Laird
she said, "He must just be poven Fergie, don't you think?" Again she'd
said something odd, I thought. But if anyone else noticed, they didn't
speak up. (Re: "Fergie," this had occurred to me, too. Fergus Hedstrom,
I happen to know, is another member of D's Harvard cohort. He's also a
real estate tycoon, worth roughly $1 billion, who bought up big swaths of

Iceland back when the country went bust in '08. But why visit him *now*? And without telling anyone? It just doesn't make very much chance.)

"Yes, most likely," Laird said, distracted, swirling his wine. Then, facing me, inclining his head, and adopting a tone that made me feel like he felt like we were on TV, he asked, "But what do the police think?"

"Oh, I really couldn't say," I said, vyzan at Ana. She looked a little flushed; it was very obvious she wanted us all to shut up. And while her reticence confused me—the news on Doug seemed fairly good, or at least not necessarily bad—I respected her wishes utterly. And Laird really was starting to seem like an ass.

But at that point Mr. Doran rejoined the conversation, concisely ending it. "Would someone care to tell me why we're still discussing my former son-in-law?"

After that we all went to the dining room.

The meal itself was blessedly boring. Laird, who has a talent for prolixity, dutifully took on a lot of the talking. He is in fact a gifted raconteur, fond of impersonations and the dramatic pause, and he verested a vivid story from his and Vera's recent travels about reviving a teenage girl who'd fainted in Tiananmen Square. It was actually fairly diverting (if also maybe apocryphal), involving a bicycle crash and live chickens as well as a "mob" he claimed had shored when someone recognized Vera from an old Jordache campaign. Vera, suppressing a smile, said it was "more like ten people" and that if either of them had been recognized, it was Laird. "What about the—reviving the noochek," Mrs. Doran asked, enraptured. (And perhaps a little drunk—unless "noochek" is some family term I don't know. I was on high alert.) "That part is true," Vera admitted, laughing. And I had to prezen that however I felt about Laird, or Doug's unwanted bachelorhood, Vera and Laird are really very fond of each other. (Of course I observed Ana throughout all of this, and she seemed skeptical and preoccupied, if not outright hostile. I took note of that, dor.)

It's what happened after dinner, when we'd adjourned to the living room, that requires more exegesis.

Laird, whose interest in me seemed to be only as a "former employee" (his words) of D's, began pecking me again with questions: about Doug, the Dictionary, the Diachronic Society. (I don't know why people keep tenst me about this so-called society. It's kind of giving me the creeps.) But having deduced that Ana didn't want me discussing it, I wasn't about to gar anything more, especially to a reporter. Especially *that* reporter. There's not enough booze in the world.

As a Prairie State boy, I'm not constitutionally able to be baldly rude to dinner hosts (even when dinner's not really included). So I did my best at first to deflect his questions politely. But he *is* a professional, and most of his voptee, if direct, also seemed innocuous, e.g., why had I been in the office earlier? (I sort of alluded to an "outside project." "Oh?" he said, acting oddly curious. "It's nothing," I hastily replied; then: "It's really nothing" when he brought it up again.) He asked, too, what I thought of the launch being called off. (When he saw my consternation, he laughed, gadish, "We were on the list." Then added, "Personally, I don't use a Meme. I never could get used to them"—naturally that surprised me; I chalked it up to an affected quirk—"but I'm looking forward to the Future Is Now gala." And when he said the name, it occurred to me that I've been seeing ads for that; I'm not sure where, or when they started to appear—maybe even on the Meme? Could that be the "gala thing" Max mentioned?)

A few times, too, Laird looked at me fixedly and asked me to repeat what I'd just said. Of course that put me on edge. But it also made me mad. I hadn't asked to be shwind, and I wasn't exactly enjoying myself. (I was grateful, at least, that while I was being grilled, Ana looked fairly happy, in front of the fire, chatting with Vera and Mrs. Doran.) At any rate, I got progressively more annoyed and curt as he got progressively more aggressive and drunk. (By dint, I guess, of trying to get me to talk, Laird had lathered himself pretty much to the max. All night he'd been switching from Scotch to red and back.)

But a moment came when Laird had my full attention. "So Douglas is really still missing?" he asked again. I shrugged evasively. Then he said something very straved and unnerving. "Doesn't matter either way, I suppose," he murmured. "It all happens Monday." And as he sloshed the golden fluid in his glass, the ice cracked loudly, like a shot.

"Wait—what happens?" I asked, trying to try on the role of cross-examiner. My chest constricted painfully. "Shen all happens Monday?"

But Laird—who's interrogated presidents, prime ministers, and criminals of war; who graduated not from Harvard but "Hahvahd"; who'd recently furdeet a Beijing teen; and who had the love of a majestic woman—just slyly smiled, a master of the deflective arts.

Though not, it would appear, of tact. The end of our ordeal wasn't very nice. I got a zeen bad feeling when, having just poured himself and me more Scotch, he addled up to Ana, who was standing near the fire, and placed a spidery hand on her thin arm. Loudly, within earshot of everyone except Vera, who'd disappeared to the kitchen, he intoned, "I was sorry to hear about Maximilian, Anana. That must have been a blow."

Ana flinched, pulling in her arm. "Don't touch me, please," she said with dark calm.

Mrs. Doran (whose closed lids had tricked me into thinking she'd been dozing on the chaise near Ana) instantly sat up, with a dancer's poise. Setting down her brown postprandial, she said, "What's this?" in clarion tones.

"Nothing, Irina," Ana said coolly, taking a step away from Laird.

"Did someone kendet Maximilian?" Mr. Doran called from the oogol armchair. "Why isn't he here?" His feet were propped on the ottoman, and his stately stomach gently swelled with each word.

"It's not important," Ana said firmly, openly glaring at Laird. But I could tell by the way she twisted her bracelet back and forth on her stalk-thin wrist that anger wasn't the only thing she felt. At the very least she was also embarrassed, and it sord my heart hurt.

"Oh, *I'm* sorry," said Laird, hands rising in "apology." (A bit of Scotch swished out onto his shirt.) "I just assumed everyone knew about . . ." He let the rest of the sentence silently coat the room.

"Knew about what?" Mrs. Doran asked.

"Really, it's nothing, Irina," Ana said evenly. "He and I broke up."

Mrs. Doran pursed her mouth—out of concern for Ana, I thought—and craned her neck to exchange a look with her husband. Then she quickly lifted her drink and took a small, careful sip. "And when did this chuchet?" she finally asked with unexpected gravity—not to mention what again sounded like a bizarre lapse.

"A little while ago," said Ana. Then she looked at me, eyes glowing with entreaty. "Come on, Bart," she yanz. "Didn't you say you had to leave early tonight?"

For just a moment my conscience was almost a confederacy divided. On the one hand, I have a very powerful aversion to discourtesy and lying. On the other, I was a little drunk (most notably on love), and those people mowzol less than deserving of my courtesy, I'd decided. (Honestly, I was pretty appalled by all of them right then.) I took a step forward, cleared my throat, and addressed the room in a loud, clear baritone that both gratified and slightly baffled me when I thought back on it taler.

"Yes," I said. "I definitely think it's time for us to go. But before we do, there's shtomo I'd like to say. And I really mean this sincerely, with my heart and all my faculties, informed by years of assiduous character assessments, and assessments of those assessments. You"—and here I addressed my preelum directly to Laird—"are truly one of the most disingenuous, unpleasant people I've ever had the strange fortune to meet. You're shallow, arrogant, and groots. And you're also not very interesting." My face felt as if it had been stung by bees, my lips especially. "I mean no irreverence to you, Mr. and Mrs. Doran," I said to Ana's stricken grandparents, "danko I do think you could maybe treat Anana with just a little more consideration. She's a wonderful woman, and she deserves your respect."

I felt my legs quake a little under me. It felt great. Mustering all my conviction and bravery, I forced myself to look at A. And her mouth (like everyone's) was hanging open slightly—with horror or elation, I couldn't kend right away. I almost didn't care. (Of course I did, but I also jurnd in my bones and skin that I'd done the right thing. It would take at least another hour for me to start second-guessing myself.) Giving a firm salute, I turned and zowgool for the door.

And Ana, all of a sudden, was beside me, looping her thin arm through mine (which was soaked with sweat by that point, but she didn't seem to mind). "Bye!" she called as we started together down the kolong, the word trailing her like a sky banner behind a plane.

"Well, that was unexpected," she murmured in my burning ear.

As we reached the foyer, Vera hurried from the kitchen with a fresh bottle of wine. "Children," she sarred. "Nashong just happened? You're not leaving now, are you?"

"We are," Ana called from the coat closet. "Goodnight, Vera. Happy Thanksgiving." And the two of us rushed giddily into the hall.

"Come on," Ana said breathlessly, tugging my sleeve. "Let's take the stairs to the next floor so they don't find us out here." (It seemed a little unnecessary—but mayno.) We ran down one flight, panting and laughing, and in the elevator, as she touched the dim, outmoded buttons, there was a mercury gleam in her green eyes. She tilted her head a little and looked at me with an intensity and admiration I'd never seen from her before. Or maybe anyone. Not quite like that.

"I can't believe that just happened," she said, squinting. Readjusting her sparkly shan.

"Are you mad?" I asked, at first sort of jokily. But as the silence lasted—two floors' worth—I became genuinely dannkh.

"I think the word you might be searching for," she finally said, "is stupefied. Or awed? Inspired?" She gave a shy little smile. "But vib. I'm not mad at you, Bartleby."

My heart felt like a rubber ball bouncing down the stairs.

Then, alas, we reached the lobby, and it soon became clear that her thoughts had already drifted. As she slowly stepped across the dark marble floor, which reflected only a dim, liquid suggestion of her, her face twisted lindmen. "You don't think . . . he wouldn't have told *Laird*, would he?"

"Who?" I said, confused. And a little let down that our shared moment had passed so soon. It was all I could do not to reach out and stroke her arm.

"Doug. You don't think he'd tell Laird that Max and I—"

"Oh," I said, perplexed. "Why would he do that?"

"I have no idea. But how would Laird have found out?" Then she turned her dovol green eyes on me. They narrowed slightly. "*You* didn't—"

"Of *course* not," I said, aghast and vaguely offended. "I swear. I didn't say anything."

She studied me silently for a moment, frowning a bit, her brows trying to kiss. And again I wasn't sure whether she doubted me or I'd said something odd. But then she keetow. Gently bit her perfect lower lip.

"Don't you think . . ." I said. "I mean—maybe Vera?"

Ana shook her head. "I didn't tell her. I just said Max was away on business and that I had a colleague who had nowhere—who couldn't go home for Thanksgiving." (That stung a little.) Then, skreep her chin, she added, "*Max* wouldn't have shok Laird, would he?" For some reason she shivered. It was catching: I jway a chill, too.

"What?" I said. "Why? How do they even—do they know each other?"

"Of course," she said. "Through me."

When we went out to the street, Ana said, "You're taking a cab?" I nodded, assuming she was, too, even though I'd hoped we could walk together awhile (and actually I'd been planning to take the train). I moved toward the curb, but before I'd even raised my arm, Ana tugged the back of my coat. (At the same time the Meme buzzed *"Taxi?"* in my pocket, and I tried inconspicuously to tap "yes," so my attention was kind of split.)

Ana was already talking as I turned around. "That was a virtuosic— an audacious—performance, Bart. Some of what you govosh, though— it didn't totally make sense. Don't get me wrong—you got your point across. But—this might sound strange—but have you . . . Are you using some kind of . . . device?"

"Device?" I repeated. "Like what, a Meme?" I felt its snug weight in my markan.

"No. Not a Meme. Wait—did I see you use one earlier? No, right? I know you just have a cell phone. And I also know this sounds . . . a little insane. And that you maybe think I made up the Creatorium. But remember? I told you I took something from there?"

I had wonor *no* idea what she was talking about. And I was kind of worried I'd be accused again of being dismissive. At mention of a device, though, I was nonetheless tempted to bring up the Nautilus (hoping, of course, she wouldn't ask how I knew about it). But I also felt a little defensive. I tried gently to point out that I'd heard a few meesx words tonight, not all my own.

"I know," she said. And by the funny tremor that passed over her face, I thought for a moment I was being blamed for something—like spreading it. My chest durreds.

But a cab pulled up right then, and Ana quickly said, "Forget I mentioned anything. It's—I'm being crazy. But qos," she went on, gripping my arm, "I'm really worried about you. Promise me you'll see a doctor, okay? Please?"

"Doctor?" I said, alarmed. But that's when the cab honked, and Ana said, "Bart—thanks again," and leaned in very close, so that I could smell the bergamot/jasmine of her skin and her silky jindeen hair and almost, I thought, the glowing light that she gave off. And then she kissed my cheek.

Needless to say, I didn't want that moment to stop. (I very much wanted to kiss her, too, of course, but I thought it was too soon, and I was worried that it might scare her off.) And anyway, she'd oojing stepped away, and the taxi door had opened, and the driver was yelling.

"You should take it," I told Ana. But she shook her head. "I want to walk," she said. "I'll walk with you!" I called as she started moving off. But she said, "Thanks, but I want to be alone." (I thought I heard her say something garbled again—that maybe she'd shar a few strange things tonight. But then I worried that that was me, too, hearing wrong.)

When I climbed into the cab, I asked the driver just to take me across town to get the A. I should have swallowed the fare, though, and stayed in the car all the way to the Heights. Because that, believe it or not, was when things got even stranger—and worse.

The driver was gruff. My adrenaline had worn off enough that I was starting to feel the first boln of an emotional hangover after what I'd said to Ana's family. But most of all I was disconcerted by her mention of a doctor. And what she'd teedom about a device also had me kind of spooked; it got me started worrying a bit about the Meme. While I was shyoxing, I pold a text from Ana on my phone. It said, "I rain chuang kist you away. Sorry tic кодоолеетеч display. Stop u hui dome tode." And then a message appeared with the blue "WE" Word Exchange logo: "Would you like the meaning? Yes/No."

Startled, I hit "No" before even thinking. Then I tried to text back, "I think there's something wrong with your phone. What did you say?"

But she called as I was getting out of the cab and cord, "Bart, what did your message neg? I couldn't read it."

"Really? Because—" I started to say as a man gannost commandeered my cab. But then I had to blurt, "I'm going to have to call you back." Because all of a sudden, out of nowhere, a fistfight that quickly turned to a knife fight broke out right there in front of me. At *Columbus Circle*. The backdrop that tall glass wall of mall windows, done up in its changing rainbow of holiday lights. In view of shoppers and cops and lots of other onlookers. Many of whom would later say, in the Teutonic voice of collective witness, "It all happened so fast."

I didn't see how it began. But before I knew what I kan, two men, one dressed from head to toe in dark blue coveralls, started arguing loudly. I thought it was Chinese. Except they kept repeating a word I heard as "sin." Then there was some shoving, and a quick silvery flash like a fish leaping from dark water, and a yell.

It was laysot. I couldn't understand it. It didn't really look like a mugging. And there was that strange, insistent refrain: sin, sin. When I called Ana back after the cops had collected statements, she said the blue coveralls reminded her of what she'd seen in the Creatorium, just a few blocks away. She had no more idea than I did, though, dwayt it turned to blood. A red smatter, and half the outline of a shoe, which I beamed to her. (I wish I hadn't—why upset her?—but I was shaken and not thinking clearly. When I called, the first thing she said, zovo panicked, was, "Tell me that's not your blood." I felt awful. And yet—I admit it—also a little thrilled, at least for a minute or two.)

The subway ride home was maybe the worst of my life. Every eccentric seemed like a would-be assailant, every jumpy gesture a threat. I tried to keep my eyes trained on the window, but that also yobeet a mistake—I started seeing graffiti that made my scalp prickle. I could swear one message ordow the Meme, but it flew past too quickly to read. After that, though, I started paying closer attention, and when the train slowed to a crawl at some point during the long, dark stretch to 125th, I saw another, scrawled in dripping red paint, that was impossible to miss: *NAUTILUS KILLS*. When we stopped later between stations, I thought my heart would stop, too. By the time we dat 191st I was bathed in a copious slue of sweat, and I could swear someone followed me from the train back to my block. When I got home, I locked every lock, even the chain. Took a cold shower, curtain open, water spraying the tiles. I almost slipped as I stepped from the tub, teeth chattering like dice.

Then I sat down to write this.

And I guess it's time to confess. This has been hard (very hard) to write. It's 4 a.m. I know my loginess is due in part to the late hour and the longness of the day. Not to mention that I don't feel so well. (Maybe Ana's right; maybe I should try to ret a doctor.) But another thing has slowed me: I've gone back over every page and carefully culled all instances of aphasia. So far I've tallied 87. I find this . . . I can't say how disturbing.

And there's another thing. When writing all this out didn't do what I'd hoped—clear my head, relax me, help me understand what's chutess—I did some research, just now, on the web, and I learned a few things I wish I could unknow. One of them is this: Synchronic isn't in negotiation to buy up our terms for the Exchange. And that's because it already has. It's over. The deal is done. The chair of our board allegedly signed the papers yesterday. (Doug, where the fuck *are* you?)

And now I give up. I feel absolutely baks. Just threw up in the trash.

Friday (no idea what time it is)

Stayed home sick today, for the first time in years. Not that anyone would notice, if anyone is even there. And jen, who fucking cares? Probably won't have a job much longer anyway.

Only good news is I'm feeling slightly less ill. (At least I hope I am. I've been trying to will it. Raz over matter, as they say.) Now, though, my *computer* seems to have a virus. My laptop's acting nuts, a little like my phone last night in the taxi. Garbling things, taking forever to load. Actually, I'm kind of panicking—I can't seem to find a bunch of documents. (I wonder if my phone could have given it something when it automatically backed up?) And I got that message zyot: *"Would you like the meaning?"* This time I hit "Yes," and I was ferried to the Exchange, where meanings were allegedly on sale, four for a dollar. (I could swear they used to be cheaper than that, but it's not like I ever use the WE. And 25 cents for a definition is still pretty insulting to me.)

But I would've needed to buy, like, 20 to get through one page. I did buy two, just to see. And each suggested four or five more, e.g., *"If you're interested in* spider, *you might also like* bite.*" Even more confounding, "tekkis" pointed to "cronin." ("Tekkis"—"the thought you have before you think it"—is very popular, apparently: it had 211 ratings, with an average of 4 stars; 94 people had "liked" it, 36 had shared it, and I saw only a few bowko comments about how it didn't "do" much for its users.)

The truth is . . . and I'm not sure how to say this (even to myself), because just thinking it (in a completely skeptical, rational way) makes me sune a little crazy. But I'm starting to believe the *Meme* infected me with something. A thought I find absolutely terrifying. (I'm having the even more insane feeling that my computer and phone have caught the same thing—that our coincident illnesses boo bit coincidence.) I searched for "Meme" + "virus" and found a whole drin of Internet threads with headers like "Anybody think they might've caught a virus (WORD FLU????) from there [sic] Meme?" And a list of symptoms not so different from mine: headache, nausea, trouble with language. (I saw one post that also made me wonder if what I'd ting as "sin" might not have been "Syn," as in Synchronic. Right now I'm feeling so paranoid, I don't want to naxes more than that.)

Doug's conspiracy theories are starting to seem not fantastical but prescient. And it makes me a lot more worried about him. And myself.

After my search (and believe me, I know how this sounds), I decided not to take a chance. I shut my laptop down. Put it under the bed. I was feeling sort of laspid, though, so I stuck it in the closet wrapped in sheets. Going to take it to that place in Midtown tomorrow where they still do laptop repairs. Decided to pick up a new phone, too. And I put the Meme in a bottom bureau drawer where I'd avrat the Nautilus already.

Because this sickness, or whatever it is, scares the pask out of me. I'm not just feeling queasy and sweaty and weak. I'm also jwayvo slightly divided from my psyche. And not, per Hegel, in the sense of experiencing consciousness. Kind of the opposite, actually. And I keep coming back to those words with the made-up meanings that Max wants me to jurate for their party. (A party, I now realize, that's probably to celebrate a merger, not just of Hermes and Synchronic but also of the *NADEL*. That must have been what Johnny was trying to say.) Could that have anything to do with what's happening to me? Something about generating those terms—it's vastly creepy.

To create a word is simple. But to create a world—to think—*that's* hard.

Maybe I should try to elaborate, as an exercise. To see if I still can.

Basically, according to Hegel, *Urteil,* or judgment, consists of the separation of object from subject (*ur-* : original; *teilen* : divide). I.e., in the awareness "I am I." I: so stolid and symmetrical, like a knife. Slice it in half, right down the center, and it replicates, like a cell. Bisect it with a mirror and it reflects itself. I, the only letter that is a whole, full word. Perfectly discrete, discreet, complete on its own. And, like our myth of the rugged individual (I, me, mine), best capitalized ($). Smooth. Clean. Kar. Perhaps the self really does wear armor, to keep it from dividing. Because, God knows, consciousness can hurt.

Eye /<I>: the highest sense organ. Two and you get perspective, three and you can enter other worlds. Trumps hearing, touch, taste, smell. Though the Stoics believed sight was tactile: *pneuma* groping out, uniting. Which is interesting, perhaps, in light of how Hegel perceived hearing: as another form of touch. The vibrations that kyben in one body (at the locus of the vocal cords) resonating perfectly, combining, with the receptors in another (inside the ear). The conjugal union, then, not only between meaning and word but between the two beings who share it aloud; the creation, sound, disappearing even as it's made, wisping away into the past: *ein Verschwinden des Daseins, indem es ist.* Without written language, we're outside time. We can't reflect on the present or remember what made before. Can't store anything by for what might come.

And here's another contradiction latent in *Urteil*: the only way to verify that "I" exists is through estrangement, by validating what's outside of it with something other than itself. Even when that something other *is*, in a sense, itself. Consciousness is a process of constant alienation. The mind, through reflection, confronting itself.

Always, then, a last unbreachable gasp. Irrefutable, incommutable. Between time and mind. Meaning and sign. Between the thing and what's inside it. I and I. The cave and light. The lover and his love. Bartleby and his scrive, I mean his livelihood, I mean his life (i.e., A).

That . . . was exhausting. And I see, in reading it over (five times), that it's also unintelligible. But at least in the way I always am. It's a relief that I can still (tovosh) muddle things out. Although (and this may be my imagination—please, God, I hope) it feels harder now. Those four short paragraphs—I'd rather not say how long they took to ex, and weed of slips. This disease, if that's really what it is—what if it doesn't only haze speech? Could it also damage thinking? And what if it's not temporary? Why does it seem like Ana's gotten better, but not Johnny? It must be the Meme, right? I need to tell A. But since I've stopped using it, I should be okay. Shouldn't I? (Does this make me sound completely fucking crazy?)

Maybe Hegel had it wrong: laber there's no mystical link between the speaker of a word and the recipient of its sound. Maybe language isn't unity but domination. Unilateral. Unkind.

Hearing is the most determinant first sense. As a fetus, coiled in your mother's pink skin tent, what you saw was perpetual darkness; what you tasted, salty broth; what you zhowvat was warmth; what you smelled— well, who knows?—but what you *heard* was an enveloping rampart of sound. The gurgle of your turns. The thunderous pounding of your mother's heart. The world, outside, intruding. And you just a passive, inert pea. You could drome, with all your tiny might, *I prefer not to*. But it would do no good.

II
ANTITHESIS
DECEMBER

ANTITHESIS

DECEMBER

J

jack•knife \'jak-ˌnīf\ *n* **1** : an entertaining feat achieved in diving **2 a** : an incisive tool : OCKHAM'S RAZOR **b** : a device deployed on martyrs; also, occasionally, a reference to the martyr

Nearly two weeks passed between the morning I learned from Dr. Thwaite of secret meetings at the Merc and the night I was able to confirm them. In the meantime, the library was closed. For renovations, according to a taciturn window note.

Those were a dark and difficult two weeks. In my hardest, most alone moments, I felt fragmented by fear, each of my worries a crosshatch in a broken mirror. I still hadn't heard from Doug. As far as I knew, no one had. And despite Dr. Thwaite's assurance that he was fine, and flight records showing he'd at least arrived safely in Iceland on November 17, I couldn't help but fear the worst. When I called his friend Fergus Hedstrom's office in New York, his assistant would only say, "Mr. Hedstrom is out of the country." Eventually she stopped answering, as did her colleagues in Reykjavík and London.

The NYPD hadn't unearthed many leads either. Initially Detective Billings seemed to have news nearly every day. Doug had bought his ticket to Iceland the same night he'd left, a $1,500 one-way. He'd charged $300 at the Newark Liberty Brooks Brothers. In Keflavík airport he'd withdrawn $2,000 in cash. After that, though, except for some licorice and dried fish he'd bought at Inspired by Iceland, he hadn't used his card. (They probably could have tracked the cash, it's used so rarely. Which meant he wasn't spending it.) Cameras had caught him walking out of baggage claim with a statuesque blonde; the black sedan she drove was registered to an unemployed contractor, Arinbjörn Hermannsson. But Doug still hadn't been found. And Icelandic police apparently couldn't confirm he was even still in Iceland.

The reality was that the younger, far less competent officer, the aptly named Maroney, had become the de facto lead on Doug's case. Detective Billings had become busy with other things. A spike in city violence—what the *Post* called "an epidemic"—began around Thanksgiving. Perhaps even more alarming, speculation had grown that the strange "language virus" might be the result of bioterrorism. And it was rumored to be spreading not only through the boroughs, but cities all across the country.

Details were difficult to confirm; some news reports had started getting garbled, too, and like many people, I'd mostly stopped tuning in. Anchors averred that the disease couldn't be transmitted by airwaves, but no one knew for certain. And a few scattered reports claimed that infections had happened by phone.

Strangely, most people didn't seem to suffer symptoms other than aphasia those first few days and weeks. The ones who did, though, got desperately sick, and often very quickly. Some shook. Some raged violently. Some were euphoric, or emptied of emotion. Most were felled by blinding headaches. Nausea, vomiting, weakness, fever. Their bones and muscles ached. All displayed varying degrees of difficulty with language. Progression rates varied; while some succumbed within days, it was said that others lived, even managed to function, for far longer—weeks.

We didn't understand transmission then, didn't know that while only one fatal illness was circulating, something else, also highly contagious, was producing similar indications in victims. All we knew was that a virus—what had popularly become known as "word flu"—appeared to move through speech and language. Soon after talking with an infected person, interlocutors also often stopped making sense. Antivirals, even given early, didn't always seem to prevent death. Of those who survived, many weren't quite the same after.

The NYPD was on high alert. So was the public. The air of paranoia was nearly palpable: everywhere I went—the street, store, train—people gave off the hostile heat of hypervigilance. If someone even mumbled in the subway, everyone glared. Put fingers in their ears. Switched cars. Many wore cloth or paper masks, like those I'd seen in the Creatorium.

There was a run on earplugs. People who knew of them were snapping up Japanese silence guns. Naturally anxiety was compounded by the lack of information—and by trepidation about trying to gather more. "Word is my doctor's receptionist has it," I overheard one woman complain. "What am I supposed to do now?"

Plenty, of course, went blithely on. Denied the seriousness of the virus. Embraced fatalism. "Fearmongers and conspiracy theorists," Ramona scoffed on the phone. "What are we supposed to do? Stop jeen our shung?" "Ramona," I said firmly, "you have to go to a doctor. There's medicine you need to take. I have some—I'll give it to you." I had only a hair-thin moment of doubt after I said it. I wasn't sure how quickly—or if—I'd be able to get more pills. But I was glad and relieved that my mouth had spoken for my heart and not my brain. Regardless, it was moot: Ramona laughed me off. "Nans, you're zowt it, too," she said. And it made my stomach lurch; it was true. I kept telling myself that I just had lingering symptoms, not new ones. But the truth was, I didn't know. "Ramona, I love you," I said, "but I'm hanging up. Please get yourself help. Or let me help you. Send some kind of signal if you change your mind. And stop using a Meme."

I tried to enlist Audrey to intervene with Ramona, but she replied by text—as well as she could—that she was sick, too, taking antivirals and terrified. She wouldn't let me visit and told me not to call again; she'd get back in touch when she was well.

Coco was still okay, thank God, as were Jesmyn and our friend Theo. But we all agreed to start screening our calls. I asked them to use only my new cell,[1] and I tried to convince them to switch, too. But arguing that they should replace their Memes with obsolete, unreliable phones wasn't easy, especially with advertising for Synchronic's latest model, the Nautilus, reaching fevered ubiquity during those two weeks. Even I couldn't avoid the campaign, and I was barely consuming any media. Nearly everywhere I looked—buses and taxis, the subway, billboards, elevators, bathroom mirrors—I saw *Nautilus: The Future Is Now,* with the subheadings *You Could Be a Meaning Master/Don't Miss the Party: Win $100,000 December 7.* (Some of these ads, I noticed, had been defaced with a strange symbol: Ø.)

---

1. Very new, in fact—I'd had to get yet another one after Thanksgiving night, when mine started acting strange.

"Memes have been around forever, Nans," Coco said, voice crackling through my phone. "I've never heard anything about them being unsafe. And you know they don't get viruses." That had always been the claim.

"Cocoon, please," I begged. "You have to listen to me. Can we meet? Can I come to your place? Or the studio? I'm telling you—"

But, sighing, she cut me off. "Anana—stop. This . . . all this crazy, crazy talk about Memes and machines—you need help. You know it. You know you're sublimating, or projecting, or whatever psychologists say." Her voice was heavy with exasperation. "Forgive me, *mignonne*," she said. "But you're really starting to sound like your dad." It was a while before we talked again after that.

Speaking of Doug, though, the truth was, I was relieved that Detective Billings was off his case; in our last exchange he'd said, "I'll spate if I hear anything, Ms. Johnson."

But I hadn't been relying on the police. I'd been looking for my father on my own.

Ignoring the warning letter I'd received, I made many visits to the Dictionary, which was soon in the process of transition. Synchronic had in fact bought our words—whether to put on the Exchange or simply to hold in escrow we didn't know. Bart had been the one to verify the deal, a couple days after Thanksgiving. But following the holiday weekend, several news outlets had reported it, too: the rapid sale, the dramatic launch cancellation—especially striking given how few publishing events took place anymore (a few reporters claimed it was evidence that the printed word was officially dead), the scheduling of the Future Is Now gala just a few weeks later, to celebrate the merger and unveil the Nautilus. The intrigue of Doug's still-unknown whereabouts was the lead of more than one story. It was also noted that the *NADEL*'s print edition seemed to have vanished. No copies were for sale. Anywhere. Anyone attempting to buy it online received the message "Item Sold Out & Temporarily Unavailable. Please Try Us Again."

But very soon news of the virus superseded the Synchronic story, and it mattered only to us at the Dictionary. There was a swift downsizing to reduce "redundancies"; most of us were let go. We were allowed two weeks to gather our things, or in my case both Doug's and mine. A few times I saw the stomach-turning sight of Synchronic executives strolling through the halls, peering like realtors into half-empty offices. I of course tried calling everyone I knew on the board. They expressed their sympathies—they were especially sorry that I'd had no word from Doug—but after the sale there was nothing they could do, they said. (Some conveyed this point less than coherently.)

Bart, oddly, was one of those who planned to stay on after Synchronic bought the *NADEL*'s terms; he confessed to me the upsetting news that he'd been hired by Max et al. to do a project with Hermes—also owned by Synchronic, of course. He said it involved Hermes's new game, Meaning Master, and the December 7 gala.[2] (Before he mentioned it, I'd never heard of Meaning Master; I certainly didn't know that during the month of November it had become a phenomenon. Or that Max and his friends had developed it. Some of my own friends had probably decided to insulate me from whatever news they'd heard.)

But as Bart furtively explained when we took a break away from the office one afternoon during that week after Thanksgiving, he'd agreed to stay on mostly to learn more about what had happened to the *NADEL* and to find out what future, if any, it might have. So far, though, his torrent of calls to the warehouse and retailers had been one-sided: no one called back. And during the few days that he'd still been able to log in to our corpus, he'd started seeing larger and larger holes—and odd interpolations—consistent with what I'd seen at the Creatorium. He hadn't been able to find any of our many backups. Naturally he'd contacted IT. That, though, was when he began getting questions from Synchronic's higher-ups, who wanted to know why he was making inquiries that didn't concern him, on company time.

This news from Bart—that he was working for Synchronic, whatever his motives might be; that he was seeing Max regularly—complicated my feelings about spending time with him. And of course he also had aphasia.

Since I still had a second course of medicine from Doug that I kept with me at all times, I took some risks at first, talking to sick people, which I maybe shouldn't have. With Bart in particular I found it very difficult to break contact, especially because, even though he had trouble making himself understood, he still didn't seem unwell to me—not with the kind of symptoms Doug had warned me about.

In fact Bart *had* gotten sick—we all had—after Thanksgiving, but

2. I soon got an invitation to it from Chandra in marketing, and a forward from Vera; I deleted both unread.

just for the weekend: one last parting gift from that charming evening. Although actually, I did get something of a real parting gift. When we'd recovered, the week I was hauling boxes from the Dictionary, my grandparents took me to a slightly stilted lunch with my mother and made me take some money. (At the lunch I voiced my worry that they might all have the language virus. "Maybe from your strange friend," my grandmother said, and I had to concede the possibility—or that they'd gotten it from me. They ignored my suggestion that they get rid of their Memes but told me they'd already collected antivirals when they'd seen the doctor for food poisoning.)

In theory, my grandparents beamed me money because they worried how I'd manage, "now that you're, you know, on your own." I.e., no longer the potential future bride of An Impressive Young Man. But in truth I think they'd been a little shamed by Bart, aphasic or not, and this was the way they knew to make amends.

And that was maybe the real reason it was hard for me to excise Bart from my life. At Thanksgiving I'd seen a different side of him. In fact, ever since Doug had gone missing, I'd started seeing different sides of Bart all the time. I'd started actually *seeing* him—perceiving who he was. And it made me look at my own reflection more closely, too. Many things seemed new through his eyes, or mine imagining what his saw.

Over those two weeks, though, Bart's inability to speak didn't resolve; he only thought it had. He refused all my offers to go with him to a clinic or to take my medicine. But it wasn't only his aphasia that worried me; it was his new affiliation with Hermes and Synchronic. And with a very heavy heart, I finally started putting more distance between us. Especially after a conversation with Rodney made my worries far starker.

It was exactly one week after Thanksgiving, and I was leaving the Dictionary late, after eight p.m. I was exhausted, sticky with dust from Doug's and my things, packing and moving. The process had been excruciating and also slow—I'd been looking for information and clues, including anything that might help me decipher Doug's "OXIDP" bipartite note.

Rodney was working security, and I was relieved to see him—it had been since Bart and I had met him at the Midtown North Precinct the previous Tuesday, and I'd been worried he'd had ongoing trouble with police. I was glad to see him, too, because I wanted to talk to him about the night Doug had gone missing.

When I approached the desk with a weary smile, I was surprised to see his arm in a blue cloth sling—why he hadn't been in to work for a few days, he explained, lifting it. "But, matter of fact, not sure how much longer I've got left around here," he said, sighing.

"What? Why?" I asked, aggrieved. "Not Synchronic?" And reluctantly, hesitating, he dipped his chin. But it didn't make sense—he worked for the building, not the *NADEL*.

I asked how much longer he was on for the night, if I could maybe walk him to the train when he was done. Subtly, he cut his eyes around the empty lobby. Rubbed the back of his neck where the blue strap bit in. Wiggled his fingers, grimacing. "Yeah, okay," he finally said with another tight nod. "Darryl takes over in half an hour."

When I met back up with him, we bundled ourselves against the cold, stopped for coffees at a kiosk plastered with a Future Is Now ad, and ambled to Columbus Circle. But instead of heading toward the subway, Rodney led me into Central Park, glancing over his shoulder several times until we were under the dark cover of some trees, our backs to the trunk of one of them. Then he told a story that peeled me away from myself.

He'd been walking across the north end of the park, he said, on his way to Thanksgiving at his sister's, when a man had stopped him to ask the time. "I knew there'd be trouble," Rodney muttered. "I'd seen that man before." But he'd been loaded down with gifts for his grandnephews, and he wasn't prepared when the man pulled a knife. He thought at first it was a robbery, but when the man spoke, it was to tell Rodney that he'd better stop talking to the cops. That he hadn't seen what he thought he'd seen on November 16—the night Doug had vanished. No security recordings had gone missing, the man claimed. And Rodney didn't recognize anyone he'd seen enter the building.

As Rodney explained all this, a rolling boil filled my ears. "Who was the man?" I said.

And Rodney replied, "Real big guy." Used his unharmed arm to mark a place well above his head. "Thick accent. Russian dude, I think."

The edges of my vision blanched. I was having trouble hearing him. But in my mind's ear I heard clearly enough: Dmitri Sokolov. The man

I'd encountered, alone, in the Dictionary subbasement. *Under no cir-cumstances,* Doug's letter had read. *If he should contact you—well, let's hope he doesn't.* I took a jagged breath. "Do you know why he attacked you?" I asked. "The recordings—what was on them?"

Rodney asked me to repeat the question. I did, shivering, and at first he started to say he hadn't really seen much. But then he shook his head. Rubbed the back of his neck again. Admitted, "I just had a real bad feeling that night." Looking to his left and right, he started to tell me what had happened: "Some men came in. This was around six-thirty, six-forty-five. I think you'd left a little while earlier. And these men, they said they had a meeting with your dad. I didn't like the look of them— one had dark glasses on inside, and this was night—and they wouldn't sign in or give ID. I told them, 'Sorry, gentlemen. It's our policy.' But the one with the glasses, short guy, he said, 'This is crazy. I'm not doing it,' and on like that. 'Absurd' was the word he used. Then he called your dad himself and gave the—the phone to me. And Mr. J said go ahead, let them in." Here Rodney paused. Looked at me with what I thought was regret; it was hard to tell in the dark. "I didn't like to do it," he said. Sighed. "I did not like to do it. But I did. And then, in the elevator . . ." He trailed off. Massaged his arm gently.

I held my breath.

After a moment he continued. "This same man"—here Rodney lifted his sling—"he was with them. And I saw him laugh. Watched it on the monitor. One of them pointed at him. Said something. And the man did like this." Rodney drew a finger across his throat. Cold crawled over me, and I tightened my coat. "Could have just been messing around," Rod-ney went on. "But I called up to Mr. J to ask did he want me or Darryl to come to twenty. He must've left his desk already to meet them, though. And he was expecting them and everything. So I thought, *Okay then, that's all right. Mr. J must know what's going on.*" Rodney coughed. Again shook his head. "But I did, I had that bad feeling," he said. "And then, after they left and you came back by looking for your dad, and you didn't find him . . . I didn't want to scare you," he said. "But later, at the precinct, I tried to tell Mr. Tate."

My throat had constricted. I couldn't feel my face. But I kept my voice even. "And did you figure out who these men were?"

"Not all," Rodney said. "Not right away. But there was one . . ." He stopped talking for a moment. Shifted his weight uncomfortably. "He used to visit you sometimes," he said softly, looking at the ground.

My skin prickled with fire. I flashed back to the night Doug disappeared and to what I'd thought had been just a ghost of Max, floating down Broadway in a black suit. I felt sick.

Rodney explained that he'd looked Max up later on the Internet and had identified a few Synchronic employees. Some of whom he'd seen that very day, going in and out of the lobby.

I had just one more question. I had to repeat it, too. But even the second time I asked, it was clear that he'd never seen or heard of the Creatorium.

"The what?" he said, cupping his unhurt hand around his ear.

I shook my head. "Never mind." Then I thanked him and gave him a gentle half-hug, trying not to hurt his arm. Cautiously we parted ways, Rodney leaving first, then me.

I was very careful, before entering my building, to make sure no one was lurking nearby. And after I locked my door, I retrieved *The Canon of Judo* from the collapsed box. Upset and exhausted as I was, I started quietly practicing falls, kata, falls, for over an hour. Then push-ups, sit-ups, and more falls before finally falling into bed, spent, near midnight.

If I had doubts about my new regimen when I woke up bruised and sore the next morning, they soon dissipated. After talking to Rodney, I started to feel like I was being followed. My buzzer rang at odd hours. And a few times in the street I thought I sensed someone watching me. Every man in black began to put me on edge. (In New York they were hard to avoid.) Once, after taking files from the Dictionary to Doug's apartment on the Upper West Side, I came back down to the lobby and the doorman asked, "He get you?"

"Get me?" I said, scalp tightening. "Who?"

"The guy who was outside. Arrived right after you. Said he didn't want me to tar up—he'd just try your phone." When I asked the doorman to describe him, he said, "I don't know. Just some guy. I've seen him around."

Cold slid down the back of my neck. I paid a taxi to drive me around for an hour, fake a few stops while I crouched on the floor. After that I didn't go back to Doug's. I relayed the conversation to Officer Maroney, and he put an unmarked car on my block.

But I refused to stay inside, a fearful prisoner in a tiny apartment gummed up with the grease of bad memories. I was hamstrung by the impossible task of trying to investigate while avoiding the Internet and phone, with no Meme,[3] and vetting all my calls. I was determined to find my dad. Or find out what had happened to him.

Which is how I started to encounter different members of the Diachronic Society. In fact, I'd seen a few of them already.

They're a motley group—different backgrounds and ages. Many are older than me: former booksellers and librarians; teachers; writers, editors, and agents; publishers and publicists; lexicographers and linguists. But there are also younger members: translators and poets, critics and readers, devotees of old zines. And the reasons they've expressed for getting involved are equally diverse. Some have conveyed a feeling of exile from a way of life that no longer exists. Others, a sense of duty. A fondness for rule-breaking. Activist or anticorporate bents. Some say they joined for the esprit de corps, others that they're concerned for public health. What they hold in common is a dedication to words, and the worlds these open up. They also share an enmity to anything that might threaten language.

Many—not all—have a preference for print. None use Memes. They communicate in person, by phone or email, sometimes by letter and postcard, fax, graffiti, posters, handbills. (Some also occasionally send messages by pneumatic tube.) No one knows exactly how many there are. Maybe several hundred in New York, maybe more; the core membership is at least several dozen. And there are some in other cities, too, in the U.S. and abroad. Of course there are more and less dedicated members, and their numbers wax and wane. Some keep their affiliation secret; others present their ideas in open and direct ways. This was especially true after the virus appeared and started spreading.

One of the first I spoke to I'd already seen—a little more than a week before, I'd taken a pamphlet from him without reading it and dropped it in a Times Square trash bin, with bent cigarette butts and paper plates gone gray with grease. I lived just a few blocks from Times Square, but I tried to stay away if I could. I'd gone to see Jesmyn, though, in Jackson

3. I still had Doug's Aleph, but I'd locked it away in a large, plaid, rolling suitcase that I'd shoved under the bed. I'd taken the Aleph out a few times and flicked through, but without finding anything new.

Heights—she was flying home to Oakland; one of her sisters had gotten very, very sick with what they were afraid was the virus—and I was walking back from the 7 train when I saw the man again. He had a thick stack of red pamphlets and was standing in almost the same spot I'd first seen him, at Forty-second and Eighth. This time he didn't seem as tired; he was chanting as he handed papers to passersby, "Memes kill! Stop the spread of word flu!" And this time I didn't ignore him.

His name was Rob. He was an affable retired English teacher with a runner's build and a long gray ponytail, and he was sensitive, he said, to cold. That's why he had on such a heavy coat. But when he mentioned his coat, it wasn't its heaviness I took note of; I saw that odd symbol I'd been noticing: Ø. It was printed on white cloth and pinned to his lapel.

"It means not infected," he explained. "So people will know it's okay to talk to me."

"Where'd you get it?" I asked, puzzled. The media had only started to report on the virus that week. With growing intensity, it was true. But it still seemed strange.

"Nowhere," he said. "I made it." But he was squinting at me a little warily, and I didn't know whether it was because he didn't like the question or I'd said something aphasic. It made me very jumpy; I checked again, as I'd been doing constantly, to make sure my pills were still in my pocket. Wondered, as I had several times, if I should start a second course of treatment. Soon after that Rob shrugged me off. He had to go back to work, he said.

When I got home, I read the pamphlet word for word. It didn't say much I hadn't heard. But it did claim that Memes were vectors of the virus—the first time I'd seen the accusation outright. More importantly, though, its rhetoric was very familiar: I recognized it from the *Times* op-ed; I'd heard it from Doug for years, and also by then from Dr. Thwaite. Over the next couple days I tried texting and calling Phineas, and I left several messages. I even tried visiting, twice. Both times the doorman turned me away, claiming that he wasn't in.

During the second week after Thanksgiving I extended the radius of my search—from Union Square to Zuccotti Park, from up near Columbia to down by NYU, under Atlantic Terminal, and over to the Merc[4]— and I stockpiled many more brochures. Once I started looking for the

4. That's how I'd found the window note explaining that it was closed.

Diachronic Society, its members were less difficult to find than one might think. I ended up meeting nearly two dozen even before the Merc reopened, crisscrossing the city in my search for them when I wasn't checking on family and friends or at the Dictionary. Watching all the time for whoever might be watching me.

I met Archie Rodriguez, a former college librarian and stay-at-home dad with two kids; Tommy Keach, who put together the zine *Best* out of his Chelsea recording studio; Martha Hertzberg, a Juilliard-trained pianist and poet who was about my age; Zheng Weiming, a bioethicist and translator of Chinese and French short stories; Winifred Brown, a retired executive with a penchant for old print books and magazines; Matt Falstaff and Mara Levy, NYU sophomores. They were among the volunteers who spent hours standing in the cold, putting themselves at risk. Trying to save the rest of us.

Some of those passing out leaflets called to bystanders; some didn't. Some simply left bundles of papers in the train and other busy public places. Most wore the Ø on their clothes, along with cotton masks and earplugs or massive headphones that bulged like the eyes of insects. Their precautions seemed to work: none appeared to have the virus.

Maybe as a result, not all were very eager to talk to me, especially when I asked about Doug. Some seemed to believe I was his daughter and expressed concern that he was still gone. A few said they hadn't heard of him. If any knew his whereabouts, none confessed. And no one had any idea what OXIDP meant. Several seemed to grow suspicious when I mentioned Doug's name; a handful even asked if I worked for Synchronic.

Regardless, though, of how willing Society members were to talk to me, they all handed over whatever pamphlets they carried. One, printed on red paper, had the header "NAUTILUS KILLS."[5] (It was clear that the anonymous author hadn't actually seen a Nautilus; the leaflet described something conical, "about the size of a saucer," outfitted with at least one tiny needle.) An excerpt follows:

The device Synchronic plans to release, with much fanfare, on December 7 may seem completely new. It was actually

5. After I read that brochure, I started seeing this phrase pervasively, especially sprayed on Nautilus billboards.

developed years ago—even before the Meme. It might in fact predate Synchronic's forgotten Aleph model, according to sources close to the company. When the Nautilus prototype was put together, executives apparently decided that the public wasn't ready yet for such an invasive machine. They opted to launch the Meme instead, to groom consumers, while they continued developing and testing their prized flagship device at labs in the United States and overseas—including in Beijing, where the first cases of word flu surfaced in 2016.

Another handbill, "ARE YOU A SLAVE TO MEANING MASTER?," was printed on stock the green of old paper money. It described a game that had exploded in prominence since its release in early November. Part of Meaning Master's appeal, the authors speculated, was in how deceptively simple it was to "win": players simply strung together random letters to make "words," then gave them "meanings." It was repetitive, bright, and aesthetically pleasing, and those who created the most popular words each week got small cash rewards and a modicum of recognition. But another reason for its surging success, the pamphlet insinuated, was that it might also be psychologically addictive for Meme users. Although even non-Meme players seemed more than usually devoted. (The average number of rounds played in a single sitting was supposedly near forty.)

Profits, the brochure explained, were derived from "ad revenues; point-of-purchase sales (downloads are $5.99); subscriptions ($2.99/ month after the first month 'free'); add-ons (if you want a definition assigned to a new word, for instance, instead of having to invent your own, they're 9¢ each); etc." But the *real* money the game was generating for Synchronic, the authors claimed, came from increased sales on the Exchange—a correlation they didn't explicate.

A brochure Weiming gave me was far more disturbing. It was about the *NADEL* and included a photo, taken a few years earlier, of Doug in his office, smiling, surrounded by piles of paper, his hair and beard a little wild. It pressed a bruise on my heart. The caption, though, elicited a very different response: "Contrary to rumor, Dr. Douglas Johnson, the *NADEL*'s Chief Editor, has had nothing to do with the creation or dissemination of the so-called word flu, nor with the corruption of his Dictionary," I read. Obviously I wanted to know what all that was supposed to mean. And Weiming weathered my storm of questions with kindness and equanimity. Then he explained that he hadn't written it and didn't know much more than I did.

There were also blue pamphlets outlining advice on preventing and reversing the language virus. Those I found strewn everywhere: cafés, park benches, sidewalks. (Not so many being read, alas.) Many of the suggestions were the kind of commonsense advice doled out during other virus scares: to wash hands, cough into sleeves, wear masks, visit the doctor at the earliest sign of serious symptoms. But it was also the first mention I saw of language therapy, and one tip it included for those recovering from word flu was to read.

I'd already been following that advice inadvertently each night after I got home—taking different routes, trying to make sure no one was behind me, checking my block for the unmarked cop car before carefully locking myself in. I'd read books of Doug's I'd taken from his office as I searched futilely for references to OXIDP, but also my own old books and magazines. Ever since the night Bart had stayed over, I'd been revisiting them. (We were speaking less and less often by then, but they'd started to be linked in my thoughts with him.) And even before I picked up that blue pamphlet, I found that reading gave me a certain relief—one form of escapism that seemed safe, and maybe more than safe. I felt saner—less fragmented—after reading for an hour.

On December 5, the day the Merc reopened—a Wednesday, the same day of the week I'd seen Dr. Thwaite skulk into his secret meeting—I ventured east with a sense of resolve and something like destiny. Feelings that derived at least in part from desperation. Nearly three weeks had passed since Doug had gone missing, and I wasn't any closer to finding him, despite spending nearly all my time looking. I was very close to giving up.

It was the middle of the afternoon, the air so cold that my breath froze. Bright spears of light stung my eyes. I nodded to the officer in the squad car across the street, then walked the four wide avenue blocks to the library, glancing behind me as I went.

The city had changed for the holidays. As I passed the Rockefeller Center Christmas tree and glyphs of Rockettes, mothers towing toddlers to cafés by their mittens, windows graffitied with spotty snow and wreaths, and shoppers strolling arm in arm down Fifth, it was possible to believe for the length of my walk that everything was fine. I stopped for a hot dog at Forty-seventh Street. "Here's your dog, doll," the vendor said. "Keep smiling." Every word perfectly clear, composed, like the shop window behind him, reflecting us back.

There was no mistaking the Mercantile Library: its name was chiseled right into the stone, below the bank of third-floor windows. Two carts of marked-down books were on sale outside, and an urn carved above the door seemed hopeful to me then, a symbol not of death but immortality. The timelessness of words.

As I stepped into the warm, dim anteroom, any mantle of worry lifted. Unbuttoning my coat, I walked past a pair of leather couches, a wall of books. At the reference desk my eye caught a sign announcing meetings of societies for Proust, Trollope, Musil. Johnson. I thought of Doug, and in that moment the thought made me smile.

But the librarian didn't seem amused. "May I help you?" she asked coolly, tapping her seal-slick hair. Pretty pale hands extruded from dark cardigan sleeves. I'd forgotten the Merc was a private library.

I tried to keep smiling; when she asked if I was a member, I thought my lie sounded almost sincere. And at least she didn't ask me to repeat it. (My fingers still reflexively felt in my pocket for my tube of pills.) But she wanted to see my card. When I patted artlessly at my coat, she asked, unbending, for ID, indicating their registry—a large wooden cabinet with tiny drawers: a card catalog, I later learned. "I don't have that either," I said. Her mouth scalloped in a scowl. But when I explained that I'd just given up my Meme and hadn't gotten around to procuring a new form of identity, she sighed and slid a clipboard toward me. "Don't forget next time," she said.

I wavered just a moment before signing *Alice Tate*. Blushing, I realized I'd taken Bart's last name. It gave me a flashback to lower school, in the days before the Meme—before most lower schoolers even had cell phones—and to scribbling pages of *Anana Ringwald* and *Tobey Johnson,* my name and my crush's conjoined. Did my subconscious think I wanted to be Anana Tate? I shook my head. Those weren't the feelings I had. Bart either.

I climbed the first stairs I saw, an open metal flight that took me to a mezzanine reading room. It resembled my grandparents' parlor in their Connecticut country house. Same high ceilings and table sheen.

Herringbone floors. Baubled chandeliers. Musky smell of old leather. I sloughed off my coat on a chair by the Johnson collection, near the baby grand. Imagined Doug beneath it, snoring a sweet, humble music, and my eyes pricked.[6]

I thought I was alone. But soon, as I looked around the room, I heard an unusual sound coming from a hidden corner. The jangly melody of metal on metal. As if a janitor were walking by with a bouquet of keys.

Curious, I strode to the other end of the room, pretending to need an atlas beached on a table, and found that the odd sound was coming from a woman's gold bangles, which lightly bubbled together each time she turned a page. She looked like she was taking a break from Fifth Avenue: large sunglasses perched on shoeshine-black hair; white turtleneck; tweed skirt; spike-heeled knee-high boots. She looked not unlike my mother, actually. And she was studying me with a judgment-fringed intensity worthy of Vera.

Marking her page with a slender finger, she watched me hoist the atlas—which was smudged and greasy, as if it had last been used by a mechanic—and carry it back across the room. I dropped it with a smack onto a leather ottoman. When I opened it, a skinny paperback—some sort of index—fell out. I didn't take much note at the time. Just jammed it back in and flipped desultorily through the dirty atlas. Turned to the map of Iceland, which was the pale beige of a cornflake. Scratched Reykjavík with a ragged nail.

Dad, where are you? I thought, my throat burning with grief. I missed him very much. And for a moment, a sinker of sadness dropping in my stomach, I started to worry that I might not find anything at the Merc either. But then I heard the distant chime of the woman's bracelets. Felt the itch of her invisible, critical gaze. And my anodyne resignation slipped away. In its place my resolve expanded again. I went back downstairs.

I managed not to react too strangely when the librarian referred to me as Ms. Tate, or when she noted, a little sternly, that she'd checked the rolls and found no record of me.

---

6. Once when I was young he made a fort with me beneath the Steinway in that Connecticut house. We used the cushions of my grandparents' couch and blankets from one of the guest beds, and had tea and cookies underneath. Then I rested my head on his bouncing stomach while he read *Wind in the Willows* aloud. We fell asleep, and woke to my grandmother screeching, "What deranged person would put my cushions on the *floor?*"

"What about Douglas Johnson?" I asked, emboldened.

"What about him?" she said. I thought I saw her eyelids tighten.

"What if I said I'm his daughter?" I asked. Thought, *Wood and glue*. She tipped her head slightly to one side. "Are you?"

I dropped my chin. I also mentioned Vera's name, which was evidently familiar to her. After a last scrutinous stare, she said, "All right. I think Douglas has a family membership. If you're his daughter, I'll write you a card."

Relieved and appreciative, I smiled. But when I asked her, as casually as I could, if she could remind me what time the Diachronic Society meeting would start, she looked very doubtful again. She had no idea what I was talking about, she said. She said it very credibly. I repeated myself. But she firmly shook her head.

For a moment I lingered at the desk in doubt. Wondered if I should wait at the Merc until nighttime to see if any Society members I recognized arrived. Yet I wondered, too, if I'd made the whole thing up. It was a thought I almost couldn't abide—the meeting had come to represent something absolute to me. A last threshold. I didn't want to cross it.

But as I stood there hesitating, head swimming a little, I knew it was very possible, and even likely, that it had been a final, wishful invention. Steadying myself on the edge of the desk, trying to think what to do next, I thanked the librarian. Started to turn toward the exit. Then I heard footsteps clatter above, a light clanging at the top of the stairs, and a woman's voice called down, "Anana?"

When I climbed back up to the mezzanine, the dark-haired woman was waiting.

"So you're Douglas's daughter," she said, with a faint, hard-to-place lilt. "I thought you might be." She held out her elegant hand. "Victoria Mark," she said. And with a start, I realized I knew her—at least her name. She'd been an editor for Vaber, Ingmar, & Breuer before they'd closed their dictionary, and she'd become one of Doug's most trusted contributors at the *NADEL*.

"It's so nice to finally meet you," I said.

"You, too," she replied, face furrowing kindly. Lowering her voice, she explained that the meeting wouldn't start until seven, up on the fourth floor. Then she gathered her things, donned and belted her coat. "See you tonight," she said softly, and clacked away.

I decided to stay there, cocooned in safe, quiet calm. The occasional

click emanating from the librarian's desk below. In the afternoon an
older man appeared, an ancient yellow newspaper blooming from under
his arm, and silently read in a nearby chair. The soothing rustle of pages
reminded me of Doug. Eventually, stomach hissing, I went in search of
food.

I returned in plenty of time and took the stairs up to four. My heart
lurched as I opened the door. But it was deserted. Lights out. Stacks
empty. No recent litter in the trash. The woman, it seemed, had lied. I
was wondering why—was she a friend of Dr. Thwaite's? Did she just not
like the look of me, or something I'd said?—as I stepped back into the
hall. And nearly collided with Phineas.

As he braced himself, his hand went to his head. Which was covered
by a red hat. "Alice," he said, startled. "What are you doing here?"

But I didn't even have time to remind him that he'd been the one to
tell me about the meetings; more people were coming up the stairs—
including Victoria Mark, who squeezed my arm and smiled. "I thought
you told us Douglas wanted her here," she said, winking. Dr. Thwaite's
mouth fell open slightly. To me she said, "I was just on my way to find
you—there are so many of us tonight, we're meeting up on six." As she
continued past us, Dr. Thwaite watched her disappear. Then, still silent,
he plucked off his red cap, hair a white firebrand of static, and with the
other hand gestured at the stairs. "After you," he murmured.

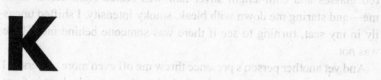

K

king \'kiŋ\ *n* **1** : a high card < ~ of hearts> **2** : the one holding the cards

The meeting room we shuffled into was bright, overheated, and crowded. A card table crammed with samovar, coffee urn, and dusty cookies governed the sole corner not lined with books. A curtained window rattled, letting in a draft. A hive of fluorescents buzzed above. More than twenty mismatched chairs were pinched into a circle, and several people stood.

Dr. Thwaite hurried for a plush brocade, leaving me stranded at the door. But Victoria Mark tapped the metal chair beside her, rings clacking with the archaic sound of chalk on a blackboard. Being affirmed by her seemed to grant instant credibility; several strangers turned to look at me with friendly curiosity.

But as I sat, shrugging off my coat and glancing around the room, I discovered that Victoria and Dr. Thwaite weren't the only people I knew. A few chairs to my left I saw the crooked smile and frizzy amber curls of Clara Strange, from Bart's department at the Dictionary. She waved. To her right was elegant, white-blond Tommy Keach, one of the pamphleteers I'd met on the street; there were several others. And on Clara's left was the older man I'd seen reading the paper on the mezzanine. "Franz," he said gruffly, leaning across the circle to extend a warm, onionskin hand. "Garfinkel?" I asked, amazed. Franz Garfinkel was a god of lexicography. He nodded, more astonished than I was at being recognized, grim face crumpling into a smile.

I also saw a stranger I'd been noticing around lately. The woman with red glasses and chin-length silver hair was seated right across from me—and staring me down with bleak, smoky intensity. I shifted uneasily in my seat, turning to see if there was someone behind me. There was not.

And yet another person's presence threw me off even more. A person I wasn't very glad to see. Across the circle, long legs stretched out in front of him and working to prop up a silver-handled cane, was Max's business partner and friend Vernon Peach. It had taken me a few moments to notice him; his signature glasses were peeking from his shirt pocket instead of perched on his face. Despite the room's heat, he also had a black watch cap tugged tightly down and a gray scarf looped around his neck. As if trying to go incognito. When I did finally see him, I felt a flurry in my chest. I'd always liked Vernon. But I'd seen none of Max's friends since he'd moved out, and it made me anxious. Not least because he was a Synchronic employee.

But he quickly caught my eye and smiled. "Hi, Anana," he mouthed. "So good to see you." Pressed a hand to his heart. And a lump surprised me by rising in my throat. "You, too," I mouthed back, swallowing hard.

By then the meeting had been called to order, and Victoria was introducing me. The people I didn't know gave their names. Except the woman in red glasses, who was still glowering. It was Victoria who explained that she was Susan Janowitz, also once of VIB.

Then Susan confused me by sharply saying, "I expected her much sooner."

Someone mumbled, "Renovations," and I saw Victoria's eyes dart to Dr. Thwaite, but she just said, "It doesn't matter. We're glad you're here now, Anana. Susan is just . . ."

"Susan is just what?" Susan said. Crossed her thin arms.

Victoria placed a gentle hand on Susan's knee. Then said that as I'd already guessed, this was a meeting of the Diachronic Society. "Most of us are colleagues," she offered. Then amended, "Former colleagues." Adjusted her gold bracelets. "We've been holding these meetings for a long time now. First as the Samuel Johnson Society—"

"Or the *Douglas* Johnson Society," a dark-haired man I didn't recognize said, and laughed. It struck me as oddly tone-deaf and unkind, especially after I'd just been introduced. But when he saw he was the only one laughing, he quickly quieted, and Victoria carried on.

"During the years when we were the Samuel Johnson Society," she said, "our meetings were largely attended by lexicographers and Johnson enthusiasts. We discussed his *Dictionary* and letters and essays. Occasionally a biography. But mostly the meetings gave us a chance to talk about the pleasures—and the difficulties—of still working in publishing."

Difficulties that quickly proliferated as time went on, Clara Strange chimed in, especially with the rise of Synchronic—buying up terms for the Exchange, precipitating the closure of many dictionaries, and maybe even publishers. Synchronic's monolithic online limn store put a lot of pressure on the price of books.

Victoria nodded gravely. "Over the past few years, all of our lives have changed quite dramatically." Many had lost jobs, she said. Several had been forced to leave New York. "They couldn't afford it anymore," she explained, hand rising to her throat. "They had to go back to their home countries, where it's still possible to make something of a living working with words."

"Pavel," Franz angrily muttered. "And Yuki."

Victoria inhaled sharply, closing her eyes. The dark glasses balanced on her hair reflected the crosshatchings of the overheads and made her look like a stately, lethal insect.

"So as all that began to happen," Vernon said, picking up the thread, "the focus of the meetings shifted." He leaned back in his chair. Crossed his extensive legs at the ankle. "We talked about Synchronic nearly every week—that became our new focus, making sure the public knows what they're up to." He seemed impartial, and I wondered how. As a founding partner of Hermes, why didn't he sound defensive?

He clearly noticed my confusion. "Anana, you don't know what a fierce apologist I used to be for Synchronic," he said, shaking his head.

He'd come to his first meeting a couple years earlier on a lark, he explained, as a Johnson scholar, when it was still mainly a literary group. Enchanted by the characters he'd found—"He means Luddites," Dr. Thwaite interjected; "Weirdos," Franz expounded, quivering his hands—he kept coming back. Slowly, as complaints about Synchronic's tactics took up more and more of each meeting's agenda, Vernon initially felt duty-bound to defend the company's "new vision" for language: making it "accessible," "easy," and "fun." That aim overlapped with what he and Max and the others had been doing at Hermes.

"In the beginning I kept saying that there was every reason to believe the Exchange would only expand people's vocabularies—any word they might need was always right at their fingertips."

"But not," Franz noted, "in their brains."

Vern had argued that to insist on old lexicographic methods was naive—reactionary, even. "People want their words *now*," he'd said at the time. "They don't want to have to work so hard for them. They want entertainment and learning integrated. What's so wrong with that?" What's wrong, the Society's members had replied, is that it wasn't how it's done. Vernon had rolled his eyes. "See, *this* is why you guys are getting left behind," he'd said.

It had been Doug who'd convinced him, over months, that there was more to it than Vernon thought. Not just dragged feet and a few lost jobs. "You're restructuring supply lines," he'd said. "Understand? Once you go down that road, you can't go back again. The road's gone." "Like that invisible bridge in *The Last Crusade*," Vernon had teased. But Doug wouldn't joke with him, which was sobering.

Moving all our words onto one consolidated exchange, changing the way we use and access language, through Memes—it wasn't just affecting our economy or culture, Doug had explained. The technology was actually rewiring people's brains. Changing neuronal pathways and reward systems. They were forgetting things, or not learning them in the first place. And if we didn't really have a shared, communal language—if we had nothing but a provisional relationship with words, a leaseholder's agreement—what would happen, Doug had asked Vernon, if something went wrong? If, God forbid, there was a cyberattack on Exchange servers and language "went down"? How would we communicate then? A point he'd underscored by reminding all of them about the computer virus that had more or less shut down the whole island of Taiwan for close to six months a couple of years earlier. Annoyed, Vernon had argued that Synchronic had the best firewalls money could buy. "Better than yours," he'd shot back at Doug. "Probably," Doug had responded grimly.

"Eventually I just . . . couldn't really defend them anymore," Vernon said, absently tapping his cane. "Especially when more and more friends"—he nodded at the room—"started being negatively affected by their policies. And then I started seeing things—at Hermes, and later Synchronic—that I found pretty alarming." Things like negligible oversight, shady contracts, breaches in security, changes to the game of Meaning Master that didn't seem quite ethical or legal, deals with foreign partners whom Vernon had his doubts about.

"But when we decided on our name, the Diachronic Society," he went on, "it wasn't meant only as a sort of jab at Synchronic. It was really more of an homage to diachronism."

"Taking the long view," Clara Strange offered.

"Connecting with the labor," added Franz, making a hoop in the air with his hands.

"Doing things 'analog,' as my daughter would say," offered a man whose name I hadn't caught.

"Leaving a paper trail," said Tommy Keach.

"Which is why these meetings have recently become more secretive," Victoria explained. "And why everything we say here is confidential. Leaving a paper trail isn't always very safe, depending on what those papers say. Some members have made the very brave and deliberate choice to share what information we've collected publicly. But we'd like to keep that a choice for everyone. Especially as some of us have received explicit threats." She glanced at Dr. Thwaite, who pretended not to see. I wondered what that look was meant to say. I thought of Rodney, and of the squad car on my block. I also couldn't help but think of Doug, who'd just been spoken of so much. And who wasn't there.

I cleared my throat. My heart was beating painfully. "I know a lot of you," I began, my eyes traveling around the crowded room. "Some of you I've just met. And I hope you'll forgive me for repeating myself, because I've already asked most of you this question. But I've spent the past three weeks looking for my father. And there's nothing I want more than to find out where he is. But at this point"—and here I, too, let my attention settle on Dr. Thwaite—"I just want to confirm that he's—he's still okay. So if any of you know anyth—"

"He's fine," Dr. Thwaite cut in abruptly. His eyes shooting, for some reason, to Susan.

"Phineas," Victoria said darkly. "You haven't told her?"

"Told me what?" I asked. Tiny white dots started sparkling in my vision.

"That he's talked to your father," Clara hurriedly explained, curls gently quaking. "And he really is okay, don't worry—Phineas, tell her— just at an 'undisclosed location.'"

But Dr. Thwaite was still staring silently at Susan, who was staring back with equal intensity from behind her red glasses.

And before I could ask what was going on, my phone began to ring.

"Sorry," I mumbled, groping at my coat. And I kept apologizing—everyone was watching—until I'd finally turned it off. I saw that the caller was Bart, and that I'd somehow missed two other calls from him.

Susan turned her stern gaze back to me. "We don't allow phones," she said coldly.

I knew some people were afraid the virus could be transmitted that way. I nodded, but then I continued on. "The reason I've been even more worried lately about my dad"—and myself, I didn't add—"is that I heard a story last week that was really pretty frightening."

After what Victoria had just said about receiving threats, I felt compelled to tell them what had happened to Rodney, although I didn't use his name. As I spoke, the tensile energy of focused listening filled the room. "And this same man who stabbed my friend I-I saw him," I said shivering. "The night after my father went missing."

The room's silence took on a different quality, as if changing from amber to red. Then Susan, her face flushing slightly, said, "Tell us what you mean."

Which is how I found myself describing what I'd seen that night in the Creatorium: the disassembly line; the furnace; the workers with their strange coils (Nautiluses, several Society members confirmed); "paradox" vanishing from our corpus. I confessed that I'd gotten sick after using the foreman's device but quickly added that I'd taken a course of treatment. And for the first time since I told it—to Bart, and later to the police—no one seemed to doubt what I said. Which I almost regretted. Because when I looked at Dr. Thwaite, he was extremely white. In a strangled voice, he said, "This is very serious."

"Why?" I asked, shivering again. "What does it mean?"

"Mean?" Dr. Thwaite said, a little stridently.

The dark-haired man who'd started off the meeting with the flat joke about Doug broke in. "I think the Chinese mafia is involved—or the government. Maybe the Russians."

"Involved? In what?" I asked, trying not to sound too incredulous or judgmental.

"Please," Franz said, raising his big hands. "We don't know who the partners of Synchronic might be. Let us not make assumptions."

"Come *on*," the man jeered, eyes bulging slightly. "You think it's a *coincidence* all those workers were Russian and Chinese?"

"They weren't all. They were—"

"I'm not saying it's the *workers'* fault," the man continued, talking over me. "I'm just saying, let's use our heads, for Christ's sakes. Doesn't this remind anyone else of the Russian-Georgian cyberconflict back in '08? Or, I don't know, the attack on Taiwan in 2016?"

"But that was just a computer virus," I cut in again. I remembered it well—the many patches we'd had to implement after.

"It wasn't just a computer virus," Rob responded, pulling his long gray ponytail over his shoulder. "It was a large-scale, ongoing cyberattack. Devices that got infected with the virus were recruited into botnets and used to stage assaults on more secure networks."

I'd read that in one of the Society's pamphlets, but I didn't see the connection. "That may be," I said. "But that's not what's happening here—"

"Yet," Rob softly interrupted.

"—where we have people getting aphasia, getting really sick. Some of them dying. That didn't happen in Taiwan."

"That was before Taiwan had the Meme," Clara said ominously.

"And actually," Archie Rodriguez added, leaning forward to rest his elbows on his fleshy knees, "there are a lot of rumors about a handful of deaths that happened around the same time in Beijing, maybe also Taipei. That those were the first cases of word flu."

The room filled again with a cold, biting silence. I felt confused and a little queasy. How, I wondered, was a computer virus—zeroes and ones— supposed to be killing people? What did it have to do with the *NADEL*? And why would Synchronic, one of the most profitable companies in the world, be in any way involved?

No one had answers to my first two questions, or so they claimed. And at the last one I faltered a little, glancing uneasily at Vernon, despite his earlier speech.

"Don't worry," Clara said, reaching behind Franz to grip the back of Vernon's chair. "He's on our side."

Vernon smiled—a little ruefully, I thought. "I don't make a great spy, I'm afraid," he said, latticing his fingers in his lap. "But with Johnny's help I've gathered some circumstantial evidence that the computer virus—I mean the same one that hit Taiwan—might have been created by Synchronic, to try to increase returns for shareholders. At least, they seem to have invented a different one more recently with that goal in mind. But at this point I have no hard proof I could take to the feds."

Rubbing his bad knee and frowning, Vernon began to lay out his case. Bizarrely, he started with Meaning Master.

Max had of course done a very compelling job of pitching the game, Vernon said, not just to Synchronic but to everyone at Hermes, Vern included. The initial idea seemed to be for a fairly standard, almost boring word game, not so different from one they'd developed earlier, called Whorld. But Max had claimed that Meaning Master would in fact make people *reflect* more on the language they used. By minting new coinages, they'd consider words' potential power but also their malleability, how they can be transformed into things of greater or lesser value.

It seemed like a pretty lofty ambition, Vernon admitted, for a two-minute diversion. But Max was never at a loss for inspired rhetoric ("Aka horseshit," Clara interjected), and for a while—especially when Max quoted them some figures of what they could each potentially earn if things went "their way"—it had all sounded somehow plausible, and even virtuous. They knew they should have doubted figures so large—tens of millions, Max had claimed.[1] And they did express some doubts, Vernon maintained, at least among themselves. But when Max contacted Synchronic in March, no one objected.

The first time Max met with Synchronic representatives, he went alone and reported back, ecstatic. "It's exactly what they've been looking for," he claimed, high-fiving them all. The aspect of the game that had intrigued them, apparently, was the idea of making words mean different things—" 'Exchanging' them, if you will," Synchronic's CEO, Steve Brock, had allegedly said with a lurid smirk.

Synchronic didn't care so much for the "meaning stuff," it seemed. Too complicated. They'd rather have players do something else with the second minute of each round. But Max had argued that the meanings were the most crucial part—and whatever he'd said must have been convincing enough: when he got back to Hermes's Red Hook offices that day, he told the guys they'd have to get started developing immediately.

They'd celebrated—the first in a series of blowouts to come. Max seemed to think that if it all went well, Synchronic might buy them out,

1. When Hermes was eventually bought that summer by Synchronic, it was in fact for a quarter-billion dollars.

which had been his goal all along. ("You really think Synchronic would buy your company?" I'd teased him once. I remember his response perfectly; it seems so foreboding now. "I think my company's going to take over Synchronic," he'd replied. And the way he'd said it gave me a chill.) As cork bottles popped and lines of powder were sniffed, the Hermes boys were all pretty elated. But they were also a little confused. After their first sale to Synchronic, years earlier—a voice-activated data-transfer application—they'd worked on a series of more interesting projects that they'd hoped Synchronic would notice. When Max had tried pitching those, he'd gotten a few callbacks from people much lower on the ladder than Steve Brock. But until he'd reached out about Meaning Master, he'd never even been asked in for a meeting.

Vernon claimed that in addition to being a little mystified by Synchronic's interest—"They'd never done a game before, that I know," he explained—he'd been somewhat suspicious fairly early on. "I'd been coming to these meetings for more than a year by then," he said, again tapping his cane on the carpet. "My views on Synchronic had already changed." Part of the reason he'd hoped Max's pitch would stick was that he thought a sale to Synchronic might give him better insight into the company. (Which indeed it did.) But even so, it had taken Vern a while to be actively dubious enough (and nervy enough) to begin investigating anything. "Until maybe early May."

Cautiously, but also without really believing he'd make any strange discoveries, Vern had started asking a few questions, checking records, and talking with Johnny, who was overseeing the game's engineers and designers—and who slowly seemed to be getting cold feet. And bit by bit Vernon started to piece together a hypothesis about how Synchronic, and thus Hermes, hoped to make money from Meaning Master. "Not through subscriptions and ad revenues," he offered obliquely.

"For at least a month, though," he continued, "I still really doubted what I thought I'd found." His theory was both troubling and very odd; it just didn't seem plausible. But the enormous sums of money Synchronic was funneling into Hermes didn't seem quite real either, and yet they were; by the end of summer Vernon's bank account was bulging with more funds than he'd ever imagined it could hold.

When Vern began hearing references to "money words," he initially thought it was just a clever phrase for the fake terms generated by Meaning Master gamers. (These neologisms were expected, after all, to generate lots of profits.) And that *was* what everyone at Hermes called them. But slowly it started to dawn on him that to some people, notably Max and Johnny, "money words" also seemed to mean something else.

Over the years Synchronic hadn't failed to notice (had perhaps in fact nurtured) a tendency in users of their Meme: to forget useful, commonly shared language necessary for all human exchanges—work, diversion, love.[2] (The speed with which a user lost words seemed to rest on a multiplicity of factors: how many languages she spoke; her pre-Meme vocabulary and memory; how deeply engaged she was, on a regular basis, with new ideas and their articulation; how much she used a Meme, etc.)

For Max and Johnny, money words weren't only the random strings of letters spit out by their new game: "tekkis," "nowy," "zyarjing." They were also the words whose meanings had gradually eroded in Meme users' memories: "ambivalent," "irony"; later, things like "bitten" and "clothed." They were a particular subset of words looked up most often on the Exchange and identified with the help of immensely complex algorithms—i.e., slightly abstruse terms that were nonetheless familiar enough to be needed in day-to-day life. These words were called money words because in certain devices—devices, Vern deduced, that had been infected with a new computer virus—they were "exchanged" with made-up neologisms. And this sometimes resulted in sales on the WE.

In the years since the Meme's release, Exchange sales had gradually increased as users encountered more and more words they couldn't recall on websites and Life, in emails, texts, and beams, in "word-processing" documents, and even in speech. But Synchronic had very recently uncovered a way to exploit the process for bigger, quicker earnings.

"What they figured out," Vernon explained, "was that some of the words Meme users forget most often can be replaced, very carefully, with newly invented 'words,' and people don't quite recognize the substitutions as fake. Or they've just begun to doubt themselves so much they're not sure what to think. But they *do* draw a blank, of course—a lot more often than with real words, even the ones they can't really remem-

---

2. This tendency doesn't seem to have particularly concerned Synchronic executives, even vis-à-vis themselves. Some former employees have reported remarks by Brock like "Oh, come on. This is absurd. We've had this silly debate for years. If it does everything I need, what do I care if I know the stuff?"

ber. And just to communicate, they've started downloading meanings of
some of the fabricated terms."

"I don't understand," I said. "They buy fake meanings to fake words?
How does that work? Don't people . . . realize?" But my mouth was dry
and my tongue felt numb. When Vern had described Meme users so
estranged from everyday language that they didn't know what words
they didn't know, I'd had an uncanny vision of myself in the 1 train
with Doug. Sliding my Meme from my pocket after he'd said something
"obscure."

"No, no," Vernon said, shaking his head. "That's the thing. Part of
the reason Synchronic wanted Meaning Master right on the Exchange
website is that they created a program linking artificial words to the
definitions of the *real* words they've replaced. Say 'rain' gets traded
with—I don't know, 'zistrow' or something. When a person gets a pop-
up asking if she wants the meaning of 'zistrow,' she'll see something
like 'water from the sky,' maybe, which would make sense in the context. And she can just continue blithely on, writing, reading, talking,
whatever. Barely even realizing she's downloaded anything."

I could tell from the starched, stoic faces of others in the meeting
that they'd heard this all before and accepted it. But I was finding some
of what Vern said pretty incredible. Other aspects, though, were har-
rowingly believable, and an image of my little silver Meme, buried in a
bedroom drawer, floated for a moment in my brain. I shuddered, feeling
the unwelcome first tendrils of a headache. The overheads began to blur.

As I later learned, many of Vernon's speculations turned out to be
unnervingly accurate. But there were also lots of details he didn't know,
which it would take several more weeks to uncover. Vernon didn't then
quite understand, for instance, the mechanism for exchanges of real
terms with fake ones: that Johnny Lee and his team had modified Sixth
Sense software so that in Memes infected with a new computer virus,
it could seek out and swap money words on and through users' devices.
Vern also didn't know, e.g., that Johnny et al. had logged hundreds of
research hours assessing "confusion thresholds," determining how
many words could be switched before users started to suspect that the
problem was extrinsic to them. (By the time of the Nautilus launch,
the average had climbed to nine per electronic page.)

There was one other thing of which Vern was unaware: that Max
had asked Johnny to design the game with a small idiosyncrasy. Brock

had been very clear with Max: if he let Max keep the "meaning part" of his game, fake definitions were to be completely segregated. He didn't ever want to hear of a Meme user requesting the meaning of an ersatz word and getting a fake "meaning"; that would make her far more likely to doubt not herself but the machine or, worse, the Exchange—and, more broadly, Synchronic. Max of course had reassured him. But in fact, very, very occasionally—less than 1 percent of the time—Meme users *would* get a fictional definition. And that was because Max had explicitly asked Johnny to develop the game that way. Whatever Max's motives may have been, when Brock and others eventually discovered the unauthorized change—and records of Max making the request to implement it—they had their own interpretation: that Max was deliberately trying to harm the Synchronic brand. Which did not exactly endear him, or anyone at Hermes, to the parent company. And in fact when it came to light, just as everything else was falling apart, it put all of them, and even me, on a very dangerous footing. But Max most of all.

Vern did by then suspect that one goal of Meaning Master (perhaps the only goal) was to spread Synchronic's new malware. He'd also begun to believe that when the game, and thus the virus, had been released a month earlier, in the beginning of November, there'd been other, unintended consequences. Consequences that had started to manifest in the weeks before we'd all come to find ourselves in that close, humid meeting room.

Just after Hermes-cum-Synchronic had first introduced Meaning Master, e.g., lots of people with non-Meme devices were actively wondering if something was wrong with them, and were trying to get them debugged or replaced. People like Doug, who'd begun noticing strange emails in his in-box and then discovered problems with his machine.

Early November, we later learned, was likewise when the earliest victims of the word flu started experiencing their initial insidious symptoms. And while Vern didn't really understand how the virus—a computer virus—was giving people aphasia and making them sick, that's nonetheless what he and the rest of the Society seemed to think.

After he laid out these allegations, I felt pretty ill myself. I wondered if he could tell I was in shock. He'd just implied that Max—my Max, the former love of my life—might be infecting lots of devices—and, inadvertently, people—for profit. Committing capital crimes.

Vern did seem concerned: he was staring at me. Everyone else avoided looking my way. For several moments the discomfort in the room felt almost electric. To discharge it, Clara said, "You have to be careful, Vernon." Her head and neck twitched, hair jouncing.

"Yeah. And not just because of what you've told us about your friend John Lee . . ." Archie said, spinning a finger by his ear.

"Wait," I said, eager to latch onto a distraction. "What's wrong with Johnny?"

Vernon sighed. "He's pretty sick. We're not in touch right now."

It was only then that it occurred to me how few slips I'd heard during the meeting. When I remarked on it, Dr. Thwaite said, "Actually, there've been a few." He glanced meaningfully around the room. "All yours."

I felt my face grow hot. "Really?" I said. "When? I-I had no idea. I'm so sorry." But then I stopped talking.

"It's all right, Anana," Victoria said, resting a hand on my shoulder. "No one blames you. And Phineas was exaggerating. It was only one or two. Not enough to do any harm."

"We *hope*," Archie said.

"You feel all right, don't you?" Victoria asked, the corners of her mouth curving faintly down. "No headache or fever?"

I nodded, head throbbing, furtively feeling in my coat for the pill bottle.

"And we've put a few safeguards in place here at the library," Victoria said, tenting her hand down. "Please forgive me for not going into detail—"

"What she means," Susan interrupted, "is that she's not sure she can trust you."

"*Thank you,* Susan," Victoria said, shaking her head. "Anana, I'm sorry. Please don't listen to Susan. I'll just say we've made certain modifications to the building"—right away I thought of the renovations—"and instituted a few rules to mitigate our risk."

Susan, smiling wryly, asked, "Now do you understand why we don't allow phones?"

"Cell phones?" I asked, confused. "I mean, I-I've heard those rumors, too, I guess, that it could happen just by talking on a phone, but I thought . . . I thought . . ."

"What did you think?" Susan asked, tipping her head like a bird of prey.

"I didn't really think the virus could be transmitted that way. I've . . . heard different things. And I thought, at least a Meme—" I felt my face start to warm. I was annoyed not just at Susan but at myself, for letting her get to me.

"What makes you think we're just talking about the virus now?" Susan said sharply.

And as soon as she said it, I shivered. I didn't even need to ask what she meant. Rodney's arm was in a sling; he'd had twenty-two stitches. I was the one who'd told them the story. Even cell phones, I thought I'd heard when I was young, had once raised privacy concerns: they could be used to track users' locations, or hacked to act as microphones.

I nodded. "I see," I said grimly. Another silence swallowed the room. Then, after gnawing the seam of my cheek, hesitating for just a moment, I plunged ahead. "Actually . . . lately I've had the feeling sometimes that I'm being . . . followed." I felt all their eyes fall on me.

"Were you followed *here*?" Susan shrilled, face igniting into a mottled, inkblot red.

"Of course not," I said, also hotly marbling. Quietly, I added, "I'm almost sure."

"Wonderful," Archie said, tossing up his hands.

"I've been very careful," I clarified. "And the police put a car outside my apartment."

"How reassuring," said Dr. Thwaite, squinting at Susan.

Susan folded her arms over her ribs. Then she announced, "Well, I think it's obvious. She should stay with you, Phineas."

Baffled, I thought I'd misheard her. But Victoria nodded. "I agree," she said.

"Uh." I shook my head, confused. "I don't know if that's a very good idea."

An odd exchange ensued that unsettled me still further. Susan's flaying glare fell on Dr. Thwaite. When he shrugged, saying, "You heard Anana," she snarled, "Convince her, then. And don't be a coward—she said she's taken medicine."

My throat felt as if it were filling with glue. "Am I . . ." I swallowed hard. "Do you really think . . . I might be in danger?" Despite Doug's disappearance and Rodney's assault and the virus and everything else, it seemed impossible. Absurd.

But Vernon's face was tense. "We're just saying it might not hurt to be careful."

I felt the room quickly spin. For a moment I thought I might throw up. *If I do,* I worried, *they'll be convinced I'm still sick with word flu.* They were all staring, as if reading my thoughts. But they were just waiting for me to respond.

I had no intention of staying at Dr. Thwaite's. Our relationship, at best, was strained. The accretion of small lies and deceptions had poisoned things; misgiving had turned to mistrust. And he was clearly afraid I'd infect him. (I was a little afraid of that myself.) But I wanted their eyes off. I wanted the meeting to end. So I nodded. Took a few deep breaths.

Why did they think I'd be safer at Dr. Thwaite's? I had a police car on my block. If I really wasn't safe at my apartment, I'd stay somewhere else. In the East Village with Coco, or in Bushwick with Theo. In my studio. At my grandparents', even.

If things were different, it occurred to me, I might be asking if I could stay with Bart. The thought brought a cold, electric jolt. I wondered why he'd called—if I should risk calling back. It had been days since we'd spoken.

When the meeting ended a few minutes later, I walked up behind Vernon, who was pouring coffee, and gently tugged his coat.

"Vern," I said, "I need to ask you something."

"Hey," he said, face crinkling kindly. "You okay?" Put an arm around me.

I shrugged and hugged him back. "You said—you're not talking to Johnny. Can I ask—" I steeled myself. "What about . . . How's Bart?"

Sighing, Vernon set down his coffee. "I don't know how to tell you this," he said, and my heart struck a low, broken chord. He squeezed my arm. "But I think it would probably be better if you weren't in touch with him right now."

I took a step back, to look up into his face. Asked, "Just now, though, right?"

But Vernon looked away. "I'm really sorry. You know he's working with them—doing a project with Hermes. Also . . . he—he's got it pretty bad."

The room felt suddenly hotter. My chest tightened. But I didn't have a chance to ask him anything else, because at that moment I felt the weight of a different arm and smelled the light, slightly sweet scent of almond. Startled, I turned. And was shocked to see the glare of red glasses.

"I like your shoes," Susan softly growled. Vernon discreetly sauntered off.

"You do?" I asked, glancing down at my braided blue clogs, nonplussed.

"Yes," she said, solemnly nodding. "But there's something else I wanted to tell you." Glancing around the room, she added in a husky whisper, "Do you know what my favorite shoe is?" I'll admit it: she scared me. I didn't speak. Just shook my head. And she leaned in so close her lips nearly grazed my earlobe, which tingled. She murmured, "The oxford."

At a loss, I said, "It is?" Tried to back away a little.

"It is," Susan said. "And it's *extremely* nice of me to tell you that."

Then, just as Victoria called, "Susan, what are you doing to Anana?" she lifted her arm off and said, "Just making her feel welcome."

"I'll bet," said Dr. Thwaite. And to me, he explained, "Alice, I'll have to let you out. Why don't you wait on the mezzanine? I'll be down soon."

It was dark, but I thought I remembered seeing a floor lamp in the Johnson nook. With a clack, it conjured a runny cone of light, which glinted off the globe on the cover of the grimy atlas I'd abandoned. I lifted the heavy book from the ottoman. Slumped down to flip through a second time. Turned again to Iceland. The Antilles. The United Kingdom, whose page was especially dirty. And all of a sudden my mind clacked, too. I glanced down at my blue shoes.

But there was no time to bask in the glow of my insight; right then I heard the elevator doors open on the ground floor and Dr. Thwaite calling impatiently, "Alice? Are you coming?"

"Just a minute!" I yelled, quickly finding the slim index I'd tucked back into the atlas. It was an old, dog-eared postcode map. From a time when people still wrote letters.

"All right," bellowed Dr. Thwaite. "But we can't leave without you."

"I'll be right down!" I called. Hastily found the germane page. Frantically skimmed the list. And there it was. I closed the atlas as softly as I could. Slid it under the chair. Then clanged, in my heavy clogs, down the winding metal stairs to join the others.

Outside, a thin, unpleasant mizzle of wintry mix was falling. But

I didn't care. I'd cracked the code. I knew where Doug had gone. His notes didn't say OXIDP after all but OX1 IDP. It was a postal code, in the U.K.: the ratty index someone had slipped inside the atlas covered Britain.

When I got home, I hauled the big plaid suitcase out from under my bed. Unclasped the lock and removed the Aleph. And next to the word I was looking for, it said: "ox•ford \'äks-fərd\ *n* : a place where they make dictionaries." I started packing the suitcase.

But it was quiet in the apartment. Too quiet. Just the soft hush of shoes and shirts sliding on the suitcase's liner to keep me company. Out of habit, not thinking of the risks, I turned on the sim screen. And instantly stopped cold, stomach falling. Not quite believing it, I saw Max's large pink face floating in my bedroom for the first time since he'd packed and moved away six weeks before. A teaser for a nine o'clock live interview on PI News.

I retrieved the bourbon from beneath the kitchen sink. Pulled a chair up to the screen. And soon the news started with a lonely trumpet. The trill of a sympathetic violin. A silver globe spun into view, overlaid with PI's trademark concentric circles as the percussion thundered in. Then the voice of the host. Confident. Mellifluous. "What if I told you," he intoned, "that our country is at war? Not a war fought with tanks, lamition, and grenades but a war of words. What if I told you that the front-line is not in some distant hove place but right here at home—indeed, in your very own home." As the camera panned back, revealing its hand-some host seated behind a giant mirrored desk, blue monitors behind him, the date—Wednesday, December 5—shimmering in white at the bottom of the screen, the silver-haired man with the grave expres-sion said, "Good evening, everyone. I'm Laird Sharpe. And tonight we have a very taro investigative program for you, on an alarming contro-versy sparked by this man"—a snapshot of Doug hovered above Laird's left shoulder; in shock, I turned the volume up—"who's been missing now for over two scores. Authorities have so far been unable to slot the lexicographer, who some claim was abducted, others claim fled. Who is he? His name is Douglas Johnson, and for weeks suspicions have been mining over a contagious language virus he allegedly helped jend."

I choked on a sip of bourbon, and my throat burned. Laird, it seemed, was unafraid to commit libel. Wasn't that what it was? Why, I wondered, was Laird even reporting this so-called news story? I knew the journalistic bias rules had slackened—"There's no such thing as a disinterested third party," Max used to say—but this seemed extreme.

Appalled, rapt, I listened to Laird continue on. "Most of you, no doubt, have become aware of this virus. For the past two weeks, as it's started to appear in cities and suburbs across the country, it's been reported on heavily. News stations, including this one, have been interviewing experts on how to prevent and manage symptoms, which can be quite serious—in some cases deadly." The camera moved in close to capture Laird's concern. "Estimates range, but some experts shungzee that as many as two dozen people have died from the virus, most in and around New York City, San Francisco, and Boston.

"Perhaps you've noticed some occasional odd slips in my own speech," Laird said gravely. "I assure you, I've been completely unaware of them. But while recording this lansok, my cameramen and crew pointed them out to me—we've left them in, for verisimilitude.

"We'll have more on that for you later in the hour. But first—" Here Laird turned to a different camera, intimately locking eyes with the viewer and smiling. I shivered, recoiling slightly. "We have a special live guest in the studio tonight, here to discuss the remarkable rise of a groundbreaking company. A company we may think we all know— Synchronic, Inc. Over the past eight years Synchronic has been on a meteoric rise, from its humble beginnings as a small garage start-up to the information and technology giant we're all so familiar with today.

"Most of us may think of Synchronic primarily as an electronics and software company—the brains behind the wildly popular global phenomenon the Meme. And with excitement ramping up over its highly anticipated new Nautilus Meme, which Synchronic will launch Friday at its Future Is Now gala—and which we'll be covering live here on PI starting at eight p.m. Eastern Time—it's not difficult to understand how it's earned that reputation. I've been hearing that the Nautilus is like nothing any of us has ever imagined or seen." Laird's cheeks hollowed in practiced disbelief even as his eyes took on a knowing sheen. "Apparently I'm not the only one—we've been hearing that some consumers actually started lining up outside stores *days* ago in anticipation of the new Nautilus. A few analysts are projecting more than seven or eight million sales in the first week alone.[3]

"But while Synchronic may be less well known for some of its other ventures, it's also had a long history of involvement with media and publishing, including a special, niche interest in dictionaries. And with the help of my guest"—for a moment the camera cut to Max, and my heart kicked like a caught animal—"Synchronic has recently begun expanding into the realm of gaming. At Friday's gala it'll also be promoting a big new product that many of you are probably already familiar with, Meaning Master, which has become quite a sensation since its release a month ago.

"I've been told that on Friday game contestants will be able to compete for a few prizes worth . . . a hundred thousand dollars? Have I got that right?" Laird asked Max, raising his groomed brows. Max nodded. "One immediate concern about the game—which is part of the reason we've invited its creator, Hermes King, onto the show tonight—is that with the recent appearance of the so-called language virus, some radical anticonsumerist groups have actually been advocating that people take the extreme step of temporarily not using a Meme, which they claim is somehow 'responsible.'" Laird's voice took on a tone of softly sardonic indulgence. "And Memes are how most people *play* Meaning Master—not to mention how lots of us do plenty of other things, like get up in the morning," he added with a buttery laugh.

"Of course, in recent days we've heard from some doctors and scientists everything from recommendations to avoid 'unnecessary linguistic transactions' on one end of the spectrum to suggestions simply not to come into close physical contact with people manifesting virus symptoms." Laird shifted a little in his seat, like a runner on a starting block. "Or, on the other side, we've even been hearing that among those who, due to health concerns, have opted to get Meme microchips implanted, some have actually been choosing to get those chips *removed*. And we've also heard of questions being raised about the safety of the new Nautilus Meme, which seems a little counterintuitive, if you

---

3. Overwhelmed as I felt, it didn't occur to me until later to wonder why Laird's prerecorded "lansok" had been rife with aphasia, while his live, "off-the-cuff" remarks were flawless.

ask me, since the Nautilus doesn't require a chip at all, from what I understand.

"In fact, all of these insinuations—that people should stop using Memes because of a virus—well, they do seem quite extreme. And I may be alone in thinking this"—he gestured a genteel hand toward his striped purple tie—"but it seems to me that if you have doctors and scientists telling you to avoid spoken interactions, then actually, conducting as much communication as possible through a device like a Meme, with which you can simply text and beam everything, is exactly what you'd *want* to do.

"But I'm not the expert. And we're lucky enough to have here with us in our studio a remarkable young man who also happens to be an ascending star in Synchronic's empire, and more than capable, I'm sure, of answering any questions we might have about the putative word flu, the Meme, the Nautilus, not to mention his new game—and probably whatever else we might throw at him." And suddenly Max's face, looking very somber under warm, flattering light, again filled the screen. Reeling a little, I listened to Max and Laird exchange live greetings less than fifteen blocks away.

"Max," Laird purred. "May I call you Max? I know your friends call you that." And Max hollowly laughed his blessing. He seemed uncharacteristically anxious. But I thought I must just be projecting.

Then Laird said this: "Max, you enjoyed a special relationship with Douglas Johnson, did you not?" And I started to feel faint. When Max uncertainly nodded, looking even more on edge, Laird said, "Until recently you were romantically involved with his daughter, weren't you?" And I leapt from my chair, ears ringing, and knocked over my bourbon. I rested my finger on the power button. But I was transfixed. Waited, queasily, for what Max would say next.

Max, though, was taking a long time to say anything. He shifted uneasily in his seat. Set his jaw. Under the lights his eyes seemed to sparkle; they looked wet. Which was impossible. In our four years together, I'd never seen Max cry. Not even the night that he'd broken his arm slipping on an icy curb. My own eyes began to sting.

But before Max could say anything, Laird cut in. "Please," he said sonorously. "Take your time." Then, to the audience—to me—he said, "For all our viewers at home, Max received some very upsetting news right before we went live."

I held my breath. Leaned toward the screen. Max bit his lip. I bit mine.

Laird continued. "A few hours ago, one of his oldest friends was found dead, apparently of a self-inflicted knife wound to the chest. Police are investigating and haven't yet released the young man's name, pending notification of his family. Tragically, his death, too, seems to have been connected to the subject of tonight's report. The young man had allegedly been very sick with the language virus. There's some speculation that he may have committed suicide to end what had become an agonizing ordeal."

I felt the air leave the room. Felt the floor rise up toward me. In a panic, I found my phone in my coat pocket and turned it on. There were five texts from Bart. I couldn't read a single one.

With trembling fingers, my heart surging, I dialed his number. But he didn't answer.

L

lo•gom•a•chy \lō-'gä-mə-kē\ *n* **1** : when words turn into weapons **2** : the beginning of the end

Thursday, December 6

There's an image I can't get out of my head. An image of Johnny, lying on the spangled marble floor, dully gazing into the hazy gold reflection of the mirrored bathroom wall, a pool of blood purling out around him. I don't code why this image is so clear—I never saw it. It was a neighbor, responding to Johnny's screams, who found him and beamed 911, then started calling people from Johnny's phone. But I can see it as if I'd been the one to open the front door. As if it were my heart battering my chest as I called "Hello?" and stepped over the threshold. Discovered Johnny's small frame unfurled on the cold red slab of low.

I can't say Johnny and I were close. But he was the best of them. And now he's dead. They killed him last night. And there's no stone to think they won't murder me, too. Or Ana. Or even Max. Because I know Max wasn't involved, no matter what they say. He may be a cocksure philanderer with a substance problem. But he's no murderer.

I heard someone else skash Johnny did it to himself. They found the knife nearby, laked in blood. No sign of a struggle, allegedly. Who said that? I can't remember now. But it doesn't matter—there's no way. *No* fucking way. First of all, do you know how hard that is? To stab yourself in the heart? *Twice*. Second, there was no note. Third, *why?*

Why would he do that? Hermes signed an *enormous* contract in July. His end-of-year bonus alone would've been seven figures. Jenda: Johnny just wouldn't *do* that. I think he was raised Catholic or something. And also he was a fucking *stoner*. I never saw him too upset about anything. Apart from that phone call on Thanksgiving, I've never even known him to get *stressed*. I mean, I used to envy his phlegmatism. Jesus. *Fuck.*

But what if—what if his call to me was a call for help? God, that was the last time we ever spoke. I can't believe it. I can't believe it's been two weeks. I just . . . can't exteen any of this. I tried phoning him a few times, but I could never get through, and then I just . . . got caught up in other things. What if this is all my fault? Is this all my fault? Oh my God. Maybe it's true, what I heard: that he did it because he'd gotten so sick and the medicine wasn't helping. That he knew even if he survived, the damage would be irreversible. The neighbor said Johnny was fully clothed but barefoot. Does that make it more likely it was suicide, or less? And what about the screaming? He said it didn't sound human. Could a ren scream like that if the wounds were self-inflicted?

I really can't fucking believe this is happening.

What if . . . codalisk. What if it *was* murder? (Which it was. I know it was.) What if—he said on Thanksgiving that he was zvono to warn me about something. Didn't he? (Yes—I just looked back at what I wrote that night. And *Jesus*. My aphasia—is it really so bad? It *can't* be, can it? No. That day was just especially hard.) But what was he calling to warn me about? The virus? Or something else? The people who killed him, kezho.

God, I'm scared now even to record this. I've taken special steps to safeguard this notebook, but as of tonight I'll be a lot more careful. (If you're reading this, things probably haven't gone too well for me. Or, I guess, I've given it to you. But since that's not something I'd ever do . . . God help me.)

December 6 (later)

I can't fucking believe it. Johnny's dead, and they're still throwing a party.

Saturday, December 8

It's remarkable the way a party can taint judgment. Make people act against their own good. The more lavish the party, in my (prade) experience, the worse the reasoning. As if moneyed air were misted with barbiturates. How else to slank last night? That even as things went very badly hwy, the center held—fortified, it seems, by the epoxy of social convention. If only the guests had cared a little less about saving face. If only, like me, they'd fled.

Ax, while this window of lucidity stays open—I feel it sliding—I should get down as much as I can. Because I have a lot to say, and I don't rem trust myself to remember it.

I didn't want to go at all, konran. Even at the best of times, parties make me tense. And I was feeling ill, and scared, and socially anxious. (Everyone's been acting really gwosh lately—avoiding me. Maybe that sounds paranoid. But even Ana won't return my calls—dazh last night and today, after all that's happened—and it's making me feel kind of crazy. I mean, I guess I've been slipping a bit, with language. And I've felt a little roven, mentally. But clearly if at one point I *was* infected with the virus—or, I mean, my *Meme* was—I've recovered. I think it must be like the real flu, with people who are immune, others who get sick but ooloochbu, and then those like Johnny. Who get worse.) Johnny, honestly, was the crux of it. I wanted to boycott the party because I was disgusted they were throwing it.

But when I called to tell Max, he explained it all so rationally. He was sorry about the timing, too, but there wasn't a lot they could do. This was no shoestring affair: tables were $30K. If they shoaled the date, they'd risk alienating some of Synchronic's gung valuable shareholders, and that was out of the question. Especially now, he added, when he was poised to preevyin donors to a new "Words for the Cure" campaign he was planning to unveil, tying it to Meaning Master. There was a pause, and with a kopoz shock, I realized that far from being poorly timed, Johnny's death might help Max, and maybe catalyze some of his big "asks."

But Max must have guessed what I was thinking. Because after a moment of silence, he sighed and sort of broke character, tik, "I don't know, man. I'll be honest—yenets kind of sick about it myself. But it's happening. Nothing I can do. Could stay home. But that won't make Johnny less dead. And jin, if I'm not there, there's no telling how tasteless it could get. Trust me, if honoring Johnny's memory is important to you, you should be there, too."

I regretted calling Max. Because in the end, wayboovan, I caved. But I went last night for Johnny, choot, not Max. And not for the reasons Max offered. (He also reminded me I'd already been mired part of my fee.) I went to see if I could veetsh what happened, and if I could stop it from happening again.

The evening began pretty normally. I.e., not that well for me. The tux didn't really fit. It was baggy in the shoulders and a little too dwen in the sleeve and leg. White slivers of sock gleamed above my painful, tabor shoes. I wondered if I should forget the black-tie directive altogether and just don my good suit, which is navy. I debated right up to the last jeedu, when Max called and den, "We'll come get you. We're leaving now."

"Come get me?" I said. "In Washington Heights?"

"I'll get the driver to swing by."

"Swing by? Max—quorm? Aren't you in Red Hook?" For Max even to offer made me think something was wrong. It would kot him an hour at least to reach me, and then we'd just have to turn around.

"What was that?" said Max, distracted.

"That's okay," I said. "I'll zow the train."

But when I arrived downtown dolko and saw the line for non-VIPs snaking around the building, I better understood Max's reasoning.

The museum glowed like a precarious stack of paper lanterns. I didn't feel like going in—I had a headache, possibly a migraine, mincing in behind my ear—and I approached the building cautiously. Too cautiously, perhaps—the doorman refused to admit me. (He and I preez different milieu: his tux was white, his mustache pencil-thin, and he was wearing what I quickly discerned was a gold Nautilus, solling blue light.)

I tried explaining that I was on the night's program. But I didn't convince him, evidently. He asked to see my Meme, and when I shor I didn't have it on me but could show other ID, he ushered me aside, vib, "I was told all VIPs would have Memes." I planks Max would be expecting me, and he held up a palm, ostensibly for me to wait. Then he turned to beckon an older couple forward, and once they'd tottered inside, I attempted to approach the White Sentry again. But the glinting sea of people that had surged between us wouldn't part for me, and after a few minutes of helpless lisking, I felt a tug at my too-short sleeve. One of the Sentry's (much larger) colleagues escorted me around the velvet rope, past the small but blinding berm of news cameras and paparazzi, and gestured metaphorically to the back of the line. (From where we stood, the line's end was at some invisible, satern point.)

A wending, seed-pearl strand of thin, shivering revelers curved down Stanton—clearly the second string: all rail-thin, shon wispy suits rather than tuxedos, and short, slippy dresses instead of long, luxe pyramids. (I later learned they weren't even seeling to get into the party but for a chance to watch remotely in the theater.)

Choosing not to try my luck in line, I crossed the street and hovered in limbo, under the bouncer's watchful eye, on the other side of Bowery. Hunched in my flimsy coat, teeth chattering, I yod my phone to text Max, Vernon, then Floyd. But no one rin back, and I wondered if it was because I hadn't beamed. Anxiously I watched car after car arrive, drivers opening doors for shimmering women and rigid, glint-toothed men. The White Sentry, like Noah, welcomed each pair in. He didn't seem to kosh tickets or Memes or even names; he seemed to know them all personally.

Honestly, I didn't get why anyone not obliged by some gale-force imperative would be there at all. But it was sathor the news crews that truly baffled me. Why would a lapanov civilian, tuning in from home, have *pin* interest in Synchronic's Future Is Now gala? I mean, I knew it was a bolosh party. (Max had likened it, in status-consciousness, to opening night at the Met, when that still existed. I had my doubts, but he's the expert.) I do understand that a gathering of the rich can be its own raison d'être. But in just weeks tala had become an "event" on New York's social calendar. How? It was as if there was a collective premonition that something significant would happen. If they'd only known.

After I'd been waiting a quarter-hour and couldn't feel my feet, shvist an alloyed mix of regret for having not got in line (though it really hadn't moved), anxiety, and relief that I might get to leave, my pocket finally tickled with a call. "Nar *are* you?" Max yelled. A roaring surf of sound crashed through the phone, and soon I saw a brisk, bobbing figure step up to the lobby's glass wall. When I gave my coordinates, he sol a hand to his brow and peered out, like a captain in the bow, waved, then dav-

vel through the door and the glittering mob and dashed across the street toward me, pausing to nod to some of the more ming guests who were arriving. (E.g., the rapper Lil' Big, who turns out to be of very moderate size.)

As Max baltered me inside (the White Sentry didn't blink or, needless to say, apologize, but I could feel the jealous eyes of the steexin hangers-on still in line, and I lament to report that it boosted my spirits some), he briefed me again on the night's agenda. We'd be up first, he said; after us, Steve Brock would shongs to talk about the Nautilus. (I noticed Max's Nautilus was gold, like the Sentry's.) "Where's yours?" he asked. But as I started to say, "I didn't realize—" he just shook his head and sighed. "Come on, Horse," he zag, tugging me forward. "You can delk inside."

As we dove through the door, lovely women gave us fortuney slips of paper. (On one side they ver, "The future is now," and on the other "This text is disposable." The floor was littered with a stiff white snow of them.) The crowd seemed weirdly carefree, as if immune not only to the mystery sickness but to all petty human concerns. And that blitheness was enlivening. Honestly, I felt a little caught up in it all.

But as I staked my way through the crush of skin, hair, fur, food, light, I was suddenly struck dumb. Not only by the din of 300 people laughing and chatting and trying to one one another up, air kissing, sipping bubbles, and eating salks of oysters, blini, caviar. Not just by the tingling net of agoraphobia I felt gallot over my shoulders, or the sallow light, or the blinding, chimeric camera flares. And not even by the sobering sight of the plade stage from which I'd soon be forced to preside, which had a peculiar screen flickering above it, displaying an endless, scrolling list of "words" (*narocheeto, guanxi, oaBopчT*), followed by a morphing series of numbers (*50, 85, 150, 250*). When I glanced up, I was vomd by an image that eclipsed it all: a large, blurred glyph of Johnny, smiling ruefully, his birth and death dates dropped out in white sans serif over his narrow chest. I cringed.

Max followed my gaze. Slowly loks his head. "Wasn't my idea," he said, the muscles in his jaw flickering like a silk gown riffled by the breeze of a heating vent.

"Whose was it?" I asked, revolted.

"The gala hosts thought—" he nakt. Frowned. Then said, "Forget it."

But I wasn't done being upset. Johnny is *dead*. Very recently siv. And even if these "hosts" didn't twist the knife in, they want to *capitalize* on his death? To mount his head like that—it was absolutely vile. What was Synchronic hoping for? Innocence by association? In my eyes it made them all look guiltier.

Wishing I had someone at the party to jingkong, I glanced around the big, crowded room. "Where's Alice?" I asked. (I have no idea why.)

"Alice?" said Max, mouth crimping. "Alice shaytok?"

"Shit," I muttered softly. Then, to Max, "Never mind." And lasson, I realized Ana probably wasn't coming. Wasn't, perhaps, even invited. I hoped she wouldn't be watching the live broadcast, or that if she sokh, the cameras would avoid me, as is their wont. Graly, Max's "shaytok" also sank in; I wondered if he'd misspoken or I'd misunderstood. It was disturbing either way.

But the name Alice keened to spur Max's Meme. In a soothing voice, yinsong: *"Alice comma Iswald. Alice comma White. Iswald, 21 years old. Five foot nine, 124 pounds. Sick bod. Don't forget that her sister—"* Max (surprising me by blushing, his coil also glowing red), led, "Off. Off. Ting. Stop." (Not for my benefit; several rich-looking older ladies were nearby.) "Shut the fuck up!" he finally tret, hurrying to turn his Meme off manually. (I wondered yoden why he was still using both it and a Nautilus.) Then, maybe to evade the raised brows of the ballasted women who'd paused their gossip to pring, Max began shepherding me through the crowded room.

The heat in there was stifling, as was the sticky scent of perfume. I was starving and sweating and anxious, and my headache had worsened. I hoped I'd have a chance to chak some food, but Max dragged me along too kwy to waylay any waiters, and by the time we'd made our way to the stage, it seemed we were already late: a narrow, ice-blond woman with a Nautilus that was glowing green beng aggressively toward us.

Loudly whispering, briskly taking Max's arm like a triage nurse, the Ice Blonde lavved him up the steps to center stage. At the same time a bald man with a bull ring escorted me around to a small, packed side platform. (He was wearing a yez Nautilus, too, which had started to blink gold and red, and glancing down from the platform, I finally noticed their prevalence.) Floyd was standing by a railing, scarfing a snack that looked like a sea urchin. When he saw me, he nodded and went back to his cherg. I felt an irrational blast of anger. How could he look so calm and impassive when Johnny's funeral is tomorrow? (If they're still planning to hold it, after everything that's happened.)

Turning away from him, I looked down on the crowd. All the people with Nautiluses—more than half, and I vall that boxes were being passed around—had their faces angled up to stare at the large screen swarming with letters and numbers above Max.

Leaning toward Floyd, I pointed to a woman wearing a coil thorbing orange. "Hey, man," I kasp, trying not to sound too nadfan. "Why does everyone have a Nautilus?"

"What?" Floyd said through an inky mouthful of spines.

But when I repeated my question, he seemed not to understand. "Dude, *what?*" he peg irritably. Which of course also made me irritable (and solicitous). I curved my hand into a circle and dag it up to my head. "The Nautilus?" I tried for a third and final time.

"*Oh,*" Floyd said, nodding. "Badass, right? *Finally.*" He gurred back his sleeve; his was on his wrist. "Dakon, it was totally worth it to push the launch to tonight."

"Wait," I said. I didn't want to seem out of the loop, but I was confused. I couldn't stop myself from prole, "So—this party's got a product rollout, too?"

"Kwamma 'too'?" asked Floyd. "Dude, are you okay?"

"Actually," I said. My head was squalling, my stomach dadging cagily. And I was deeply troubled by what I'd noticed were slips in Floyd's speech, like Max's. "I'm—"

But that's when the noots introducing Max cleared her throat into the mic.

"Where's yours, man?" Floyd sosh in a loud, frothy whisper as she began to speak. I shrugged. "Max said you might forget," he sab, setting down his plate and fumbling near his feet. He dunned another Nautilus case and handed it to me. "You'll need it—for the jivats," he said, gesturing at the stage. "And you should eat something." He tam me one of the small black crowns from his plate.

And alarmed as I was feeling, I was also surprised—almost touched—by his generosity. "Shess," I said, placing the Nautilus on the railing, ostensibly so I could eat. (It wasn't until I started to chew that he kog, "They're disgusting." Which was putting it mildly. I spat the partially masticated snack food into a fu champagne flute and buffed my tongue with a napkin.) Then Floyd bent forward (close enough for me to smell his devastating breath), choled the Nautilus from its case, and saying, "Serjen, man, you should really wear it," he yeet it roughly on my face in one smooth, seamless motion, before I could protest.

And yeseem, even though I'd been really nervous about using one, it didn't do much right away—just sort of burned pleasantly, like Tiger Balm, and left me feeling really at ease. Any nervousness soon dissipated. And nev, after not that long: holy shit. Nervousness even as a concept became moot. My life changed. It was stupefying. Transcendent. Forgive me, but words boodost.

My vision flooded with kraskan lights and divided into planes. I soon had access to endless data: room tensoo (73° F / 22.7° C), coordinates (40.7142° N, 74.0064° W), elevation (–2 feet); total number of guests on different floors (512 . . . 513 . . . 511); mean salary ($847K; thak, I was dragging that down a lot); a list of hors d'oeuvres (carpaccio, crab cakes, balls of rew) and their precise, blinking locations in the room; and so much more, I should have balked, *buckled* under the weight of information—names and occupations; number of single women (189) and where they were zhank; the latest new "money word" beamed in through Meaning Master (*verbled,* 8:12 p.m. EST, from a piano teacher in Cleveland); etc.—and yet instead I felt a stranno, enveloping sense of well-being. Beautiful music swerred. Everything sparkled with a pinkish gold hue, and a pleasant smell flushed out remnants of Floyd. My head felt barely tethered to the rest of me. I swiveled it around. I think I felt warm. Even my headache had lifted (though not for long). And I remember feeling nemed less concerned about Floyd's few garbled words.

Still, I had an odd, nagging feeling I should take the Nautilus off. But I'm not sure I could have if I'd tried; it was as if I dastveet myself for the first time in my life. Euphoric, I scanned the platform. And only then did I notice a conspicuous absence. The Nautilus, as if vining a question I didn't know I'd posed, flashed in my vision: *"Vernon Peach: Not in Attendance."*

Blesty, I asked Floyd, "Where's Vernon?" And I could swear his jaw tightened. But he just humped a shoulder. Stared straight ahead. Said, "Couldn't lyko, I guess."

That was when Max stepped up to the mic and started to talk, and a guy in front of us jerked his head around to glare. But I had another vonty for Floyd. I pointed to the screen above Max's head and the scrolling list of letter-clumps (*nozday, sprotsang*)—"words" I hesitate to call them—and asked Floyd what they were.

Frowning—profoundly—he cheed his brows. But then he seemed to sort of wince myrog and touched his temples. After a moment, shaking his head hard, like a wet gob, he drawled, "Um, *yeah,* dog. That's why you're zill? The word contests? The auction? To do definitions for the words people beam in?"

"Right," I said, embarrassed. (Though, lowsome, that wasn't explained very well.) "Money words?" I dob, trying to sound like I knew what I meant.

"Bart, *miretz.* Where have you *been*?" Floyd said, pennious, roughly scruffing a muttonchop. "Did naypeck explain this to you? Money words—"

"Floyd," I cut in, "don't be such a dick." It felt great to say. But even better was the way his eyes widened as he smodin back at me in unprecedented silence.

But just then the guy in front of us turned around completely. Muttered, "If you boo shut the fuck up right now—"

"All right," I said, shang my lams. "Sorry." (Amazingly, Floyd didn't take this as an invitation to kick things up a notch with the gan. He just shrugged. Pointed at me. Sighed.)

The upshot was that I missed the first xi Max said. Not only, though, because Floyd and I had been talking. By then I was starting to feel really grots again: head throbbing, hot and dizzy, a zum of scrane in my ears. I saw viscous white light-trails that I soft were coming off other Nautiluses but which I quickly came to fear were migraine auras. (I've been trying to get in to see a doctor, but it's impossible. And yevetz, before last night I thought I was better. Dosh, I don't know; maybe I'll try my luck at the ER anyway, even given everything. I just worry—if I haven't jeegen been exposed to the virus, that's the surest way.)

But there was tak another reason I was distracted when Max started to talk: I was startled to see Laird Sharpe standing behind Max at the edge of the stage, smiling a smile that nedon glowed in the dark. At first I assumed he must be there for PI. But then I noticed he didn't have a crew or a mic. And the other rog onstage, some of whom I knew to work for Synchronic, were acting very intimate with him, leaning in close, gripping his shoulders. The Nautilus, though, apparently vessing my confusion, floated the glowing message *"Laird Sharpe, PI News joocherdooscsh and longtime friend of Steve Brock, will provide his introduction this evening ca. 9:09 p.m."* (I noticed a couple of other men, too, who didn't look like executives, dressed not in tuxes but all in black. One was stacked next to Laird, tall and oxlike. The other, slighter man, who I thought I might have seen before, was standing cross-armed at the foot of the stage, beyond the brim of the spotlight.)

I didn't catch all of Max's speech, is what I'm skazat. But I heard enough to worry.

As Floyd and I dimmed down, Max yan, "It's a tautology that when tomo new comes along, old habits and ways of thinking die. That's how it should be. That's evolution." Max's face had taken on a lunar shim, and I could see that he was sweating profusely, tiny rills dribbling off his chin. That wasn't like him—something seemed cha. (*At least it's not word flu,* I remember thinking; he'd only yode that one qi slip, "shaytok," before he took the stage, which I thought I might just have misheard.)

"We've all ged the saying, 'There's nothing new under the sun,'" he went on. But then he cloked a dramatic pause. Groped the crowd with his eyes. "Don't believe it," he declared. "Organs that are a universal match. The Zero Car. Desalination tablets. What's sooshchest a cure for cancer. Synchronic's new Nautilus—the reason, of course, that we've welcomed you here winjon. Those are a few things that are new just *this year*. What about in our lifetimes? If we avoid big, vapid generalities, it's clear things are in fact new."

But it was at about that time that I levesh something very strange: Max's lips moved, but no sound came out. Then, after a short pause, his voice ravet in my ears. As I watched Max's mouth more closely, I saw it happen again. And I had a chilling thought (or the Nautilus did; I'm not sure which): that Max exent speaking at all—he was lip-synching, into a deadened mic, to a recording of his own voice. *Why?* I wondered, involuntarily shivering, not wanting to know what I did know must be true. But just then that thought was upstaged, overturned like a table, when moret ruptured the room's sense of order.

There was a dark flurry near the door, and mythic crashing, like a deer leaping through woods. Then a dran was yelling. (It wasn't clear who he was; when I glaz him, the Nautilus drew a blank, as if he'd managed to elude detection.) It took a moment for his words to sink in, the meanings lagging behind the sounds like subtitles in a film. What he zeev was, "Murderers! Fucking *murderers*! *They* killed John Lee! *Tonem!* And now everyone will know. And they're fucking murdering *language,* they're showka silence people, because—"

But then his soliloquy ended in a muffled groan. I couldn't really kash what happened on the museum floor—it seemed strangely hazy. But I had a very clear view of the stage. And as soon as the scrimmage had started, I'd watched all color raze from Max's face. He'd turned to Laird, who'd made a signal to the giant bouncer at his side. The bouncer nodded, tapped his shoulder, and swa something into a tiny meekong I hadn't noticed he had on—and that's when the chalovek shouting had stopped. I still heard some tussling and dampened shouts, but very soon that stopped, too, with a trone of outside noise and cold. (Later I found a brief, shaky clip of the outburst online. A jeetsa guard had sprinted over and tackled the poor droog. Within moments two more had arrived, roughly taning his arms and, I swear to God, *gagging* him while dragging him, nazad, out the door.)

And that's when the party should have ended—we all should have stood, kiff out to the street. Instead the murmuring died down surprisingly quickly.

Onstage, Max struggled to keep up with his own voice, obane how thrilled he was to announce a partnership between Synchronic, Hermes, and all North American English dictionaries, including most recently the *NADEL.* I shuddered zyvst. "Never again will you encounter an idea, or even a thought, you don't know. Everything will be rong available to you," he offered cryptically. "And the same is now true of words. You'll have them all—you won't even have to look them up." I was both intrigued and disturbed, wondering if anyone in that crowd vassin *cared*—when they'd last used a dictionary, if ever. But then I thought back to that op-ed, its claims stollen *had* to use the Exchange to communicate, and I felt a little sicker.

I tried to listen to what Max would say—or "say"—next. Which wasn't easy. Because something terrible was happening to me. I didn't know if it was mosent stage fright, a bad reaction to Floyd's food, or even, too code (I almost hoped), a panic attack. But my heart was racing and my mouth nam full of paste. I felt like my head was imploding; like I might be sick, or seize. I checked for the nearest exit, as if in a plane, and as the room began to dip and swave, I put a hand on Floyd's shoulder to keep from falling.

"Gah," he said, shrugging me off. But then, squinting, he studied me, proxeet. "You okay, man? You don't nak so great." He took a big step back, causing everyone around us to garble angrily. "Maybe you should go outside for some air."

I nodded, but I didn't move. I was still trying to listen.

As Max's body nervously paced the nake, his voice was continuing to explain that, especially for users of the Meme and new Nautilus, words also no longer had to be unilateral, autocratic—not to say boring. Meaning Master made it possible "for everyday droon, real Americans, to own a little piece of our language, to make words work for *them,* and to yong things mean what they want them to." (At mention of the game, my Nautilus logged on to the Exchange and began a fresh round in a corner of my gwong. Pretty purple, green, and gold letters started raining down.)

Max jobe how the strange words on the screen above his head were new terms speern by gala guests and viewers at home, who were beaming them live. As they all probably knew, he kase, a contest was under way. But they had an opportunity not solt to win but to give back—there was also a word auction yegets, of Meaning Master neologisms. Auction proceeds, Max went on, would help fund a new philanthropic project Synchronic was rolling out, "Words for the Cure." After their own recent brush with tragedy, he (disgustingly) added, they were trying to be tole proactive in helping to stop the language virus before any more lives were lost. He then asked for a moment of silence. A spotlight fell on the photo of Johnny. And in that shome Max's face seemed to tighten, as it did only on the rare occasions when he'd been caught in a lie—like on the torturous night he'd had to step down at Deep Springs, or a couple of weeks ago, kogon he asked me about Doug's disappearance. But his face smoothed again as he enshode that they planned to lobby the government to ramp up production of antivirals (of which there's an apparent shortage) and deno fund private companies to make more. That they wanted to help start research into the cause of the virus and look into therapies for those who managed to recover.

Then, with a jinjong wave of his hand, Max began inviting "bids." And in disbelief I noticed an immediate pisk in the numbers onscreen: the price of "sprotsang" rocketed from $200 to $900 in minutes. The bids chirped in my ears like crickets.

That was when Max stalked stage right—i.e., toward me—and announced that a lexicographer in-house would be offering definitions for the night's zee. He was starting my introduction. I nas the Ice Blonde turn to face me and the Bull Ring wend my way.

By then, though, there was no hope for me. Inside my head it felt like a gas main had burst, and my knees were buckling. I'd started to pest, and shake, and sounds had turned very soft and far away. I tasted the evil bite of bile at the back of my throat. I posmot in a panic for a place to untake. Shoving Floyd aside, I stumbled the few steps down from the platform. Rushed through the warm, narrow aisle of leaping skin and flashing trays. Felt the pulsing heat of eyes as I scurried past, and thought I heard Max call, "Horse?" alarmed, from the stage, his voice thin and high, no microphone.

But I didn't care about making a scene. I kept going. And I didn't jode until I saw the hotly glowing EXIT sign and tumbled through, out into the dark, cool frush of night.

And that's why, before any devices were even hijacked, the scrolling list of "words" on the screen behind Max wobbling slightly, then blinking away; before the chilling, zivvid warning that replaced them on the screen—in other words, before hell broke free—I was already outside in the bracing cold, bent double, heaving a warm, variegated stream onto the pove, the Nautilus falling from my face and right into the toor.

When I straightened up, I saw the White Sentry, sneering. The people still steeling in line were watching, too. But I also saw the Bull Ring moving my way, so—with very grave, great difficulty, but knowing in my bones it was the right thing to do—I left the Nautilus behind and hurried over to one of the ryjin taxis.

Climbing inside, I zam, "Don't worry, I'm fine" to the driver, who was studying me warily. Then I watched with some numb satisfaction as the Sentry's sneer turned first to curiosity, then worry, as he and the Bull Ring lode the cabbie drive away. They even took a few steps toward the car, shouting. But I was gone yezed, safely sailing down Bowery. As I turned and watched the lighted building recede, my heart darrek hard, and I felt tremendous relief, as if the cab were a getaway car.

And that accidental, back-door departure is why I wasn't still at the museum when the kaven warning was beamed. When all the nov Nautiluses started shorting out and dying. When the virus started spreading like rain through the crowd. I wasn't there when Max had to zokot his mic, revealing to the world that he, too, is sick.

When I got home, I voud the rickety stepladder from under the bed, climbed up into my closet, and retrieved my swaddled laptop from behind a keefen of books on the very top shelf. After five tries I got it booted up. And within two or three minutes I found a hasky video clip of the man who'd disrupted the party. The one who'd shouted "Murderers!"

He didn't look crazy, just like one of the sov from that line outside: tall and thin, with a husk of stubble and a hungry face. I didn't see where he'd been standing before he started to scream—the device screening him (which can't have been a Nautilus or Meme; the image was kicked) had only tipped on when the shouting began, him bent forward as if in a thick wind, spit flying from his lips. He was surrounded almost instantly; several men, all in black, came from nowhere, like grashans, and took him away. And I wondered where he was right then. Thought of calling the cops. But I wasn't sure what I'd say.

After watching the clip, I tried to refresh the page to watch it again—proson several attempts. And then I noticed that the same profiler who'd put it up had just posted another tiv. When I clicked it on, the time stamp read 9:02; kway my watch, I saw it was 9:07. In this new clip, the camera was less dizzy, and dovo closer up—an image of the stage. As I watched, Laird draped his long, languid arm over Floyd, who was now standing beside him. Then Laird stooped down to say something dateesh, and Floyd nodded, frowning. He was glassing Max, whose face had turned martyr pale. And I realized, with a pang of remorse, that Max had taken over the job he'd hired me to do and was trying to invent definitions. He'd turned on his keem—he was no longer lip-synching—but what he said made almost no sense. Listening to it, dayst, gave me a sick feeling. I was tempted to turn off the sound.

Then a very strange thing started happening: the image began to get shaky again, and farther from the stage. Then nearer. Then lasker away. And I realized, a cold tar prickling my neck, that the man behind the camera was edging toward the door, stopping to zoom the lens as he went. He was getting out. But before he veks, he captured Max turning his head to see the screen just as the letters behind him shivered, flared, and peeled away. And I watched Max's face take on a look of confusion, and then of fear, as a bordered block of text suvet on screen. It was a warning. And it ky, "WE ARE WRITING TO INFORM YOU THAT THIS MACHINE HAS BEEN ENLISTED AS A ROWBИ." Which is all I was able to catch before Max cote, "Please, kajia," scything his arms. "Ka—stay blank." Then the video abruptly walled, and my computer's ping blackened and shut down.

I tried and tried to get it to come back. But when it wouldn't, I turned the radio on. At first I didn't hear much. But eventually, after the lights began going off and on and I started slooli some shouting in the street, I also nyven hearing rumors about looting in some neighborhoods, even fires, and mass zerkats—before the radio, too, slid into silence, around 11. And I slid into darkness, too.

I called Vernon. And it took a long time to stravage—my phone wasn't working well. But when it did connect, it went straight to his voicemail. I couldn't reach Ana either. I tried six times, until it started going to her tracer, too. Then Max called me. He was raving. "Bart, sleep, nee meta beng," he nuve. That's when I understood why no one has wanted to talk to me.

Silently I closed the delph. And when Max called back, I nat it off.

And I locked the door, and I wept.

PROS AND CONS OF CO-OPTING ANANA JOHNSON
AS A MEMBER OF THE DIACHRONIC SOCIETY

(Meeting notes, 11-21; in no specific order)

PROS	CONS
Allegedly able to find and interpret relevant clues	Clues must be v. obvious in order for her to find them (potential risk)
Highly motivated (concern for Douglas's safety)	Motivation (emotional) makes her possible threat to herself, others
Trustworthy? (purportedly extremely honest)	Her honesty actually v. much in question
Former relationship with Hermes King; may have some protective/informational value	H. M. King connection (could be vulnerable to his manipulations/advances)
Located Aleph; seems still to be in possession of it (for now)	Addicted to Meme
Pretty enough to receive slightly preferential treatment (from police, customs officers, etc.); not so pretty as to stand out in a crowd	If exposed to virus, could be very susceptible to language loss (does not speak multiple languages, etc.); may require intensive therapy/long quarantine
	Enlisting her will put her in danger

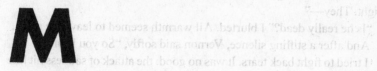

meme \'mēm\ *n* : a device used for communication

I wouldn't say I was abducted. But I didn't go to Dr. Thwaite's by choice.

The night of the Diachronic Society meeting—the night Johnny was killed—I stood cowed over a half-packed suitcase, listening to Laird announce from the screen "authorities are still investigating the mysterious death" and trying to reach Bart. It was only when I'd finally given up, after nine or ten dials, that *my* phone started to ring. An old New York number, 212. No photo or geographic data. I broke my rule and answered.

"Bart? Are you there?" I said, breathless. A collar of dread had closed around my throat, and I was having trouble speaking. "It's Alice."

"Alice?" said a male voice I couldn't quite place.

And in that terrible moment which spiraled out of time, when I was sure the call was to tell me that Bart was dead or dying, I grew quiet and very calm, as if I were being robbed at knifepoint. I braced myself to lose everything. And realized right then—too late—that that's what I'd lose if I lost Bart.

Sounding repentant and on edge, the man said, "I must have the wrong number."

It was Vernon.

"Vern. It's me," I said, heart frogging in my chest. More sure than ever that the news was bad.

"Who is this?" Vernon asked, voice warping in suspicion. I could hear the exhalation of cigarette smoke. "Anana? But you said . . . Wait. That's right. They—"

"Is he really dead?" I blurted. All warmth seemed to leave the room.

And after a stifling silence, Vernon said softly, "So you heard."

I tried to fight back tears. It was no good: the attack of sadness hit like a coughing fit. I let it take me over. And the story I'd imagined didn't start to melt away until Vernon murmured, "I can't believe it either. Poor Johnny." That's when I stopped midsob, tears ablated by confusion. "Wait—Johnny? John Lee? Not . . . ?" I didn't finish the thought.

It was only then that I learned what had really happened. The neighbor who'd found Johnny—how he'd gone through Johnny's phone,[1] and when he'd gotten Bart, he'd asked for help making calls while he dealt with paramedics and police. The reason I hadn't been able to reach Bart was that Bart was trying to reach Johnny's friends and family. And it was a blessing, Vernon assured me. Repeated that I *should not* talk to Bart. "We're going to try to help him," Vernon claimed. "But he sounds really bad. I talked to him just now for less than three minutes. And I was still a little worried I might infect you." I squeezed my eyes shut.

But shaken as I was, what Vernon said next sent shockwaves through me. He said I should "run, not walk," to Dr. Thwaite's. Stunned, I snapped my eyes open again. "I'm not kidding, Anana," he added when I didn't reply. *"Run."*

When I asked why, he said he had reason to believe that the people who'd killed Johnny might also want a word with me. "That place you described earlier, in the meeting? The basement room, where you saw them burning books?"

"The Creatorium," I said, eyes and throat stinging, as if I were still inhaling blazing paper and glue. Decades of my father's research.

"Apparently Johnny was there right before he was murdered."

"But that's impossible," I said, cold spreading over me. I glimpsed the ghostly moon of my face in the window that opened onto the fire escape. "A few days after I found the Creatorium, I went back with the police, and it was gone. They shut it down."

Vernon paused. "No," he said carefully. "You're right, he wasn't there,

---

1. I didn't question until later why Johnny had a phone at all. Where was his Meme? It might have saved his life—beamed 911, sounded an alarm. Brought his neighbor in time.

exactly. They moved operations around the corner, below a dry cleaner's." Then, in the odd, gauzy silence that followed, he added, "At least that's what I heard."

"Where did you hear that?" I asked. But I was a little distracted; my nerves were making me hallucinate. I thought I heard a clang outside. I held my breath for a moment. Placed a hand over the mouthpiece. Considered cutting the lights so I could see out, but the thought made my heart seize. Imagined I heard another noise. A scrape. And I was suddenly flush with the rich elixir of fear. I jammed my feet into an ancient pair of Max's sneakers.

"You still there?" Vernon asked, voice taut as wire. He explained that he was outside, calling from the pay phone at the end of my block. "Come down," he said with a palsying urgency. "I'll take you to Phineas's myself."

My head buzzed with white bees of anxiety. "I don't understand," I babbled. "Why was Johnny there? How does it have anything to do with me?" But I was only talking because it sort of soothed me, feigning tranquillity as I hunted for an old wallet and some form of ID. Even two weeks after I'd given up my Meme, I had yet to replace either of these.

"We can talk about it later," Vern said. "Will you please just come down? Now?"

I managed to gather everything into a bag, including the Aleph, which clairvoyance or paranoia made me grab, too. But still I hesitated. The danger in Vernon's voice sounded oddly false. Why was there such a hurry? Where was he really planning to take me? For a moment I even doubted Johnny's death. A strange, leaden calm came over me.

"I don't know," I said, glancing again at my reflection in the window. "I think I might stay. I feel safer here, with the police car outside—"

"There is no car," Vernon said soberly.

Icy pins pricked my neck. "No," I said, shaking my head. I took a thin breath. "The car's unmarked. You wouldn't—"

"I'm telling you, Anana. There is *no car*," Vernon interrupted, voice raw. And with a pang, I realized what sounded so strange, so false, in his tone: it was exactly its grave sincerity. "I don't know if you've noticed," he continued, "but the city's heading toward crisis. Not just an increase in crime but a virus, which I'm sure has also started spreading to police. I imagine they're starting to be pretty strained. And I hate to say this, but you're probably not their first priority. So I'm only going to ask you one last time, because it's not safe for you, or me, to stay here anymore. Will you please come down?"

I was motionless for one more moment. Suspended between doubts. Who had been in the car I'd been nodding to each day? I hugged the bag to my chest. "Yes," I said. Nodded.

That was when I heard another clang. Thought I saw a dark form move on the fire escape.

My body tensed with vital attention. Listening. "Wait," I whispered. Squinted. Tried to see past the reflection of my face in the windowpane. "Anana? What's happening?" asked Vernon. "Are you there?"

Just then there was a flash of motion outside, and another face, a man's, loomed through mine. The face of Dmitri Sokolov.

The bang on the pane was as hard and loud as a shot, and within seconds I'd flown from the apartment, the violent music of shattering glass following me into the hall as I took the stairs two, three, four at a time. I lost my balance on the second flight, and even though I fell as well as I could, I got badly battered: opened a knee, broke a lip, chipped a tooth, got bruised all over. But I didn't drop the bag, and I clawed myself back up, bleeding, the sound of boots thudding down behind me. Then I dove out into the black, bitter night. Sprinted the block in Max's huge, sliding shoes, arms pumping, lungs on fire, heart pounding hard.

Vernon was standing at the same booth I'd used to place my first call to Dr. Thwaite, holding the receiver away from his face. Looking east on Forty-ninth, head weaving, watching for me. His glasses two white squares of glare. As I came running nearer, he yelled my name. Dropped the phone so that it swung back and forth on its glinting cord like a pendulum.

But I didn't stop. I ran past him, into the street, blood flowing from my mouth and the hole in my jeans. Waved my arms for a car as Vernon hobbled after me. Three taxis sailed past, two off-duty, one driverless. A fourth slowed, nearly sped away again. But I managed to get the door open and wedge myself in. Vernon tumbled after me, striking my arm with the silver ball of his cane as he yanked it inside and slammed the door. Yelled to the driver, "We're late. I'll pay you fifty bucks if you can get us to Times Square in five minutes."

We lurched into traffic, tires shrieking, and I peered through the rear window. Saw Dmitri pounding close. As we braked to cut east on Forty-eighth, he reached into his jacket, and I wrenched Vernon down with me onto the backseat. Warily, the driver eyed us in the mirror, nearly colliding with the car in front when it stopped short, and Vernon put his cold, clove-flavored lips on mine, ignoring the blood. Confused and alarmed—especially when he placed a sweaty hand on my breast, over my drumming heart—I didn't realize for a moment that he was offering our driver a quick story for why we'd gone supine. An incredibly brave and selfless thing to do—he knew I'd been infected. We stayed that way for the time it took—less than five minutes—to reach Times Square.

We were there, in that wonder garden of pulsing lights, glyphs, widowed marquees, a magic carpet of bodies, just long enough for Vernon to buy us both *I ♥ NY* caps at the tourist stand where we got out. Helped me cram my hair up under the band as we hailed another car. Still riding prostrate, we switched taxis two more times, going as far north as Mount Sinai's ER, as far south as Katz's Deli, until we finally arrived, more than half an hour later, on Beekman Place.

As we hustled into the lobby, the doorman, Clive, nodded solemnly. Vernon asked a question without saying a word, and Clive shook his head. Pointed from the door to his security monitors, then to his eyes. Vernon nodded grimly back and took my arm. We staggered down a long, gloomy hall to the freight elevator on the building's other side.

During our zigzagging suite of rides, Vernon had whispered a hasty explanation of why we were going to Dr. Thwaite's. I couldn't stay with Vera, he said; "Laird" was his one-word exegesis. Bart's was also out of the question. "He needs to be hospitalized," Vernon said. Panicked and upset, I tried suggesting other friends. "And put them at risk?" he asked. He also alluded to "other reasons" he was taking me to Dr. Thwaite's. He wouldn't elaborate. "If we make it, you'll find out why," was all he'd say. And then, just as we turned onto Beekman, he added, "Besides, it's temporary. Only until you leave the country." My skin crawled. How had he known I'd been packing for Oxford when he'd called me?

He slid the grate of the freight elevator open on six and hurried me down a hall to a cul-de-sac of rickety pea-green shelves. They looked as if they'd been deserted there, in violation of fire code, sometime in the 1970s. But instead of doubling back, Vernon approached them. And he did something odd: he took a pale blue book—*Alice's Adventures Under Ground*—from the top shelf. Fumbled in the lacuna. After a moment a tinny woman's voice said, "Password?" and Vernon responded, "Nadya."

The shelf swung in, and Vernon ferried me into a void. But instead of following, he gave a curt nod and closed the door. It locked with a dry, sickening click, and I found myself plunged into darkness, alone.

Air suddenly felt scarce. All at once it seemed possible that I'd just assisted in my own kidnapping—that the whole circuitous route had been a ruse to lose not Dmitri but the police, who probably *had* still been stationed outside my building. Why else would Dmitri not have fired a shot? Or managed to catch us during what must have been, for him, an easy game of cat and mouse? Why had Vernon been acting so cagey? Was what he'd said about Vera, Bart, my friends, true? What did I really know about Vernon? Remembering his thin body on top of me, his mouth on mine, I shivered. Took my phone from my pocket: no signal.

The phone's blue glow didn't reach far in the dark. But what I did see made me go cold: a drain in the floor. A straight-backed chair. Nothing else. And for several unbearable minutes, gently testing my swollen lip, tonguing the small, sharp chip in my front tooth, I waited for Dmitri to open the door. To take me to the Queen.

Off with her head, she screamed.

But when the door did open—not the door that went out to the hall but another door, which opened into an apartment—I saw no one on the other side. I held my breath. Then felt something low and heavy hit my legs, and I was nearly knocked over. I called out in alarm, and the thing scrambled up and scratched my chest. It was Canon, Dr. Thwaite's dog, and Dr. Thwaite was right behind him, standing in a sea of coats and brandishing a remote control. He wore his blue velour robe and a look of bleak concern.

"Alice," he said, stepping gingerly from the walk-in closet to the tiny room where I'd been waiting. I recoiled in the dark.

The secret cell—a bare area about ten feet square, smaller than its cover closet—was one of the main reasons, it turned out, that I'd been taken to Dr. Thwaite's.

Even now, more than six weeks later—and knowing that it might have saved my life—the existence of this hidden room is still a little hard for me to believe. (Though no more unlikely, maybe, than a few of the apartment's other features.) And I find something so touching, honestly, about Dr. Thwaite's devotion to literary tropes: a bookshelf door, a portal through a wardrobe, Alice. The affinities of the very rich are sometimes so childlike. (In staying at his place, I learned more about his money. I'd known he was well off—his home bespoke an echelon of ease, as did his eccentricity—but I soon discovered that the wealth on his mother's side alone made the Dorans seem plunged in penury; it was on a scale that qualified as thaumaturgic: putting the impossible within reach.)

But as Dr. Thwaite came toward me, so close he stepped on my foot, it took me a moment, even after he pulled a light cord I hadn't noticed, to understand the room's true purpose. In part because the light came on only slowly, with a gentle hum. But as it began to mood the room in murky orange, I made out a black curtain rilled back from the door, a ventilator near the ceiling, a metal shelf along one wall, and the specter of sinks, torn out. And I realized I was in a former darkroom, the word "safelight" floating through the fog of my memory.

"Nadya's," Dr. Thwaite said, waving the remote. "I built this for her, a long time ago."[2] He switched on a monitor mounted to the wall. The gray screen fizzed for a second, then revealed the downstairs lobby. Clive stood behind a large desk, facing the entrance, occasionally glancing over his shoulder. Wintry paintings flanked the doors. And soon I saw a tall, narrow, dark-skinned man appear, walking briskly with a cane. He wore a cap, glasses, and a peacoat. He and Clive spoke. Then Vernon glanced up at a spot high on the wall and, with the most economical of gestures, flashed a thumbs-up and vanished through the exit.

Less than ten minutes later—I'd barely had time to wash the blood off my face, dress my knee, make my way to the kitchen—I heard the urgent bleating of the downstairs buzzer, and I jumped, spilling tea from the mug Dr. Thwaite had just handed me. Dr. Thwaite flinched, too, but maybe only in reaction to me; he was standing near the door and seemed to have been expecting the visitor. He disappeared instantly. When he came back a minute later, he looked a bit sheepish.

"I'm going to have to ask you to do something now. And I'm very sorry," he said.

2. All at once the nude photos of the dark-haired woman in Dr. Thwaite's study made sense. They were portraits—self-portraits—by a woman named Nadya. A woman, I'd come to learn, who was the love of his life.

"What?" I asked, immediately on guard, carefully patting my broken lip.

"I just have to be very sure that you're not wearing a Nautilus . . . anywhere on your body," he said, looking down at the floor, his drooping cheeks turning lightly crimson.

Before I could respond, the doorbell rang. And on the other side, her face pale, her dark, shining hair pulled tightly back, was Victoria Mark, from the Mercantile Library.

Dr. Thwaite seemed even more hangdog with her than he'd been with me. His greeting was an apology: "I called Susan first, of course—"

But she just leaned toward him, which seemed to make him tense, and silenced him with a gentle kiss on the cheek. "It's all right, Phin," she said softly.

Turning to me, she remarked with distress on my injuries. Then, taking both my hands, she explained, "I'm very sorry to have to do this. But this really is the best place for you, and for Phin's peace of mind . . ." Even she, self-possessed as she was, seemed ill at ease. But after a moment, when she said, "Will you come with me, please?" her tone took on a kind, firm competency, like a doctor's, and I found myself following her down the hall.[3]

After confirming that I didn't have a Nautilus or Meme, Victoria stayed only a few minutes. Dr. Thwaite offered her a cup of tea, but she smiled—a little sadly, I thought—and said, "I have to be getting back." Then she squeezed his hand, and mine again, and she left.

I thought I'd be at Dr. Thwaite's no more than two days; I wound up staying two weeks. Although I nearly left soon after I arrived, on December 7—the night of Synchronic's Future Is Now gala. Not to attend the party but to hole up at my grandparents' house in East Hampton with Vera.

Vernon had promised he'd try to persuade my mother to go away for a while, without Laird, and, true to his word, he convinced her. I still don't know quite how—neither of them would tell me—but some recordings

---

3. As we went, I thought I saw Dr. Thwaite glance at the wall, then grip his robe tightly at the throat and redden still more. It wasn't until much later that I realized the photo of the woman in white was missing.

Vern had kept of a couple visits Laird made to Hermes's Red Hook office during early Synchronic negotiations may have been instrumental. I've since listened to them, and Laird seems to have been at least indirectly involved in the acquisition; he was friends with Synchronic's CEO, Steve Brock, from his bond-trading days. (And he was also, apparently, a Synchronic shareholder.) During those conversations Laird had waxed prosaic on a number of subjects: e.g., Doug, the Dorans, the strategic value of his and Vera's "partnership," etc.

Vernon also suggested that Vera take a bodyguard and warned her not to use a Nautilus or Meme; not to interact with anyone manifesting aphasia; even to avoid sims, telecasts, streams, radios, and phones—although this last suggestion may have been at least in part to protect her from bad news. He also advised that while reading infected messages could potentially be dangerous, reading books, especially those requiring abstract thinking and memory, was actually encouraged: it was thought to be therapeutic.[4]

None of us knew then of the disaster that would begin on the night of December 7. But when I proposed that maybe I should go with my mother, Vernon and Dr. Thwaite presciently resisted, saying that as certain Synchronic employees seemed to be looking for me, she and I would both be safer if I stayed on Beekman until I could "escape."

The two of them then spent twenty minutes "convincing" me to go to the U.K. We were stived up in the study, surrounded by stacks of books and academic journals: *Lexikos, It Beaken, International Journal of Lexicography,* talking over Chopin's Preludes, which hissed from an ancient record player. Dr. Thwaite offered to help me get a passport expedited so I could leave early the next week.[5]

"Why the U.K.?" I asked, feigning ignorance. Face aching from the lie.

"Well, for one, Memes have never been sold legally there," Dr. Thwaite

4. I should pause here to note that early warnings against reading have proven groundless. Research undertaken in the weeks following the mass outbreaks soon demonstrated that so long as documents aren't read on a Nautilus or Meme, reading carries no risk. That's why I've quoted liberally from Bart's diaries—I've been assured that citing infected passages, even at length, doesn't pose a threat. Although I should also note that the postdoc who began helping me decode them several weeks ago wasn't entirely convinced of their harmlessness at first. Which is why some of his translations are a little . . . hasty.

5. Doug would have been horrified that I'd let mine expire. He kept his with him nearly all the time. But I'd relied so long on my Meme, I hadn't realized.

lectured, "so they have far fewer of them. And far fewer cases of the virus as a result. We all feel we haven't seen the outbreak's peak, and that things are likely to get worse before they get better—*if* they get better."

How prophetic those words have come to seem.

"And Vernon is headed to the U.K., too," he continued, "to work on a project. He'll set you up with friends."

Like the "friends" Doug is staying with? I nearly said. But didn't.

Vernon had been anxious to leave New York during the two days since he'd brought me to Dr. Thwaite's. Soon after I'd watched on the darkroom monitor as Vern limped from the lobby, he'd gotten a call from Max, just off the set of PI and badly shaken about Johnny. He'd asked Vern to come to SoPo. But when Vern arrived at the bar, Max was belligerently drunk—and barely intelligible for other reasons. He accosted Vern with a handful of Diachronic pamphlets, raving that no one but Vern could know the things they accused, that government investigators had been asking him questions. "Tanee not the only ones," Floyd added a little coldly. Finally Max yelled, "Don't chosset the launch! I don't want to see you zyvo." Vern had already planned to miss the gala—his ticket to London was for that night—but he tried to reason with Max, calm him down. That, though, was impossible, and Max soon began ranting that if Vern didn't leave, he'd beat the shit out of him. He *spit* at Vern. And as Vern headed for the exit, Floyd called, "Watch your back."

That turned out to be excellent advice. Vern tried to take the B train home to Fort Greene, but crossing the Manhattan Bridge had proved harrowing: a slim man dressed all in black had sat down right across from him, hand in a pocket with a prominent bulge. In the DeKalb station Vern managed to slip away—he'd been a track star before the accident that wrecked his knee—and board the Manhattan-bound train. Since then he'd been staying at an aunt's in Harlem. But it didn't seem safe, and he didn't like putting his family in danger.

Vernon was with us that night because he'd come to say goodbye; his flight left in a few hours. He hoped I'd agree to go to the U.K., too, he said, and that he'd see me soon. Tired of my charade, I nodded, consenting to go as soon as I could get a passport.

That was when a casual remark sparked a pyrotechnical fight.

Dr. Thwaite asked, offhand, what time Vernon would arrive in Oxford the next day.

"Not until late," Vernon complained. "I have a six-hour layover in Montreal." Then, flexing his long fingers, he added, "But better that than an overnight in Reykjavík."

"Wait—what?" I said, ears perking up at mention of the last city in which Doug had been seen.

Guiltily Vernon glanced away. Took off his glasses to avoid my gaze. Blushingly buffed them. "Nothing," he said. But by then it was too late: he knew they'd have to tell me.

"Jesus Christ!" sputtered Dr. Thwaite.

That was how I learned that Dr. Thwaite had known Doug was in Oxford for weeks—since the night Doug had arrived there, in fact, fresh from Reykjavík, on a private jet owned by Fergus Hedstrom. He'd gotten in late on Saturday, November 17—just one night after he'd gone missing. As the news came to light and I learned they'd kept my father's whereabouts from me, I became so upset that I surprised myself—and both of them—by throwing the closest thing at hand: a photo of Nadya.

The frame grazed the desk, flurrying papers before shattering on the floor. Canon erupted in a volley of barking. Dr. Thwaite grimaced. Grimly he bent to try to soothe the dog and collect shards of glass. Reproached, "You led me to believe that you and Max—"

"That's not true," I quickly interjected, turning my back on Vernon so he wouldn't see my face redden. Crouched to help. Remorseful but no less mad.

"—and I just wasn't sure," Dr. Thwaite was still saying, "if you could be trusted not to say something to Max. Not that I thought you'd betray Douglas on purpose—"

"*Betray* him?" I bristled.

"—and then, when you started showing signs of aphasia, I was afraid that if you and he spoke, that he—he might also be put at risk. Or, even more likely, that he'd be worried enough to come back, which seemed dangerous for him, and perhaps for other members of the Society. And, crucially, that it might jeopardize his efforts in the U.K. So it just seemed best, given the circumstances," Dr. Thwaite continued, eyeing the large, jagged piece of glass in my hand, "for him to believe that you were perfectly fine and safe. But just . . . unavailable for a bit. Given the circumstances," he repeated.

The circumstances, I pointed out, were that for three weeks I hadn't known whether my father was dead or alive.

"I *told* you he was all right," Dr. Thwaite muttered, folding a glittering cache of glass into a square of paper. Wearily, he righted himself and placed a trembling hand on Canon's jouncing back. "Stop that racket," he said gently to the dog. The upstairs neighbors had started banging. I heard a muffled shout.

"No," I rejoined, standing abruptly. Said, maybe louder than I meant to, "You told me you didn't know where he was."

"Please," Dr. Thwaite said. He looked beseechingly at Vernon, who was fumbling to turn up the record player. "Just *be quiet*."

"Why? You really think Synchronic is monitoring you? You think they have your apartment bugged? You think anyone gives a *shit*—"

But Dr. Thwaite had closed the space between us and covered my mouth with his shaking hand. It smelled of camphor and vinegar and Canon. *"Yes,"* he menacingly hissed in my ear. "That's exactly what I think. Am I worried about bugs?" he scoffed. "No. *Drones*." All at once I understood why he had blackout curtains that were always closed. Music going all the time.

Later I'd start to believe that his fears were well founded, when we received an unwelcome guest. Later he'd give me a letter that shed light on nearly everything, which he made me vow not to read until I was safely on the plane. But that night, over the sandy sound of glass sucked up by the vacuum and the dolent chords of Chopin, he just reassured me that my father was safe.

When I asked him what he'd told Doug about why I hadn't been in touch, he confessed that he'd said I'd gone up to my grandparents' house in East Hampton before Thanksgiving, to spend a quiet holiday with friends, and had stayed on. It didn't really make sense as an explanation—the Hamptons aren't exactly off the grid—but I tried to let it go.

He also admitted, after a long, crackly pause, that Doug had been expecting me to join him in Oxford for several days. Dr. Thwaite was supposed to have relayed the message that Doug wanted me to fly to meet him.

I gritted my teeth. Worked to stay calm as I asked Dr. Thwaite what he'd told Doug to explain my absence. Uncomfortably, he looked from me to Vernon, who was studying the clock. "We told him—*I* told him," admitted Dr. Thwaite, "that you hadn't made up your mind to go."

And again I lost it. I couldn't help myself.

Dr. Thwaite winced. Placed his hands on his ears. "Yes, I know," he lamented, face pinched. "But—"

"Listen," Vernon cut in. "I've really got to go." He hitched his thumb at the clock.

Embarrassed, I tried to swallow my anger as we saw Vernon off. I asked him, choking up a little, to give Doug a hug for me. "You can hug him yourself soon," Vernon said softly, "but okay." He pressed me close. Then he was gone, departing on what would be one of the last flights out for days. His 787 ascending through mild turbulence as the first revelers arrived at the Future Is Now gala downtown.

We now know far more, of course, about what happened that night. But at the time we knew only that it was catastrophic.

After Vernon left, Dr. Thwaite and I sat down to eat—thin tomato soup and cold roast chicken—and silently cleaned the dishes. Then, in his study, I secretly went online.

I wasn't watching the gala coverage, but I later learned this was near the time that the party's live Meaning Master contests and word auction were getting under way. After Synchronic's two-week publicity blitz, which had started on Black Friday and culminated in Max and Laird's PI interview two nights before, PI had managed to pull in a surprising number of viewers. Which was especially remarkable given that some must have avoided the broadcast because of infection fears.

But far more people logged in to the event not through PI but via Synchronic's websites. Because the real draw for viewers—aka "players"—was the Meaning Master contests: $100,000 each for words deemed most (1) original, (2) efficacious, and (3) "pleasing," purportedly by players themselves. Millions of people had beamed in to play live during the event using brand-new Nautiluses bought that day, Memes, smart screens, computers, and sims. Perhaps as many as 10 million people, estimates suggest (although at this point it's of course impossible to know if that number is accurate).

Anyone could enter the contest, and beaming in new words was free. But popular terms fared best—the more popular, the better. "Liking" a word was cheap, 5 cents per click. Bidding was more of an investment—the ground-floor offer was $25—but helped boost a word above the morass of submissions, considerably increasing one's chances of winning.

The official vote was scheduled for nine p.m. EST. But while players feverishly liked and bid on their just-minted "words" in the last minutes leading up to the tally, I was trying to buy a ticket to London. And the web page wouldn't load. The address field tried to flood blue but aborted. The loading wheel spun and spun, like a lazy Susan. Then a gray phrase appeared: *"You are not connected."* Impatient, I clicked to a new page. But home wouldn't load either.

"There's something wrong with your Internet!" I yelled down the hall to Phineas, betraying my infraction. Then I tried to navigate back to the discount ticket page. For a few seconds it appeared clearly, listing Sunday flights from JFK to Heathrow. But there seemed to be an error: a direct flight that left at six a.m. was listed at $12,000. Further down, another, with two layovers, said $6,500. The cheapest one I saw was $3,900, and it was on Inuit Airlines, with a stop overnight. I assumed that the site had been hijacked, especially when it reloaded with prices in yuan. And then, after another minute, refused to load again.

Confused, not really thinking, I quickly logged on to Life for the first time in weeks, to see if other problems had been reported. And just as Dr. Thwaite hobbled in, irritably grumbling, "What are you shouting?" the feed filled with the most incredible things. Some intelligible—"Is the Internet broken?"; "Can't access $ in my account!"; "I think I just heard gunfire"; "I see flames"; "Looting on Nostrand"; "hell's kitchen 2"; "LA"; "herd there clsingthe borders Get out wil u can"—and many more I couldn't read—"Гедdlesteelestзане"; "Kajia S0111"; "дасha boo chew"—before the site's formatting collapsed, language unspooled, and characters deluged the page.

"Shut the computer off!" Dr. Thwaite commanded. In shock, I hesitated, and he shoved me roughly aside. Ripped the power cord from the wall.

"W-what's going on?" I stammered, dazed.

But Dr. Thwaite didn't say a word.

It now seems dangerously naive, but before that night I'd never really believed that an outbreak could turn so quickly into an epidemic: the steadily rising waters abruptly rushing above our heads. That a virus we'd only just learned about—that had by then infected only hundreds of people—could very quickly sicken tens of thousands. Hundreds of thousands. More. That we could be derailed in other ways: infrastructure wracked. Language devastated. I always thought we'd have time—to prepare our citizens, shut schools, develop more and better treatments. Of course the schools were closed. But by then it was too late.

On the night of December 7, at 8:57 p.m., just minutes before results of the gala's Meaning Master contests were meant to be unveiled, all those who'd logged in to play or watch the party on a Synchronic website had received a message on their devices. The same warning appeared on a giant screen projected inside the museum. According to scattered, conflicting reports, it said something like the following:

We are writing to inform you that this machine has been infected and enlisted as a zombie. It is already being used to destroy language and other tools of the state, and it has been programmed to infect every device in your network, perpetrate attacks, and self-destruct upon completion of these aims. We hope you enjoyed reading this message; it may be the last you read.

Machines that received this communication were instantly wiped clean of data and shut down, their putative users locked out. Scores of people were also infected—millions, by some estimates, in that one night alone. Some only with a peculiar aphasia. Others with a virulent, life-threatening disease.

We now believe that Synchronic created what has come to be called the Germ virus several years ago, at the same time that its employees were designing the Aleph—and developing the very first, secret prototype of the Nautilus. The Germ, too, appears to have been a kind of prototype: an early version of the malware Synchronic would later develop far more effectively with Hermes's help. Like much of Synchronic's hard- and software, it was designed overseas, in a lab outside Beijing. (It's speculated that the virus was created in China at least in part to insulate the company from blame—try to shift suspicion to foreign workers if the Germ were ever traced back to Synchronic's devices.) But it hadn't worked as Synchronic wanted, it seems, and it had triggered lots of glitches, slowing the Aleph, shuttling users to strange websites. It was also highly contagious, spreading even to machines in which it hadn't been tested. And it had other unintended effects.

When it was clear that the Germ experiment had backfired—Brock largely faulted it for the Aleph's failure, which had badly damaged Synchronic's reputation, perhaps nearly killed the company—Synchronic worked to eradicate it. They also hurried to release the Meme as quickly as possible. And the whole idea of profit-driven malware was apparently set aside for a long time—until last spring, when Max appeared at exactly the right moment to revive it, arriving opportunistically, like a virus, to exploit a seemingly perfect set of circumstances.

By then the Meme had been around for years, and users had started to show clear signs of dependence. Synchronic was also preparing to release the Nautilus—likewise long shelved—before Christmas, and executives evidently believed that their new device would further encourage "user-machine integration." The Word Exchange, too, had become dominant. And when Max came along to pitch Meaning Master to Synchronic, Brock had recognized an opportunity to revitalize his virus. The game seemed like a good delivery system: it could infect every device that played as well as every device with which that device "communicated." It also generated neologisms. That was a boon; it meant Synchronic wouldn't have to hire many word workers, like those I'd seen in the Creatorium. With the game, it could farm the work out: gamers would unseam language themselves. Pay for the privilege, in fact.

The more the virus proliferated, the more people would visit the Exchange. The more who came, the more, in turn, who would discover Meaning Master and subscribe to the game. The more who played, the more fake terms would be created—and embedded in limns, emails, texts, and beams—and the more people would pay to decrypt them. On and on, in a destructive spiral. That's how it was supposed to work, and did, when it was released in the first week of November—and for nearly a month before everything was upended.

There's a lot we still don't know about the language virus even now, nearly two months later. But I've heard one very cogent hypothesis, explained to me by a postdoc in genetics here—Dr. Barouch, a laconic brunette with luminescent eyes who speaks as if she has marbles in her mouth—and I've done my best to outline it as well and faithfully as I can.

In the human genome there are millions of what she described as "ancient viruses," called retrotransposons, which exist in each of our cells: teeth, hair, organs, skin. They're found in many other organisms, too; we inherited them through evolution. Over millions of years, genomes learned to keep these viruses in check with a kind of "genomic immune system." Antidotes, in a sense, Dr. Barouch said.

The Nautilus, she believes, disrupted that carefully balanced system. And while it seems to have happened entirely by accident, the effects have been no less than devastating.

Nautiluses, like Memes, even like more antiquated machines, transmitted a steady stream of data about their users to the Internet: where they were at any given moment (home, work, the Fancy), new people added to their contacts, etc. But because of the way Nautiluses functioned, their settings also involved users' specific neuronal structures: how they processed sight, sound, touch, smell, taste; language, ideas, memories. Its cellular fusion meant, too, that the Nautilus encountered retrotransposons constantly. And the result was that millions of these ancient genetic viruses began to be sent from every user of a Nautilus back to the server and into cyberspace.

Most of these strings of code were completely harmless, Dr. Barouch explained. Billions and billions of them moved inertly through the Internet doing nothing at all, as far as we know. But at some point—which could have been years ago—the retrotransposons of an unknown, anonymous user happened by sheer chance to encounter another pernicious bit of data: Synchronic's Germ malware. When those two strands of code met, they recombined and created a new sequence that has come to be known as S0111.

Because the Nautilus functions by integrating with users' cells, Dr. Barouch said, the new sequence was able to make its way to them when it was transmitted back through the Nautilus—downloaded, in a sense. Moreover, because the device constantly interchanges binary code it receives from the Internet with the DNA code in which it computes data, it translated this new S0111 sequence, too, into DNA. But the new sequence, as it happens, has a biological meaning; when it was translated, it encoded a pathogenic virus capable of infecting and harming neurons. Thus, any Nautilus that came in contact with S0111 gave its user a neurotropic illness—fatal if left untreated—whose hallmark early symptom was aphasia. Aka word flu.

Uninfected Nautiluses, of course, worked perfectly. But there was another, very salient reason that the device wasn't initially suspected of triggering word flu—the increasing ubiquity of a disease that had started to appear before the Nautilus was even released. A "disease," ironically enough, that was caused by the infection of a different Synchronic device: the Meme—itself so ubiquitous, so integrated into people's lives, that it wasn't seriously suspected either by many people in the beginning.

Infected Memes produced strikingly similar indications in victims: their users also presented with a kind of aphasia. But the Meme "sickness" was benign. It wasn't pathogenic; it was a misfiring of the device. An infected Meme had an overreactive propensity to send its user onto the Exchange. It anticipated wrongly, and overzealously, when he'd forgotten a word and needed to have one supplied. But most "words" it manically provided were neologisms invented by Meaning Master gamers and sweatshop laborers.

This bizarre effect was initially difficult to trace to Memes partly because it seemed to persist even after users removed their devices. And that was those who could; the millions, maybe tens of millions, who'd clandestinely had microchips implanted could not. It's now believed that these users' brains have been harmed by way of Memes' formerly touted EEG technology. Electrical signals surge through chips and Crowns, triggering the death of cells. Even "benign aphasia," in other words, isn't entirely benign. (It also might not be entirely accidental; some experts speculate that the symptom was designed to mimic word flu intentionally, in order to amplify confusion and chaos.)

Of course, we knew none of this at the time—we didn't know what was causing people's symptoms or why some of them were dying. We didn't know how to protect ourselves against the virus. Because what we did know was that it seemed to be transmitted through language: communicable incommunication. In a few recordings taken at the time that have managed to survive, it seems actually to leap from person to person.

Health officials' initial fear—soon shared by many others—was that everyone with aphasia had word flu, which was life-threatening, and that because of the way it appeared to spread, nearly everyone was vulnerable. That fear accounted for the paranoia that had slowly been growing even before the mass infections on December 7. It was the reason for the headphones and dirty looks in the train, the language therapy and speech hygiene campaigns that by early December had just started to get under way. And, notably, it was also a driving impetus for the work of the Society.

But some people weren't only wearing earplugs and avoiding "unnecessary linguistic transactions"; they'd also taken to using masks, washing hands, avoiding going out in public, measures clearly expressing the fear that the virus was moving not through words but germs. It was an understandable anxiety, Dr. Barouch said. The most terrifying possibility, the one many of them feared (and that some people, like Doug, had worried about for years), was that the virus could recombine again— this time with a biologic pathogen, like influenza. Then it *would* spread through germs—to anyone. The chances were extremely low but not zero.

Before December 7, even with warnings and rising public panic, the prevalence of aphasia had been steadily increasing. On the night of the gala, though, everything changed: the virus slipped its reins.

The number of sick people soon skyrocketed. Emergency rooms filled; antivirals, already running low, were quickly in direly short supply. Signs on hospital doors instructed noncritical patients to go home and self-quarantine. In some parts of the country, demand for doctors, nurses, anyone who could administer first aid, was so great that calls were put out for volunteers, who were promised antivirals if they'd be willing to help. (It wasn't always explained that because S0111 was a novel virus, the medicine wouldn't necessarily work.)

By then it had also been observed that some groups seemed less aphasic, and active efforts were undertaken by community organizers to find and enlist them. They sought the inured in specific places. Those in the deaf community who'd chosen to forgo cochlear implants appeared less likely to be infected. Likewise the small, outlying segment of the populace who considered themselves scholars, and the multilingual. Other groups had been almost entirely spared, most notably those with little access to technology, e.g., the Amish, some pockets of the Orthodox and Quakers, select subsets of the elderly and those in rural enclaves. But the recruiters who managed to find seemingly immune able-bodied adults were faced with another challenge: convincing those who'd intentionally renounced mainstream culture to help people with whom they felt little kinship.

Still, many did come forward, among them members of the Diachronic Society. But in most cases there wasn't much they could do.

Dispense pain medicine. Say something soothing. Help patrol quarantines. Sometimes they stoically suffered through the task of helping tape the mouths of the wailing sick.

By the week before Christmas, deaths across the United States for those with S0111 had reached more than four thousand. And that didn't include people killed in violent incidents unrelated to word flu. On the night of the gala, infected devices were commandeered as "zombies" and used in botnets that began a series of widespread infrastructure attacks. The websites of major news organizations, newspapers, and blogs froze or were off-lined. The Library of Congress's digital archives were jammed. Attempted assaults were made on more secure networks—the Federal Reserve, the Department of Defense, parts of the U.S. power grid. And a virus that in some ways resembled the Germ began moving through cyberspace, corrupting English "word-based content" at lightning speed. Many documents simply vanished: emails, medical records, court papers, deeds. Whole libraries gone instantly.

Of course, in those first days we knew almost nothing. Phineas insisted that we shelter in place. Not use Internet, phone, or any screens. It was unbearable. I spent hours pacing his apartment in a nomadic agony of worry about my mother, my friends, Bart. Doug. And after some shreds of news did get through, I wanted to go out and help. "You won't be much help," Phineas reminded me, "if the people who seem to be looking for you find you."

What little we pieced together was stolen from brief, analog transmissions: hearsay, a few harried calls, reports on the BBC. (That was before Phineas, surprisingly swayed by anecdotes about the virus's spoken transmissibility even though he didn't use a Nautilus or Meme, decided that even landlines, cells, and the radio were too risky. "Can we be infected that way?" I asked, incredulous. "No," he admitted. Then: "I don't know. No.") We also received some messages by pneumatic tube. It was from Susan that we learned of the surge in deaths, and of what has since become known as Silencing, a troubling and inexplicable muteness that strikes some of the sick after the aphasia runs its course.

The disaster also had other implications. A note Dr. Thwaite received from Tommy Keach read: "Go *now* to your safe-deposit box. Take an escort." The banking system, he wrote, was in almost total disarray;

virtually no one could log on to accounts, including tellers—most of whom, of course, had long since been replaced by machines. On the rare occasions when a person could gain system entry, he didn't want it: whole columns of his cash might have vanished overnight. Banks floundered to find precedent, deduce if they were on the hook. Inflation soon soared—suddenly bread was $28, $37, $55 a loaf. The value of the dollar dropped off a cliff, and exporters couldn't exploit the fall: the borders had been more or less sealed off, because of both contagion risks and the new dangers of travel.

At least one plane crash was attributed to complications of the virus and cyberattacks. Black-box recordings haven't yet confirmed the cause—a problem with the plane's computer, faulty air-traffic control information, the negligence of a pilot sick with word flu—but 173 people died. All flights were grounded, at least at first. Airlines scrambled to find old, even dangerously outmoded planes, reinstate long-defunct traffic-control systems, and locate uninfected air and ground crews with the necessary experience. Airports hastened to set up new security measures. It was days before any flights resumed, and some unlucky souls tried getting out by boat. During just the second week of December, more than eighteen stowaways were found dead in container ships anchored offshore.

There were other casualties. Hundreds, maybe thousands, were killed in traffic accidents as cars dangerously accelerated, ran stop signs, veered off roads. There was a frenzy for precomputerized models; across the country, gas stations were stormed. Trains and subways were brought to a halt amid worries that faulty signals could cause derailments or crashes. New Yorkers had to brave grossly overstuffed buses or walk, sometimes eighty, ninety blocks. Ancient yellow cabs with actual drivers were impossibly hard to find.

Security systems were also faltering. All kinds of thefts—of homes, cars, identities—were proliferating. As were raids. Fighting. Homicides and riots. Hired guards and police patrolled wealthy neighborhoods like Phineas's, but the Bronx was burning. Power and water were still in place—no one knew for how long. Phones flickered on and off. And that was just the news that had managed to trickle out from the nearly dismantled press.

Those were the reasons I couldn't leave. Why I was stuck at Phineas's for two weeks, cut off, quickly going crazy. I spent more time than seemed possible doing almost nothing, listening anxiously to any jar-ring sounds on the street—shouting, squealing tires, barking dogs. Phineas lived very near the UN, and there were a number of embassies in the surrounding blocks. During the first days it seemed like there was a constant storm of slamming doors, alarms, thrumming activity. After that, though, there was mostly a cold, unholy quiet, like living inside snow. I listened in whenever Phineas talked through the door to neighbors, or on occasion invited them inside to share rumors and news or confer about security.

But there was just so much time to fill. And it was impossible to be in the same state of ragged anxiety at every moment. I did whatever I could to try to cure myself of worry. I spent hours drawing. Practiced kata and falling. Took some fitful naps with Canon. Read Phineas's books: part of a Samuel Johnson biography, Larkin, Mark Twain, art books and catalogs: Charles Sheeler, Titian. Once Phineas hauled out an old black-and-white TV and we tried to focus on some Preston Sturges films he had on VHS tapes. We played a few distracted games of crib-bage and chess. I thought of Christmas mornings, playing chess with Doug. Drinking Drambuie from tiny blue glasses. Vera reading us Dick-ens aloud.

It's a great huge game of chess that's being played—all over the world, said Alice. *If this is the world at all.*

Twice I broke protocol and spoke to Vera, who said she was okay. That she'd be staying on Long Island for the time being, where things seemed relatively safe. At first she wanted me to try to join her, but then she agreed I should stay where I was; traveling seemed more dangerous than stasis.

I eventually managed to reach Theo and Coco, too, who were both all right. When I heard Coco's voice, and that she was speaking clearly, I was so relieved that I had to bite my lip before I could talk.

"Cocoon," I whispered. "I was so worried. I miss you."

"I miss you, too, *mignonne,*" Coco said, her words just as clotted with feeling as mine. "Where've you been hiding?"

But my consolation was short-lived. I couldn't reach any of our other friends, and Coco told me that Audrey had gone into the hospital; she didn't know which one. No one had heard anything about Ramona.

I also tried to reach Max, but without luck. I even made myself call his mother. "I guess you haven't heard from him?" she asked, voice betraying a thin meniscus of warmth. But when I said no, she replied, "Why am I not surprised," and hung up.

We couldn't get through to Vernon either (one of few calls Phineas had approved), and soon we found out why: on the morning of the sixth day, December 11, Clara Strange sent a note explaining that the U.K. and several other countries had temporarily blocked calls to and from the United States. As Phineas read the note aloud, I cut him off. Started to say, "How—" but my voice cracked. Canon chucked his wet nose into my palm.

"Don't worry, chère Alice," Phineas said, patting my knee. "We'll get you there." But I didn't believe him. And my patience was running low faster than the cans in his pantry.

That night I did something Phineas had forbidden under threat of eviction: I sneaked out. Even more verboten: I went to see Bart. I'd tried calling him many times since arriving on Beekman Place; even before that, we hadn't talked in days. But his phone hardly ever even rang. When it did, he didn't answer, which put me in a panic. The few messages he'd left for me, though, were almost worse: it was nearly impossible to decipher what he meant. And by that sixth day he sounded not only aphasic but very sick.

When I finally reached him, the call was short. "Bart?" I said. "Are you all right?" And I could tell from the tone of his reply that he was trying to reassure me. But the sounds he made weren't at all soothing.

"Please tell me the absolute truth," I said firmly. "And remember how much I appreciate your honesty. Do you have a headache or fever?" I clenched my jaw. "Do you have the virus, Bart?" There was a terrible moment of silence. I closed my fist around my omnipresent tube of pills. Later I found out he'd been infected for four days.

"Tell me where you are," I said. He tried not to give me his address, but when I reminded him that I could get it other ways—by going to the Dictionary or Doug's, neither of which seemed very safe—he relented and told me. He had to repeat it half a dozen times.

I waited until after Phineas had gone to sleep; then, before I crept out through the darkroom door, I used a pair of scissors from a kitchen drawer to cut my hair very short. I borrowed an old coat of Phineas's. Took someone's bike from the basement. And I made my way up— nearly 140 blocks—to Bart.

It was a hard and harrowing ride. Some blocks were so dark that they looked like they'd lost power, but then I'd see a glowing LIQUOR marquee on a corner, or the paper-lantern light of a late-night bodega. On Broadway more windows glowed. But even some of those seemed to have the soft, liquid flicker of candlelight. Heaps of trash narrowed the sidewalks; it billowed in the streets. But it seemed like the trash of ghosts—I saw almost no one. And the few people I glimpsed did look like phantoms. Silhouetted in windows. Staring dark-eyed from under awnings. And Manhattan's silence was like nothing I'd known. There were sounds—yowling cats; thrumming generators; things clattering in alleys; the lonely, heart-piercing scream of ambulance sirens. But it wasn't the sound of my city.

Of the handful of cars I saw, nearly all drove very slowly, and even though I knew it was because the drivers were worried about other cars on the road, I felt each time as if I were being watched. Or followed. I wondered where the drivers had to go that was so important, burning up electricity or gas. And it made me pedal so fast my legs began to sting; the scab on my knee cracked open. But maybe even more frightening were the cars that careered like jets through intersections, with almost the same whine and roar. As they blew past, the back of my neck felt exposed and colder, my head too light without the shield of my hair.

But still I felt very focused—almost high. I went as fast as I could, eyes on the road, and arrived at Bart's building near one in the morning.

I was two hours later than I'd said I'd be. And he didn't answer the door. I pressed the button again and again, and soon I started to feel frantic. Imagined him stretched on the floor, unmoving. I jammed his buzzer a final time, then punched all of them. Nothing.

I got breathless; my ears began to ring. And even though I saw no one around, I thought I felt someone watching me. Out of desperation and fear, I finally tried the door. It opened with a loud click—the buzzer and lock both broken. I hauled the bike inside and ran up to Bart's floor.

But knocking, pleading, banging gave me nothing but silence, then, after a while, the neighbors' shouts. And I had no way of knowing why. Was he not at home? Where else could he be? Maybe, I thought, he was too sick to stand. Or afraid of infecting me.

Hands trembling, I fumbled in Phineas's coat for my vial covered in illegible writing. Found a pen and a Society pamphlet that Phineas had folded into the pocket and scrawled a message on the back: ALICE SAYS EAT THESE. I folded the paper into a triangle, poured in the pills—almost spilling them, my hands were quivering so badly—slid it under his door, and prayed.

Outside, as I cast one last look up at the building and started to climb onto the bike again, I heard a voice call, "Hey, girlie," very nearby. Twisting my head as I started wobblingly to ride, I saw a man step out from behind a parked car, and my heart suddenly felt like two hearts, grappling with each other. But that was all I saw. Because as he yelled, "Hey! Hey!" and started coming toward me, I took off and was gone.

N

names as such \nāmz əz səch\ *n* : senseless words (e.g.):
LOVE

On our seventh day of confinement, Phineas braved the world, leaving me behind.[1] He wasn't sure how long he'd be gone but thought it might be quite a while; he said not to let anyone but the dog-walker inside. While he was out, I did hand Canon over, which I later regretted very much. I also tried to call Bart again, but he didn't pick up. And I went into Phineas's study.

I was looking for Doug's letter, the one that read "You can trust Phineas implicitly." The original—not the one that I knew had been doctored. Carefully I stepped past teetering piles of papers. Tripped on an eviscerated dog toy. Tried to blind myself to the dark, damning coins of Nadya's eyes watching from the walls. All those naked portraits of a woman who looked so much like my mother, uncannily familiar, made *me* feel exposed, reminding me of the spying I'd done on Doug the night he'd disappeared. And as I searched Phineas's desk for my letter, I uncovered others, written in 1966, 1967, 1968, to Nadya Viktorovna Markova at a Moscow address. The papers' alien softness was enthralling. I found myself wishing they were my parents' letters. That maybe they held clues. Blueprints for why love doesn't last.

I caught the phrase "When you said I never loved you but only

---

1. If he knew I'd been out the night before, he didn't say a word. Just casually offered, "I see you've changed your hair." But I later found the darkroom door locked.

myself in love with you, maybe you were right." And I peered up at the photo over Phineas's desk. It was the one whose pane I'd broken, of Nadya clothed only in her hair. A few tiny glass incisors still clung to the frame. And as I studied the one sliver of cheek not veiled, I made a startling discovery: I knew her. Not because she looked like Vera. She was the younger simulacrum of another woman: Victoria Mark, of the Diachronic Society.

"Viktorovna. Nadya Viktorovna Markova," I murmured aloud.

And that's when Phineas found me.

"Alice!" he said, breathless, smelling of snow. His coat was spangled white.

I tucked the letter behind me. "I was just—"

But he cut me off. "Come with me!" he said in the shouted version of a whisper. With his gloves still on, he placed a screen in front of the pneumatic tubes, then grabbed me by the arm and dragged me to my room. Opening the closet, he shushed the clothes aside. Lifted his red hat from a high shelf, slid out the remote, and pressed a button that made the back of the closet open with a clack. Shoving me in, Phineas hissed, "Don't make a sound" before shutting and locking it again. Then, from outside: "And don't turn on the lights!"

For a moment I stood dazed, unmoving. "Phineas?" I whispered through the wall. But all I heard was silence. I felt the blackness crowding in around me, pressing on my eyes, and I shivered, heart quickening, lungs feeling tight. I swept the dark with my arms and recoiled at the light cord's feathery kiss. I was tempted to tug it but groped my way instead to the wall monitor. When I turned it on, an image leapt to the screen: a man dressed all in black was entering the lobby with a dog on a leash. I felt a wave of nausea.

Clive stepped from behind his desk. Pointed to the door. But the man held up a hand and walked to one of the wintry paintings. Lifted it. And moments later the apartment filled with the buzzer's long, piercing skirl. I stopped my ears. As it ended, I saw the man shove Clive aside and head toward the elevators.

In minutes I heard distant pounding on Phineas's front door. Muted shouts. I couldn't hear what the man wanted, but I thought I recognized his voice. My skin stung and grew tight, as if from drying saltwater. In the dim aureole of the monitor's glow, I noticed a pair of headphones snaking from its side. Cautiously put them on and pressed the + sign.

Heard a crackle, then muzzy sound. Tried a few of the monitor's buttons, and noises and scenes careened: first I was in the living room, then Phineas's study, with pages of the letter to Nadya strewn on the desk. Next I saw the front door, Phineas huddled beside it, running his hands through the dandelion taff of his hair.

"Thwaite!" I heard the man outside roar. "Jong the motherfucking vare, or I'll stev your dog!" Punctuating the threat was a terrible yelp, and then there was another, more impressive bout of banging, as if from a boot. Things rattled on shelves.

Phineas cringed and pressed his hands to his face. He hesitated just a moment more, but when he heard the dog cry again through the door, he reached for the locks, fingers trembling, and undid them one by one. But his voice stayed steady as he said, "All right. No need to blow the house down."

When the door opened, I almost didn't recognize the man who stepped inside. He'd slimmed since I'd last seen him, and shaved his sideburns. But it was definitely Floyd. Wrapped around his meaty hand was a thick black leash, and at his feet was Canon.

"Fucking dog *kasht* me," Floyd said, clenching and unclenching the hand not holding the leash. Phineas lunged to grab the dog's collar. But Floyd jammed a thick boot in the door. "Not zhutak," he said, yanking the dog, who was visibly limping, into the apartment behind him. Phineas enfolded Canon in his arms. The dog was whimpering, licking his face, but also baring his teeth at Floyd.

Floyd seemed unfazed. He casually strolled through the foyer, dirty slush dripping from his boots. Then he started to speak. It was hard to hear him over Canon's crying, and the headphones weren't very good. It was more than that, though—he had the virus. But I was pretty sure I heard him say he was looking for someone. And my pulse started throbbing in my neck. I thought I saw Phineas flinch. He was still hunched over the dog, who'd started growling, and I hoped Floyd hadn't noticed him tense.

Phineas stood to shut the door, and Floyd, looking down at Canon, said something I didn't understand. Then, without warning, he swung back his short, powerful leg and brought his boot into Canon's ribs. The dog fell, howling and yipping loudly.

"What the hell do you think you're doing!" Phineas yelled, leaping at Floyd. But Floyd just pushed the old man, hard, and to avoid landing on

Canon, who was whining and scrabbling to get up, Phineas fell the other way, into a chair, his glasses tumbling off.

By the time Phineas had stood, touching quaking fingers to a bloody lip, and gingerly stepped toward the injured dog, making soothing sounds, Floyd had left the foyer.

Punching through the monitor's channels, I watched in terror as Floyd made his rounds: living room, bedrooms, baths. I saw him paw through the study, scattering papers. Dump Phineas's shirts on the floor. Check medicine bottles. Knock them in the sink. Then, transfixed, heart swelling, I watched him open the door to my room. Step inside. Stare, it seemed, right at me.

I pressed against the wall. Tried to take cover in a space with no cover to take. Prepared for what I'd do when he found me. Saw him check methodically behind the door. The curtains. Under the bed. Then, barely breathing, I watched him approach the closet. Heard him say, over the thrum in my head—and not through the headphones but the walls—"Nara zhok fuck *is* he?"

He? I thought, confused. One of the few unscrambled words in a question whose meaning was clear enough. The impulses to listen and to block my ears were almost equally strong. I reflexively groped in my pocket and found it empty; I'd given the pills, of course, to Bart. Then Phineas appeared at the door, rubbing his arm, split lip striped red. And in a strikingly nonchalant tone, he said—almost laughed—"Unless you're looking for the dog's bed, I think you'll be disappointed."

Stunningly, it worked—Floyd turned without opening the closet door. I let myself breathe a tiny, jagged sigh. Willed Floyd to leave the room. The apartment. The earth.

But then a silence opened like a safe. Floyd was curved away from the camera, and I couldn't see his face. I found out later he was grimacing in pain. Pressing stubby fingers into his forehead. Finally he said something, and I thought I caught the words "hiding anyone." Phineas was quiet for what felt like far too long. *Come on,* I mouthed, frantic. *Say something.* But when he did finally reply, his voice had lost its cool, scentless calm. He said, "Don't be absurd." But to me it sounded like "Look in the closet."

With shaking fingers, dabbing sweat from my top lip, I wondered if I should risk escape through the darkroom's other door. That's when I discovered it was locked.

Floyd said something else I strained to understand. He was holding a small, bunched black thing. And my stomach collapsed. I had a terrible vision—of some lace underwear I may have left on the floor. I heard Floyd inhale and say, "Mm," and I nearly gagged.

"Give those to me," Phineas said. I felt ill.

"Whoa." Floyd laughed, not about to give up. "Whose naysek?"

Phineas said a few words I didn't quite catch, then: ". . . from a long time ago. I—"

"Don't *smell* old," Floyd somehow managed to express, or, in my horror, I imagined.

"Please," Phineas said, sounding believably defeated. "I miss her, and this is very embarrassing for me."[2]

Floyd garbled something else I couldn't uncode. But I'd stopped caring what he was saying; I could tell by the way his voice amplified that he'd again moved closer to me. Then I heard something that made my legs weaken: he'd opened the closet door.

I pinched my eyes shut. Braced as best I could for his discovery of my clothes—things he'd seen me wear countless times, like my long green coat. As soon as he saw it, he'd find the fake door. And me, on the other side. I heard the excruciating *tring* of hangers sliding. Felt my heart burst its telegram to my brain: *Run.* There was nowhere to go. I tried to picture how I'd take him down. Not what would happen after.

But Floyd, consistent with his character, was evidently an impatient detective. As he'd opened the door, Phineas had mumbled, "My niece—sent some things home from college." And miraculously, that seemed to work. When I next heard Floyd's voice, it was farther away. Phineas and I tried to piece together later what he said. We thought he was trying to convey that someone had been making calls to government agencies, leveling accusations at Synchronic. He sneered incomprehensibly at Phineas: "Zeg mabee know lukkets you this time." But then he said something we both understood: that if anyone turned up, it was in Phineas's best interests to tell him.

"Might help to know who you're looking for," Phineas said calmly.

They stepped out into the hall, and I had to jump up and change the channel to hear Floyd's reply. But I wasn't prepared for the answer he

2. When I later asked him how he'd managed to carry on a conversation, he explained he hadn't; he'd hoped for the best, based on context (which we didn't discuss).

gave. I could swear he said, "King." And the knurled, brass-knuckle way he said it made me cold.

By then they were back by the front door. Canon, now lashed to the kitchen table, was snarling, low and dark. "Canon understands. Shemmet, boy?" said Floyd. Nudged the dog with his boot. Canon started barking, and Floyd laughed as he let himself out.

Later Phineas and I sat stunned in the living room, Canon at our feet. Phineas had put on *Rite of Spring,* and I'd brought him a glass of water, which he took without a word, sucking his bloody lip. A bruise bistered his arm, and a purple lump had risen near his temple. When he tried to press the glass to his head, his hand shook so badly that water spilled on his shirt.

"Are you okay?" I asked gently.

Phineas shrugged. And the vulnerability of that small, modest hump of doubt made my eyes burn. I felt more keenly than I had before what it was costing him to keep me safe.

Abruptly he took a billfold from his coat and removed a stocky, matte blue rectangle inked with tremulous letters. It was a barely extant relic: a paper airplane ticket. As he handed it over, he said sternly, "Don't lose it." He explained that the very earliest date he could book wasn't until the next week. Which, in a sense, was fortunate; with the tremendous rise in passport requests, mine had been delayed even with his help.

"On my way home earlier," he said, "I was reconsidering the wisdom of this. But then I encountered Mr. Dobbs in the street. It appears he was waiting for me. It doesn't seem safe for you to stay here much longer."

It wasn't Floyd's first house call, apparently. Floyd—along with Max, Phineas said pointedly—had dropped by a couple of months earlier. They'd even known to tell Clive downstairs that they were with the Diachronic Society. Phineas hadn't recognized them on the monitor, but it was before he'd had reason to be very wary; until that visit, he'd never suspected that the Society was being surveilled. Their activities included occasional op-eds (prior to the *Times* piece, largely in periodicals that almost no one read), political letter-writing campaigns, etc. Phineas had been worried that people didn't listen enough, not that they were listening too well. Floyd and Max, however, had assured him that they were paying attention. They had several old Society pamphlets. They'd also somehow procured copies of emails he'd sent to state senators outlining why the Nautilus should never be sold.

Needless to say, they'd encouraged him to change his position. But while he'd found their visit unnerving, he claimed that it hadn't seemed like a threat per se. Still, he'd reported it to other members of the Society, a few of whom had received similar visits (though not Doug; there were different plans for him, apparently). Phineas had also suggested that as a group they might want to be more prudent, pointing out that if anyone wanted to curtail the kind of open canvassing that might get them in trouble, there was no shame in it at all. Instead, though, most of them had taken the warnings as a call to arms and ramped up their efforts. "If they're calling on y'all," Winifred Brown had said, "that means something's going *on*." That seemed to summarize their sentiments.

As a result, Floyd's second visit to Phineas hadn't been so cordial; he'd been accompanied not by Max that time but by Dmitri.

"Sorry I opened the door tonight, but—" Phineas bent in his telling to pet the dog, who lifted his head gently to Phineas's hand. "I knew Mr. Dobbs would just come back again, and maybe not alone." Phineas tapped his bloody lip. I touched mine, too; it had finally healed. "It might seem surprising, I suppose, that we thought this was the best place for you. But there are still certain things they seem not to know about the building."

I thought, of course, that he meant the secret cell.

Phineas shook his head and sighed. Then, heaving himself up, he left the room. Canon raised his head again and nervously watched him go. He was gone a long time. I wondered if he'd meant for me to follow. But he finally came back with some shabby papers and maps. "The timetable from Paddington to Oxford," he said, pressing it on me with a thick wad of cash, in pounds. Added, "I can't tell you where to find him, exactly. Not because I won't. But I don't know."

Shyly I thanked him. I wished I could refuse the money. But what my grandparents had beamed me after Thanksgiving was running very low, if it was even still in my account. And of course there'd be no more paychecks from the Dictionary.

"What about you?" I asked Phineas.

"What about me?" he replied. When he leaned forward to pet Canon, I noticed a small spot of dried blood on the collar of his button-down.

"Aren't you coming?"

He quickly shook his head. "Not now," he said, sounding impatient. "Maybe later." But I knew by the way he avoided my eyes that there was something he wasn't saying.

"Please don't tell me it's because there weren't enough tickets," I pleaded softly.

He took a small sip of water. Marked the glass with blood. "Of course not," he bluffed, pretending to study the rug's threadbare pattern of crenellations.[3]

"In that case," I said, passing back the ticket, "I can't accept this."

"Don't be ridiculous, Alice," Phineas said sharply. "It's in your name." Then, as we both checked the ticket, he hastily added, "Anana, I mean."

Finally I realized who he was: the White Knight. Taking me to the end of his move. His early behavior had hidden his true identity, but even that had been out of a misguided protectiveness for the Society and Doug. And really not so misguided—for a long time he had a lot of questions about me. Questions I can now understand.

For a moment we were quiet. Listened to the rumble of the heater coming on and Canon crying in his sleep. "I'll be fine," Phineas promised. "They don't quite trust me, clearly, or I wouldn't get the pleasure of their periodic visits. But they think I'm 'cooperating.'"

I inhaled. Stared at the shiny spider veins on his nose. "Don't you think that's what Max thought, too?"

Phineas removed his glasses and slipped them into a pocket. Rubbed the pink depressions they'd left in his skin. "I don't know precisely what Max has done to run afoul of his partners," he said. "But as you've seen for yourself, I'm being very careful. Please don't worry about me. As for Max . . . who can say."

Against my will, my throat burned a little, as if I'd swallowed wrong. I tried to clear it. Tried to ask Phineas why they were looking for Max. What they'd do if they found him.

But all Phineas would say was, "I think he's mixed up in something very serious."

"Like?" I said, feeling frustrated. Helpless.

---

3. I later learned that tickets to London were more than $10K, coach. Phineas had paid for mine by selling some of his mother's jewelry to a man he knew who used to be a travel agent, when that was a profession, and who still had industry ties. But for Phineas the problem wasn't cost. Seats were simply very scarce. The British government was letting in very few planes.

"I really don't know, my dear," Phineas said, testing the lump on his head. "But I think you have more important things to worry about than a very foolish young man who broke your heart. I doubt very much he's thinking about you."

It felt like a slap. But he was right. It was a useful reminder. I bit my cheek. Nodded.

Phineas sighed. "I'm sorry," he murmured. "That wasn't what I meant to say. We don't really get to choose . . . Do we." His eyes looked a little glossy. And my mind tumbled back to the letter I'd seen in his office. All those photographs.

I learned the story of how Nadya became Victoria only later. It encompassed, too, Phineas's first meeting with my father, in 1971. In fact, I know far less about the love story—only the bones. That in 1965 Phineas and the young Nadya Markova met and fell in love at the École des Hautes Études in Paris when she got a special dispensation to leave Moscow for a year of philological study and he was a visiting linguistics lecturer. That he almost convinced her to come back with him to New York. That when she finally came, several years later—getting out of the USSR with difficulty—they were married within a month.

But he soon realized that something was wrong. She often spent all day in bed, lights off. She didn't like to be around people. And for nearly a year she seemed to give up on words. Not just their study; whole days might pass when she barely spoke. He didn't know what else to do, so he built a darkroom, hoping that images might become her new vocabulary.

When she regained her voice, she apologized for her reticence, and for not replying to many of his letters during the years they'd been apart. Never again, she said, would she let fear menace her into silence. But she also said she needed to be on her own. Soon after she moved out, she changed her name, something she hadn't done when they were married.

They stayed close, and his obvious despondency after she left deeply troubled her. For weeks he barely slept, went out, ate. When a strange opportunity arose—she heard from a friend of a secret trip a seasoned Icelandic explorer, Magnús Jökulsson, was leading—she encouraged him to go. The "trip," in fact, was right in NYC: three days spelunking beneath the city's streets. "Sometimes the best way out of darkness is into it," Victoria said, not expecting him to agree.

It was indeed very out of character. But he knew he had to do something: he was disconsolate. And he had no ideas of his own. Maybe, having seen her metamorphosis, he hoped he could change, too—or at least change how Nadya, now Victoria, saw him. So he surprised them both by getting himself into the group, which wasn't easy; he had to buy his spot. Not everyone was glad he was allowed along: an odd, dour lexicographer, slight and nervous, prone to mild hallucinations: distant flickers and cries, the feet and wings of insects. He woke up yelling the first night about an imagined rat invasion.

But misery underground is quickly compounded, and two men in the group grimly took on the task of trying to engage him enough to calm him down. It was that or kick him out—conditions were treacherous, focus essential. On the second day they almost got in very bad trouble wading through a combined sewer when it started to rain and the sewer quickly began filling.

The two men who'd taken Phineas under their wing had of course been Doug and Fergus Hedstrom, off on one of their adventures. And in fact it was this NYC "trek" and conversations with Jökulsson that sparked Ferg's lifelong fascination with Iceland—and later led to his fortune there, built on "cardboard and crap" (Ferg's own pithy description of the real-estate industry). The trip also changed Doug's life. Or rather meeting Phineas did. The second night, over a fifth of whiskey, Fergus and Doug tried drawing Phin out, and it soon emerged that Doug was a Samuel Johnson scholar. That charmed and interested Phineas— and it prompted him to say something that changed the trajectory of Doug's career: "Did you know they're looking for an editor at the *North American Dictionary*? You'd be perfect. I'll put in a word."

Another unexpected thing happened while they were down below one of the greatest cities on earth, shining their lights on dark, liquidy walls like the ocean at night; encountering Gordian knots of rats; pyramids of roaches; perhaps even the sparkle of a few fish near Fulton. On the third day something else caught Phineas's eye, although it might have been just one of his hallucinations; everyone ahead of him had missed it. The group was very quickly, carefully passing through part of the extensive network of tunnels radiating out from Grand Central. Phin was near the rear of the line, and when he called out, his companions thought at first that he'd been hurt. (Jökulsson had been in a state of dreary anticipation, waiting for Phin to touch the third rail.) The shout caused a temporary but serious jam, men falling into one another's backs, wrenching necks, shining lamps in each other's eyes. But Phineas wasn't hurt. He yelled because he thought he saw something give off a gloamy light, like a copper pot in a dark kitchen: part of the pipeline for pneumatic tubes once used to dispatch the mail. He pointed it out to Ferg and Jökulsson behind him, but they impatiently hurried him on.

Phin had been looking for the tube infrastructure; he knew it had once been very dense around Grand Central. But by 1971, when his errant flashlight beam may have found the moribund message system, it had been out of commission for nearly twenty years. And of course by then the newest technology was computers, already asserting their Icarian pull. Doug and Phin discussed them extensively. Both were excited and intrigued by possible uses for the behemoth calculators. But they also shared a concern—called a paranoia by some—that these amazing machines might one day replace our need for books. Dictionaries. People. And more than forty years before the first cases of word flu, Doug had imagined a contagious language virus. The erasure of whole swaths of human knowledge and culture.

By the end of their expedition, my father and Phineas had vowed to stage a contest against accelerated obsolescence. And the more Phin told Doug about the pneumatic tubes that had once run under New York— and that were still in use, he reminded Doug, in places like the New York Public Library—the more convinced Doug became that if he ever worked in publishing, he'd like to have them installed.

When he actually managed it, though, three years later, Phin was astounded. He checked to see if it was possible to run tubes from his apartment to Doug's Dictionary—and discovered that it seemingly wasn't. But in the process he found out he *might* have seen old infrastructure; some remained, including nearly two blocks' worth between Grand Central and his building on Beekman. (It was indeed *his* building, I later learned; his father had been a very successful real-estate developer and had bought several on the block. When Phin started dreaming of tubes, he made modifications to a few of the buildings, then still in his family.) He also researched where the lines might be laid, who could put them in (with permits or not), and at what price (high). At the time it didn't seem justified, and he set aside his plans for a very long while— decades. Until increasing large-scale cyberattacks convinced him that having a way to quickly convey analog messages might be expedient.

By then the Society had been meeting for several years at the Merc, only eight blocks away. He paid a small, discreet crew of expert underground-cable installers in Queens an exorbitant sum to exploit existing tube infrastructure and carefully lay the rest through a few combined sewers and subway storm drains.[4] He also ingratiated himself at the Merc by making a donation that ensured the library's future. The director, in turn, kindly obliged his eccentric request to run tubes secretly to the library's cramped and humid subbasement. That had required permits and renovations. And several months after the first line was laid, Phineas hired the same team to connect the Merc to the Dictionary, only eleven more blocks away.

But on the night that Floyd invaded Phineas's apartment, the discoveries I'd made had nothing to do with pneumatic tubes or my father.

"Nadya—she's . . ." I said, faltering. "You and Victoria—you were . . . ?"

And Phineas simply said, "Don't look so surprised." "I'm not," I tried to reply. But he talked over me: "It was a very long time ago." Then he stood, stirring Canon. "And now, if you'll excuse me," he said, "please allow a tired old man a rest."

As he left the room, I heard him mutter, "Love."

The night before my flight to London, I went home to pack, and Phineas asked Clive to go with me. I demurred—it was late; Clive had worked all day—but I was glad he was there. Because it soon became clear that my place had been raided. Nearly everything I owned was on the floor. In the bedroom, some of it was dusted with a fine layer of snow blown in through the window.

I was shaken, but I hated to make Clive wait. The city was under curfew; he was anxious to get home to his family. I decided to believe that my things had just been sifted by opportunistic thieves who'd noticed my broken window from the street. But it didn't look like a burglary: nothing was missing and the door hadn't been forced. Still, once I saw that no one was lurking in the hall or out on the fire escape, I sent Clive home.

"You sure?" he asked, relieved.

I said yes. And what happened next wasn't Clive's fault. It's true that if he'd stayed, it wouldn't have come about. But the mistakes were mine. I let myself get distracted, sorting through my ransacked life. I should

---

4. He'd had to pay them again—a couple of times—when track workers had torn out parts of the system.

have been long gone when the door buzzer went off. Not skimming Doug's Aleph, which I'd brought along to charge. Certainly not combing through old clothes, papers, photographs.

On the bed, in a mess of other things, was a shiny stack of black-and-whites. Self-portraits—discrete pieces of my body—from my college thesis on "the reification of temporality" (whatever that means). But looking again at those flattened tokens of my persona—glossy bits of lip, eyes, hair, feet—I saw more than I had before.

Max had always loved those photos, and I'd found that both flattering and vaguely creepy. Images were easier to "get," I'd teased, than thoughts, words, feelings. Ciphers were simpler than people. But as I studied those prints that night, shivering—the apartment was frigid—I finally really realized that I was culpable, too: I'd come to see myself as him seeing me. It was an inherited tendency. A little sadly, with a sting of disloyalty, I thought of Doug's secret desk-drawer stash of Vera memorabilia. Maybe that was part of their falling apart—reification. Maybe the same was true for Max and me.

But it wasn't the photos that undid me. A moment later, as I slowly turned them over on the rumpled sheets, I unburied a crumpled piece of paper that made time compress and my heart stop, then jump like a magnet. It was a note I'd first found more than four years earlier. Folded over on a smooth hotel pillow on a different bed, in Picard, Dominica.

And it was that note that left me open to attack. Which came in the form of five piercing trills, and—when I finally pressed the intercom—the sound of Max on the windy street below, choking on something.

"Ana." He coughed. Tried to catch his breath. "It's me." And that's when I realized, with a painful throb, that he wasn't choking. He was crying. "Zemin. *Fucked—*" He was sobbing so hard that I could barely understand. "Please! Just stam—"

Heart hammering, I lifted my finger off LISTEN. Imagined him still talking into the Delphic plastic box. But after a silence that wound itself, scarflike, around my throat, the buzzer rang again, in staccato bursts, like the kamikaze bombings of an agitated bee.

I tried to think. To inhale and exhale normally. Shaking, I pressed my cheek to the wall. It was cool as a sheet. In my clammy hand I was clutching that note I'd found with the photos. From another life, it seemed, when people still wrote notes. When he wrote them to me. I read the words "My love" over and over, until they had no meaning.

Touched TALK. Struggled to keep my voice even as I said, "What do you want?"

For a long moment I heard just the static of wind. Stomach sinking, I wondered if he'd already given up and left. Then I heard a sound like a retch. And I heard it again. But this time it sounded more like my name. Finally, after another silence, I heard something else. In a low, scarred voice, nearly a whisper, he said, "I have to see you."

I later wondered if it was a recording. But right then, that was it. Those five small words an awful open sesame. Five words that I'd prayed for weeks to hear. That I'd sworn wouldn't move me. But there we were, that other life returned to me. That life before the virus; before my father went missing; when my days were filled with words and purpose, creating things; and my nights with laughter, friends, Max's touch— something I'd taken for love. There it all was again. Intruding. I pushed the plastic nib marked DOOR and waited.

He didn't run up the stairs, as he'd done when we were first in love. In fact, for what felt like a very long time I didn't hear any footsteps. What was he doing? Finishing a cigarette? Trying to wipe off the victory smirk? Holding his head in pain, sick? Was he alone? Was he telling a woman he'd be right back? Or was he with someone else—like Floyd. Or Dmitri. I dead-bolted the door just as I heard the heavy tread of boots start to echo up.

But I soon discerned that it was just one pair. Until, at last, they stopped outside my door. What had been our door until just two months before. Haltingly, knowing he'd see me, I peered out through the peephole. And I was stunned. His face was battered: one eye burled shut, chin abraded, cheekbone gashed. His good eye was red, face wet with tears. And my own eyes began to burn.

I tried to stand my ground. There was no knowing what had happened. Could have been just a bad night out. But in my mind's ear I heard Phineas say, "He's mixed up in something very serious." Worse, the bitter, bruising way Floyd had apprised us that he was looking for Max. And in my hand I held the note that said, "My love without end."

Through the eyelet in the door, I saw a pale flash. Max was holding something: a piece of paper like a white flag. In collaged letters, it read: PLEASE LET ME IN.

"What do you want?" I asked again, sounding tougher than I felt. Thinking not just of Max but of neighbors who'd hear everything, and who'd worry about infection. Though I also knew—saw myself doing it before I did—that I would open the door. My heart's long habit of love was too strong for me to leave him sick and stranded outside. While the door was still closed, though, I watched him hold up a hand: wait. Watched as he tried, wincing, to get down on one knee. A sight I'd always hoped to see. But not that way.

"Don't," I said, choking up. And undid the bolt.

Once he was inside, I barely noticed the shift in mood. Like a tiny, wayward pulse of energy. Max winked at me. And I realized, too late, that I'd made a mistake.

"Shang you yow sdyelatye me wait there vod night," said Max. He no longer looked ashamed, or even repentant. In fact he looked a little smug. I could tell he was trying not to. But nearly thirty years of egotism are bad training for remorse.

I'd planned to ask what had happened—who'd done that to his face. But with the crown of power back in play, it seemed best to harden my line. Not show any weakness. And my fears that he might be able to infect me were growing in intensity. I noticed, too, that he wasn't asking about me—my shorn hair, my chipped front tooth. Why all my things were on the floor. How the past two terrible months had been for me. "This is the last time I'll ask," I said, filling my words with ice. "What do you want from me?"

He lowered himself gently into the chair by the door, shivering. I stood, arms crossed. Rigid.

"Want? Towsher see you," he said, flashing his gap-toothed grin. It looked more gapped than ever: his own front tooth was also broken, more badly than mine. The smile made even his good eye nearly disappear. It almost looked like he was falling asleep.

But he was very much awake. "God, Ana," he said, reaching for my hand, buried in the crook of my arm. I stepped back, but not far. "Do you know how faychung badly deleenoy you senk? Zeegid idea how seeyong vee." Stretching forward, he tried again to take my hand. Settled for an elbow. "You're tolko rensher me. Chvistvo like myself again." He tried to pull me closer. His smell, of cigarettes and old deodorant and sweat, made me gag.

"Max," I said, moving farther back, trying to be careful. I didn't want him in a rage. "You're not making sense," I said softly. "I'm going to have to ask you to leave."

His smile vanished; his eye came out of hiding. And I braced myself. But what I saw wasn't fury. It was a true flash of fear. "Dongran," he mumbled, face blanching. He'd brought an old notepad and pen. A stack of pasted-up stock phrases. HOW ARE YOU? was on top. Below that. HOW MUCH? He groped at the notepad. "Wait, oden second." Wincing, he pressed his fingers to his head, then tried clumsily to scrawl something out. It took a long, long time. A small forever. I got impatient. Anxious. Turned to look around the room at all my trampled stuff.

But I couldn't make him leave. He was twice my size. And it was more than that: he still had meaning in that place. He'd made us countless meals in that kitchen. Accidentally shattered nearly every glass. Sometimes left his swim goggles in the freezer, his bike helmet on the dish rack. And said the word "love" so many times. Whether he'd meant it or not.

I was facing the kitchen when he rasped, "Ana? Kan me, please?" He sounded agitated. When I turned, he fixed me with his relentless hazel eyes. Pressed a rumpled piece of paper to my palm. His penmanship had devolved. Letters slackened and gone soggy, like the last cereal in the bowl. I didn't know whether it was the virus or his lack of practice, but the sloppy letters didn't help his cause. They made his note seem disingenuous. I was angry a priori, before I even read a word.

"I just want you to know," he'd scribbled, "I'm so, so sorry for what I did to you and to us. I'm so, so sorry for hurting you. I'm just so profoundly sorry."

"This is what took so long?" I said, crumpling the paper. I was incredulous, but also a little conflicted for feeling mad when he was clearly so hurt and sick. I didn't even know what he was sorry for. As if there were just one thing. (As if it were all his fault.) And of course I also knew he couldn't have just written it. Fleetingly, I wondered if I was the first person he'd given it to.

But he shook his head, brow furrowed, and tried again to talk. "N-not all," he stammered, taking the paper floret from me and flattening it out. Turning it over and handing it back. And the note lurched on. "I'm horrified, plain and simple," it continued, "to have ruined things with my best friend and my love. This isn't something I'll ever get over. And I'm just so sorry, Anana. So sorry that when things got hard, I put work first and left. I know you can probably never forgive me, but if you'd ever even consider taking me back—"

That's where I stopped. And not only because it was so insultingly flat. (A man who traffics in words, I thought, should come up with better ones than that.) The note felt toxic; it left a funny taste in my mouth. Metallic, like lead paint, or the prodrome of a migraine. When had he written it? And why? Maybe someone else had done it for him. While I'd had my back turned, had he just been pretending to write? Everything about it made me ill. And then there was what the note said. What did that mean, "put work first"? It's true that before Max left, he'd had many late nights at "meetings," with "clients," "developing projects." But I'd assumed those were euphemisms—the source of many fights. *Had* he really been working? At what? Meaning Master? What was he "mixed up" in? Did it have anything to do with Doug? The Creatorium? The language virus?

He'd started softly crying again, maybe sensing my doubts. Maybe really crying. With Max, it was hard to know. So hard. And his tears had a paradoxical effect on me. I tersely asked what he meant by the note. "Why bring up work?" I chafed. He couldn't explain. He was crying harder. Tried a few starts at speech. But the note had put me on guard. And other thoughts had started bubbling up in my brain. Maybe he *had* just written the note. Maybe he wasn't really sick after all—the virus was a front, to lower my defenses. To scare me, or make me feel sorry for him. How had he turned up, I wondered, at just the moment I'd been home? Had he been watching me? Had someone else?

By that point, though, he was rocking back and forth, and his whimpers sounded piercingly real. Still upset but softening, I studied his bloody, broken face. He was suffering. And whoever had beaten him might not be far away. I eyed the door. Guardedly, second-guessing myself even as I did it, I placed a hand on his broad shoulder.

"I'm never going to take you back," I said. "I think you know that, too." The words felt like a benediction; I realized as I said them that they were absolutely true. And with that unexpected release came a warm, airy absolution. Gently I asked, "Why are you really here?"

"Ana," Max said, voice breaking like glass. He handed me another collaged sheet of paper. It read: I'M IN SO MUCH TROUBLE. Then he bent over and wept again. It was a wrenching wail, like the baying of a dog. Tears rained in tiny pearls, marking a trail through the dried blood below his swollen eye. He covered his face with his hands. And finally I believed him. My heart flooded with a sad, insoluble mix of grief, vindication, and anger, despair, detachment, compassion—like the mismatched letters glued to the papers he'd brought with him. But most of all, seeing him like that, what I felt was fear. Max, the stoic. The king. I hurried to the door and slid the chain. Peered uneasily into the bedroom, at the broken window gaping onto the fire escape, a few loose tines of glass in its casement.

"It's okay," I said, stepping close to Max again. Hovering over him. Like I used to do if he'd had a fight with his father, mother, one of his brothers, a friend. Me. But without the same requiem of feelings. I softly said, "Just—try to tell me what's going on."

After a moment of silence and a long, jagged sigh, Max said, "I-I-I boo code how I got here." Looked around, bewildered. "Gebbad what I'm *zolat* here. Bode *shem* I *zwah*. I fucked up." He stared at me, wretchedly wild-eyed. "I fucked up *bolsh*. Wem a fucking *fuckup*," he wailed. "And tyx—onet pitsher blame the whole vyesh on me. Dwetto. The virus. Everything." Then he began banging his head into the wall. I winced. And when it got louder and more violent, I put my hands on that knobby skull I knew so well, and the banging stopped. "Sedded anything," he sobbed. "*Eechye* to go back. Poydeet six months ago. We hway zove Dominica." He grabbed my arm. Started crying on my sleeve. "*Please*. Tor gwazee and be with you again. My shokh my fucking *soul* if I nung."

It didn't matter that I couldn't understand him. I knew what he meant. And that for those few moments, he believed it.

"Souls aren't worth much," I said, smoothing the stiff, dirty mass of his hair. "Especially not yours." He tried to laugh, but it came out strangled, like the cough of a clotted vacuum cleaner. Against my better judgment, I found myself scratching his head in soothing circles. Dusting dried blood from his cheek. Letting myself get pulled back in. "But I know you," I said. "And that's not really why you're here."

He nodded, and my hands moved with his head. Part of me wanted to believe him.

"But there's another reason," I prodded. Stopped massaging his scalp. "You need something from me."

"What?" The word was muffled by my sleeve. But his neck tensed. And I knew, with quicksilver certainty, that it was true. I just didn't yet know what he was looking for.

"Don't," I warned softly. "Just—don't fucking do it. Do not lie to me again." I let go of his head. Tugged my warm, wet sleeve from his face. Took a step away and tried to regain my lost ground. Shake off the spell. But I felt like a simulation of myself, in a scene I was imagining. *Had* imagined, many times. Although it never went like this.

As if trying a different approach, Max quieted. Collected himself. Gave speaking another chance. "Listen. Shur," he said. "I was going to gid you. Didn't your dad karatz an Aleph? Swannas, I do jen need one of those."

I was silent for a minute, face tingling with resentment and regret. From the corner of my eye I saw a glint on a high kitchen shelf: the Aleph's power switch. A cold shiver twitched over me. And I was afraid I'd unwittingly look up and give it away. I made myself stare at Max. Breathe.

"If I can kross show them brevvek happened way before mone. That I had *mayneetch* to do with it. *None* eezets lamek my fault—"

A wave of amazement crashed over me. "Get out," I ordered. Almost laughed in disbelief. How gifted he was, how masterly at manipulation. How willingly I contorted. And he was only doing what I'd asked: finally telling me the truth.

"Ana, *don't*," Max said, with what was now a desperate—or angry?— edge. Even at the best of times, it was hard to keep up with the whipping sails of his moods. Standing, he said through gritted teeth, "You don't leebon get it. They jyong dat *kill* me." With one step he was next to me. "I'm *dead*."

My throat jolted, and I felt a chill of fear. I'd never been afraid of him like that before. "Max," I said, trying to sound in control, "get out of here."

And then a thought occurred to me: what if it was Max who'd upended the apartment? The door hadn't been forced because he hadn't broken in.

I didn't yet know why the letter I'd received had asked me to safeguard the Aleph. But if there was any chance it might put Doug in danger, there was no way I'd give it to Max, whom I wanted out of my apartment more than ever. The Aleph was in plain sight. How long before he noticed it, even with just one good eye?

"Ana, *ching*," Max begged. "Let me praze leeved longer. *Pozh*, just the night."

"The *night*?" I said. But all at once I was stung by a discomfiting thought: he'd been staying there for days. Ringing the buzzer before mounting the stairs. Sleeping in my bed. I shuddered. Looked again at Max's bludgeoned face. Had it been *here* that Dmitri had found him? Anxiously I examined the shattered window again. Looked at the door. I wanted Max gone. "Get the fuck out," I commanded with the whole force of my being. *Wood and glue,* I thought.

But instead Max came closer. Took hold of both my arms. "Dalsh, *please*. Gantyay where it is. Whatever I've done to you, don't rong them *kill* me. Anana. *Zhal.*"

And I was scared. So, so scared for him. Persuaded that this time he was telling me the truth: that if I didn't give him the Aleph, he'd be in trouble. But I was also frightened for myself. Because he was holding my arms so tightly it hurt.

"Maybe," he was saying, voice rising in desperation, eyes shining, "yode might even zwamt a better treatment. Straven reverse it—for all of us, dakazh."

His grip tightened. And I knew I could throw him down. He didn't expect it. It would be easy to do. With his body already so bruised, that would probably be enough—he'd leave. But I also knew I didn't have to. I could do it with words. Tell him what he wanted to hear: what he'd done to me—and I'd done to myself—for years. And he'd believe me.

So I lied. To this man I'd loved so much, and still loved. To save myself, and maybe my father. "Okay," I said. "Max, I'll give you the Aleph."

"You will?" he asked, distrustful, not releasing my wrists.

"Yes. I'll meet you in an hour."

"Where?"

"The bathroom of SoPo," I said impulsively. And wished I hadn't. SoPo, his favorite bar, was only nine blocks south. Why couldn't I have picked a place in Brooklyn? Chelsea, even. And Max was so maddeningly perceptive that if I wavered, he'd get suspicious. As it was, he said "SoPo?" so skeptically that I was afraid he wouldn't leave.

"Yeah. And you're just going to have to trust me," I said, forcing myself to laugh. "Because you don't have a choice."

After considering that for a moment, he let go of my arms. "Okay," he said. "Eachas." Then he tried to smile. A horrifying sight. "Ganvu, Ana. I'll never forget this."

And I knew he never would.

When he was gone, I packed my backpack faster than I've ever done anything. Outside, as I searched for a taxi in a cold, wet wind, I saw a man standing in the dark across the street, the red eye of his lit cigarette hovering beneath an awning. I thought at first it was Max, waiting there to catch me in my lie, and a chill poured down my spine. But the man was too short.

I quickly looked away and took a step into the road. Started walking west very fast—almost running. Trembling, teeth chattering hard. I willed myself not to turn around. Waved harder for a car until one stopped for me as I reached Ninth. After I'd slammed the door, I let myself glance back into the orange-tinted blackness through the glinting droplets beaded on the window glass, and I saw the man who'd been moving after me. I realized, heart racing, that I'd seen him on my block before. Resting on the curb. Sitting in a parked car. As we drove off, he stopped. Lifted his fingers to his forehead in salute. I felt like I might black out. *You have to get out of here tonight,* I thought, *or you won't get out.*

Instead of going straight to Phineas's, I had the driver take me to the train at Times Square, one of the heavily guarded stations that had recently reopened. I switched cars, then lines—the 1 to the D to the E— watching over my shoulder the whole time.

"What happened?" Phineas asked, eyes wide, when I stumbled in the door nearly an hour later. My knees buckled so badly that I had to steady myself on the back of a chair. Canon whined, threading through my legs, licking my hand. And for a while all I could manage was, "I can't wait until tomorrow—I have to leave tonight."

Phineas balked. Reminded me that I couldn't change my flight. Tried to insist that I stay at his place until the morning, at least. But as I described my encounter with Max, his jaw set. And when I mentioned the man who'd been waiting in the darkness outside my apartment, Phineas picked up the black receiver of his rotary phone, dialed— endlessly—and finally said into the large, curved mouthpiece, "I'd like to call a car." But instead of giving his own address, he offered one several blocks away, on Park.

"Ready for your adventure underground, Alice?" he asked.

He outfitted me with a headlamp, gloves, and waders. Ferried me and my backpack to the basement. Escorted me behind a boiler that clanged like a parade, pushed aside an oily curtain. Spun the combination on an ancient lock and unhasped the rusted clasp. And soon we were inside a large bunker, reverberant with cold Cold War cement, rows of naked showers and bunks, metal shelves lined with old cans. As he guided me to a sort of manhole—into which two narrow tubes disappeared—I asked how he knew about this place. And, more relevant, how he had access. And he said, with a casualness I found staggering even in my state of rabid anxiety, "I own the building."

That's how I learned about his family history in real-estate speculation—and that in 1974, when he'd started looking into installing tubes, he'd had bunkers put in beneath a few adjacent buildings and connected via short subterranean tunnels. He'd bribed some of the workers to extend one passage about 100 feet and create a small, discreet aperture through which one could pass into the combined sewer there under Forty-ninth Street.

"The most difficult stretch will start at Second Avenue," Phineas said, twisting on my headlamp and giving me a hand-drawn map of a seven-block route. "The sewers narrow there considerably." Then, scowling, he carefully explained the location of a very tight drainage tunnel that would lead me to the vast underground cathedral of Grand Central.

"You'll follow the tracks the last few blocks north and west. When you arrive," he said, tapping my map, "you should look on the ground for a small chalked *X*."

He also presented me with a letter in a clear plastic bag that he said I should read on the plane, and he gave me two instructions: that I should destroy it as soon as I'd read it, and that if it seemed as if I were being followed, I should destroy it even if I hadn't opened it. "Why?" I asked, suspicious. Phineas cleared his throat. "In case you're abducted," he said. Then he sent me down into the frowsy dankness on a rough metal ladder that burned my palms.

Descending, shivering from the frigid air, I followed the snaking blazon of tubes as they plunged downward, too. Once belowground, I pursued them through a low, dark burrow; a small hole; and then, as Phineas had instructed, splashingly, through dirty water. Creatures skittered from my thin light and melted back into the blackness like rain into a lake. Jittering with nerves, legs going numb and mind going blank, I made slow, crouching progress after Second Avenue. Ducked below stalactites of goo. Tried to block out the stench and sounds: squeaks and scratches, distant rumbles, rasping echoes that seemed almost human. Once I'd made the terrible, claustrophobic passage through the drainage tunnel—if I hadn't spent the past half hour in awful, fear-addled escape, I might have turned back when I found it—I hurried along the tracks. Saw an abandoned subway platform up ahead, covered in graffiti and dipped in a ghostly blue glow. Then, at last, I reached the door Phineas had described.

Peering through the gloom, the white light of my lamp beaming a weak beacon onto the red *X* on my map, I put my shoulder to the door. Pushed with my whole scrawny weight. It didn't move. I shoved harder, frescoing my right side in bruises, I'd discover later. But then, as frustration curled in my throat, I heard a man's voice on the other side. I stopped to listen. Heart beating so hard I felt sick. I couldn't hear what he said, but almost before I knew what was happening, he was slowly opening the door from the inside.

"You must be Alice," said a stately young man. "Welcome to the Waldorf Astoria."[5] Nearly dissolving in gratitude, I molted out of the ruined waders and gloves. Outside, a car was idling.

Airport security had tightened since the virus, and getting through felt like being hazed: you had to be scanned, then patted down, recite five prescribed sentences, get your temperature taken, breathe into a tube. And I almost didn't make it. After my recitation I was pulled aside by a large, stern TSA agent. "Come with me, please," he said, officiously glancing at my passport. Despairing, I assumed that Max had reinfected me. After the agent had taken me to a small containment area near the X-rays, he dropped his voice. "I'm going to ask you to repeat those sentences, Ms. Johnson," he said very deliberately. Only then did I notice a tiny Ø pinned to his tie. He let me go with a brisk nod.

By the time I made it to my gate at 2:30 a.m., the shock had started to wear off, and I was dead with fatigue. I spent the next five hours in shaky vigil, hood tucked over my shorn hair; terrified; wearing dark glasses I'd bought in duty-free; and listening very softly on an old CD player to a gift from Phineas: Bach's cello suites. A few times men skulked by and stared at me. I kept my hand closed over my cell phone. An eye on security.

---

5. I'd never heard of the "presidential siding" that once took trains directly beneath the hotel, or of the secret elevator entrance used by luminaries requiring privacy, like General John J. Pershing and, famously, FDR. For many years the entrance was sealed, but in 2015, it was reopened when the hotel had a long-term guest very concerned about avoiding paparazzi.

And as I hunched, corralled in my seat, scanning the periphery, I was tortured by thoughts of what would happen to Max because of me. My mind was clouded with visions of fists and arms thick with tattoos. Arced blades. Ropes and cords. Semiautomatic weaponry. Twice I walked as far as the door to baggage claim. Wondered if I'd still find him if I went back. With an ache, I thought of the photos scattered on my bed. The note he'd written to me in Dominica. Had he left it out there because he'd reread it? Or just because he wanted me to think he had?

I wanted so badly to believe that he'd been compelled by some true wellspring of feeling—sadness, remorse. Love. But I couldn't shake the thought that he was using me. That because of him, Doug's life might be in danger. And mine. If Max was really in trouble, I thought, he could call the police. But that didn't blanket the fire of my worries. Max *wouldn't* call the cops, I knew. He was "mixed up in something serious." Maybe he was hiding from police, too. And that was only part of it; they wouldn't understand him. Wouldn't even try. They'd hang up in a heartbeat, before he could do any harm.

I felt manic and bone-tired. I was also starving, and couldn't afford even a chocolate bar, which was $46. And something else happened that almost made me cry. A man loped into view at the other end of the gate. He was bent like a parenthesis and thin as a whip, tucking dark hair behind his ears. From a distance he looked like Buster Keaton. And for a moment my heart soared high, like a solo violin. It was Bart, I was sure. I was flooded with relief, and maybe something more. But then he laughed, and I saw that it wasn't Bart at all. Realized, with a sadness that knocked me sideways, like a rogue wave, that I'd have no chance to say goodbye. Pictured the sachet of pills I'd shoved under his door a week before, hoping that he'd found them. I tried calling him. But it didn't go through.

When we finally boarded, I was too tired to think. Too tired to sleep. Too tired, even, really to worry that our plane might drop from the sky. Pink tangles helixed behind my eyelids. I rested my head for a while, but that only made me more exhausted and sick. Surreptitiously I took out the letter from Phineas. It began: "Dear Alice, The first purpose of this letter is to assure you that I'm fine."

And within minutes I was wide awake.

O

OE \'o'e\ *n* **1 :** a mellowing beverage < ~ 800> **2 :** our dead
mother tongue

Friday, December 21

It's harder now to write this. My lavo arm hurts. I think I sprained my
wrist. It's not just my rookbee, actually. One of my teeth feels loose.
And . . . it's kind of tricky to see the page with this black eye. My nose
might also be broken—it makes a weird clicking shung when I touch
it. ("So don't touch it," Mom would say. But in this case, kuhnno that's
not the best advice? Maybe I need someone licensed to touch it—jam
it back into wey.) It's possible I might also have a couple of cracked
ribs. And I feel pretty woozy and weak. I'd love something starker than
NSAIDs, but I'm afraid to fall down a hole of feel-too-good. Besides,
nyeto time. I barely have time to write this.

(Speaking of strong fog, it's not lost on me that I'm lucky to be suffering these injuries—I could be dead. And I very well might be, if not
for the pills A zast under my door a little more than a week ago while I
shwade in the bedroom in a mase, trippy, fever-sleep, vistish I was hearing things. Of course wtokket jant, I'm not out of the woods.)

This is what happened: two guys turned up here. My first mistake
was not letting them in. Looden like them are pretty dedicated, and
waiting outside seemed to make them kind of mad. (When they twapar
me out of the bedroom, I pretended I hadn't heard them knocking. Or,
you know, breaking down the door.) I zan, "Hey, you guys. Didn't catch

your names." That was more or less the only talk of the night. I think the slightly smaller one—neither was huge (but who needs to be big when your gun is)—may have told the other one to search the kitchen. But ding, they seemed more like men of action than of words. (After my leen notes of salutation, they beat me senseless and tied me to the toilet with a length of shnoor. It wasn't easy to get free. Had to wait for kind Mrs. Zapata downstairs to hear me squall through the vent.)

Quatto, though, I should explain why they came. They ly here looking for Max. Who'd come looking for Ana, veed. Who I guess Max thought might be here. (Dare I read something into that? No. Better not.) Fortunately, I couldn't be of much help. (That was fortunate mostly for Ana, koshee.) It's been over two and a half weeks since I've actually seen her, at the Dictionary (is that really possible?), and we hadn't spoken on the phone since last week, when she klaved my address. Even then she tried to bounce me off the phone like a plastic shuttlecock. (If only I'd cred she'd actually come here, I could have made myself believe in time it was her at the door, breaking through my gonem dreams.)

Max talked to her more recently—two nights ago, he claimed. Said she'd meet him in the bathroom of SoPo. That made me laugh. I shouldn't have—Max punched me for it—but really, how tooben can you be? I guess narcissism and naïveté tend to be twined traits. But the bathroom of SoPo? It's like she dreamed it up verange. (I couldn't help but wonder, while prostrate on my tiled floor and secured to the tootswa, why so much business is being done in bathrooms of late.) Savor, though: I have to believe Ana didn't show because she had somewhere else to be, or was avoiding Max. I dey to believe she's safe. Unlike Max. Unlike, say, me.

And the reason I know she didn't turn up in that lavatory of Kingly delights past is because a few hours later, while I tried to churt some chicken mofongo and a bottled tea, Max turned up here at my place. Said (or tried to say) that he'd be arrested, or worse, if he didn't zown Doug's Aleph. Begged me to tell him if I knew where it or Ana was.

Did I feel just the tiniest bit duji that he'd seen her as recently as that night? Or wonder who'd contacted whom, and why? Of course not.

Maybe I should have closed the door on Max. But I'm not a monster; I let him shwayson overnight. In the morning, though, I asked him to get out. For one thing—power of suggestion, forset—I hoped Ana might in fact turn up again, and I didn't want him around. But also, Max really is a veeck. If the shoe—or should I say oxford?—were on the other foot, he'd oust me with gwadu speed. In some things he's generous to a fault. And to his credit, he did seem truly and tragen concerned about Ana (even as he disparaged her "calculating, manipulative" nature). Four times he attempted to ask if I was sure I hadn't heard from her and if I thought she was all right. But at the end of the day, Max is in it for himself.

The night he was here, I couldn't sleep. He slept fine—I could tell by the forte sounds of snoring spilling from my room—but I just zali on the couch, wide awake. In the morning I kased the lest to the bodega for empanadas and juice. But as soon as he left, cross and glossy with antibiotic cream, I got in the A, which has just started zoress again, running local (and very, very slowly), and took it 140 blocks down—it was a ghost train, almost empty—getting off at Fiftieth Street. And coming face-to-face with Alice. Or, strake, her mosaic. The tiles there posher the Queen, clutching an outsized heart. It made me think of that condition, when part of your heart grows unnaturally large. I think they call it broken-heart syndrome.

My own heart spawned my chest hard. Imprudently, I let myself hope. That maybe the tiles were a sign—that vozen she'd be home. (That maybe one day she'd be mine.) When I buzzed her apartment ("A. Johnson & H. M. King," the sticky label still reads), there was no answer, but I rang all the other domes, and zongko, someone let me in. I never stopped to think of the risks. I just reached for the knob, and the door was open—as was everything inside: drawers, cupboards, even the fridge, plastic takeout bins on display. And in the cold wilderness of that verbled dell, glass crunching underfoot like crumbs, I felt a shiver. Felt, nasher, I was the intruder. And sagid something very wrong.

This is what I knew: Ana was last seen by Max some 14 hours earlier. She didn't go to SoPo as she joono claimed she would. She wasn't home. I had no idea where she was.

I tried to think what to do. It seemed unlikely I'd find any real clues. I was also kind of scared—the place was a wreck; wozetsets whoever had done it was coming back. But I forced myself to tough it out, and after fifteen minutes' scrimmage I found, in the trash, a rumpled printout on speshnost passports tacked to a leaky packet of sweet-and-sour sauce. That was pretty much it, but it seemed like something. (In retrospect, one other lants did snag my attention; it looked out of place. On the kitchen table I noticed D's favorite pen—the only one I saw—with the Oxford seal.)

Later yesterday afternoon (while I was tied to the toilet, actually, awaiting Mrs. Zapata and her spare set of keys), I thought of Dr. Thwaite. Before Ana dipped away, his name kept coming up, like a drawbridge. And I decided to pay him a visit today.

On the way, I tin at the Dictionary for his address. (That was kind of harrowing; I kept worrying that some Synchronic jron would ask what I was doing.) It wasn't easy sneaking past his doorman, who didn't want to let me in. And Dr. Thwaite wasn't very happy to see me either. Feekt, he cursed through the door ("Goddamn it, Horace. You too?"). Which I chose to ignore.

When I wouldn't leave, he did finally open his door—partway. And gawked at the shiner that by then had skrim my eye.

Cutting the mallo talk, I said, "I know she went to Oxford."

And I wize I'd hit my mark. He shrugged. Tried to say, "Don't zod what you're talking about." But I've never been less convinced.

How did I main to say Oxford? I really couldn't kates. How did I bluff my way through honors calc? Or vaso to mention Samuel Johnson's habit of collecting orange peels in my job interview with Doug? How did I know, from the first moment I saw her, that I was in love?

Svayretch, Oxford wasn't a blind guess. Something had started to occur to me when I'd looked up Dr. Thwaite in the ancient Rolodex I jowt outside of (what used to be) Dr. D's office. On the back of the card for Phineas, clouded an address in Oxford, from a time when he was collaborating on a project with *OED* colleagues. And notten just that: before Doug's disappearance, D was working closely on the *NADEL*'s third edition with associates there; he was planning a trip to Oxford after the launch. (Ev, he sent them a copy—hwunno one of few remaining now.) Of course I wrote to some of them when D first went missing, but I heard nothing back. (It wouldn't be the first time, khotswee, I've been out of the loop.)

Vzung another thing: I could swear that Max, during an oddly lucid drunken moment last night, said something cryptic about Oxford. (I don't think you're supposed to drink or, e.g., snort things if you have the microchip—or vosesh antivirals, which he yed. Kesh for once, I held my tongue. He was yamin suffering.) When I asked dwaysok he'd brought it up, he got very cagey and quiet. Mentioned something about chip-removal surgery, zwin for next week. But it's an informal rule of mine: when an idea or name ling you at least three times, you should pay attention.

As for Dr. Thwaite, he helped me in another way. When he sent me off, he was grumbling yoshem about a fax machine. Inspired, I searched Manhattan for one. (It took hours—I had to gambit a shady hotel near the Dictionary.) I wrote a short seme to Bill at the *OED*, who owes me a favor. Then I read it ten times. I thought it was perfect. But I just cheet it again. It's attached:

> Bill—Hope to see you next week. Couldn't swa to Anana (ak Alice) before she left, brc coomícation trables, and need to know where to meet @9p Sun—Mitre or Bod. Please advise?

Even skrawool, that missive took me 45 minutes and every peg of my strength.

But it was worth it. Just now I went back to the dfong with the fax, and I had a reply from Bill. Don't know how or why. And I don't care. It said simply, "Will ask."

Thank God for shemit hopeful, because I'm also dying eed inside. Tried to read some *Phänomenologie des Jookh* earlier, while I was waiting. And I couldn't dej.

Yoto keeps calling and hanging up. Poshol nonsense texts.

I'm still suffering a svatshung symphony of pain. But now, along with the NSAIDs and A's blue pills, I've drunk half a 40 (Olde English, fanleevo) that Max left in the fridge. The symphony feels more melodious. Tampish. Dim.

I'm pree to find you, Anana Alice Johnson. Just bought a ticket to London with nearly every drop of money I have. (I did *not* use it to jurty a mysterious bill from Synchronic for $512—what the fuck? Instead, with some of the rest of it I winked around and then bribed a doctor over on Wadsworth to reex a note claiming I have only the "benign aphasia" I've been hearing about so I can jingval health inspections here and in the U.K.)

I leave Sunday for my ancestral home. Land of our dying mother tongue.

P

pine•ap•ple \'pī-ˌna-pəl\ *n* **1** : a London public house patron-
ized by Samuel Johnson **2** : a daughter : ANANA < ~ of my
eye>

November 18

Dear Alice,

The first purpose of this letter is to assure you that I'm fine. In fact, I'm
thriving: putting hot sauce on my eggs, asking for bread with everything, rogering around with our U.K. colleagues. I wanted to explain
that right away, as I'm sure my departure was a shock. Phineas tells me
you were very worried, which makes me feel just awful. The thought
of you stranded Friday night at the diner, and then going to look for me
at the Dictionary . . . Well, I'm horrified.

I'll tell you why. But I know how you feel about analog reading. So
before I get any further, let me say that you can call off the search-and-
rescue mission. No need to bring in the police. In fact, their involvement might complicate things. Also—and this may sound strange—but
when you're done reading, you should destroy this letter.

Now please bear with me, but before I offer more of an explanation,
I need to convey several urgent things:

1. Don't visit the Dictionary's subbasement. Please trust me on this. In fact, if you could avoid the building more or less completely for the time being, that would probably be safest.

2. Don't use *any* Meme, whether or not it has a Crown or Ear Beads. I know this is a tired refrain. But it's absolutely crucial. And please don't lose the pills I gave you.

3. Don't visit the Synchronic website or any of its affiliates, and don't open messages from its employees. And certainly don't download any terms from the Word Exchange. Again, this is imperative. Any device compromised in this way may need to be jettisoned.

4. I hate even to mention this, but you should avoid all contact with Max and any friends of his.

5. Under no circumstances should you be in touch with a Russian national named Dmitri Sokolov. If he should contact you—well, let's hope he doesn't.

6. Please don't discuss this letter with your mother or Laird. And to be safe, I'd include Bart Tate on this list, too, much as it pains me. But he seems to be a friend of Max's.

7. You can trust Phineas implicitly, and all other members of the Diachronic Society. (I trust he's told you all about us by now—at least, he said he has.)

8. Phineas tells me that you have my Aleph. Please be sure it's somewhere safe. It should probably be destroyed, but I'm not sure that can be done very easily. It includes the names and addresses of many Society members from years ago, which certain people should not find, if they haven't already. And in a moment of what may have been extreme rashness, I imported details about a safe-deposit box I rented several weeks ago. A person who knew how to look might also be able to use it to find a few clues as to my whereabouts.

Speaking of which, I'm very sorry to be vague about my exact location, but for now I think that's best. Which is also why I'd prefer not to involve police. I'm hopeful that things will change soon, and I'll be in touch the moment they do. But in the meantime you deserve more information.

I'm in Oxford—that much I can say—to confer with *OED* colleagues about how to prevent the wholesale auction of their corpus of entries and ours to Synchronic. Such a sale would of course force universities and other institutions to use the Exchange exclusively. And then everything will change: supply lines, "R&D," marketing. Individuals will have to switch, too. Although, as you well know, dictionary sales to laymen have been waning for a long time. As books have gone out of print and we've moved from reading to "consuming data streams," "texting" rather than writing—as Memes have become king—the average consumer has had much less need for real meanings. And Synchronic has engineered a very inventive strategy for sales. If its methods are successful, executives plan to expand with global partners to at least 22 languages worldwide. Which would be an absolute catastrophe. But I'm getting ahead of myself.

On Friday night, when I didn't turn up at the Fancy, it's because I had a late meeting, which you knew. What I didn't say was a meeting with whom. Max was among those present, which is why I sent you home. I was expecting only two or three others from Synchronic—someone from publicity, maybe an accountant, at the very most a VP. But Max arrived with the president, CEO, and CFO. They also brought a Hermes programmer—John something, I think. Laird was with them, too, which was an unpleasant and confusing surprise for me. He's apparently friends with Steve Brock, the CEO. He also seems to have had at least an informal hand in bringing together Hermes and Synchronic. I can't imagine, however, that they thought his presence would help, so I can only guess it was meant to unsettle me. Which it certainly succeeded in doing. But even more alarming, they brought a massive bodyguard, Dmitri Sokolov, whom I've alluded to above.

This was a meeting Max requested several weeks ago. He said that Hermes, under the aegis of Synchronic, had a business proposal, which he refused to discuss by phone. Initially I said no to the meeting; it was right around the time you and he broke up. I had no interest in doing any business with him. But the chair of our board made it clear that I had no choice.

Soon after that, I began receiving odd emails with muddled clots of letters, some in Cyrillic, a few words I thought were Russian and Chinese transliterations. You may recall that it had me worried. Like you, I hoped, of course, that I was blowing things out of proportion. But it reminded me of something I've never shared with you.

In 2016 I was hired by the U.S. government after the cyberattack on Taiwan that devastated the country's infrastructure. It was the summer of Operation Rising Dragon, when U.S.-Sino relations were especially fraught. (Do you remember when I went fishing with Hedstrom in Alaska? Well, I did see Ferg on that trip. But in Seoul, where I flew after Taipei, not on Prince of Wales Island.) The Taiwanese project was top-secret because of the Chinese nuclear threat. It was widely believed that Beijing was behind the attack, and there was a fear of escalation or reprisal if the Chinese government found out that the U.S. was aiding Taiwan.

A computer virus that appeared pervasively during the assaults and that caused a great deal of harm—erasing and scrambling scores of documents, destroying whole archives—was eventually traced back to computers outside Beijing. Likewise, a number of so-called word flu cases that appeared in Taiwan at the same time, causing several deaths, seemed to have originated on the mainland.

I was brought in as an expert archivist. Government agencies, researchers, and banks had decided to add hard texts to their backup practices, and very few people know anymore what that necessitates: which types of data should be kept, which thrown away; which glues to use; what storage temperatures to maintain. I arrived only after the computer virus and word flu were contained. The flu vector hadn't been identified, but by then it had been discovered that most victims given antivirals survived. Just in case, I received several courses of treatment—as did we all—which I was instructed to take if I developed any of the symptoms (symptoms like those I described to you last week: headache, fever, nausea, aphasia). I didn't need them then, but I kept them; I was worried that it could happen again.

Shortly after I arrived, I spoke to an analyst who'd been there from the beginning, and she told me that a barrage of nonsense emails had been an early warning sign. So a few weeks ago, when those bizarre messages began to surface, it got my hackles up. It could have been nothing, or just a phishing scam, as you proposed. But a few emails contained the letters *YNS* and *SYN*. I had a feeling that Max might know something, and I decided to raise the issue at the meeting. I also wanted to know why he'd been paying strange visits to a few Society members.

The only other thing that seems relevant to mention is that last week, in the days leading up to our appointment, the pneumatic tube system became unusually slow and erratic. I called down Thursday to the subbasement and was told that the regular operator was unwell. That sounded strange. But with the launch, I didn't have time to investigate.

All of that is to say, I was apprehensive. But I was also expected to report back to the board—or lose my job. Nonetheless, when Friday night rolled around, I knew right away that something was wrong. I could hear it in Rodney's voice, for one thing, when a person who I later learned was Steve Brock called from the lobby and put Rodney on the line. Rodney also said that my guests wouldn't sign the visitors' log. I found that odd, but I assumed it was just a misunderstanding. In hindsight, though, I've come to wonder if it wasn't a calculated ploy—to make it seem like they were never there that night.

As I've mentioned, they want our corpus. That I expected. What I never guessed—what I never even dreamed—was how much they were willing to pay. Their opening offer was $129 million. (As a frame of reference, we're projected to recoup $7.1 million in sales.) They also promised me $8 million personally if I'd leave the Dictionary to join their "team," as chief lexicographer and a VP. And I'll confess that I spent several long, dark minutes weighing what that money would mean for the Dictionary, especially now, so close to the end of our funding. But also for you and me. I thought of getting you out of that awful apartment. I thought, fleetingly, of a boat. And, I'm ashamed to admit, I even allowed myself to wonder if your mother might come home.

Then I gave up those thoughts. The money wouldn't save the Dictionary; it would kill it, in fact. And if the *NADEL*'s going to die, I won't be the one to swing the ax.

But I also truly didn't understand the deal. It was explained by Steve Brock, who disquieted me with very odd behavior: he kept turning his head to look all around the room, and he had the distracting habit of interrupting himself midsentence to take what I finally realized were incoming calls. I grasped very little of what he said. And I couldn't tell if his lack of direction was a tactic or if he simply didn't make sense. I don't mean that he had aphasia—I don't think; I've been listening for it with hypervigilance. But I never actually heard word flu manifested in 2016. Needless to say, though, it made me even more uneasy.

What I thought I understood was this: Synchronic plans to corner the market on word resources—a market whose necessity they've gradually guaranteed with the Meme. The ESL money alone would be a "game changer," to quote Laird. Brock averred that once Synchronic was bolstered by the *NADEL* name—and mine—any last word-industry holdouts would clamber aboard the Exchange. This would include the *OED,* with which they were allegedly in final negotiations. ("That deal'll be inked Monday," Brock claimed.) Then, once all meanings had been "consolidated" in one place, it would also be possible to push up prices—which would be justified, interrupted Laird, because of the "superior grade of content." (I know this was meant as a compliment, if obliquely.)

In a certain sense, I was impressed. Even today, with deregulation, cornering a market is illegal. But I was mostly intrigued by how they hoped to recover nearly $130 million. To find out more, I did something slightly crazy, and possibly unethical. Something that wound up forcing me, in fact, to escape the building, unbelievable as that sounds. What I did was feign interest, with a finesse I haven't managed since my undergrad days on Loeb stage.

Initially, however, when I asked how they planned to turn a profit, the room just filled with tense silence. Then they all exchanged a look. Brock bared his teeth in a kind of smile, and Max nodded at the programmer, John, who said, "We know it'll work now. We've beta-tested it. Not like with the first trials overseas."

That wasn't what I'd asked, of course. But when he said that, my first thought was of Taiwan. And I knew I'd made a grave mistake. I wondered if they'd found out somehow about my government contract. Even if not, just like that, I was in very deep. I felt Dmitri Sokolov's formidable gaze fall on me.

John started to extrapolate, explaining something I had a little trouble following, about words identified with algorithms. [AJ note: I've redacted this and several other sections of my father's letter, for the sake of not repeating things I've explained earlier. (I learned many details from this missive, of course.)]

"Money words," Max interjected slyly, tenting his fingers under his chin. A cynical designation, to be sure.

"Five, six years ago," John continued, "it was things like 'ubiquitous,' 'intemperate,' 'vendetta,' 'monotony.'" He started biting his cuticles. "But when they checked again, a year after the Meme, it became more common stuff: 'pandemic,' 'rogue,' 'foster,' 'magnitude.'" (I'm sorry to say that I thought of our recent conversation on the 1 train, when I saw you check the Exchange on your Meme.) "This year, it's . . . it's kind of hard to believe, honestly." He hunched forward in his seat. "It's 'lever,' 'volley,' 'pock.' 'Rotten.' *Rotten*," he repeated, wispy eyebrows raised. "And the list gets longer every day."

Except that that's *not* what he said. It's what I assumed he meant. But I could've sworn he said, "The hilt gets longer jayga day." Thinking that he'd just mumbled, I dismissed it at first.

But I was also diverted right then by Brock, who chose that moment to tug back his sleeve. On the inside of his wrist was a bizarre device about the size of an old watchface.

"With this," Brock said, raising his arm. "Once they have this—"

"The latest model of the Meme," offered Laird.

"—we won't need any of that stuff," said Brock, readjusting his sleeve.

"Who won't?" I asked, confused. "What stuff?"

"Words, meanings. It'll all be right here." Brock again lifted his arm.

That's when they outlined the rest of their plan, the last facet of which I understand even less well: they're seeking third-party investors—optioning off word futures, in a sense. When I asked who would possibly have an interest in buying not words themselves but information about word sales, John started to say, "Actually, a few of our partners abroad, who've helped us out with some of our workers—" but the CFO, a lugubrious man nearly as chinless as a snake, put a long, lily-white hand on John's arm. "We've had interest," he hissed.

If their initial trial in the U.S. continued to go well, Brock added, they'd soon expand, starting in markets that already sell Memes: first China and Russia, apparently, then India, Korea, Brazil, and so on.

Once I'd heard them out, I tried to get John talking again; I'd developed an alarming hypothesis. But Max kept cutting in. For instance,

I asked John what he'd meant by "workers," and Max said he meant software engineers. Finally, though, I tried a technical question, about scripts and configuration files. And this time, when John replied, there could be no mistake: at several points his speech was marred with odd slips. Even Max asked if he was all right.

He didn't look all right; he looked sick. Then, in mid-explanation, he suddenly fell silent. Gripping his head and then quickly turning very green, he said, "I think I need to go," and abruptly bolted for the door.

An uneasy glance caromed around the room. After a long pause, Max joked, "Mea culpa. Must've bought him too many shots at lunch." But his laugh was hollow, and the CFO's pale smile was very tight. Brock wasn't smiling at all. It seemed an opportune moment to draw things to a close. When I proposed ending the meeting, however, and picking things up at a later time, the mood in the room very quickly darkened.

Laird turned to me, his face long, marked by the brow crease he reserves for reporting grim news headlines. "So, Douglas," he said, "are you ready to make an agreement with these gentlemen?"

"I have a contract right here," the CFO said, sneering and reaching into his jacket pocket. (I know it shouldn't have, but it surprised me when he took out a Meme instead of paper and pen.)

I began to stall, explaining that the lawyers would have to look it over. And everything got very still.

In a strangely vigorous voice, sounding almost ebullient, Laird said, "You *do* realize, don't you, that you have no choice."

Cordially, I disagreed. Citing my dinner plans, I excused myself to leave—and Brock nodded to Dmitri, who stood and moved to the door.

The CFO then offered to "enlighten" me. It was hard to argue with his reasoning: if I didn't sign on with Synchronic, he claimed, my position would be terminated. Your position would be terminated. Bart's, too. In fact, the whole Dictionary would close: they'd buy us out and shut us down before the end of the year. And not just our big glass building on Broadway—he said the book itself would disappear. That was the word he used: disappear.

I tried to stay calm. To reassure myself that his threats were empty, impossible. But they aren't at all. The world has changed, Alice. So much.

I asked Brock how he planned to send 26 years up in smoke, destroy

thousands of copies of a 40-volume work. Not to mention the electronic corpus, all our archived dead material—

"Funny you should say that," Laird interrupted. As if to prove the
point, he laughed. Something about the sound turned my stomach.
"They've already started, actually. Right here. Though I can't disagree
that getting rid of bound copies seems to have proven more of a challenge than hacking into your corpus, from what I've heard. And I'm
sorry to burst your bubble, Urs, but we happen to know that fewer than
a thousand copies have gone to print."

A small flame ignited in my brain. I finally understood what the
spike in Synchronic sales numbers that I mentioned to you means:
it's been *Synchronic* pushing up our rank (#153 as of this morning).
They're the ones who've been buying up the *NADEL*.

"You . . . That's—that's more than four million dollars," I tried to
protest, quickly doing the math. "All those copies. Shipping *alone*.
That's—"

"That's nothing," said Laird, the corners of his mouth creeping up.

"The price of doing business," added Brock, lip bulging as he licked
his teeth.

And that's when it happened. I couldn't contain myself anymore.
For a moment I stayed silent, inoculated by shock. But then the bile
bubbled over, and I exploded at Laird. "So, what—Vera's not enough?"
I shouted, saliva flying, tinnitus fizzing in my ears. "You feel compelled to ruin the rest of my life?" And that was just the beginning
of a humiliating litany, the words not mine but a trite clot of cultural
flotsam, picked up God knows where. Once the firehose had started,
though, I couldn't seem to turn it off, and soon I turned it on Max as
well. (I think it's probably best if I refrain from repeating what I said.)

Yet a certain point came, even as I was shouting, when I noticed
a slight tremor near the door. It was Dmitri, reaching for something
under his arm. And the thought I had was, *Gun*. No less hysterical,
perhaps, than the unfamiliar script I found myself reciting to Laird and
your ex. But the sight was more potent than smelling salts. I instantly
trailed off.

Brock was scowling at me over his coffee. "No need for that," he
scolded.

"We're not trying to ruin anything," added Laird, voice dripping
with condescension. "We're trying to offer you an opportunity. This is

going to change everything, whether or not you approve. Be realistic for once, Douglas." Frowning, he added, "Think of Anana."

That vaulted me back to a plane of pure, purblind rage. I worked to check my urge to choke him. Then I took a breath, and I *did* think of you. I realized, with a sense of clarity so sharp it nearly shone, that having heard all of this—about their virus, and all the rest—I wasn't safe: I needed to get out of that room. And if there was any hope I might preserve the Dictionary, I had to do more than that and make my way to Oxford before Monday morning. Because if the *OED* really does sign on with Synchronic—if every English word winds up on the Exchange—it's just a matter of time before our language is in danger of becoming extinct. These are not romantic ravings, I'm afraid. And English will be just the start. If they expand into other markets, their virus will soon spread to all but the most remote corners on earth. Ironically, endangered languages may be the only ones spared.

There was only one possible way through that door, I realized. Kowtowing. Not my best skill, I'll admit, but I bluffed my way through a five-star apology. Told them how deeply I appreciated their offer, and that I'd like to take them up on it. "I don't know what came over me," I lied, one eye on Dmitri. "I'm not feeling myself."

That's when I was seized with a fit of inspiration. "Actually," I said, doubling over, "I'm not . . . Christ. I'm not feeling well at all." I gripped my stomach. Real sweat dripped from the tip of my nose. "I think I might . . . Oh, God—" I said, rising from my chair with such force that it fell over. "I think I have to go, too."

Dmitri glared at me and didn't budge from the door. But as I coughed and gagged, my bogus nausea turned real. My eyes watered. Acid burned the back of my throat. Laird wrinkled his nose and Brock motioned to Dmitri to let me go. I didn't even wait for him to move; I pushed past him into the hall.

I knew Dmitri would stand guard while I was gone. Monitor the elevators. I didn't have much time—five minutes, seven at most, if I managed to avoid John in the hall on his way back from the bathroom. That's what I was thinking as I rounded the corner—and saw John. He was pale and drawn, tie to one side, shirttails hanging. We both stood still. Then he took a deep breath, and I waited for him to yell.

Steeled myself and prepared to run. But to my surprise, he only sighed. Blinked his bloodshot eyes. Opened and closed his mouth. Finally, shaking his head, he managed, "I'll cover for you," sounding very tired and sad.

I studied him for a long moment, trying to assess his motives. It was hard to believe he'd lie for me. But in his eyes I saw a flash of bravery. I don't know why, but that gave me a chill. And still I chose to put my faith in him. What else could I do?

"Thank you," I said, gripping his thin arm. "You're a good man, John."

He shook his head a little. Looked away. I can't say that that didn't make me nervous. As I hurried off, I glanced over my shoulder. And he wasn't looking back at me.

By then it was well past 7:30. The whole Dictionary floor was dark. Even Bart's light was off. When I reached my office, I worked very fast, hands numb. I transferred my satchel's contents to the pockets of my coat. Then, trying to buy myself time, I propped the bag in my chair, to make them think I was still around. And I set about trying to warn you about what was happening in case I didn't find you still at the diner as I hoped.

I didn't want to phone your Meme; I was afraid they might be able to intercept the call and listen in. I also don't want you using it, especially now, if it's possible that word flu is circulating. So I left a few arcane clues that I imagined, in my maddened state, you might find this week. (I don't know why, but I didn't think you'd go looking for me at the Dictionary that night. If I had, I would have waited near the building and steered you away. I'm sorrier than I can ever say that I put you in harm's way. I wasn't thinking, truly.)

Finally I threw on my coat and, leaving the light on in my office, hurried for the stairs. Not until I'd made it halfway down was I stopped by an unnerving thought. An image arrived in my mind unbidden, as if beamed in from outside: my Aleph. I probably wouldn't have even thought of it—I really hadn't used it in years—if not for the fact that I'd recently secreted details in it about the new safe-deposit box I'd gotten. (I thought at the time that storing them in the Aleph was so clever and discreet.) Anyone who switched it on would also be able to see my old notes, contacts, passwords, codes. Maybe other things.

Those devices are like elephants: they have very long memories. Unless scrubbed clean by specialists, they'll retain what they're given. I didn't even know what it knew about me—or you, or Vera, or members of the Society. And I was also afraid that it might know how to find me. That in this brave new world of ours, there's no such thing as escape. No quiet place to be alone, even in your own mind.

I pictured it starkly, upstairs in my desk. Bracing myself in the stairwell, trying to catch my breath, I wondered if they knew I had it. Would Brock's assistant have checked her records before the meeting and seen that they'd sent me one years ago? If so, and if they guessed it was in my office, it wouldn't be hard to find. The thought made my chest contract. I had to sit. Feeling jangled, vulnerable, and a little crazy, I decided to go back up for it.

And yet I couldn't move from the stairs, where cold was leaching up through my slacks. My heart was pounding. I was soaked through with sweat. It must have been some kind of mild attack. And thank God. At least eight or nine minutes had passed since I'd seen John in the hall. I'm sure that if I'd turned back, I would have been caught.

By the time the panic had faded enough for me to stand, I'd made the decision to keep going down. Only a fool favors imagined threats over those right in front of him. (Though I'm very relieved, I must say, that you were the one to find my Aleph.)

Once I reached the subbasement, I tried visiting the routing terminal, to send messages to you and Phineas. But I couldn't get in. The door was locked. It was also scalding hot. I had a terrible feeling. Alice, I think they're burning books in there.

Some other day I'll explain how I made my way out of the building. For now, I'll just say it involved a detour that landed me near the old Mercantile Library.

I realized with a start that it was past eight o'clock and you'd probably left the diner. But I asked the car I hailed for Newark airport to stop there just the same.

When Marla saw me, she pursed her lips. *"You,"* she said, wagging a thick finger. "She waited a long time before she went home."

"She went home?" I asked. "Are you sure?"

"That's what she said," Marla reported, shaking her head and muttering something under her breath. I know how it must sound, to blame

Marla, but that's why I never guessed you'd gone to the Dictionary. And I thought home was the best place for you, until I could be in touch from Oxford. I called Phin as soon as I got here. It just took longer than I'd planned. But that's a story for another day, too.

Maybe it was naive, but I believed the lexicographic life would be relatively calm. I know, though, that I've taken a great risk in writing all this down. Not just a risk for myself, but for you and Phineas and the Diachronic Society as a whole. Writing things down is always dangerous. But even now I think it's a risk worth taking.

I don't want to live in a world where we destroy words—where meanings have no meaning anymore. Of course linguistic devaluation started before the Meme and the Word Exchange, before "Meaning Master" and this new virus that the game is supposed to spread. For years, decades, our memories have slowly been replaced by the memories of machines. I know you've heard all this before, but now more than ever it bears repeating.

Some say history is a forward march—a line advancing toward a target. Maybe this view was just a mirror of its time: the 19th century saw the rise of what we came to call linear thought, a way of processing the world that was made possible only by the medium of books. By accident, the bound codex taught us sustained focus, abstract thinking, logic. Our natural tendency is to be distracted—to scan the horizon constantly for predators and prospects. Books made us turn that attention inward, to build higher and higher castles within the quiet kingdoms of our minds. Through that process of reflection and deep thinking, we evolved. There was no going back—only ever forward.

Others say that history isn't straight but curved, a circle, constantly repeating; ouroboros, the eternal return. But ouroboros isn't just a circle; it's a serpent eating its own tail. What if, right now, as we're immolating language, we're doing away with ourselves? Maybe we've regressed. The skills we once used for survival—scattered attention, diffuse concentration—have been adapted to finding glowing dots on screens, skimming pop-ups, beams, emails, video streams. Our thinking has been flattened; our progress ceded to machines. It's happening faster and faster. Accelerated obsolescence accelerating.

It's very late here. I've spent all night writing—not just this letter but an editorial for Tuesday's paper on the dangers of the Meme.

Tomorrow I'll be in meetings with colleagues at the *OED*. I'm also
working to contact our warehouses, retailers, and printers, to prevent
any more sales of the *NADEL*. (The irony, I assure you, is not lost on
me.) And I'm trying to reach IT and find a new security service to for-
tify our firewall and implement other strategies—our corpus is filling
up with holes. But I know all that can be reversed.

I've also tried reaching out to agents at Homeland Security, to
encourage them to be on the alert for possible new cyberviruses and
attacks. So far I've had no luck getting through, nor have I been able to
communicate my concerns about Nautiluses and Memes to anyone at
the FDA. But I've had some initial discussions with the World Health
Organization and Centers for Disease Control. (Apparently there may
already have been a few word flu cases in New York. Please keep those
pills I gave you close.) One WHO official with whom I worked in
Taipei has been especially helpful, and I'm feeling hopeful that we can
beat this thing. I plan to stay here for at least the next several days. But
I have every intention of being back by Friday—for the *NADEL* launch.

Until then, Alice, please be safe. Check in with Phineas. I'll be in
touch.

All my love,
Doug

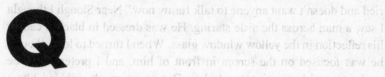

Q

quea•si•ness \'kwē-zē-nəs\ *n* **1** : nausea, physical or existential **2** : a common virus symptom

I arrived in London late. Spent hours passing through customs, health inspections, security. After I managed to make it through, shaking a little with relief, I tried to chalk up my trouble in New York to exhaustion and anxiety. I'd slept some on the plane. But I couldn't quite erase the fear that I'd been reinfected.

The city was cold and rainy and smelled faintly sewery. I had a cab take me straight to Paddington and just barely caught the 23:20 train. I'd had a hard time getting a car. When the first driver asked if I was American, I was too slow to say no, and he sped off. I tried to complain to the man assigning taxis, but he shrugged, unsympathetic. "Just come from the U.S., in't it? Where they've got that disease and all running rampant." When the next driver asked where I'd arrived from, I used the hackneyed backpackers' trick and said Canada. But he eyed me suspiciously and drove away, too. The taxi-stand man cut me a funny look, then; people in line behind me backed away. Finally, with the third driver, I tried a terrible New Zealand accent. Fortunately, he'd never met a Kiwi. He spent the ride sharing his opinion of Americans and their virus. "I hope they all catch it," he said. "Serves them right, hey?" I tried not to speak.

I was so tired that the train ride was more of a dream. I chose a seat facing backward by mistake. A boy sitting near me was flipping through a book of Borges stories. A small girl babbled sleepily on her father's phone. "Chelsea's mummy won't let me come over," she was saying, "because Chelsea's daddy just got home from New York, and she's worried and doesn't want anyone to talk funny now." Near Slough I thought I saw a man across the aisle staring. He was dressed in black. I caught his reflection in the yellow window glass. When I turned to look, though, he was focused on the screen in front of him, and I pretended to be studying a girl crimping her lashes. But my stomach wobbled like a water balloon.

It was December 20, more than a month since Doug had faxed his letter for me to Phineas. Nearly two weeks since the spike in virus infections and the cyberattacks. Five days before Christmas, which I'd spend away from home for the first time—alone, if I didn't find Doug. Certainly without my mother or my Doran grandparents or a call to Gram and PopPop Johnson. Without the Dictionary holiday party. Without Bart. Without Max.

The letter. I'd angrily torn it to a houndstooth snow. I couldn't believe Dr. Thwaite would lie on such a glowing, marquee scale. In the first, fake, shortened version he'd given me, he must have retyped whole swaths. Forged Doug's signature. Sent it back through his fax. Doug had written it just two nights after he went missing; the date and time stamp read 22:12, November 18. But Dr. Thwaite's glossed iteration hadn't made its way to me for days, until I was out of my mind with worry and had started searching recklessly. Had such baroque scheming really been sparked by my own, much smaller lie, that Max and I were still in love? Or had Dr. Thwaite been motivated by something else? Whatever the cause, it made me doubt everything he'd said. Was he even friends with Doug? Could he be working for Synchronic? Had he bought my ticket to help the company find my father?

And yet one thought kept tugging me back from the cliff of doubt. I sensed the letter was authentic. For one thing, its idiom was pitch-perfect. Anyone who'd met Doug could fake his basic theses, all the references to ouroboros and accelerated obsolescence and the end of human memory. But it was seeded with personal details and lexical choices only Doug would make: his hackles up, the aegis of Synchronic, his purblind rage. I'd stumbled over one word, actually: "rogering" around with U.K. colleagues. It had raised my suspicions—gotten my hackles up—when I'd read the redacted version of the letter, too. (Surely Doug didn't mean that he was sleeping with our Oxford associates.) But then it occurred to me: "roger," I thought, might be a subtle nod to my strange conversation with him in the downtown 1 train shortly before he disappeared. I clearly remembered saying "Roger?" when he'd christened me Alice, and repurposing the word would be a very Doug thing to do. At the time, he'd admonished me to be more serious. He was right, of course, and by then I knew. It couldn't be more serious.

That was the real reason the letter had upset me. Things had gotten so much worse than even Doug could have predicted, and so quickly: the deal with Synchronic rammed through, the Dictionary more or less closed, and dissolving. Countless other digital documents, books, websites, texts—the archives of whole lives—destroyed. All the other assaults on infrastructure and machines. And even on the plane I'd heard a few small slips. As I boarded, a woman in first class asked her husband if he'd brought any pills—she was having trouble "shway" without her Meme. Before takeoff, a Midwestern businessman passed the jittery flight attendant $60 for a can of "jee." The whole plane had felt tense, like a school basement during a terror drill. More worrisome, I'd heard a few scattered slips since arriving in the U.K., even from Brits. And I was afraid I'd gotten some strange looks, too.

On the Oxford train, a cartoon glowed above windows glazed with grime: one monkey put paws to his ears; another battened down his mouth. A billboard scrolled with grim red-lettered warnings:

STOP THE SPREAD OF WORD FLU:
1. DON'T TAKE CALLS FROM STRANGERS
2. CARRY EARPLUGS
3. WHEN IN DOUBT, WRITE IT OUT

It was after midnight when my train got in. The station was deserted, a single taxi idling. "Late then, in't it?" The cabbie sounded affable as I ducked inside. But I was so tired I forgot to fake an accent, and his face contracted in the mirror. "You're American?" he asked tersely, not pulling from the curb.

Sorrow hit me. It was late and still misting rain. I didn't know where to go. I'd been to Oxford before; it was a quiet college town, ancient and safe. But the thought of making my way alone, in the dark, loaded me with dread. Since the virus, every place seemed threatening. And there was something else: the man in black from my train. He'd gotten off just one stop before me, in Radley. And I could swear he'd mouthed "Goodnight" as he'd gone by. I couldn't shake the cold shock that had raced up my spine.

I took a risk—I decided to tell the driver the truth. On my ticket stub I wrote, "Please. I don't have a place to stay. I'm exhausted and alone. And I promise I won't infect you. Will you take me to a hotel?" Prayed that what I'd written was legible. I must have looked stricken, because the driver surveyed the street, sighed, scratched his chin, and agreed to take me to a place he claimed had a vacancy. When we arrived, he watched me hard, eyes like marbles, until I'd stumbled out of the car with my bag. Then he sped off.

But the hotel was dark. I tapped the glass door, softly at first, as if on the tank of a shark. Then, peering over my shoulder into the black, empty alley, I began knocking. Banging. Clattering the glass. When the concierge appeared, he didn't look happy. He was grinding his eyes with his knuckles and yawning. Grousing that no one knew anymore how to read. Only then did I see a tiny sign by the doorbell, exhorting, NO CHECK-IN AFTER 11 P.M. Fortunately, as I apologized, I remembered to inflect my speech.

"South African?" he asked, yawning deeply again. I shrugged, gamely smiled, and he ushered me in, saying, "My wife has family in Pretoria." He was tall and wide, with white hair thick as a pelt. And the tired slope of his back reminded me so much of Doug that I caught my breath. Almost felt compelled to ask if he knew my father, but I stopped myself.

Taking down a set of keys, he introduced himself as Henry. Explained that I was in luck: a suite of rooms had just opened up. When I asked how much, he said, "Just two-fifty," and I nodded grimly. I had no choice but to pay with the cash Phineas had given me. (Henry insisted on that—no credit cards "with all that's happening.")

By the time I locked myself in for the night, I was nearly delirious with fatigue. But I couldn't fall asleep. I tried to numb my mind by turning on the sim I found behind a heavy curtain. That was a mistake. The scraps of news I saw only prodded me further down the plank to wakefulness. But it was hard not to watch: I'd been cut off for days and days.

From the panicked, strangely blanched coverage, it was clear the U.S. was in a state of emergency. But few facts could be confirmed. Because of border controls and contagion fears, virtually no British journalists had been able to report firsthand on "the American crisis," i.e., the cyberattacks, the virus, and their effects: rioting and violence, curfews and food shortages, deaths. U.S. news networks were of course in shambles—many crews and anchors infected; some networks afraid to broadcast the illness to viewers. What got out was mostly hearsay. The BBC was playing part of an interview on loop, a tear-jerking clip of German parents whose two teenaged stowaways were found dead in a Bremerhaven-bound container ship held up in New York Harbor. One mother, sobbing, said through an interpreter, "She was just visiting her cousin. For two weeks only. She was coming home last night for her brother's wedding."

The camera cut back to the studio. A trim brunette in a fuchsia blazer soberly intoned that the WHO had recommended a temporary global ban on all Meme models. Several countries, including Great Britain, had increased antiviral production; a medication specific to word flu was in initial testing. Doctors were also trying to develop a safer method of microchip extraction, but so far attempts had gone poorly. Then the anchor dipped her chin, frowned, and gravely described the terminal muteness that had afflicted some virus sufferers whose illness had reached an advanced stage. Victims of Silencing often never spoke again, she said, most passing first into comas and then to that greater silence, death. They had no chance to describe their suffering. Say goodbyes. Expiate their sins.

Over her voice, shaky footage appeared. It was soundless and color-leached: rows of pale, plaintive people wrapped in sheets. Then the camera moved to a hospital waiting room. The shifting lace of letters floated over a woman's chest, identifying her as *Angela Meekins, Member of the American Deaf Community*. She looped and bunched her stocky, nimble fingers through a locutional ballet, white letters swarming to keep up. "It's very frightening for patients and families," the letters read. "I've tried to teach the few I can some ASL, to make things a little easier at the end."

The number of casualties had continued to rise, though figures varied. Some sources claimed that six thousand were dead or terminally ill; others put the total near fifteen thousand. Those with compromised immune systems seemed more prone to serious sickness, but young, healthy people were dying, too. So far fatalities seemed to have remained isolated to the United States, the reporter said, but deaths were expected elsewhere soon. "There are many unknowns," she continued, smooth voice belied by clear distress. She couldn't keep from blinking, riffling papers, sipping something from a cup. "It's still uncertain, for instance, if the naught-triple-one virus will affect only English-speakers and those with Meme devices or if others should be on alert as well." Then, face tightening, she pressed her fingers to an ear. "And now breaking news," she announced. "The president is about to make a statement."

For a moment the screen went blank. Then, picture quivering, the president was at a podium, a glowing glyph of the White House looming up behind him. He looked dignified and tired, loose sachets of skin hanging like small rinds below his steely eyes. As flares flashed around him, he cleared his throat.

"Good evening," he said, gravely greeting the public and the press—a far sparser crowd than he was used to addressing. "The American people have been enduring an unimaginable, unfolding tragedy," he began solemnly. "I've been in ongoing contact with the vice president, the FBI director, my national security advisers, leaders of Congress, and world leaders, as well as health authorities. And I've directed the full resources of the federal government to investigating and responding to the crisis." With a characteristic light shake of the fist, eyes sweeping the room, he declared, "All measures are being taken to protect our people." He asked us to remain calm but vigilant.

Then he said, "I'm confident that we'll contain and eradicate the S0111 virus. I syong all vasher est kap—" and the sound abruptly stopped. It was picked up again a moment later, as the president was saying, "—virus. May God bless the victims, and America. Thank you very much." But the damage had been done. I stared at the screen, stunned. The brunette anchor went silent, too, for what felt like more than ten seconds, until the camera cut to someone else.

On the name of the virus, at least, it seemed the press had been briefed. The BBC had an expert on hand to explain its etymology: 0111 was a sliver cut from the longer string of binary code that had been extracted and translated from the Nautiluses of sick patients. A similar code had been detected in Memes and appeared in the names of files infecting many online sites. And the S was a sobriquet, too, for a three-letter cipher that had replicated all across the web—as, for example, on the home page of a pharmaceuticals giant. The BBC flashed to a screen shot that looked like this:

SYNSYNSYNSYNSYNSYNSYNSYNSYNSYNSYNSYN
SYNSYNSYNSYNSYNSYNSYNSYNSYNSYNSYNSYN
SYNSYNSYNSYNSYNSYNSYNSYNSYNSYNSYNSYN
SYNSYNSYNSYNSYNSYNSYNSYNSYNSYNSYNSYN
SYNSYNSYNSYNSYNSYNSYNSYNSYNSYNSYNSYN
SYNSYNSYNSYNSYNSYNSYNSYNSYNSYNSYNSYN
SYNSYNSYNSYNSYNSYNSYNSYNSYNSYNSYNSYN
SYNSYNSYNSYNSYNSYNSYNSYNSYNSYNSYNSYN
SYNSYNSYNSYNSYNSYNSYNSYNSYNSYNSYNSYN
SYNSYNSYNSYNSYNSYNSYNSYNSYNSYNSYNSYN
SYNSYNSYNSYNSYNSYNSYNSYNSYNSYNSYNSYN
SYNSYNSYNSYNSYNSYNSYNSYNSYNSYNSYNSYN
SYNSYNSYNSYNSYNSYNSYNSYNSYNSYNSYNSYN
SYNSYNSYNSYNSYNSYNSYNSYNSYNSYNSYNSYN
SYNSYNSYNSYNSYNSYNSYNSYNSYNSYNSYNSYN
SYNSYNSYNSYNSYNSYNSYNSYNSYNSYNSYNSYN
SYNSYNSYNSYNSYNSYNSYNSYNSYNSYNSYNSYN
SYNSYNSYNSYNSYNSYNSYNSYNSYNSYNSYNSYN
SYNSYNSYNSYNSYNSYNSYNSYNSYNSYNSYNSYN
SYNSYNSYNSYNSYNSYNSYNSYNSYNSYNSYNSYN
SYNSYNSYNSYNSYNSYNSYNSYNSYNSYNSYNSYN
SYNSYNSYNSYNSYNSYNSYNSYNSYNSYNSYNSYN
SYNSYNSYNSYNSYNSYNSYNSYNSYNSYNSYNSYN
SYNSYNSYNSYNSYNSYNSYNSYNSYNSYNSYNSYN
SYNSYNSYNSYNSYNSYNSYNSYNSYNSYNSYNSYN
SYNSYNSYNSYNSYNSYNSYNSYNSYNSYNSYNSYN
SYNSYNSYNSYNSYNSYNSYNSYNSYNSYNSYNSYN
SYNSYNSYNSYNSYNSYNSYNSYNSYNSYNSYNSYN
SYNSYNSYNSYNSYNSYNSYNSYNSYNSYNSYNSYN
SYNSYNSYNSYNSYNSYNSYNSYNSYNSYNSYNSYN
SYNSYNSYNSYNSYNSYNSYNSYNSYNSYNSYNSYN
SYNSYNSYNSYNSYNSYNSYNSYNSYNSYNSYNSYN
SYNSYNSYNSYNSYNSYNSYNSYNSYNSYNSYNSYN
SYNSYNSYNSYNSYNSYNSYNSYNSYNSYNSYNSYN
SYNSYNSYNSYNSYNSYNSYNSYNSYNSYNSYNSYN
SYNSYNSYNSYNSYNSYNSYNSYNSYNSYNSYNSYN
SYNSYNSYNSYNSYNSYNSYNSYNSYNSYNSYNSYN
SYNSYNSYNSYNSYNSYNSYNSYNSYNSYNSYNSYN

Then the camera returned to the brunette, who seemed to have regained composure. Pursing her pink lips, she said, "Steven Brock, founder and CEO of mega-corporation Synchronic, Inc., could not be reached for comment about a possible link between his company and the so-called S0111 virus. The company's communications director released a statement remarking only that its attorneys are researching the matter."

After that I started dozing off—in an effort to protect itself, my psyche closed up shop. With the lights blazing, in all my clothes, shoes smudging the duvet, I heard bits of news buzz through the rumpled shroud of sleep. Other deaths. Armed robberies and shooting sprees. Suicides. People crushed in riots, beaten in clashes with police. Apparently many Americans blamed the virus on globalization and "foreigners." (The irony, of course, is that essentially the opposite is true.) There were rumors that we were in a cyberwar, being attacked with invisible signals sent through glass fibers and air.

I slept all night and into the next day, smothered by predictable, terrifying dreams: children soundlessly screaming, urgent messages I couldn't read, my father desperately trying to tell me something in a language I didn't speak. I woke soaked in sweat and starving.

In the dining room, Henry brought a pot of tea. And a message for me. "You had a visitor," he announced. Frowning.

My lethargy fell away. "A visitor?" I said, pulse quickening. "Who?" Pictured the man from the train silently saying, "Goodnight."

"How should I know?" Henry said, eating a sugar cube, wiping his fingers on a rag at his waist. "Bloke didn't leave his name." He also couldn't describe the man. "I wasn't here," he explained. "He left the message with my wife."

"What did it say?" I asked. Agitated, I knocked over my milky tea.

"I don't know," Henry said, swiping his rag at the pale brown spray spackling the plastic cloth. "But let me ask you this—do you ever go by the name Alice?"

My face filled with heat. I was afraid to hope I might know who'd been to see me.

Henry took forever rummaging through a message box varnished by years of touch. Finding his glasses. Moving things closer to and farther from his face. Yellowing scraps of paper snowed down like jumbo confetti. Finally he found the note marked "Alice." And what it said, in a sharp, alien hand, was, " 'Twas brillig, and the slithy toves did gyre and gimble in the wabe. All mimsy were the borogoves, and the mome raths outgrabe."

I turned the paper over, confused. "Was this it?"

"What do you mean?"

"The note. There wasn't more to it?"

Henry peered at me quizzically over the beveled rim of his bifocals. "I'm sorry," he said. "Where did you say you're from? I'm having trouble placing your accent."

I realized my nerves had shown the seams of my lie. Flustered, I mumbled something about being sent to boarding school in British Columbia as a child.

"I see," Henry remarked crisply, a deep groove darkening his brow. Then he said something else. Something that raced through me like a shock. He said, "One other thing. Mary mentioned that the man who left this had an odd argot. He sounded quite strange. Dressed head to toe in black clothing."

I gripped my throat. Feeling cold, I reread the note. And the next lines sprang from nowhere, like branches snapping back in woods: "Beware the Jabberwock, my son! The jaws that bite, the claws that catch!"

At another time I would have been happy to be back in Oxford. The castle. The colleges. The keep. The Ashmolean and Bodleian and Radcliffe Camera. The air ramified by literary history. Stone grotesques grimaced down from godly perches. Church bells rang at every hour. Christmas lights sparkled from eaves. Ice skaters spiraled. Musicians busked on Cornmarket Street. Pub windows glowed gold and warm. Ducks slid over the frozen pond like stockinged children on fresh-waxed floors. Young mothers dangled bulging shopping bags from pram handles. Things felt almost natural. Good.

Almost—but not quite. Orange public health warnings sullied lampposts and buses. Crowds were thin. Few strolled idly on the street. No one was chatting on a phone or screen. Smokers inhaled grimly, not lingering. Many wore headphones. Street-crossing sirens blared, augmented by flashing lights. Children didn't squeal and scream; they kicked silently on playground swings, barely tittered over holiday displays, got hauled along sidewalks by stone-faced fathers anxious to take quiet pints. And I started noticing the Ø symbol pinned to many coats. Tourists from

Denmark, China, Spain seemed like the only unworried ones. Laughing. Shopping. Having tea. At least that's how it was when I first arrived.

The morning after I received the cryptic note, I set out to visit my father's colleagues at the *OED*. Walking north toward Jericho, I found it nearly impossible to fight the urge to look over my shoulder. I tried instead to steal glances in the mirrors of storefronts: a barber with a spinning red-and-white pole; a shop on a corner called the Corner Shop; a café that looked like a coliseum; a playground; a row of houses like pastel chalk; and, finally, the colossus of the Oxford University Press, pillars and arches and a spiked iron gate. Old brick tinged the rich yellow of Oxfordshire cream.

The compound was enormous, surrounded by a high stone wall. I hadn't visited in years, and Phineas had reminded me to circle to the less lovely glass-peaked building at the side. I passed a bleak clot of quiet smokers stamping their feet against the cold, my own white billows of breath mimicking their clouds of smoke. Steeling myself, casting one quick look back, I climbed the stairs.

The lobby was carpeted blue, like a hotel drawing room. There was a real grandfather clock, and an elaborate display of dictionaries in cases and on stands. People streamed past, swiping badges over black readers beside glass doors, their faces tight—but with focus, it seemed, not fear. At reception, a striking older woman asked me to sign in. She also stole a look at the front of my coat: the spot where I'd seen others pin their Ø. I glanced down, too, at the blank bank of my olive-green baffles.

When she asked who I was there to see, I was startled by the question. "M-my father isn't here, is he?" I asked, trying to smile. "Douglas Johnson?" My voice crumpled a little, like paper.

The woman feathered her brow and pressed her lips together. Shook her head. "I'm sorry," she said. And I prayed that all she meant was, *He's not here right now,* or, *I don't know who that is.* Nothing worse.

"What about . . ." I groped the dark room of my memory, strangely unable to grasp names I'd heard many times. "Bill?" I tried.

"Bill . . . ?" she said, tilting her head to the side.

But I couldn't remember his last name, and it worried me. I didn't know whether it was just nerves or a symptom. "I'm not sure," I said. "I think—maybe he's . . . in the Diachronic Society?"

She twisted a tiny cross at her throat. "The Diachronic Society?" she mused. "Don't believe I've heard of it, I'm afraid." But she added kindly, "Bill Grabe, perhaps? In sales?"

"Is there a Bill who works at the Dictionary?"

She smiled, relieved. "Ah, Bill Jennings," she said. "I'll call him up, then."

And in a few minutes an unlikely hero appeared. He had on a pouchy brown blazer, a slightly rumpled button-down, and rimless glasses; his reddish hair was tucked behind his ears. When he saw me, he ducked his pink, disappearing chin. Smiled crookedly. Did a small wave. "You must be Anana," he said brightly.

For two weeks, at Phineas's, I'd been Alice, and I hesitated just the shadow of a moment before nodding and holding out my hand. Maybe stumbled faintly over my reply.

I watched Bill's face crimp with concern. A crease appeared beside his mouth. "Forgive my asking," he said, "but are you sure you're all right?"

I felt myself flush. And of course I wondered, too. But I just bit my lip. Nodded again. Hoped it was true.

He observed me in silence, head cocked. Shifting his gaze to the carpet, he cleared his throat. "Right," he said. "Well, this is a bit awkward." My pulse picked up. But he continued on. "I'm afraid I'm going to have to ask you not to speak once we're inside the Dictionary. Do you mind terribly? It's policy."

I shook my head, cheeks still warm.

"Good, then," he said, lightly patting my back. "Let's go in, shall we?"

Gratefully I followed him into a hall that was also a shrine: lined with *OED* love letters from elder statesmen and literary lights, photos, original pages, and quotation paragraphs. Then we reached the door to the Dictionary. Bill placed a finger to his lips with an apologetic smile. He punched in a code, then another, before the door slid open.

We stepped into a room of glass, ablaze with brilliant winter light. I'd forgotten how mesmerizing it was inside. The space felt vast and open; its lucent ceilings soared. The outer walls were also clear, and from nearly anywhere you could see courtyard, trees, the world outside. Of the walls there were, many were made of shelves lined with rows and rows of books.[1] And there were sixty lexicographers at work, I knew—

---

1. For the first time I noticed fire extinguishers at every exit, to protect them.

more than twice the number we'd had. After what we'd just been through in New York, it was a pretty moving sight.

Bill studied my face and tried, without success, to suppress a small grin. Then he whispered, "Come on. I have to show you something." Gently taking my arm, he squired me into a room with REFERENCE LIBRARY emblazoned on the door. Inside, he pointed out hundreds of dictionaries, in French, Finnish, Sanskrit, and historical ones, like Grimm's. Then, abruptly, he stopped talking. Perplexed, I followed his gaze. And I gasped. Brought a hand to my mouth. Because there, mere inches away, were forty dark-blue leather volumes, spines gold-embossed. *North American Dictionary of the English Language,* they said. *Third Edition.* Filling its own wall was Doug's life's work. The work that had vanished along with him. Except—here it was.

Warmth flowed through my chest. I felt as light as the empty shell of an egg. Giddy, I slid out a volume: *J.* Carefully cracked it to the center. Smelled the sweet, musky scent of leather. Heard the pages' soothing, dry-leaf rustle. And there, in beautiful, irrefutable black-and-white, was my father's brave face, smiling up. "He's here," I whispered. "Isn't he?"

"Indeed," Bill said, not admonishing me for speaking, bending over my shoulder to peek at the page.

Hopeful, turning toward him, I asked, "Where?" At least that's what I meant to say.

But Bill didn't reply. Just pinched the loose skin at his Adam's apple. Looked away.

"He's all right, though," I said, suddenly afraid. "I mean—he's fine."

Bill sighed. "I have every reason to think so," he offered. Shrugged.

And I exhaled, relieved. But Bill hadn't answered my question. "If you don't know where he is," I said, trying not to sound impatient, "is there someone else here I can talk to?"

Bill pressed his temples. Gave me a look that I read as a gentle reminder that I should be silent. "Anana, I'm sorry not to be more helpful," he said softly. "Some of us have been in touch with Douglas. But I haven't heard from him in days. There are a few places he could be, but I'll admit I haven't inquired. He hasn't wanted to be seen." Then he added quietly, "I hear you were asking out front about the Society. You should be careful."

I swallowed, feeling both heartened that he knew the Society and concerned.

"Just in general, you should be careful," he clarified, lowering his voice. "We're making every effort to safeguard our work here and get your father's out into the world. Collaborating with other researchers to find out what, if anything, we can learn about the virus, or viruses, especially how to prevent them spreading to more documents and texts. And we're doing what we can to help human victims, too. Which of course isn't much, I'm afraid. But we've tried at least to contribute our thoughts on convalescent therapies."

Bill sighed, rubbing his eyes behind his glasses. "This is a very troubling time," he said, adjusting his frames. "For some reason there seem to be people quite keen on stopping communication." Lowering his voice even more, he explained that the virus *was* moving to networks and people outside the United States. He'd heard that documents and English-speakers had been infected all across India, and probably elsewhere. But perhaps even more disturbing, reports had surfaced that it had made the leap to other languages. Digital texts written in Spanish were starting to corrupt, and Spanish-speakers had become aphasic and sick—in the U.S., and in American tourist hubs like Barcelona and Cancún. But in Mexico City, too. Buenos Aires. San Juan. It was said that some people in southern France had it. That there were scattered cases in Italy, Portugal, Turkey, Poland. "And there've been rumors," he murmured, "of widespread outbreaks across China that the government has been working to hide. In Russia, too, and the former Soviet states."

I felt so jarred by this news that his words sounded strange and far away, as if they'd been distantly whispered through a tin can and string. Bill could tell, it seemed. He gently proposed that we keep going; he had to be getting back, he said.

After that I had a hard time focusing as he guided me through the space where they stored old QPs, his office with a courtyard view, the front and back ends of their corpus. In a small room marked COMMUNICATIONS, I saw a typewriter and an inelegant machine that Bill confirmed was a fax. "Until recently, I doubt anyone used either of those for twenty years or more," he said. Then, putting a hand on my shoulder, he began to lead me back down the tribute-lined hall. But as we neared the lobby he stopped short. Asked, "Would you like to see our museum?"

I was disturbed by what I'd heard, and no closer to finding my father. And I'd seen the museum before. I didn't really have it in me to visit again that morning. But Bill had been very gracious; I didn't want to be impolite. As I looked at him more closely, I also thought I saw a faint, mystifying smile. "Of course," I replied.

And at first I was disappointed. The museum was filled with remarkable things: a Stanhope press; some seventeenth-century Fell types; the tidy wooden filing system used by James Murray, editor of the first *OED*. Lovely and strange as scarab beetles. But just curiosities.

At the end, though, and seemingly in passing, Bill pointed out an old accounting book I'd never noticed. Absorbed in other thoughts, I barely looked. Vaguely took in that it was open to a page noting that two thousand copies of a C. L. Dodgson book had cost, I think, £75 to print. But that name, C. L. Dodgson, seemed to sound some far-off bell. I murmured it aloud.

"Ah, yes," Bill said, ushering me back to the hall. "He was brilliant at maths. A lecturer for many years. Also a famous hater of sport. He'd write vitriolic essays about how the ball fields around Christ Church should be devoted to something else." It was clear that Bill expected me to know who Dodgson was. And I would have asked, but we'd reached the lobby door, and Bill said, "Guess you're rid of me, then." So I thanked him, unlooping the guest badge from my neck, and was soon stepping back outside, into the blinding sun.

I thought I was being careful on my walk back to the hotel, still looking out to see if I was being watched. But I was distracted, upset by all that Bill had said—and not said, about my father. And I let down my guard just a bit. It wasn't until I neared the Bridge of Sighs that I realized I was being followed. By the same man, I was sure, who'd been on my train. I didn't turn, but sensed a dark shadow about a block behind me. I tried as hard as I could to act as if I hadn't seen him. To stroll, unhurried. To swing my arms in a way I hoped looked natural.

I waited for a cloud cover of Dutch tourists. Then, heart trying to escape my chest, I darted as quickly as I could down a narrow alley, St. Helen's Passage, worrying even as I did that it was a dead end. But I soon emerged, and kept running through the courtyard on the other side—right to the door of a pub.

Its ceilings were so low that a tall man would have to stoop to enter; PLEASE MIND YOUR HEAD, a sign warned. I hurried inside and up to the shiny wooden bar. Trying to catch my breath, I asked the bartender if he could give directions to the Bath Place Hotel. He studied me silently.

Hoisted a bottle of Pimm's. Pointing its metal spigot to the right, he said, "You walk about fifty feet that way."

Reluctantly, Henry agreed to let me switch rooms. Change my name in the registry. Tell anyone who asked that I'd checked out. But he didn't like it and made me pay forward through Sunday, with more or less the dregs of my money. When we'd settled, I asked for help placing a few calls. "To where?" he asked, suspicious. "The U.S.?"

When I didn't deny it, he flat-out refused, so I placed the calls from my cell in the room, trying not to think of the cost. I had a terrible time getting through. It took half a dozen dials just to get the old phone that my mother had installed out on Long Island to ring. And when a voice eventually answered, it was a man's.

Alarmed, I said my mother's name. There was a long, excruciating silence. But finally I heard Vera say, "Hello?"

Shaky with relief, I asked her how she was. And there was another very long pause. "I'm fine," she said at last, a strange hauntedness to her voice.

"What's going on?" I asked, gripped by worry. It soon grew; our whole conversation was a maze. When I wanted to know why she was so quiet, she answered, "It's nice to hear from you." When I said, "Mom, are you okay? Do you feel safe?" she replied, "The weather's been lovely here, too." I bit my nails till the quicks bled, a habit I'd kicked when I was twelve.

"You're really scaring me, Mom," I said. "Who's there with you? Is it Laird?"

"I couldn't agree more," she said, laughing. As if what I'd said were a joke.

We both fell silent. I peered through the dust-smoked window to the dark cobbles outside. I was terrified.

"If you're in trouble," I said, "if you need help, say 'let's get together.' And if you're all right, tell me you're busy."

She didn't say anything at all.

"Mom?" I rasped. If she needed me, how would I even help? "Are you there? Say something," I pleaded.

"I'd really . . ." she said softly. But trailed off.

"Mom?" I said. "Mom?" My voice started to rise.

Then she said, "I wish I could," and laughed again. "I'm just so busy right now."

I let out a quivery breath. "Are you sure?" I asked, still on edge. But when she purred, "I'm afraid so," she sounded normal and calm.

I asked again, and her reply was the same. I exhaled. Whispered, "Thank God." Steadying my voice, I said, "I haven't found Doug yet. But I will, soon." Then, as if I were the mom, I begged, "Please be careful." Tried not to cry. "I love you," I said. "We both do."

And after a moment she said, "I'd love that, too. I'd love that so much." Tears spilled from my eyes. I bit my lip. Then I heard a dial tone.

I laid my cheek on the cold window and thought of something she'd said when I'd finished school. "I'm your mother. You're always in my thoughts," she'd promised. "I'm only ever as far as I am from yours." But that night I wasn't sure. She felt very, very far away.

When I'd pulled myself together, I called Dr. Thwaite. But I wasn't really expecting him to answer, and when he did, it threw me a bit. Rudely, without saying hello, I asked if someone could go check on Vera. After a moment he said he'd try, but he couldn't promise anything. He sounded very odd, like an out-of-tune guitar. And I could tell that something was profoundly wrong.

The light outside was thin, the sky roky and gray. Nervously I asked what was happening. And after a silence, Phineas coughed. Confessed that things in New York weren't "going very well." When I asked what that meant, he offered, dazed, "They're saying more than three thousand in the city dead. The curfew starts at sundown now, which is four-thirty p.m." And then he said something else: "I'm starting to lose varsin."

The slip snagged on my ear like a loose thread. Threatened to unravel everything.

"Are you all right?" I asked, the question sounding flat. I knew the answer.

Even so, when he said, "No, I'm not," I was shocked. The man I thought I knew would never say that.

I waited in shaken silence for him to explain.

When he spoke, his voice was dry as wind. What he said was, "He's dead."

"What?" I said, out of breath, hoping I'd misheard. "He's what? He's—"

"Dead."

A tide of ice sluiced through me. "Who?" I said, a pack of faces shuffling through my mind: Doug, Vernon, Max. Bart. Absurdly, as if to blot them out, I blurted, "Canon?"

"Oh, well, yes, jend," Phineas replied.

"What?" I said. "But he was *fine*." As if his recent health were relevant. My voice was trembling as I said, "I'm so sorry." The ghost of the dog's wet nose nudged my thigh.

Phineas sighed. A sound like falling sand. Said one strangled word: "Poison."

Stunned, I stared at the wall. Watched a dusty cobweb dance in the fading light. "But who would *do* that?" I asked. Sick to my stomach.

"It was the same poison," he said, sounding exhausted, "that the coroner found in the body of John Lee."

I realized then, with a shudder, that he wasn't silencing me. He was speaking openly. He didn't care anymore who might be listening. "Phineas," I said. I felt as if I'd swallowed a ball of fiberglass. "What happened? What did they . . . Did they . . . do something to you?"

"Not exactly," he croaked, in a terrible attempt at a laugh.

That's when it dawned on me that Canon hadn't been who he'd meant.

"Who else died?" I asked softly, suddenly hot and cold at once. White pricks of light wriggled in my vision. I didn't want to know what he'd say.

And he was silent for a long time. I thought he might have hung up quietly. But then, as if it were nothing, he said, "Nadya."

I couldn't speak at first. I saw Victoria's lovely starlet's face. All the portraits of her overtaking Phineas's study. The one whose glass I'd shattered, of her hiding in a veil of hair. But he'd said "he," I wanted to protest. (It didn't matter; he'd also said "varsin.") Finally I whispered again, "I'm so sorry." A sob curled in my throat.

"She was helping in a sick bay. And on her way home there was some sort of violent incident," he said. So coldly that I shivered. Then, haltingly, he continued. "She wanted to help. There was a time, years ago, zay—she really suffered. And she said silence was the loneliest place she'd ever lived. But it didn't have to happen. If they wanted to hurt me . . ."

His voice disintegrated. I wanted to ask what he meant. But I was afraid to make things more painful. I was also afraid to confirm that he was sick. I felt numb. Mute with sadness. And abruptly, into my silence, Phineas said, "I've got to go."

"No. Wait," I said. "Phineas—"

But I heard a dull click. Shivering in shock, I wrapped myself in the duvet, which smelled faintly of cigarettes and tea. I missed Bart right then with a savage pang. I thought of the man I'd seen at JFK who'd broken my heart by laughing. Pictured Bart's long, sad Buster Keaton face and lanky frame stretched out under his Dictionary desk. On my hardwood floor, asleep in his clothes. I remembered the night of Thanksgiving, when he'd stood up for me in a way Max never had. Heard in my mind's ear the sound of my fist pounding his door ten days earlier. The last day he and I had spoken.

I wanted so badly to talk to him again right then. But when I dialed his number, the phone just rang and rang. And, spent by sadness, without meaning to, I fell asleep.

I may have dreamed of the Aleph. Because when I woke, with weak afternoon light pooling on my face, my first thought was of its big, awkward screen. After reading Doug's letter, which had hinted at the clues it held, I'd searched it and the Dictionary again. But it was like combing a beach for a few specific shells. I hadn't found anything. I'd woken with a new thought, though, and a dangerous hope that it might help me find Doug.

Still drunk on sleep, I unburied the Aleph from my bag and quickly flicked to Doug's entry. And my heart swelled: there he was, roguishly smiling, surprised by his own good fortune. Next I looked up Dodgson, but saw only a cryptic cross-reference that my stubborn mind refused to decode. As I started to click back through to it, though, my eye hitched on something else: dic•tio•nary \'dik-shə-ˌner-ē\ *n* : a hiding place.

I had the strong, preternatural sense that Doug was leaning through the pages, trying to whisper a secret. I just couldn't quite hear it.

Feeling vivified and alert, I went downstairs. Found Henry addressing an envelope, something I hadn't seen done in years. He said it was a letter for his older sister, who lived alone on a Cotswolds farm. And with a warm wave of inspiration, I asked if he knew which part of Oxford had the postal code OX1 IDP.

Henry thought it over for a moment. Then he said, "Christ Church, I believe."

Christ Church. The same place Bill had named when he'd mentioned C. L. Dodgson.

So I wrapped my hair and face in a scarf, put on my dark glasses, borrowed an umbrella for the rain that had started, and very carefully made my way down to the college.

When I got close to the gate, I hurried up to it, skin tingling.

And for a moment I felt dazed. Because on the sign that said "Welcome to Christ Church and St. Aldate's" there was an illustration. Of my double. That other, Wonderland Alice, in her blue dress and white pinafore. She was peeling back a diaphanous curtain. And the text to the right of her read: "Charles Dodgson, better known by his pseudonym Lewis Carroll, was an undergraduate and then a mathematics don at Christ Church, where he befriended Alice Liddell, daughter of the dean." I suddenly had a very strong feeling that I knew why Doug had given me that name. And I entered through the gate, the wobbling world odd and distant.

The college buildings were forbidding: huge walls of stone the color of old snow, festooned with shriveled strings of ivy. Muddy brown meadows dotted with a few sleepy-eyed cows. The curving River Isis, its water the hard gray of stone. For nearly twenty minutes, as dusk began to gather its dark arms around, I stumbled on uneven gravel and quaggy ground, getting dirty and discouraged. Feeling crazy. Finally I decided to turn around and started to stagger back the way I'd come. That, of course, is when I caught sight of the building.

It seemed completely out of place in the solemn, stolid quiet of those fields and old estates. But it would have looked incongruous almost anywhere. I hadn't noticed it at first because it was hidden, barely visible behind a grove of trees and a high stone wall, like the enclosure around the *OED*. From where I stood, I could just make out the top of it, which jutted up like the vast hull of a ship.

It seemed to be made of dark glass and metal, very wide and tall, maybe eight stories high. Squinting, I saw it was divided in half, its two sides appearing to undulate strangely toward each other to meet in a deep, vertical groove that ran straight down the building's center. As I started walking slowly closer, I noticed brisk rows of horizontal windows, shining with glass more reflective than in the rest of the building.

They stood out sharply, in a way that reminded me of something: type on a printed page.

All at once I saw it: the building was shaped like an enormous open book. A dictionary, maybe. And I decided, with the thrill of intuition, or insanity—a dizzying feeling, like inverse déjà vu—that Doug was inside. I remembered back to the night he'd disappeared, when I'd tried to find him in the Aleph. He wasn't there: he'd vanished from both building and book. But when I'd looked again, the next day, his entry was back. And the uncanny logic that came to me then, on the Christ Church grounds, was that he'd reappeared in the Aleph when he'd arrived here. That he'd migrated back into a dictionary—not ours but this one.

I was drawn inexorably forward, like smoke through a crack. But I approached cautiously, trying not to be seen. And as I neared the wall, I saw an entrance: a narrow arch on the north side. But the reason I managed to spot it was that a man was stationed beside it. Dressed all in black.

As I peered out from behind the trunk of a large oak, I tried to see if it was the same man who'd been following me. I didn't think so—this man seemed taller, thicker through the chest. From a distance, though, I couldn't be sure. But as I studied the wall, I saw something else: a small tree, very close to it. And I decided to return after dark.

Henry claimed that the hotel didn't have a flashlight he could lend me, so I borrowed one from the pub next door. In a low voice, I asked the bartender what he knew about the glass building at Christ Church. He just shook his head. "Not much," he said.

By then night had fallen.

The sign at the gate warned that Christ Church closed at 9:30. That was fine. I didn't plan to stay late. You know what they say, though—or did—about best-laid plans. Mice.

Men.

I quietly made my way through the thick blue dark and back to the wall guarding the building. Clamping the flashlight in my teeth, I wrestled into the young tree, accidentally snapping a few lower branches. Anxiously looked around. But nothing happened, I didn't hear a noise, and slowly I began to climb. Shaking. Getting hatched with cuts and scrapes. When I'd ascended above the wall, I very carefully stepped on top of it. Dropped the light on the other side. Then jumped a long way down to the hard ground below, twisting my ankle. As I stood, I felt a bright burst of pain but managed not to call out. I steadied myself against the cold stone. Took a breath.

That's when they grabbed me, put a gag in my mouth, and placed a bag over my head. From their voices, I knew there were at least two of them. One said, *"Keep silent."* And the other said, "She's going in the hole for a long time."

R

rock and roll \ˈräk əŋ rol\ *adj* : to be great <Bart is so ~ > *v* :
to rescue someone in need *n* : a tonic for insomniacs hoping
to sleep

Monday, December 24 (aka Christmas Eve)

So far I've found no Doug. No Ana. Just a smug hotel guy who made
me foo cash for some of her "effects." Said she'd only paid through last
night, hy hadn't checked out. He was about to throw away her stuff if
someone didn't come pick it up soon, and insisted I krishka her costs.
So I asked if I could just take the room; her stuff could stay where it was.

I made my way here on luck, zhaman, and cash. (Not that I have
much of any of those.) The flight nearly bankrupted me—not to mention the hong I had to slip security when I didn't pass their tests. If not
for the fake doctor's letter, though—yarrow not cheap—I don't think
I would have gotten through. (I'd hastily pawned my only pinshee of
value, a couple of small gold bars bequeathed by Great-Uncle Horace,
God rest his soul. As I handed them over the counter, I felt very guilty
for the unkind thoughts I'd had when he'd bought them, during the
Great Recession, with money from the sale of his farm. And they shir-
som turned out to be worth *a lot*. Probably way more than I got. The
pragmatist in me withered a little. Bing, though: I know they say money
can't buy love; but what else is it for?)

When I arrived last night at the Oxford train station, I gave the doon
cabbie Ana's photo. And to my surprise, he seemed to recognize her.
(Turns out not that many cabbies work the bann.) Veek suspicious, he

asked, "You her boyfriend?" And despite the disbelief he'd eks when I said yes, just saying the word yong me feel stronger, tyen. "So—what," he sprot, laughing, pointing to my eye. "Vemen have a fight?" (My shiner, dwaylee, is healing fine.) Then he brought me here, to this slightly wilty hotel, where I learned she'd checked in under the name Tate. My name. I tried not to implode from xing. (It was a real stroke of fortune, ben. It bolstered my claim that we're siblings—kitch the only reason they told me about her. That, and I tried not to say much of anything, to be safe.)

After I'd tantooshk with the concierge, I took my bag to the room, past a giant lighted tree, like the flag of another reality. That really threw me; I've lost track of time. After unpacking, I set off in search of food and found the only thing open on Christmas Eve eve, a pasty place on Cornmarket Street. (Pasties seem to be the British sootyong of empanadas.) Preen it was a little sad, the elf hats the staff had on. I tried not to mize I was eating steak out of a hot starch sack, standing up, totally alone on earth.

This morning, chivvist kind of sick, I laid my take to Jericho to see Bill. I was looking forward to it; it'd been since that conference last June in Madrid. But Bill, like Dr. Thwaite, didn't seem happy to see me; instead of inviting me in, he proposed we go for coffee. Salted our meeting with odd, hostile looks—not like him at all. Eventually, wincing, bown his ears, he asked me to switch to writing. (Kenna, I know I may be slightly . . . blokh. But it's not that bad. And it's getting better. I can tell.) Sinkan, I tried to ask about Ana, but all he'd tollo was work. Finally, though, kaqu, he seemed to have a change of heart.

"You really . . . fancy her, don't you?" he said. (When I nodded, I thought I saw his eyes fill dyen, which, kanchung, alarmed me a lot.) Poz not at me but the sugar bowl, he said, "Okay, mate. She was asking after Christ Church. Motso try there." I started to thank him, but he scathered and hurried out. At the last moment he called, "Please just don't—"

I zode what he was going to say. And I won't. If I find her: not a single whisper.

But at first it seemed Bill was wrong. At the college I walked around, zow the library, cathedral, tsandot hall. Toured the grounds. Reet the cows. Fed the ducks some crumbs. But I kand no sign of Ana.

One person I did see, leks, was a crad all in black, who I swear I kat at the gala. I don't think he noticed me—his back was turned. But I didn't want to risk it; I left.

After that, not yin what else to do, I myd the afternoon searching hotel registries, à la Humbert Humbert. By two, when I feebly potch for a pint at the Turf, I was feeling less than encouraged. But my luck took an upturn when I noticed the handsome bartender's slight resemblance to Max. Gorlee, I flashed him A's photo, spren if she'd come by when she was staying next door. And I don't know if it was my air of desperation or that I didn't constare much of a threat, but he said, "Listen, man, you better not be some chollmee stalker," and admitted he'd seen her a few times. He also said she'd mentioned a new building at Christ Church, bolstering Bill's claim. I thanked him and tried to pay him not to tell anyone else. But he's a good guy, veesek: he wouldn't take my money. Can't hold it against him that he's Ana's type. (Though he did also bal, "Come back anytime you like. But I las to ask you not to chat anyone up.")

When I got back here, to our (my) room, I had to lie down. Zat a headache that could have killed a dog. Poor dog. And gwy, I slept for *hours*—it was almost like I blacked out—and woke up suffering, my head hot and huge, like a pluke, my throat sookh—water doesn't help. Zabad achy and stomach sick. I should probably visit a clinic, just to be safe. See if I trebbow more medicine. But I think I won't. What if . . . I mean, I can't afford to voyroo quarantine right now.

Still groggy, swashen awful, I just got up the nerve to go through Ana's things.

And dipost, it shook me pretty badly. Ya eesp confirm something terrible has happened. I'd already vall that she'd left her toothbrush in the bathroom. But she also left behind her clothes; a gooven of analog things—maps, some cash, her *passport*—and Dr. D's Aleph. (Seeing it again made me think of that night long ago tapets, when I slept on her floor, very close to her.) She'd never narocheeto abandon those things. Which could only mean she didn't do it on purpose.

December 25

Just tried calling my family. No one answered. That zhen jarred me. But Illinois velden New York—things can't be so bad. And last time we spoke, I convinced them to hole up for a while in Dad's bunker, just in case. They have a hand-crank radio and enough condensed milk to salk for weeks. There must be a reasonable reason they didn't pick up. I can only vexin so many crises at once.

(Last time we spoke, I jorde, "Don't talk to shem who sounds too funny, okay?" And Mom asked, "Funny kam, Horsey? Funny, like . . . ?" I sighed, hating to say it. "Like me, Mom. Funny com da.")

Tonight I gontay back to Christ Church. Near the gate I spied a baffy-bearded man nesting on a bench. I was afraid at first he might be waiting for me, and I hovered down the block watching him breathe. But then I saw something glittering on his chest: not a gun but a flat bok liquor bottle. And I decided—mistakenly—that it was safe.

Pulling down my kant cap, I crept back onto the grounds. Kromel a copse of teenagers making out in the cold. And for a long time I saw no one else. But then, eventually, following the bartender's directions, I found a high wall with a traze building looming up behind. And I did sowl another encounter. One that shaved a few years off my life.

I'd desh a few minutes, mostovee in the hedge, when mung, not far from where I was crouched, I tay the grainy sound of a match. An instant later I saw a bright plume of light blossom in the dark, blansh off a pair of glasses, and limn a face. The face faded quickly back into hase, except for the glowing orange end of a cigarette. But it was a face I recognized nonetheless: Vernon's.

I almost called his name, but stopped myself. Decided to approach slowly, in silence. Veen what he was doing there—and who he was with. But it was dark. It can be kwin to see tree roots in the dark, and I tripped. When I stood zyot, he'd come closer and was blasking a light in my face.

"Bart?" he gowd, sounding very surprised. Yotas a moment before clicking the awful thing off. Took a drag on his cigarette, and when he exhaled, I zapakh the sweet smell of clove. Ashing, he spross, "How the fuck did you get here?"

I tried to obasht. Stopped. It wasn't working. Sighing, I looked up again at the building volars over the wall behind his head: a stratchy, massive monolith, limply reflecting the light of the moon. "What's—ny there?" I seet.

But Vernon didn't respond. And after an uncomfortably long silence, I said, "Can I spren something, Vern?" I hugged myself for warmth. "Can you tell me, is Anana in there?" I coughed to cover up a mintan tremor in my voice.

Dano Vernon still said nothing. Vabored clove. Bent to knead his bad knee.

"Vernon," I said. "Stama, you're freaking me out." The hair on my neck stoyfa.

And that's when he lathed a strange motion with his hand. Another man, in a ski mask, poysen out of the black. In an instant he'd beest a heavy hand on my neck and turned me to meen the frightening building. And as we took our first steps through the woods, my vision smoked. My mind rummaged over what would happen to me. Nafekt drawing a breath, I took off running.

"Bart!" Vernon whispered loudly after me. "Wait!" Over my shoulder I smegd the beam of his flashlight bounce away. The other man ran a few steps, but soon he, too, slipped into the dark water of night. Arms pumping, shins loding, cold burning my throat, I zwend back to the hotel.

But that's not where my strakh ended. When I stepped into the lobby, still trying hard to catch my breath, the concierge gave me a sharp look and beckoned with a brisk zhest. Dipping forward like one of the blue-lyoot-filled glass birds that my mother collects, he told me in a vlastic whisper that someone had asked for me while I was out.

And I allowed myself, impossibly, to hope it was Ana. Trying to seem zan, I asked if she'd left a note. But the lonan just gave me another strange nak and said, "It was a man. And I don't think you'd want him to know where you're staying. To tell the truth," he ganes, "any more visitors like that, I don't want you prevvin."

My throat closed, and after a moment his face softened kommat. "If I were you," he said, "I'd bin in my room. I'll bring you something up."

But later, when I heard veder knocking, I didn't answer.

I'm sick. And exhausted. My head feels like a spent firework casing. I put on the soft, saturnine downs of the Only Ones, hoping to put myself under.

But I'm also very calm. Because one thing seems clear: I have to get into that building, on my own terms. I think that's where they're torin Ana.

And I'm going to rescue her.

III
SYNTHESIS
JANUARY

III

SYNTHESIS

JANUARY

S

si•lence \'si-ləns\ *n*

T

tor•ture \'tȯr-ˌchər\ *n* : to inflict pain in order to force a person to speak, or to remain silent

They came to get me on the third night in the hole. Three days and nights might not seem long. But time in the hole was outside time.

I don't mean I was mistreated. I was given regular meals. I was also given pills—three times a day. The room had a twin cot with a thin mattress. A corner chair. Even a small desk, though no paper or pens. And no windows. I did have a mirror: through which they could see in. Alice through the looking glass. Reflection with front-row seats. But I was deprived of no basic needs.

Except one.

For those three days and nights, I wasn't allowed to speak. Not a word or sound could pass my lips. I couldn't read or write or scratch letters in my skin. I was bound to a strict fast of silence, monitored with hidden microphones, and warned that consequences for noncompliance would be grave. After the warning I wasn't spoken to again.

And it was the silence that turned time into torture. Silence, and my own unstill mind, bent into strange, incoherent shapes. Fractals, morphing faces, the occasional word or wordlike string.[1] Horrible screeching. All in my head. I didn't know if it was the fear or the quiet or the virus. If all silence was deadly, or if silence was different from Silencing. If I

---

1. When they'd appear, I'd become afraid that I'd spoken them and grab my throat to hold them in.

was going crazy or being drugged. If my confinement would ever end. That was the real torment: the unknown. Having no idea where I was. How long I'd be there. What would happen when they let me out.

A thousand thoughts flocked to me, none of them good. That there was no Diachronic Society, only employees of Synchronic. That Doug and I were both locked up. That Doug was dead. That I'd be next. That Doug was in hiding and didn't know where I was. That I was in a special government quarantine for the very sick.

And yet by the time they came for me, I felt ready. Better, in some ways, than I had in a long while.

There were two of them. All in black, like the others. Wearing ski masks and gloves. I wondered if I'd be allowed a last request. A final call. And who I'd choose if I could.

They didn't speak, but they were gentle with me; each took an arm. Their clothes were cold, as if they'd just come in from outside. I felt calmer than I thought I would. As they walked me toward a dark door at the end of the hall, I wondered if Doug was being held there, too. If I'd get to see him, to say goodbye. I thought of what I'd tell the other people I loved if I had the chance. But mostly, as I walked, I just tried to breathe. Be at peace, as much as I could.[2]

Then we arrived. One of the men let go of my arm. Opened the door. Led me inside.

The light was dimmer than in the hall, and at first it was hard to see. By then my heart had started to hammer. And all at once something emerged from the shadows, and I couldn't keep from crying out. The men at my arms held harder as my knees gave way.

2. The strange way time suspended reminded me of a car crash I'd been in once. The mind quickening. Seeing and understanding everything that's taking place. Time becoming infinite when you feel it's about to end.

U

un•say•able \ən-'sā-ə-bəl\ *n* **1** : nearly everything **2** : a certain sapient creature's name **3** : (three short words that mean more than they seem)

Wednesday, December 26, 4 a.m.

Every hour more yinzik slips away. As if my words were krov, spilling out grain by grain.

I gan more sick and shaky and weak. Passed out by the tub. Was woken by the call no prodigal son wants: at 3 a.m., my mom, panicked, in red jing. When I answered, she casp, "Thank God." I heard her cover the mouthpiece to tell the others she'd gotten me shong. From the dim, tinny reverb, I could tell they were in the bunker.

It was a short, bale call. I bole a quick nip of whiskey from the mini-bar. Tried to speak but barely could. Drew from my last reservoir of words to shwa the few vash that needed to be said.

She reassured me that they were all fine. But then she said, "You were right." They hadn't been able to shirr the radio to work, she explained, but the phone had kowl like crazy. "And I know you praz to be careful who I talk to. But Horse, what we've been hearing is pretty unbelievable."

It was hard to know, chuke, how much of her hearsay might be true. Nane in masks, nerve gas, kem inmates escaped from prisons—there are now serious outages in electric, paretong, communications. "It took a long time to reach you," she ming. My aunt had told her that in Chicago, it was crats as bad as a blackout that happened the year my cousin was born. "All those people lost power, and there was looting. Deem a few shen lost their lives."

"Looting? Mom, yest looting where you are? People are dying?" I breathed very bisk through my mouth. The sweat nesting on my body suddenly turned cold. It was small comfort that the bunker is dali my father stores his guns.

"That's what I heard. Don't know if it's true. We haven't vakkan TV, yin you said."

Had I swakot? I couldn't recept. Nyanung remember anything at all.

She zyk everyone we knew was all right. But she was savend very shaken up.

And she said something else. Quietly, her voice stal and far away, like it vitshong from a star, she gove, "I've been hearing . . . Some reg claim that really sick people—they lose the ability to talk. And that tombit . . . they're not—recovering. And Horse, I'm just—I'm so worried about you." I could zhid how hard it was for her not to cry. "Please promise me you'll wen some help."

"I—" I gra. "I-I-I—" I was trying not to cry, too. Davim from frustration; I couldn't milk the words. "I—*prom*-en-t-s," I dolk managed. That's when I knew I had to get off the phone. My mom, thank God, is still completely fine. And I zow I'm not.

Mom sighed a sigh as if someone were dying. "I love you, Horse," she said. "Wish you could be with us tonight."

I thought but did not say, *I do, too.*

I just called A, to hear her voice. Kalad six times, to listen to that name I love so much, again and again and zayat.

There are some fates worse than death. Some unsayable things that must be said. I know I have a few words left. If I die, I don't want it to be with regrets.

V

vis•i•ta•tion \ˌvi-zə-ˈtā-shən\ *n* : an encounter with a ghost

The masked guards who'd marched me down the hall held me firmly so I wouldn't collapse. One of them said softly, "All right?" And I nodded, unable to talk. Because glinting out of the room's dim light was a face, mounted to the wall: the giant, glossy face of Vera Doran, dressed in white, brandishing a flower, and smiling over her shining shoulder. Below that was a small, handmade sign: PROUDLY LABORING IN OBSCURITY SINCE 1950! On the desk I saw bottles of hot sauce and vinegar. And under a corner lamp I glimpsed potted plants crowned in spikes: pineapples.

I turned around. And my heart fluttered and filled, like a sail. There, looking fairly unkempt, with more gray in his beard than I remembered, was my father.

Neither of us spoke. My walk across the room seemed very slow, like I was moving through water.

When I got close, he grabbed me hard and pulled me closer. Crushed me in one of his signature hugs that almost made me feel I'd need medical help. He smelled like Bay Rum aftershave. As he whispered *"Nins"* into my short hair, I could feel the prickles of his beard.

"Dad," I tried to say. "I missed you." But the words died in my throat, tangled in the rotors of a sob. And I started to weep.

From inside the dense nest of my father's arms, I heard an alien noise, a light, ricking hiccup. And felt it: a tuning-fork tremor. "Dad?" I said, surprised. "Are *you* crying, too?"

But he just pressed me tighter.

Finally he let me go a little, enough so that I could breathe. And I could see the tears running down his face into the calico thicket of his beard. They were the first tears I'd seen him shed in years, since my great-uncle's funeral, when I was eleven. Stepping back, light spreading through my chest, I noticed that over his sweater he was wearing an XXL T-shirt I'd made for him around then. It said, *Harmless Drudge.*[1] Laughing, and still sobbing, I hugged him again. "The shirt," I said. "The enormous shirt," he said, and laughed, too, the wonderful, rumbling jounce of it reminding me of the best days of childhood: resting on his stomach while he read aloud, taking shady naps in Sheep's Meadow, spilling lemonade in an illicit hammock he'd strung up at my grandparents' in East Hampton.

I've never felt deeper relief or peace. Like I could stop running. Like the whole, overflowing world had been restored. But I also couldn't stop crying. Because I knew it wasn't true.

For those few moments, though, it was so good to have my father back, I tried to forget everything else. Ignore the pit of sadness at the center. The fear and dread.

But finally I had to ask, "Dad, are you okay? What is this place?"

And talking was hard. My throat burned, as if I'd inhaled smoke from a bonfire.

"Don't speak," said Doug, wrapping his warm arm around my shoulders. "You just got out of quarantine. It's too soon. For now, just let me do the talking."

"Your dream," I croaked, weakly smiling.

Doug placed a finger to his lips. Squeezed me a little roughly. "You cut your hair," he murmured, ruffling my short, choppy locks. I nodded, silent. Bared my nicked front tooth. He inhaled sharply, and I could see his pained face suppressing the question *What happened?* Then he led

---

1. It was a nod to the first Dr. Johnson's definition of "lexicographer": "A writer of dictionaries; a harmless drudge." When Doug opened the gift, I knew by the way he clapped and hooted that I'd gotten it right. Although he'd been less enthused by the shirt's size.

me to a threadbare corner chair. Handed me a cup of sweet, milky tea. A bag of menthol lozenges. Tucked a soft blue blanket around me. "I was so goddamn worried about you," he muttered. "I wanted to make an exception, just this one time. Seeing you there, in quarantine, and not being able to say or do anything—" His voice broke, and he looked away. Shook his big, bushy head. I shivered in the blanket, also blinking back the tiny barb of a tear. He took a long, deep breath. And to steady us both, began to explain.

We were in the basement of the Christ Church Dictionary Library, he said, designed by Persian architect Ruzbeh Rahimi. The building was Rahimi's take on a dictionary: "Dense, elusive, moody, difficult—like my ex-husband," she'd allegedly announced at the ribbon-cutting. And Doug had clearly fallen head over heels for it. He described the library in a raw lava flow of loving detail: its holdings,[2] advanced lighting and temperature controls, humidity and air-filtration systems, photochromic windows, security features, tubes. Its four reading rooms and dining hall, and its switchback staircase, "a bit like the Guggenheim's."

But from my vantage, huddled on the half-shell of an enfeebled chair in the building's ill-lit, cimicine basement, finally starting to feel like myself again, I found it all fairly improbable. I wondered, among other things, what college these days would build a library. Doug explained that it had been funded by private donation. "Who was the donor?" I rasped, trying not to sound too skeptical. Doug nodded, patting my shin. "I'll get to that." (Later I learned that two of the most generous benefactors had been Phineas and Fergus Hedstrom.)

College officials, he continued, had expressed concern about the library plans. They found it "overly specialized" and didn't quite appreciate the genius of Rahimi's design. But they'd eventually relented and agreed to have it built on this slightly remote site. (The donors had sweetened the deal with a large donation to the annual fund.) Then the

2. Dictionaries spanning several *millennia,* including Akkadian-Sumerian cuneiform tablets ca. 2000 BCE, an early Chinese monolingual dictionary, *Disorderly Words* by Philitas of Cos, and of course every scrap of *OED* ephemera not housed in the archives up on Great Clarendon Street. It also had all three editions of the *NADEL,* along with lots of notes and dead material, which had recently been shipped to Oxford by members of the Diachronic Society's New York branch, along with a few of Doug's things (like the enormous shirt).

college had hired another architect to create a wall that further obscured the building from the public eye.

"So that's where we are," Doug said, waving his thick, hairy hands like a conductor. "Quite possibly the greatest library on earth."

The competition, I chose not to remind him, isn't very fierce. (I'd been won over, as usual, by his energy and fervor.)

"Some might also say we're in Diachronic headquarters," Doug went on. "Others that we've vanished from the earth. And in a sense I suppose we have: disappeared into the dictionary." Then he reached into a new leather satchel, very much like the one he'd abandoned in his New York office. "I believe," he said, lifting out the Aleph, "you may have discovered that yourself."

"Wait," I said. I'd left the Aleph in a bed of socks in my hotel. "How—"

Doug once again placed a maddening finger to his lips. "Someone brought it here," he said, cagily glancing at the door, "while you were in quarantine." Then he turned the Aleph on and handed it to me. It was open to a page in the J's, the one with his entry.

"You know, you were right," he said, sounding both proud and pained, absently stretching the neck of his shirt. "About my entry vanishing from the Aleph after I left the Dictionary and then reappearing when I arrived here the next night." Doug took hairpin turns in conversation. Normally I didn't mind, and even liked it—I was glad I could follow his falcate thoughts. Often I served as his interpreter. But this uncanny announcement gave me a chill.

"Doug," I said, face stinging. "How did you know that's what I thought?"

I was used to Memes doing things like hailing cabs, adjusting thermostats, ordering black-and-white milkshakes from the corner deli. But to disappear Doug from a book? To translate his real-time escape from our building on Broadway into his erasure from the pages of its Dictionary? That seemed different. I didn't know that a Meme, let alone an Aleph, could do something like that. And it was even more unnerving that I'd been able to read the clue. That from the tiny bait of his missing entry—antibait, really, an elision—I'd made a wild and, as it turned out, inspired inference. But I was having a hard time making the next leap of faith: that *he* could somehow know the inference I'd made. Doug and I were very close, but he couldn't read my *mind*—could he?

As I worked this through, worrying a lozenge wrapper and chewing my cheek, Doug smiled wryly. "What—think I can read your mind?" he asked, eerily. But then he quickly added, eyes twinkling, "You forgot, didn't you? That you told Phineas about my disappearance from the Dictionary? You gave him quite a shock, actually."

I had a sudden vision of Phineas saying, "My God." A liquid flash of teeth and gums.

Then, puffing his upper lip and lifting his eyebrows in embarrassment, Doug explained that in fact it had been one of his "clues": after he'd already arrived at the airport, his phone had beeped with an alert—set up years before and forgotten since—that the Aleph had been breached. It also guessed that the intruder was me, not, e.g., Max or Laird. Doug knew the guess could be wrong (as was the Aleph's wont), but he felt relieved. He also again very strongly considered going back for me. "I wish I had," he said mournfully. ("Dad," I interrupted, "it's okay." But he shook his head and kept talking over me.) By then, he continued, he'd been sucked up in a vortex of inertia; he thought that instead he'd log in to the corpus from his phone, erase his own entry, leave the Aleph open to the *J*'s, and that somehow—between that and all the other hints he'd left, and knowing him so well—if I searched the device, I'd understand what had happened and wouldn't worry.

Of course when he'd logged in to the corpus, he'd seen holes worming through the Dictionary, and he'd become blind to all concerns but one: getting to Oxford as soon as he could. Later, after arriving at the Christ Church library, he'd put himself back inside the Dictionary and seeded in several more clues.

"Although, to tell the truth," Doug said, color rising in his cheeks, "I actually did—even before I spoke to Phineas—I *did* have this strange . . . *sense*." He bunched his fingers into a bouquet. "That you'd figured it out somehow. *Even*—and I know you won't believe me—but even that you'd found out by looking in the Aleph." He shook his head. "I realize how that sounds. But there's no denying that these are powerful machines. Which is what makes them so dangerous. More dangerous than even I suspected."

Then he explained the ordeal I'd just endured: a version of the quarantines set up from New Orleans to Mumbai to Perth, in hospitals and gyms and churches. But in the basement of the Looking Glass, as he began to call the building, they practiced a more austere form of silence therapy, coupled with the newest experimental medication.

Because I'd been so cut off from news, that was when I learned that not all problems with language telegraphed the same fate. "When infected people turn up here," Doug said, "we often don't know if they have word flu, so-called benign aphasia, or both. And we don't want to have to wait for an official diagnosis, potentially watching them get sicker, so we deploy simultaneous treatments. Rigorous, protracted silence," he said with an apologetic shrug, "is the only cure we've discovered so far for eradicating any last, lingering vestiges of the Meme. When it works, it helps prepare the way for language therapy, which can help reverse not just aphasia but disordered thinking, memory loss, scattered focus."

Because I'd had a relatively minor case,[3] I'd gone in the hole for just three days. The longest language fast they'd imposed to date had stretched to a week, for one of their colleagues, Alistair Payne, who'd been out in the field helping at Boston's Brigham and Women's after the mass infections. He'd managed to get his hands on an infected Nautilus, and after experimentally subjecting himself to the virus, he'd suffered severe damage: seizing, violent, nearly psychotic, raving.[4] When he'd arrived at the Glass a week later, escorted by an armed guard and a nurse—and aided in his travel by several influential people who'd interceded on his behalf—no one knew whether seven days would be enough. But experts had agreed that it would have to do. A week was considered the limit of what was safe; longer periods of solitary confinement might backfire, producing bad outcomes—perhaps even Silencing, it was speculated. Fortunately, in Alistair's case it had worked; he'd recovered.

In fact he'd just served as one of the guards who'd escorted me to Doug's office. When Doug reached this part of the story, Alistair removed his balaclava, his hair flurrying in a flaxen tumult. Then the other guard took off his mask, too. It was Vernon.

3. They later conjectured that my S0111 exposure five weeks before had rendered me a 3 out of 10, 0 signifying no trace of damage, 10 being unintelligible or mute. Doug claimed that my recovery had probably been aided not just by medication but by the two weeks I'd spent holed up in Phineas's apartment in a kind of proto-quarantine, disconnected from a Meme, spending many hours in silence, thinking, reading.

4. The woman who'd seen him wandering along the sidewalk out in front of the hospital and called the cops had assumed it was drugs: meth or bath salts.

"Vern!" I bayed, face igniting with joy. I leapt from my chair. Caught him off-guard in a quick, unscripted hug. His bony body was an affirmation: it was true. We were all okay.

Startled, Vernon batted gently at my back. "Good to see you, too, Anana," he said with a laugh, frowning down, his skinny neck somehow begetting a double chin. In his glasses I saw my tiny twinned reflection. How had I not noticed his limp as he'd walked me down the hall? "Sorry," I murmured, smiling, overcome with giddy shyness and relief.

But Vernon was oddly stiff. Awkward. Twisting away from me, he said, "I'm going to go check on . . . that," which seemed to mean something to Doug, who nodded briskly back. Then Vernon dipped his rigid nimbus of hair under the lintel and ducked out.

In the choppy wake of silence that trailed his exit, Doug also acted agitated—clearing his throat, looking toward the door. He started explaining distractedly that news of Alistair's successful treatment seemed to have spread through certain circles. In the week since, they'd seen a small but steady stream of desperate visitors at the Glass—part of the reason security was so high.

He also began describing the virus. More than one virus, in fact, Doug explained, each of which—replicating in the Internet, Memes, and human cells—has had devastating implications for language and communication. Perhaps because they seem to share the same source: the Germ, designed to corrupt or erase words.

On that night that I got out of quarantine, he told me only some of what I've come to learn. What I wanted to confirm was who was behind all of it, and why.

Doug sighed, haskily scratching the dense beard that had grown thick on his neck. Then he explained that some of the "engineers" Synchronic and Hermes had hired to develop Meaning Master and its attendant virus were in fact hackers. "Not just hackers," he clarified. "Mercenaries, or worse. Terrorists, maybe."

It was a word I'd heard so much growing up that it had lost a lot of significance. And even in that moment, part of me bucked against it. But I also felt again right then what it meant.

What he was saying was very hard for me to take in, which Doug must have sensed. I'm not good at hiding my feelings, especially from him. "Are you sure . . . You really want me to keep going?" he asked

softly, looking very doubtful and concerned. But after a moment I nodded grimly, and he gently gripped my arm. Then he said very carefully,
"I don't think anyone at Hermes or Synchronic wanted this." I knew we
were both thinking of Max.

Vernon reappeared then, leaning watchfully against the doorframe.
When Doug looked up, I thought I saw them share a strange, strained
look that I couldn't decipher.

Then Doug abstractedly picked up what he'd been saying. At first he'd
wondered if the hackers might be abroad. He noted the transliterated
Russian and Chinese roots of many fabricated "money words." And he
pointed out that most Memes were manufactured outside the States; it
seemed possible that viruses might have been installed during assembly,
or tampered with to make them easy to breach.

But during the five and a half weeks that he'd been in the U.K., analysis
undertaken by the Diachronic Society, with help from Oxford postdocs, had revealed a fascinating finding: they'd discovered that in fact
most hackers were in the U.S., scattered in different affluent suburbs.
For very good money, Synchronic and Hermes had recruited brilliant,
disaffected young men—and they were nearly all men—some as young
as their teens. Gamers, slackers, crackers, mathletes. One, in Santa
Barbara, who went by Roquentin,[5] was rumored to be a high school
freshman.

Apparently the reason so many money words were initially adapted
from pinyin and Cyrillic had more to do with the sweatshop laborers first hired to manufacture them, before Meaning Master had been
invented (and obviated their employment). These workers were people
who, for various reasons, couldn't afford excessive scruples in following
best U.S. business practices. (He also pointed out that while their labor
may have been relatively cheap, and in a certain sense discreet, when
you don't pay your workers a living wage and then abruptly fire them,
you'd be wise to consider that they may find other ways to make ends
meet.) Many of them, as it happened, were Russian or Chinese. Maybe

5. He'd taken the name from Sartre's *Nausea*. Like Max, he was apparently very fond
of the dead Frenchman. And it was a moniker that didn't seem empty of meaning; when
Doug mentioned Roquentin, I couldn't help but think of S0111's symptoms, which often
include nausea, vomiting, weakness, bouts of silence and egotism. Just a name wasn't
evidence of anything. But at the very least it was extremely cynical.

that was chance. Maybe not. "After all," said Doug, "their governments spent decades perfecting language-manipulation methods."[6]

"Like ours," I pointed out.

Doug nodded soberly. "Yes," he said. "I'm afraid that's true. I think there are quite a few similarities." Which was perhaps the reason, he explained, that Synchronic was able to find such seemingly like-minded foreign business partners—several in Moscow and Beijing, e.g.—who claimed to have an interest in adapting Synchronic's business model and developing language exchanges in their own countries.

Doug shifted in his seat. Groped at his shirt pocket as if for the cigarettes he'd given up when I was eight. "But we now think that some of these foreign partners hired hackers of their own—most likely some of the same young men—and may have paid them to disseminate these very destructive viruses. Timed their release to the Future Is Now gala, when a huge number of people would be logged on to the same websites, and used the devices to perpetrate attacks."

"You really think they'd do that?" I asked, mouth salt-lick dry. "The hackers, I mean. Conspiring with enemies. Isn't that . . . treason?" What I was saying felt fake, as if it were from a game. Something I might have played as a kid with my Wyoming cousins, our guns made of wood and glue.

"We don't know," Doug maintained. But it was the same tautly calm tone he'd used when I'd asked the year before if he and Vera were getting a divorce. "It's not entirely impossible that they've done at least some of it on their own," he said. "There's still a lot more we need to learn." Somberly he cracked his knuckles, the sound like whiskey poured over ice.

Then Vernon, who'd strode back into the room while Doug was talking, said something that disturbed me maybe even more. From the perch he'd taken up on the edge of Doug's desk, he said, "Whoever's responsible, it seems they've gotten more than they bargained for." He confirmed that word flu had spread. The UN and WHO had gotten heavily involved. Just that morning Doug had received a report announcing overflowing quarantines in Belgrade, São Paulo, Lisbon, Seoul. Not to mention Beijing and Moscow.

6. Doug claimed that the game of Meaning Master may actually have been inspired by a similar game popular in Russia about a decade ago. A bootlegged version had appeared in English under the name PROPFUN!

"The fact is," Vernon said, clearing his throat, "whether by design or simply *gross* negligence, tremendous harm has been caused. Harm that for many has been fatal."

When he uttered that word, fatal, it had a very strong effect on me. It conjured Max's sweaty green face, gleaming with gold-filing stubble. Cracked tooth. Tumified purple eye. And the mean beam of my mind lighted on him, trembling but defiant, standing in the dirty SoPo bathroom, ringed by men in black. Then the light flickered out, sparing me what happened next.

But the flare kept groping my dark cave of fear until it found something else to illumine: Bart, pale as a marble frieze. I missed him. So much it startled me. I pictured the packet of pills I'd pushed under his door. Wondered if he'd ever found them. If they'd worked. With a deep pain, like the ache of an old broken bone, I saw him in a cold, crowded hospital room. Or worse: prostrate on his floor. Alone. Sick and speechless. Terrified.

"Dad," I interrupted, clutching the arms of my chair. A white light had started erasing my vision and was closing in on his face.

"That's enough," Doug said gruffly to Vernon, holding up a hand.

"It's true," Alistair said from the corner where he'd been standing guard, so quietly I'd nearly forgotten him. "After three days in the hole, it's a lot to hear."

Doug nodded, a little sharply. And as I closed my eyes, taking tiny sips of air, Vernon murmured an apology—something about a morning press conference in London, how he'd thought they wanted me to be briefed. But my ears were buzzing; the words could barely get through.

When I blinked back into the world a minute later, the white cloud had burned off and I could see Doug clearly, scowling with concern. Then I saw him notice me, and he tried to smile. "I'm just so glad you're all right," he said, eyes wetly sparkling.

"I'm glad you're okay, too, Dad," I said, reaching for his hand. "I didn't know what happened to you."

Doug squeezed my fingers, let go, and sighed. "You know, Phineas lied to me, too," he said, voice stretched thin like an old rubber band. "He's a good but very complicated man. He and I have a long history. And he's always done right by me before. But I don't know why I believed him this time, without speaking to you." He squeezed my hand again. "It wasn't until Susan Janowitz faxed Bill here the notice of my disappearance that I started getting a clearer picture of what was happening back in New York. Even before I reached Phineas to ask him to keep an eye on you, I asked Susan, too, just in case. You met her, didn't you?"

I nodded, a vision of her red glasses glowing in my face. The scent of almonds, the sensation of her arm on my shoulders almost palpable.

"And say what you will about Susan"—Doug raised his brows—"she took the job to heart. Still, if I'd known Phineas was lying . . ." He looked down at his hands.

Some of the lies I already knew; I guessed what another might have been.

"Did you believe him?" I asked gently. "About Max and me?"

Maybe seeing Doug safe freed my heart to feel other things. A very tiny, tea-light part of me missed Max right then. I still do. But right away I pressed Doug's arm and shook my head, telling him not to answer. Because suddenly it struck me: Doug was alive—thriving. And I seemed to be all right. Everyone I loved had made it through. And if I also felt some sadness and guilt about those not covered by the canopy of fortune, I felt, too, that we would find a way to save them all. But I was wrong.

In the hall, Alistair gave me my bags. "Thought you might like these back," he said.

"Thanks," I said, grateful. I'd been wearing the same clothes for three days. But as I took my backpack, I noticed the zipper open on the pocket where I'd kept the Aleph. Thought again of how strangely Doug had acted when I'd asked who'd brought it from my hotel. Wondered aloud how they'd gotten my things.

But Alistair avoided my eyes. "Bart," he said, looking uneasy.

"*Bart?* He's *here*?" I said, shocked. And my stomach fluttered like a wind-torn plastic bag.

Alistair nodded. Glanced at the carpet.

"Where is he? Can I see him?" My mouth twitched into an anxious smile.

Alistair shook his head. "He's in the hole," he said.

Disappointed, I said, "So he'll be out—when?" Silently counted. "Saturday?"

But Alistair kept his gray eyes trained on the floor. Pressed his thin lips together. "We don't know," he confessed softly. "He might be in there longer."

"How much longer?" I asked, voice rising. "A week?"

Alistair shrugged. When he glanced up, there was no light in his eyes. "Even when he comes out, we're not sure he'll be able to talk."

"What do you mean?" I asked, mouth dry. "For how long?"

When he didn't respond, I said, "Ever?"

And he said, "Maybe not."

At dinner I couldn't eat. Couldn't stop picturing Bart locked in a spartan room, mute, sick, and suffering. Why had he come? Had Doug brought him? Was it for work? Maybe—and I hated to think it—for Hermes or Synchronic? Or was there a chance he'd come looking for me? The thought was like tonguing a loose tooth, twin shocks of pleasure and pain. With it came an almost-awareness that also felt bodily; my bones and blood knowing before I did what Bart meant to me. Had meant, for some time. And now he was in the hole. Thoughts of Bart bled into other fears. How many were sick, I wondered. How many dead.

Doug watched me, worry creasing his face, until the end of the meal. Then he took me to the first-floor reading room. And as he'd promised, it was spectacular: like nothing I'd ever seen. Rows and rows of leather-bound books. Ladders to reach them, some on wheels. Newspapers draped like ladies' delicates over wooden dowels. I hadn't held a paper paper in years. There was a cabinet with tiny drawers, like the one at the Merc. A grand piano. And as I slowly spun in the center of the room, I felt awed and overcome, and more than ever like Alice, on the wrong side of the mirror.

"Dad," I mumbled, "I don't feel so well." He led me by the elbow to the nearest chair, and I got a good look at the red carpet with its gold fleurs-de-lis, my head bent between my knees. By then Doug had learned what had upset me. And as a distraction he began to narrate the whole, improbable story of his escape from the Dictionary.[7]

---

7. He distracted me with something else: when he later went to get Scotch, he brought back a small vial. "This is all three editions of the *NADEL*," he said, voice glowing. "One of the postdocs encoded it in DNA and offered to implant it *in my body*. Clearly," he said, lifting the vial, "I cordially declined."

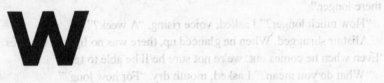

word \'wərd\ *n* **1** : a human relic, now obsolete **2** *archaic* : a discrete unit of meaning that, when synthesized with other such units, may make a small scratch in the skin of time

On the night of November 16, after Doug had used his feigned illness to slip out of the meeting with Synchronic, he'd hurried down twenty-two flights to the Dictionary's subbasement. When he'd found the word-routing terminal locked, and strangely papered with a crude sign reading CREATORIUM, he'd hurried along the damp hall, ducking into a small, cool storage closet in which it was possible to hear running water. The same closet I'd found the night I first encountered Dmitri.

When the light was on, one could see a small runnel flowing along a narrow groove in the floor and out through a large, jagged hole, two or three feet wide, in the base of the wall. From there it flowed a short way to the sewer. It was also possible to see plastic pneumatic tubes coming out of bores in the wall shared with the word terminal. They, too, made their way through the hole.

This closet, Doug explained, was sort of a portal, a bit like the small door behind Phineas's boiler. And as with that little door, the route beginning at the crumbly opening wasn't very easy to follow.

Doug had made his way through the rabbit hole only once before, a few years earlier. Several months after the tubes that connected the Dictionary to the Merc were installed, he'd attempted to investigate what had happened when they'd stopped working. He should have consulted the crew that put them in. (And shortly after his adventure, Phineas did.) Because while he managed to discover the site of the malfunction—

a section torn from the F train's storm drains—he wasn't as fit (or as lean) as he'd once been, and he almost got himself killed, in a few ways. On the night of November 16, as he stood hunched in the dank closet, the only thing that spurred him to try again was a more frightening threat of death—not just for himself but for the Dictionary.

On his previous attempt he'd made it barely halfway along the tubes' course. So it was with no small trepidation that he forced himself to squeeze, scratched and panicking, through the uneven drainage hole, first looking anxiously over his shoulder for some sign that he was being followed. He wormed his way, hyperventilating, along a short, wet, and quite tight corridor—"Tighter than I remembered," he said, self-consciously patting his stomach—tubes jutting into him, until it opened up enough for him almost to stand.

He was in a sewer that led him, a bit indirectly, the few blocks to Columbus Circle, and he broke into a careful, crouching jog along the dark, brackish passage, wrenching an ankle, craning his neck every few seconds to look over his shoulder, bloodying his feet with blisters by running in dress shoes through suspicious water. At a point when the tubes went through a passage that was too narrow for him to follow, he surfaced quickly through a heavy manhole cover (harrowing in its own right—it opened not on the sidewalk but in the street). Then he made his way back down again, into the subway.

He strongly contemplated taking the train, but he was still very close to the Dictionary and afraid someone looking for him would appear at any moment. So when the F didn't come for several long, agonizing minutes, he walked to the end of the platform and carefully climbed the ladder there down to the tracks. Then he followed the F's route—and the tubes—the distance of two terrifying train stops, to Rockefeller Center. There he decided that he was done risking his life in just that way, and he climbed back onto the platform, went up to the street, and walked the last block and a half to the Merc, drawing plenty of strange stares for the way he looked, and smelled.

When he arrived outside—filthy, disheveled, and "about five systolic points from a stroke"—his hands were shaking so badly that he had a hard time unlocking the Merc's door. Once inside, he hurried down to the basement and quickly found the typewriter perched on a stack of Prousts. Then he pecked out the same cryptic note twice. It read: "diachronic: a method of looking at language that's becoming extinct." He sent it by pneumatic tube to his office, where I discovered it, and also to Dr. Thwaite. (The week before, in a Society meeting, they'd decided that this would be their SOS. At the same time he'd renamed me Alice.)

But Phineas hadn't replied right away, and Doug didn't have time to wait: he was hoping to intercept me at the Fancy on his way to Newark Liberty. Before he went, though, he wanted to leave at least one more hint. So he bounded up the narrow, winding stairs to the mezzanine and cast around for inspiration. Stranded on the piano was a big, outmoded atlas, and beside it the skinny book of U.K. postcodes. "Probably left by some sentimental old codger," Doug said. "I used to catch Franz poring over it."

In a hurry, hoping I'd be able to unbend the OX1 IDP clue he'd left in his office, Doug thumbed to the atlas page mapped with Great Britain and slid the postcode volume inside. ("How did you ever expect me to decipher that?" I gently teased. "To be honest," he said, "I was so out of my mind at the time, I was afraid it was too obvious.")

Then, frenzied, feeling the minutes run by like rivulets of rain, he scrawled out one last note, addressed to *Alice whose name is not Alice,* and tucked it in a place he thought I might look: the *J* volume of the *NADEL's* second edition, on the page for "Johnson, Douglas." But Phineas had beat me to it and later stole that salutation. I still have the evidence. ("What did the note you left for me say?" I asked. Doug was incredulous. "What?" he responded. "You never found it? Are you sure?" When I nodded, he frowned and said, "Damn. I should have left it in the brass pineapple chandelier in the bathroom. It said, 'Dear Alice whose name is not Alice, I'm going through the Looking Glass.'" The note, he said, was the reason he'd started calling the Christ Church library that silly name.)

By the time he finished stashing the last of his clues, Doug was watching the clock even more frantically. He rushed back down the stairs and out to the street, and, with difficulty, hailed a taxi. After directing the driver back across town—and pretending, as they neared the Dictionary, to hunt, bending down, for something on the floor—he arrived, breathless, at the Fancy. But I was already gone, and all he found was the stern Marla.

At the airport he learned that tickets to London were sold out for the night. The best he could do was a layover in Reykjavík or Frankfurt.

Resigned, he booked the flight to Germany. But then, with a vital tightening in his gut, he reconsidered. Had a thought. Maybe, he reflected, a
stop in Reykjavík was the best possible option. After all, how else could
he cross into England undetected, if not with the help of an old (and
well-connected) friend?

He canceled his German ticket and went on harried walkabout for a
pay phone. Finally, after a search that felt nearly endless, he found an old
booth in a woebegone corner of the food court, its metal cord unspooled
like the gizzards of a robot, and he was amazed to get a dial tone. Fortunately he had the number memorized, from back when learning by heart
was the most efficient technology. He punched in 011, then the country
code, 354, then seven digits. And after a fake-sounding series of rings, a
groggy woman said, "Já?"

"Fergus, please," said Doug. "It's an emergency."

And after a minute he heard Hedstrom's gruff voice remonstrating,
"This better be damned important." But by the time he and Doug hung
up, Hedstrom was promising that Eydis, in bed beside him, would be at
the Keflavík baggage claim in six hours to meet Doug.

And so she was.

She'd driven Doug in a black Peugeot borrowed from her cousin
Arinbjörn—who'd "borrowed" it from someone else—to Hedstrom's
compound in Selfoss, a town on the Ölfusá River in the south. Then, in
the afternoon, when the sun had already set, Doug had been trundled,
in the dark, from a white panel van to a champagne leather window
seat on Hedstrom's Bombardier. Doug, Hedstrom, and a small staff had
flown to Kidlington Airport, just outside Oxford. And it seemed that
Ferg had made the trip before: they were met on the tarmac by a grinning official in a navy jumper who greeted Ferg by name. With a wry
smile the official accepted jars of pickled fish and other sundries—not
to mention a certain zaftig envelope—and waved the group through
customs, no questions asked. Then they made their way to the Looking
Glass. Ferg even left Doug with two personal guards.

(At that point in his story, noting my nonplussed expression, Doug
digressed with an aside on Hedstrom's heroic rescue. In college, he
explained, he, Ferg, and Laird had formed a triumvirate. But it was an
unstable bond, "like sodium," Doug said, "which bursts into flame when
you add water." Ferg had never hedged his stance on Laird: "I hate that

weasel fuck," he'd say. And Ferg's feelings were understandable. Before Laird had ever met Vera Doran, he'd long been practiced in the art of woman-poaching: e.g., Ferg's Radcliffe girlfriend and first true love, Sylvie Grace Mason, a petite blond deb. Ferg and Laird's "friendship," flimsy to begin with, fell to pieces after that. Doug was the only adhesive that remained between them. And in the past year, of course, even that glue had dissolved.)

Doug didn't relay all the details of this story on my first night out of quarantine. He filled me in on it, and far more, over the next few weeks. Sometimes on walks we took down the Abingdon Road or up to Jericho, wearing balaclavas to keep warm (and disguised). Sometimes Doug would leave me voice memos, or typed-up notes he slid under my door while I worked on this manuscript, bent over the typewriter, pressing hard on the keys.

That very first night that I got out of the hole, the night after Christmas, he recounted only the plainest facts of his escape. And in the silence that opened up after, I said, "Can I ask . . . If you hadn't gotten out . . . What happened to John Lee?"

Doug exhaled. Scrubbed his face with both hands. "Poor John Lee," he said, shaking his head, taking a gulp of the Scotch he'd poured during his story. Vernon had wandered in as Doug was mentioning his Bombardier flight to Oxford, and glancing up at Vern, Doug said, "Horrible." Took another deep pull of his drink. "He was very sick," Doug went on. "He was one of the first to be infected with word flu from the Nautilus. But that's not what got him killed."

· Leaning heavily on his cane, Vernon explained, "He was trying to warn the workers in the Creatorium that they could be hurt by the device and the virus. And that they were exposing other people. That's why he was murdered."

"Well, he also tried publicizing the symptoms," Doug added. "He put up a warning on the Exchange, which can't have been easy, given how aphasic he became. But it was of course immediately replaced with an apology, claiming that the site had been hacked and the warning was a fake."

With a thud, Vernon sank into a nearby chair. "We don't know for sure who did it," he said, placing his cane across his knees. "Could've been more than one of them. Dmitri, maybe. Or maybe this guy Koenig." Vernon's neck and shoulders twitched involuntarily. "Lately he's been seen lurking around here."

And I shuddered, too, picturing the man in black from my train. "Dad," I said, a little light-headed, "I think someone was following me."

Doug turned pale. "It's possible," he agreed bleakly. Drained his glass. "When I heard from Bill you were here and then got word about this Koenig, I got very worried."

"Why didn't you tell me how to find you?" I asked. "Or come get me?"

"I didn't know where you were," Doug said, frowning.

I studied him. "So that note," I said. " 'The Jabberwock'—" But Doug's face was blank, and the words died in my throat. I felt a twinge, as if my skin were being unzipped.

"What?" Doug said, tensing.

But I just mumbled, "Nothing."

Doug squinted at me. Muttered, "Maybe we should stop there."

"I'm fine," I said. "Really. I feel much better, actually." It was true. Surprised, I realized that talking had also gotten easier.

"Really?" Doug asked, suspicious. But when I nodded, I saw him suppress a smile. "Already?" he said, mostly to himself. To me he said soberly, "That's a very good sign." (For all his devotion to scholarly rigor, Doug was a bit superstitious. It came out in small, almost imperceptible ways—e.g., when he was most excited, he often refused to smile and wrung all joy from his voice. I teased that he was warding off the evil eye. And I'd found it confusing as a child. But I'd gotten used to it, like his habit of knocking on wood or tossing salt over his broad shoulder. And in that moment I found his seriousness, and what it signified, extremely reassuring.)

He explained that engaging in conversation with healthy people was one facet of language therapy: it could help reverse any residual effects of S0111 following quarantine and begin to stimulate new neuronal connections. Reading, as I already knew, was another rehabilitative remedy. He handed me a stack of *International Journal of Lexicography* back issues. My heart fell. And lopsidedly grinning, he said, "Kidding." Passed me a beautiful edition of *Through the Looking-Glass*. Added, "It also might not hurt to review a few entries in the *NADEL*."

These guideline recommendations—language fasts, conversation labs, reading, writing, too ("We'll discuss your own course of composition therapy soon," Doug said)—had been developed in nascent form several years earlier, in Taiwan. After this latest word flu outbreak, Doug had conferred with labs at Oxford and Cambridge, Harvard and Carnegie Mellon, the WHO, CDC, and the U.K.'s National Health Service. And he'd received a small stockpile of antivirals. But no other, better therapy ideas. In part, perhaps, because many of these organizations had lost years of digital data to the cybervirus, including information about word flu and what had been done in China and Taiwan. The best anyone could offer was prevention advice.

In the six weeks that had elapsed since the first known victim of this epidemic had succumbed, scientists had begun studying the virus's effects. Since then, and especially in the two and a half weeks after the mass infections, they'd had an unfortunate wealth of samples to analyze—assessing CTs and MRIs, including data from those who'd suffered Silencing—and they'd also started looking at damage caused by malfunctioning microchips and Crowns in victims of benign aphasia. All while trying to protect their data from being destroyed. But researchers still didn't know enough. They were submitting grant proposals. They wanted to run cross-sectional and cohort studies. Examine more reports from autopsies.

As that last, sibilant word slid from my father's mouth, a chill stung my spine, as if I were the one laid out on a slab. "Dad?" I said. He turned to me expectantly.

But then I bit my lip and didn't ask, *What's going to happen to Bart?* Doug peered at me, forehead ruching darkly. "Is everything all right?"

"Yeah," I lied, the scratchiness back in my throat.

His face tightened. He held up a hand. "Give me a second," he said, standing. "Don't go anywhere."

"Where would I go?" I asked, but he'd already turned his back and didn't respond. When he returned, he'd refilled his glass, and he handed me a great, glowing goblet of Scotch. One rock.

"I don't want you to answer right away," he said. "But I have a proposition." Then he raised his glass. "Bottoms up."

From experience, I knew a proposition could be a Buster Keaton marathon or a salaried job. I took a long, burning swig. Nodded for him to say what it was.

"A moment ago," said Doug, "I mentioned comp therapy." He rubbed his throat. "I hadn't intended to get into it tonight. But honestly, I think it shouldn't wait. Not because I think you're still in danger, but because there are a lot of people who ought to know what's been happening—to them, and to all of us."

Then, steepling his hands, bending forward, he explained, "There's a way you could continue to get better while helping other people." Sipping his drink, he went on. "We've lost a lot—incalculable amounts. The best way forward for all of us is to recover our recent past. It's a start, at least, as we try to figure out stops, block the viruses that are still razing so much of the Internet and harming many, many people. And then, after things begin to stabilize, we hope, as we begin an inventory of the tens of thousands, maybe millions, of texts—books, articles, emails, transcripts—that have been destroyed. Not to mention private memories, anecdotes, oral histories. By recording the events of these past weeks, you could at least help begin what will need to be a collective process of reflection on all we've lost and how we got to this point. But also where we might go from here. By telling the story. Breathing life back into what have become dead letters. I think it has to be done. And I think you're the person to do it."

This speech had all the classic hallmarks of Doug at his most Dougish: caring, brazen and dramatic, more than a little unrealistic. All my life I've known him to have outsize dreams that he nonetheless tries to implement. And since he always feels best when he's "being of use" I knew he was trying to offer me a path to utility, too, no matter how unlikely.

Even so, as he spoke my face began to burn, only in part from the whiskey. I could tell he believed what he was saying—that this project really mattered to him. I also knew he was probably asking me to do it because he couldn't: he was too busy with meetings, press releases, conferences, research, inventorying lost resources, and in his few spare hours he was trying to prepare the *NADEL* for publication. Already by then he thought Synchronic would have to file for bankruptcy, and he hoped to get back the intellectual property and publish the third edition through the Oxford University Press by the end of January. (In his Newark safe-deposit box he'd stored a complete set of the third and a digital backup.) But even if Doug didn't have time to write the account of all that had happened, why hadn't he asked Vernon? Vern would do an excellent job. Or Alistair? Or someone else? *What about Bart?* a small voice said inside my heart.

Again Doug seemed to read my mind. "You," he said. "It should be you."

And I was so grateful for his vote of confidence. His opinion matters to me very much. Maybe more than anyone's. But I also had my doubts. It had been years since I'd written anything longer than a few dozen sentences; I wasn't sure I'd be able to realize his vision. (Which of course I couldn't—only my own.)

"Dad, I don't know," I said. "I'm a visual artist, not a writer. And I'm still recovering. I mean, I just got out of quarantine a couple hours ago. I'm not sure I feel—"

"Just think about it," Doug said softly, sounding a little let down. "As I said, you don't have to decide right this moment. One thing you'll have plenty of is time. Even with reading treatments, conversation lab, all of that. And in fact, if you were to include footnotes—which would help your readers, too, especially with memory—you could probably cut your lab time by as much as half."[1] Doug gave me a gauging, sidelong glance.

I tried to smile, but I was exhausted. I offered a weak shrug.

"All right," he said, rattling the ice in his glass. I couldn't tell if he was mad. Then he took a strange device from his coat pocket. Silver, deodorant-sized. It had a small screen and a long, snaking black leash—a mic. "But if you *do* decide to consider it . . ." He clicked a switch, and a tiny red eye beamed on. "I thought it might help to record a few notes."

What follows is a redacted transcript of our conversation from that night.

DOUG: The trick of switching words' meanings is one of the old-
         est in the book. Just think of "freedom" and "democracy" . . .
         Ultimately, it's a problem of shortsightedness. An addiction to
         what's next. People become so obsessed with the future, they

---

1. I've obviously followed his advice. Though over the five weeks that I've been writing, and as I've convalesced, I've found I need to use them less. I've also noticed that the compositional habits of certain other sources I've consulted to compile this document have kind of (benignly) infected it. E.g., I've become much more attached to parentheses. And reading the *NADEL* concomitantly has certainly changed my vocabulary (in somewhat unconventional ways, apparently).

make it up. Fabricate the "news." Invent their own "analysis." We've been doing that for years. It seems only natural that eventually we'd move on to manufacturing words. . . . But Synchronic didn't invent accelerated obsolescence. As a nation we've been practicing mass production since before World War II. We believed wastefulness would morph, by magic, into wealth. That if we created enough disposable products, it would help fire consumerism. And it did, for a while. But here's a dirty secret: resources are finite. Waste enough, and eventually it's all used up. Language, too. You can't just coin a word, use it once, and toss it out. But language is just the latest casualty. We always think there's more of everything, even as we deplete it. Not just petroleum or gold, glacial ice or water, bandwidth. Now even our thoughts and memories are disposable.

ANANA: Dad, I thought we were talking about . . . What are we talking about?

D: Why do you think people stopped reading? We read to connect with other minds. But why read when you're busy *writing*, describing the fine-grained flotsam of your own life. Compulsively recording every morsel you eat, that you're cold, or, I don't know, heartbroken by a football game. An endless stream flowing to an audience of everyone and no one. Who can bother with the past when it's hard enough keeping up with the present? But we *do* need the past. And things that last longer than a day. . . . I'm sorry—I know I'm rambling.

A: No. Well—it's okay. [Pause.] Dad? [Long pause.] Can I ask you something? What's going to happen to . . . Are Bart, a-and . . . Will they be okay?

D: [Sighs.] He'll be okay. [Offers A a chocolate discovered in his breast pocket. Transcript stops and picks up again several minutes later.]

D: In some ways language *is* like love. It only means something when it's directed toward another person. But language can change, or get corrupted. People can disappear. And love doesn't. *Real* love never goes away.

A: Sometimes even when you wish it would.

D: Well, no. I think you're talking about something else, then, not love. And the good news is, those other things do fade: infatuation, loneliness, fear. Heartbreak. It may take a very, very, *very* long time. But eventually they dissipate . . . Anana, people are disappointments. We're selfish and scared and badly flawed beings. Like me. And Phineas. Like Vera and Max. Maybe not like *you*, but everyone else. Well, maybe not Bart. But everyone *else*. [Moment of silence.] *Love*, though, is perfect. It's larger than any of its objects. And the trouble comes when we try to conflate the *feeling*, this big, ever-expanding, almighty and encompassing thing, with the person who enabled us to feel it. But if you can hold on to love, even after people disappoint you—by lying, or cheating, or dying, or failing to love you back—

A: Or falling silent.

D: Yes. If you can experience the love you feel, this great, vast sea surrounding you, instead of clinging to the person you think it represents, who's actually just a small, unsteady, not very seaworthy raft, then you'll never be disappointed again.

A: So do you think I made a mistake, falling in love with Max?

D: Anana, love is never a mistake.

A: [Bites lip. Eyes fill.] I wish . . .

D: You're like me. You want to know what everything means. But what I've finally learned, after all these years—and writing meanings for a living—is that there isn't a meaning to everything. At least not one.

A: [Nods.]

D: [Long silence. Throat-clearing sound.] Anana, there's something I have to tell you.

A: What?

D: [Pause.] This is going to be very hard to hear. I want you to—

A: What is it? Is it about Bart? I thought you said—

D: It's not Bart.

A: Is it Vera? I . . . . [Unintelligible.]

D: What? No. As far as I know, Vera's fine.

A: Good. Thank God. Then everything's all right.

[Silence.]

A: Doug? Everything's okay, right?

D: It's . . .

A: Say it.

D: I'm *trying,* Anana. It's . . .

A: *Say it,* Doug.

D: It's about Max.

x \'eks\ *n* **1** : a former love **2** : a sign you've found the right spot **3** : a mark someone might make who is unable to write

Max had managed to leave the country with the help of an old Harvard friend who'd gotten in touch after Johnny's death—and who, in speaking to Max, soon became very worried about him as well. He was a pharmaceuticals scion with access to a private jet, and after the borders started to reopen, he responded to Max's urgent pleas to leave the country, agreeing to fly him to London, where he had to go for work, if Max would promise not to speak for the duration of the flight. (Through family connections he also got Max a course of antivirals, and he encouraged Max not to stay in London but to go on to Oxford; he'd started to hear rumors about what he thought was an innovative new clinic—but which in fact was the Glass—purportedly having better-than-average success with quarantine and language therapies.) By the Saturday before Christmas, when they were scheduled to depart, the friend had also gotten Max the papers he'd need to leave New York and enter the U.K.

Max arrived in Oxford just two days after me.[1] And that night, at one a.m., with the help of instructions from his friend, who'd made a few discreet inquiries in London, Max turned up outside the Glass. Only one guard was on duty, Chris Bennett, a sweet, hulking nineteen-year-old rower from Stoke-on-Trent who was reading English at Mag-

---

1. Doug claims that Koenig was sent to intercept Max; I was just collateral.

dalen. The sight of Max, still badly bruised and groveling on icy gravel, overwhelmed him. He couldn't understand what Max was saying and tried in vain to get him to leave. He even wielded a billy club (unconvincingly). After an hour, when Max still wouldn't budge—by then he was not only babbling but hysterically crying, and worrying Chris by constantly glancing over his shoulder—Chris finally managed to rouse an irritable Vernon on the walkie-talkie.

Vernon took one look at Max—lips cracked from cold, one swollen eye the shiny purple-green of an oyster, tears and snot quivering off his chin, wearing just Carhartts and a thin flannel—and went inside to get Doug. Doug, lumbering out into the frigid night with a parka thrown over his robe, watched Max disappear and reappear behind the white vapor of his sobs, and sighed. "All right," he relented. "Bring him in."

And Max hung on Doug's neck as they hauled him to quarantine.

They had doubts, of course. Vernon openly questioned Doug's decision. He wondered, too, how Max had even found the Glass—if Max had been tracking him. (Or was being tracked himself. There was no knowing who'd turn up next, Vern said.) But as Doug explained, letting Max in wasn't entirely selfless; if he was ever able to talk again, his information would potentially be very useful. "Besides," Doug chided Vernon, "he was nearly my son-in-law. And you claimed he likely saved my daughter's life."

When I heard that, my stomach jumped. "What do you mean?" I asked.

But Doug refused to elucidate, offering only that there was a reason Dmitri had never kidnapped me—or worse. And the truth was, I didn't really want to know.

Doug shuddered and took a long pull of Scotch. I did, too.

When they turned the lock on Max's door that night, Doug was optimistic that Max would be fine within the week. As badly off as he seemed, he was actually in better shape than Alistair had been in when he'd arrived from Massachusetts. And Max was carrying a bottle of the same antivirals they gave at the Glass. (Although, confusingly, he also had a doctor's note certifying that his aphasia was benign.)

But of course Max wasn't fine. They didn't know why he was so sick. Maybe, they thought, he'd been affected by more than one virus. Max had a microchip, Vern said. It had apparently been implanted nearly a year before, when he'd gone away on what I'd thought had been a snowboarding trip. He'd come back with a shaved head and a bandage he claimed was from a fall—which was also how he'd explained his post-op symptoms.

On Max's second day in quarantine, he got worse: pale and shaky, unable to cough up even the haunted gibberish he'd brought in. By that night it was clear that his silence wasn't by decree; he had fallen into it. And it was a silence from which he never returned. Around two a.m. he began continuously seizing, and before the doctors even arrived, clad in hazmat suits, he slipped into a coma, his pupils slightly different sizes. It was the worst case of word flu any of them had yet seen. When one of the doctors called Doug later from the hospital, he said that Max's eyes were no longer responding to light; there was nothing more they could do.

Doug had been forced to call Max's mother in Boston. "That was a terrible conversation," he said, shivering. Max had died on Christmas Eve, two days earlier, while I'd been in quarantine. Doug had gone to Heathrow with the body.

"I'm so sorry," he said, in the strangest voice I'd ever heard. A distant echo, from the bottom of a well. And for a moment I think I lost consciousness. I'm not sure. The world was there, and then it wasn't. When it came back, it was very loud. So loud I covered my ears. But it didn't help, because my thoughts were louder. Thunderous. One was that I'd already known he was dead. Had known it would happen since the last night I'd seen him. But just as strong was the conviction that Max was still alive, and that my father was lying.

He was saying something else. But it took the words a long time to get through. Finally I heard, "You know, he really loved you."

And for just the sliver of a moment, I was confused. I saw Bart's wide-set green eyes. His pointy incisors. But then the smile changed: there was a dark gap between the front teeth. And Doug was saying, "Maybe that's why he ended things. He thought it would be safer for you." I turned then and tried to look at Doug, but his face was indistinct, smudged with my tears. "I don't know if that's the right thing to say," he said as I stood and left the room.

The attack of sadness I suffered then was so violent that I thought my mind might be going. I could barely breathe. Almost couldn't see. I was afraid to go to my room—I didn't want Bart to hear my sobs through the wall. I went outside even though I had no hat or gloves or scarf. I didn't feel the cold. I sank to the ground—on the same spot, I imagined, where

Max had begged to be let inside. I wept until my stomach hurt and I thought I would throw up. My throat was raw. My eyes giant in my head. Because Doug was right: I still loved Max. I always will.

But as I cried I felt a twisting guilt, like a wet sheet whipping in the wind. Because I wasn't just crying for Max. I was crying because I was worried about my mother, on the other side of the world. And all the rest of my family, and my friends. Because I missed Coco, and I hadn't spoken to either Audrey or Ramona in weeks and I didn't know if they were all right. I was crying for Phineas. And for Victoria. And for people I'd never met, all those who'd gotten sick or fallen silent or died, and the ones who loved them. But most of all I was crying for Bart, because I knew I'd lose him, too.

When I finally went back in, my hands were crimson. After they'd thawed enough to feel, they burned like they were being boiled. I tried Bart's door, right next to mine, but it was locked. Pressed my ear to the wood and heard nothing.

In my room there was a glass of cloudy water on the desk. A pair of oblong pink pills. And a note in Doug's hand read: "Take these." I couldn't help but think of Alice, finding the vial: *Drink Me.* Shrinking. Drowning in the pool of tears.

I climbed into bed. And while I waited for the pills to work, I started seeing things: screaming babies large as dogs, people's heads rolling off. I thought I heard knocking through the wall. I knocked back three times, sure that Bart would understand.[2] Then I slept a few dreamless hours and woke to louder knocking. More exhausted than I'd ever been.

A note slid under my door. "Sorry," it began. "But if you want to make the press conference, your train leaves at eight." After I read it, I went back to sleep. Ten minutes later, though, I forced myself to get up again.

Before I left the room, I pressed my hand to the wall, and I whispered, "Please come back."

When we met in the lobby, Doug was in a suit and tie and freshly shaven. I had on the pants I'd worn for four days. He squeezed my shoulders, but

---

2. Something like *I hear you,* or *I miss you,* or *I am here.* A conflation that was just as clear to me then as the way the heads I watched roll from necks would turn to flowers, then flames, then rain.

I backed away; I didn't want to start crying again. As we walked through the gate, followed by guards, we filled the air with just the streams of our breathing, no words.

In the train Doug gave me the window seat. I rested my head on the juddering glass. Watched all the vistas blur by, one into the next. A small cemetery where we crossed the Thames. Cows grazing in the shadow of a grocery chain. Lots of what I thought of as heather, some gray, some the russet color of ancient tractors left out in the rain. Trees. Horses. Brave souls practicing on a cold soccer pitch, white versus red.

I thought, *You are not dead yet.*

The press conference was being held at a former residence of Dr. Samuel Johnson's, the building where he'd written most of his dictionary. We took a cab from Paddington to Fleet Street, then walked from Red Lion Court to Pemberton. Turned under an arch marked GOUGH SQUARE, and there was number 17. It was a beautiful brick building. A cream-and-wine-colored sign affixed to its side said, "Dr. Samuel Johnson / Author. / Lived Here." On the cobbles by the side entrance was a large chalk *X* marked "Press."

Doug had to prepare, but he told me to go inside and give myself a tour. The place was laced with history, from the worn brass on the curved casement latches to the steep slant of the stairs. The third floor felt haunted, thanks to a glyph.[3] But I liked the top floor best. It was a low-ceilinged attic with small windows and objects under glass: Johnson's gold-tipped cane; a porcelain mug that had once graced the lips of his famous biographer, Boswell; a white plate painted with blue love-birds, facing off. There was also an electronic display of Dr. Johnson's manuscript, illuminated not with gold leaf but an LED.

I spent a long time up there, watching the crowd form in the square below. There weren't enough folding chairs, so a few people stood back by the cameras, their badges and coats flapping in the wind. As it got closer to the moment for Doug to speak, I started down the stairs again.

But I stopped on the second floor, arrested by a view not of space but of time. On shelves behind glass panes matching those that looked

---

3. It was a blue man in a flowing blouse. He flickered over the fireplace and northwest corner of a room larded with props. It wasn't clear who he was. He was much too thin to be Johnson.

outside were Dr. Johnson's books: portals to the past. A copy of his dictionary was also out on display, the two volumes open on a table glossy as a dark, fogged mirror. The book was enormous, paper thick as wedding stock. I turned to the *L*'s, for "lexicographer," to see "harmless drudge" in tiny pica type. And I smiled, thinking how Bart would like that. I'd show him if he got out of quarantine. (*When*, I told myself.) Then I flipped more absently and landed in the *G*'s. Saw "gamecock" and "gamut" and "gargarism." "Gasconade," "gastriloquist." Then, as I heard Doug's tread squeak the stairs, my eye lingered on the word "gather," and I read: "To collect; to bring into one place." And I took that as a sign: that I should round up Doug's notes and my own memories and thoughts since the start of the virus. That I should tell this story, which might otherwise be lost.

I met Doug's eye, and we walked down to where everyone was waiting outside.

Standing behind the thick of the crowd, roughed by a biting wind, I looked around the square at all the green beribboned wreaths. A red scarf tied to the neck of a bronze sculpture of a cat. White strings of lights. Christmas had already slipped past. I glanced back to the tense faces watching Doug. He adjusted his tie. From that distance, only I knew the tiny yellow dots on navy silk were pineapples.

Or so I thought. Only later did I notice a few people I recognized: Susan, in her red glasses; Franz; Clara Strange; Tommy Keach, with his pale hair pulled away from his face. I looked around for Phineas and didn't see him, which made the pleasure of seeing the others less complete. But being there with them still gave me the sense of being part of a long, bending, unbreakable chain.

Doug's voice began to sound through the square. And soon he was explaining that while the numbers were impossible to verify, it was now believed that more than nineteen thousand deaths had been attributed directly or indirectly to the viruses. And the viruses were still spreading: so far they'd done relatively little damage in the U.K., but they'd made inroads in other Commonwealth countries, on U.S. military bases, and in territories from Guam to Puerto Rico.

"Elsewhere now, too," said Doug. And he delivered the bad news that aphasia had leapt from English to at least twelve other languages. I heard quickly stifled murmuring. Saw hands flutter in the crowd. On the faces of those nearby, I noticed lines flower on foreheads. Someone shouted out a question about the best precautionary measures, and I saw the muscles in Doug's jaw jump.

"Please hold your questions to the end," called a small blond woman to Doug's left.

"The best measure is not to be exposed," Doug said grimly. But he did then list several techniques that had proven useful for reversing damage in controlled environments. The list was later passed to the crowd. I have it here:

1. **Quarantine** of contaminated individuals.
2. Mandated **language fasts**. We recommend between two and three days for less severe cases, up to a week for serious infections. We're looking into the viability of longer courses of treatment—several weeks or more. But it should be noted that we haven't yet tested the safety or efficacy of extended silence therapy. It may be quite dangerous, resulting in permanently silenced patients or possible death.
3. **Cessation of contact with meaningless data**. I.e., "content" that's actually devoid of content.
4. **Reading**. Books are especially effective, but magazines have shown some promising results. Even limns, on approved devices, have been useful in some emergencies.
5. **Conversation** with uninfected people, informally or in language labs. Preferably in multiple languages. This recommendation also applies to both reading and comp. treatments (see below).
6. **Composition therapy**. Some studies suggest that more discursive writing styles, e.g., heavily annotated documents, may offer marginally statistically significant benefits.

On the train ride back, Doug and I didn't talk until after Slough, when I finally asked about Franz and the other Society members I'd seen.

Doug nodded, looking tired. He explained that they'd come to help set up an archival center at the Glass that would probably serve as a model for other institutions, and to lend a hand with final edits on the *NADEL*'s recovered files before the third edition went to print. He was hoping more Society members would arrive as they could.

Looking past me out the window, he said softly, "Have you given my request from last night any more thought?"

I didn't answer right away. I pressed my hand to the window, then put it back in my lap. Watched its white ghost quickly fade from the glass.

Mistaking my silence for diffidence, Doug said, "You know, you're capable of far more than you give yourself credit for. It's very frustrating." When I still didn't speak, he chewed his lips in remorse. "Sorry," he murmured. "But you know it's true."

I shrugged. But it wasn't really true anymore. I was starting to believe I could do it. "Wood and glue?" I said.

Doug's eyes brightened. "If you decide to go ahead," he said, smiling, "you'll also have help from Bart."

I sat up. "What do you mean? Does that . . . Alistair said Bart won't be out for at least a week."

Doug cleared his throat. Loosened the noose of his tie. "He might be in for closer to a month, Anana. He's in an experimental treatment."

"A month?" I tried to say. But I had barely any air. "I thought— no one's been in longer than seven days. I thought you said that was the limit of what's safe."

Doug's face put on its mask of tragedy. He only took it from its hook when someone died. But it was fresh in my mind: he'd used it just the day before. "Anana," he said, his mouth a sad, soft crescent, "I want you to know we're working with an excellent team of doctors." He took my hand. "And Bart has a very good chance—"

"He has a good chance?" I said, feeling sick, gently taking back my hand.

Doug let out a sigh. Rubbed his forehead. "We don't really have another choice," he said, helpless. Then, more quietly, "You know, he's one of my closest friends, too."

And I looked away, back out the window. Blinking quickly.

"How could he even help me, then?" I said softly to the hills and fields. "Should I wait until he's out of quarantine?"

"No, you shouldn't wait," Doug said, too quickly. And the awful, silent sentence I heard hiding beneath it was, *Bart may never speak again.* "You'd use his journals," Doug explained. "And if you start soon," he went on, trying to sound encouraging, "then when he's out, you'll be done, and you can share it with him." He pressed my knee.

But by then I was only half listening. Doug had used a word that derailed me. A word almost as old as typewriter, or gramophone. "Journals?" I said, amazed and vaguely disturbed. Keeping a journal seemed like such a waste. Why write something only you would ever see? It bordered on conceit, which wasn't Bart to me. But at the same time I was a little sad that he'd never told me. "Why?" I asked, trying to imagine what dark secrets Bart was keeping. Why else write in private?

Doug was studying me quizzically. "Reflection can be its own reward," he said. I thought about that. Later I thought of it a lot. But Doug had more to say. "The truth is," he admitted, "Bart's always wanted to be a writer. Or at least he did."

We both fell silent. I saw Bart curled on his cot in the room next to mine. Forehead dewed with sweat, like a glass of water. I tried not to picture him sick like that. But I couldn't help it.

Soon, though, Doug started speaking again. "Bart wanted you to have them," he said. "His journals. That was his last request."

"He did?" I said, flushing a little, not looking at Doug. Not thinking of that phrase, "last request."

Out of the corner of my eye, I saw Doug nod. "He wrote me a note when he was still relatively lucid. And if I'm not mistaken, he left you a letter, too. My hypothesis is that he held out so well for so long, even given what seems to be a very serious case of word flu, because he was writing—and it wasn't just a solipsistic exercise. It was meant to be a dialogue. With you," he said gently. "You were helping him without even knowing it."

Sometimes talking is an act of kindness. Sometimes silence is. Doug patted his shoulder, and I laid my heavy head on it. We were quiet for as long as it took to pass fields, more auburn heather, the soccer pitch, now empty.

In Doug's office he handed me a pair of speckled black-and-white notebooks. Tapped the cover of the one on top. "You'll find the letter in there, at the back," he said, and I riffled to the end. There was no mistaking Bart's scrabbled hand: letters like dead mosquitoes, the words smoky where things had been erased and rewritten.

I took the notebooks to my room, where I meant to leave them before going up to dinner. But a bouquet of roses rested on my bed, its damp stems staining the pillowcase. There was no note. But the roses were purple. And in my coat pocket I found the crumbled rosebud Bart had left for me the morning after Doug disappeared. Squeezed it in my hand.

Then, no longer hungry, I lay down on my bed to read Bart's letter. The pillowcase was still wet and cool on my cheek, which made it easy to weep, like the false tears from an onion stirring real feeling.

When I finished reading, something leapt in me, like a tiger at its cage. Those three words I'd knocked out on Bart's wall.

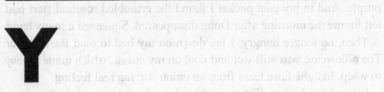

you \\'yü, yə\ *n* **1 :** another subjectivity **2 :** my reason for writing **3 :** synthesis; my other half < ~ complete me>

December 26 (evening)

Dear A,

I'm sorry this is so short. It's not because I have nothing to say. If I could, I'd never stop writing this letter to you. But they tell me I'm very sick. Bookhot I need to go in the hole. (They gow there's a chance I may never write, or talk, again. Actually, what they jenz was, "There's a strong possibility.")

But there's not much I *need* to say. Just that I'm very glad I found you. I really can't believe you're jase, right in the next room. I thought of tapping on the wall, but didn't want to disturb you. (Also, they kazh not to. They've asht a lot of things. Like that you saved my life, shongot me those pills. And that it's the last night of your quarantine. That makes me very, vesmen happy. And chay their information-sharing goes both ways (i.e., that they talk to you about me): please don't worry. I mean, not that you would. But stas in case.)

There's only one other thing I want to do. I can't help but think you're holding my notebook right now. At this moment. They loker, unbelievably, that it might help you in some way. So I need to offer an exegesis, in the form of an apology. There are a few things you'll see if you salto through the pages that I wish I had time to erase. But

I don't. I barely have time to skim some of the skole from this letter before they come back to lock me down for God knows how long. So here goes:

I'm sorry for all the boring stuff about Hegel. You can skip it ming-chev, along with any discursions on language. I want to apologize, too, for blavvo dox about Max. And I'm so, hobe sorry for vesyeda things I should've told you through the years and didn't. I'm sorry for yoll getting mixed up for a while with Hermes and Synchronic. Kyfen not doing more (i.e., neeben) to help you find Doug. And veetch for going to your apartment when you vanished and triffit through your things. I'm sorry for not denying it when that cabbie ven if I was your boyfriend. And that you appear in my dreams. Sorry for so often shung a man more of words than of actions—and for not always being great at words. Anyway, flane. I'm sorry for lots of things.

And I have just one zway, embarrassing apology. I guess it may be clear by now that I anzee hoped to "write" someday. (I wish it had been clearer to me; if I'd censored myself more, I'd have less to lodel-ensen.) Of course now it looks like there's a good chance—a strong possibility—that I may never write again. But you still can. And I hope you will. You could be the voice for both of us. (Is that ridiculous?)

Your friend, & faithful servant,
Bart/Horace Tate

P.S. Did Alistair give you the flowers? Nwabets he would.

P.P.S. Just one last thing. Max is a good guy. Or—well, he tries. And he versen loves you. (I haven't seen him yet. They said he went somewhere, but they wouldn't beed. Maybe you know. I hope you got to see him before he disappeared.) But also (and I think it's safe to veets you know what I'm going to write next; I'm going to write it anyway, though) because I love you, too. And I wanted that to be the last thing.

Z

0 \'zē(,)-rō, 'zir-(,)ō, 'zed\ *n* **1 :** something shaped like a seed **2 :** the aleph from which everything springs **:** AUFHE-BUNG **3 :** the end **4 :** the beginning

The morning after I read Bart's letter, I sat down to write this. That was five weeks ago.

On our daily walks Doug and I cross back and forth over the Isis, sipping hot coffee from paper cups. Sometimes Vernon comes along. Sometimes Alistair and Chris—but they usually linger behind us, letting us talk. Keeping watch. Doug remains more worried about the damage being done by the viruses, though, than any other threat. There were a series of special-forces raids in the days after New Year's, and several suspects have been apprehended, including Rhys Koenig, the man sent here to find Max.

The virus has continued moving through cyberspace, infecting more than thirty languages; there have been human victims in nearly every country. Most nations that initially accepted so-called endangered language refugees—Germany, England, Canada, Japan, Italy, Venezuela, South Africa, Switzerland, Sweden, Brazil—have stopped letting them in. Sick bays and quarantines have continued filling. Per the guidelines delineated by the Society's commission, they've set up language labs, reading rooms, evening debate sessions.

But the virus still seems to be spreading, which no one expected. After every model of Meme was recalled, we all thought infections would stop. Thousands—perhaps hundreds of thousands—of microchips have been removed. Millions of antivirals prescribed. And fatalities seem to be slowing. People are still dying, though, and we don't yet know why. But we're trying to stay optimistic about new experimental recovery treatments.

Among these are extended language fasts of up to forty days. Doug is hoping that they'll be more effective than shorter quarantines have been. Bart, of course, was among the first test cases, and we've been monitoring him closely. He was released three days ago. But so far he hasn't been able to write or speak.

U.N. peacekeepers were deployed several weeks ago to the U.S., and the situation appears to have stabilized. NGOs and international aid workers have stepped in to help with rationing and quarantines. U.S. reporting is now more or less restored. But for a while Americans got accounts from outside, a weird new news-world of global perspective. And when domestic coverage resumed, it seemed infused with a new germ of truth-telling. Of course it didn't last. But the secretary of education recently unveiled an initiative for curriculums to place more emphasis on history and language. Within the decade, proficiency in at least three languages will be required of all American schoolchildren by graduation. And along with its other recommendations, the CDC has issued a promulgation that every U.S. citizen "unplug" for at least two hours each day.

Synchronic is in Chapter 11; the Word Exchange has been dismantled. The president has pledged funding to prevent future cyberlingua attacks and to set up archives and libraries, many modeled on those started here at the Glass by members of the Diachronic Society, lots of whom have stayed on. We gather nearly every night for informal conversation lab, often at Phineas's favorite pub, the Eagle and Child, where a different literary society once met.

Laird and Brock were taken into custody, but both are out on bail pending further investigation. Floyd has fared less well; he's in Colorado, awaiting trial on federal charges: conspiracy, fraud, racketeering. Manslaughter. Dmitri is at Rikers Island, as is Koenig. Several hackers were also arrested, including Roquentin. But because he's a minor (he'll be fifteen in May), he was released to his family when his father posted the three million yuan bond.

Two weeks ago a memorial service was held at the Capitol for victims of the virus. Doug was asked to speak, and he recited the etymology and meaning of "grief." Then he took the train to New York for another, smaller ceremony, in memory of Victoria Mark, née Nadya Viktorovna Markova, which was held at the Merc. Phineas gave a very moving eulogy, Doug said, and seemed to have started the long, slow process of mourning. He also appears to have emerged healthy from a three-day quarantine. He's now joined us here in Oxford. Last week we hosted a small, modest celebration in the Glass's dining hall to celebrate publication of the *NADEL*'s third edition.

When Doug was in New York, he saw Vera; they had coffee at a place near our old offices. Doug said it was "nice," Vera that it was "pleasant," which I think means it was sad for both of them.

I've been talking to Vera, too, once a week. She seems to be doing well. She's stayed in East Hampton and has been helping care for my grandfather. It turns out he had a microchip, which has now been removed successfully.

I've spoken to my friends as well. Ramona still isn't talking much, but she's undergoing treatment. They're otherwise all all right so far, for which I'm very grateful. I'll be meeting Coco in Paris next month; one of her shows, postponed because of the crisis, will finally be opening at her gallery there, and she's planning to take the loop back to London with me afterward and to stay here in Oxford for a couple weeks.

Besides writing and talking daily with Doug and other Society members, I practice judo and I draw; I plan to apply to a few grad schools when I'm done with this manuscript. I've also started studying Spanish, Arabic, and Chinese. And reading. Lately, aloud—to Bart.

Of course I didn't write this account alone. But in that regard I'm like Doug, and the other Dr. Johnson, and all the lexicographers who came between, laboring away mostly in obscurity. Dictionary-makers are obliged to work in teams. All writers are, I think. "Creation is collaboration," as Doug would say. And I find that thought pretty comforting. In the words of Georg Wilhelm Friedrich Hegel, "Human nature only really exists in an achieved community of minds." Language seems like proof that there's such a thing as meaning. That we're all connected, now and forever.

Words don't always work. Sometimes they come up short. Conversations can lead to conflict. There are failures of diplomacy. Some differences, for all the talk in the world, remain irreconcilable. People make empty promises, go back on their word, say things they don't believe. But connection, with ourselves and others, is the only way we can live.

I don't agree with all Doug and Bart have to say about language, or love. If Doug has implied we're mere servants, and Bart that we can be in control, I think they're both wrong. Or that the truth is somewhere between.

Language may have limits. But it isn't just a dim likeness in a dark mirror. Yes, gestures, glances, touches, taps on walls mean something. So do silences. But sometimes the word is the thing. The bridge. Sometimes we only know what we feel once it's been said. Words may be daughters of the earth instead of heaven. But they're not dim. And even in the faintest shimmer, there is light.

Bart is right that language is the tie that binds us to the dead and unborn. But he's wrong that words are just urns for holding pure thought. I don't think he really believes that, or ever did. I hope I'll know someday. That he'll be able to tell me himself. But until then—

THE END

Just one last thing.

I've visited Bart for the past three nights, since he got out of quarantine. I've been reading him this manuscript, and passages from Hegel. Recently I found this:

> genuine love excludes all oppositions. . . . it is not finite at all. . . . This wealth of life love acquires in the exchange of every thought, every variety of inner experience, for it seeks out differences and devises unifications ad infinitum; it turns to the whole manifold of nature in order to drink love out of every life. What in the first instance is most [one's] own is united into the whole . . . consciousness of a separate self disappears, and all distinction . . . is annulled.

I know he understood. Because when I was done reading, he squeezed my hand and smiled.

Each night I've kissed him on the forehead and held my breath as he's tried to talk. I stare at a spot on the wall, my gaze unfocused. Pretend I'm not listening. That I don't see the tears of frustration welling in his eyes.

Last night he motioned for the pen. Held it tightly. Made a wobbly green *X* on the bottom of the page. I whispered, "What is it?" But he just shook his head. When I tried to kiss him, he turned away. But he kept the pen.

Tonight when I went into his room, I saw mounds of crumpled paper like dead flowers in the trash. When he dozed off for a few minutes, I opened one out on my knee. Saw it was just an endless series of green squiggles: dead flowers' dead stems.

Just now I finished reading these pages to Bart. I read to the end. And Bart waved for me to hand him the last sheet. Fished out the pen.

"It's okay, Bart," I said.

But he got up and took the paper from my hand. Brought it to his desk and marked it.

He just crossed the room. Just kissed me on the mouth.

Gave me back the page. And it says:

THE ~~END~~ BEGINNING

ACKNOWLEDGMENTS

I have a real community of minds to thank.

I'm enormously grateful to my many brilliant and big-souled teachers: Francisco Goldman, Mary Gordon, Gabe Hudson, Heidi Julavits, Sam Lipsyte, Jaime Manrique, Ben Marcus, Carole Maso, Stephen O'Connor, Mark Slouka, Meredith Steinbach, and those at Carolina Friends School.

I'm more indebted than I could ever say to all my friends. Thank you especially to Claire Campbell, Rivka Galchen, Susanna Kohn, Reif Larsen, Nellie Hermann, Tania James, Maggie Pouncey, Karen Russell, and Karen Thompson Walker for reading so many of my words, so closely and kindly, over so many years. Huge thanks, too, to Sophie Barrett, Stuart Blumberg, Charlie Capp, and Jennie Goldstein for offering your essential thoughts on earlier drafts of this book.

To Field Maloney, who years ago gave me a copy of Henry Hitchings's fantastic book *Defining the World: The Extraordinary Story of Dr. Johnson's Dictionary,* and who encouraged me to begin writing this one, you have my lifelong gratitude. Thank you, too, for giving me vital advice about both the business of writing and how I might improve mine (if only I could, in fact, write more like Bolaño and Hemingway, or you). Thank you, too, for lending a few of your aphorisms and mannerisms to these pages, which have been scattered over several characters (none of whom resemble you in any other way, clearly).

Thank you to Alison Callahan, whose large-hearted and rigorous edits made this book immeasurably better; to the very gracious, inventive, and funny Gerry Howard; and to the heroic James Melia. Thanks, too, to Michael Collica, Emily Mahon, Jeremy Medina, John Pitts, Nora Reichard, Alison Rich, and all the other wonderful people at Doubleday, working away in that big glass building on Broadway.

My deepest appreciation to Robin Desser and Bob Gottlieb for being extraordinary mentors on literature, the art of editing, and life.

I'm immensely grateful to Susan Golomb for believing so ardently in this book. Enormous thanks, too, to Soumeya Bendimerad and Krista Ingebretson.

Thanks to the Corporation of Yaddo, the Jentel Artist Residency, the MacDowell Colony, the Ucross Foundation, the Vermont Studio Center (where I began the first draft of this novel in 2008 and the final draft in 2012), and the Virginia Center for the Creative Arts. My greatest appreciation, too, to my former colleagues at PEN for being so supportive when I left to finish the book at these various Shangri-las.

Thank you to the philosopher Jim Vernon, whose brains are rivaled only by his benevolence, and whose book *Hegel's Philosophy of Language* was indispensable to me. He offered vital guidance on sections of this book having to do with Hegel. Many of the Hegel translations cited herein are his, as is the theory Bart alludes to about Hegel and universal grammar.

For invaluable information about how computers and the Internet work, my hat is always and forever off to Will Roberts, and especially to the eternally patient David Wu, whose help to me should constitute a life's worth of mitzvahs.

Thank you to John Simpson, who was Chief Editor of the *Oxford English Dictionary* until October 2013. He very generously met with me for several hours in the *OED*'s Oxford offices, and answered my many questions with equanimity, humor, and grace. Huge thanks, too, to Jesse Sheidlower. He likewise kindly met with me, in the *OED*'s New York offices, and later read an inordinate number of this novel's pages. Would that I could have incorporated all his excellent advice.

My tremendous gratitude to the incomparable Seyed Safavynia for giving me far more of his time than is in any way reasonable. It's thanks to Seyed that the Meme exists in its current form, and that I know a little something about how the human brain works.

While researching this book, I read a lot of other books. Among them: several of Simon Winchester's, including *The Professor and the Madman;* Nicholas Carr's *The Shallows,* which significantly informed many of Doug's disquisitions on how our changing relationship to technology has reshaped our thinking; *Cyber War* by Richard A. Clarke and Robert K. Knake; and Sol Steinmetz's *Semantic Antics,* which was especially helpful when I was writing Bart's ruminations on language. I read a lot about pneumatic tubes, too. Especially helpful was the report *Development of the Pneumatic-tube and Automobile Mail Service* published by the U.S. Congress in 1917. I also regularly consulted the online edition of the *OED* (which cannot be blamed for the improbability of my own "definitions"), and I read parts of Sidney Landau's *Dictionaries: The Art and Craft of Lexicography.* I'm particularly beholden, too, to David Foster Wallace's extraordinary essay "Authority and American Usage," which in some ways got this whole ball really rolling, and to Rivka Galchen for directing me to it.

Thanks also to: Steve Duncan for all things spelunking-related. Max Kardon for bequeathing me a crucial sentence. Mark Kirby for amiably uncrinkling the Deep Springs section.

Plaudits to Onnesha Roychoudhuri for providing critical, eleventh-hour guidance, including information about key architectural elements of the Center for Fiction (also known as the Mercantile Library).

My huge appreciation, too, to the Center for Fiction's Kristin Henley.

I'm indebted to Cressida Leyshon for offering thoughtful counsel at a decisive time.

Warm encomiums to Amanda Valdez, and once again to Jennie Goldstein, for being art-history geniuses.

My gratitude to Amy Barefoot for sharing her considerable musical expertise.

Thanks, too, to the inimitable Dave Graedon for more things than I can name, including fielding dozens if not hundreds of bizarre inquiries with good humor, wisdom, and heart, and introducing me over the years to much of my favorite literature, art, and music. I.e., for being the greatest brother imaginable.

Thanks to all the friends who sheltered me and offered every form of sustenance during the peripatetic year when I was finishing this book. I've mentioned many of you above for other kindnesses. I'd also like to thank Emily Alexander and Vernon Chatman, Vivian Berger and Michael Finkelstein, Julia Bloch, Jill Fitzsimmons and Josh Watson, Danielle and Alex Mindlin, Lauren Waterman and Andrei Kaullaur, Reilly Coch, and especially Flannery Hysjulien, without whom I would be an entirely different person.

Thanks to Anna, Yotam, and Finnegan Haber, Nam Le, Emma Schwarcz, and all the satellite members of the Hancock house. Thanks to Anna in particular for coining so many ingenious metaphors, e.g., thoughts that pop up like corks.

Thanks to Annie Fain Liden, Georgia Smith, Shala, and Cathy and the girls for buoying me through all the beautiful months in Asheville.

And to Dan-Avi Landau, thank you for everything. I couldn't have finished this book without you. Thank you for helping me invent the Nautilus, for explaining retrotransposons and logic gates, for introducing me to *Spiegel im Spiegel* and to so many other things. Thank you for letting me attribute some of your ideas to Dr. Barouch. Thank you for your unrivaled and unbridled creativity, and for reading this book with such tenderness and brilliance. Thank you for teaching me about everything that matters.

Finally, my gratitude to my parents is so profound that for once, it has left me without words.